THE SECRET KEEPER
CONFINED

(THE SECRET KEEPER SERIES #2)

BREA BROWN

WAYZGOOSE PRESS

Cover design by Keri Knutson at alchemybookcovers.com

ISBN: 978-1-938757-62-4 (second edition)

CONTENTS

*For the ladies in my life who make me laugh,
lift me up, always look "quite pretty," and give me more material than I
could ever use. Love you, Cara, Laura, Karen, and Sonya! Get your
passports ready, "just in cases!"*

1

THE WEDDING PLANNER

I need to touch a cow. It's not something I'm proud of, but there it is. I think it's the only cure for this constant desire to scream until the veins pop out in my neck and the blood vessels in my eyes burst. And if touching a cow doesn't work, I'm not sure what I'm going to do.

I never considered myself a control freak, but my panic at the current lack of control in my life is hinting at a personality trait that may have been lurking undetected my whole life, like some sort of latent cancer. Or maybe all brides-to-be feel like this. I'm starting to experience a scary affinity with those detestable women on that *Bridezillas* show.

What started out as a simple plan for an understated Lutheran wedding with family, close friends, and the members of our church (you can't really get away with not inviting the congregation when you're marrying their pastor) is turning into—frankly—a cluster-fuck. And it happened without my even realizing it was getting so out of hand.

It started with the dress. When I showed my mom what I had in mind in a bridal magazine, she looked up at me as if she thought I was kidding. After it was apparent that I was serious about the ivory, simply cut garment, she smiled across the dining table at me like I was a simpleton.

"Oh, honey. You can't wear *that* dress."

"Why not?" I asked.

"That dress says that you're getting married because you *have to* get married."

I grabbed the magazine from her hands and practically pressed my nose to it so I could examine the size-zero model wearing the dress. Neither she nor the gown was saying that to me, but... what do I know? "What are you talking about? I think it's nice."

"Ivory? Really?" Again with the patronizing smile.

Though now I understood what she was getting at, I didn't agree with her. "Oh. Well, Mom... I mean, everyone *knows* about... you know..." I fumbled around, trying to get her to understand where I was coming from without spelling it out. When she unhelpfully blinked blankly at me, I sighed. "Everyone knows I'm not a virgin."

"Those are old-fashioned rules!" she insisted. "If everyone followed that convention, nobody would get married in white anymore. It's not like the wool's being pulled over anyone's eyes. But ivory! It's just so... yellow."

The irony of her talking about old-fashioned rules while worrying that people would think that I "have to get married" wasn't lost on me, but I didn't bother pointing it out. Instead, I sighed and gave her the magazine. "What do you suggest, then? And just so you know, I won't consider anything with puffy sleeves or cascades of tulle or bows or anything like that."

Eagerly, she flicked through the pages, licking her thumb occasionally for better traction. Finally, she stopped and pointed to a long-sleeved, off-white lacy dress on a model about five sizes (at least) smaller than me. "There. That would be perfect. Understated, elegant, not bright white. But you'll look like a princess."

That's probably because it looked almost exactly like the dress that Kate Middleton wore when she married Prince William. As a matter of fact... I looked more closely. It *was* pretty much the same dress.

"Mom, I don't know——"

"Oh, come on! It's perfect. Timeless and classy."

I do love that dress, I thought wistfully as I stared at the glossy picture.

She noticed my weakening and said, "Oh, come on! You only get married once—well, at least I *hope* you do. Especially you."

"No pressure."

"*Yes,* pressure! As it should be." She grasped my hand on top of the table. "Too often, people go into marriage with divorce in the back of their minds as a safety net. But when you marry a pastor..." She smiled shakily. "Well, you're going to be a role model for all couples at the church."

I could tell that the idea filled her with trepidation but tried not to take offense.

I gulped. "Yeah, well, I'm not worried about that. Brice and I, we're solid."

"Oh, I know that!" she said, squeezing my hand. "But it's not just about the two of you. You'll have to remember to find time for each other and put each other first, even when everyone around you is vying for your attention and telling you that their needs are more important. Plus, Brice is already married—to the Church."

My chair squeaked on the hardwood floor as I pulled my hand from her grip and abruptly stood, but I was still relatively calm when I said, "Mom, I know all this stuff."

Unfortunately, it's a topic I've avoided discussing with

my future husband, because I don't want him to think I'm worried that he won't know how to balance everything. Even though I do worry. A lot. I wasn't going to tell her any of that, though.

"Okay. Well, then. Cake tasting! When are you and Brice available to do that?"

Which brings me to the next issue: the reception. Originally, Brice and I envisioned a cake and some champagne in the church fellowship hall. Maybe coffee, too, if we felt like going wild. But when Mom heard that, she said, "What about your first dance as a married couple? What about the father-daughter dance?" On this occasion, we were talking about it on the phone, but I actually heard tears in her voice when she posed the question.

I told her we weren't planning on doing any dancing. I may as well have told her we weren't getting married at all.

"A wedding is supposed to be a party, a celebration! Celebrations involve dancing and laughing and plenty of eating and drinking," she said. "Plus, Brice's friend, Vince, is coming all the way from Florida to perform the ceremony for you two."

"So?"

"'So'? You have to show him a good time."

I hadn't really thought about that, but I said, "Mom, I don't want this to turn into one of our family's drunken parties where people get out of control and say and do embarrassing things."

She snapped, "You make it sound like we're a bunch of white-trash drunks!"

"Who said anything about 'white trash'?"

"You need to relax." In her best realtor tone (probably the same one she used in her prime when describing a dump as a "sweet fixer-upper" to prospective buyers), she wheedled, "Why don't you just leave the reception to me? I'll find a venue that can accommodate plenty of people and has room for dancing and a nice open bar area."

"Mother."

"Your father and I will pay for everything."

"It's not about the money!"

Well, that's not completely true. Things are pretty tight with the church budget right now, and Brice thinks it'd be in poor taste if we spent a boatload on our wedding, so it is *sort of* about the money.

She knows it, too. "I don't want you worrying about that. You guys deserve a good time, and your dad and I will do whatever it takes to make it happen. So stop worrying and have some fun!"

Honestly, until Brice, I didn't really think of myself as the type of person who ever wanted any kind of wedding to anyone. So when we initially agreed as a couple to do something low-key, I was all for it. The thought of being the center of hundreds of people's attentions makes me itchy, anyway. But when Mom started mentioning all of her ideas, she woke a sleeping bear that I didn't even know existed in me. And that bear wants to be a princess. Go figure.

Every time she calls with another one of her extravagant ideas (the four-tiered chocolate fondue fountain, the cross-shaped ice sculpture, the adorable miniature wedding cake-shaped petit fours, the string quartet, the live deejay, just to name a very, very few), I have to conjure a picture of Brice listening to me tell him the latest detail so that I don't immediately and enthusiastically agree to whatever it is (except for the ice sculpture, which I vetoed on the grounds that it's not only tacky but dorky). Most of the time, the expression on the fiancé in my head is one of dismay, so I politely remind her of our "no frills" policy. (I couldn't resist the petit fours, though. I love cake of any size, and you can never have too much cake.)

Now, in her latest call, practically in the middle of the night, I've once again rejected the string quartet in favor of having the church organist, Carol, provide the accompaniment, and I'm trying to talk her down from a ledge regarding another of her incorrect assumptions.

"What do you *mean* you're not serving a meal?"

I thought "We're not serving a meal" was a pretty unambiguous statement.

Impatiently, she says, "Peyton, we don't have time to argue about every detail, if you want this to happen on October twenty-first."

Oh-ho! This thinly veiled threat immediately makes me clamp my teeth together. "That's your deadline," I say firmly.

I'll wear the dress she wants me to wear, eat the cake she wants me to eat, dance to the songs her deejay plays, drink all the alcohol she pours down my throat, and do it all with a smile, but we're getting married on the twenty-first, so help me God.

"I know it's important to you, since it would have been her first birthday and everything, but—"

"No buts." I ignore her reluctance to say Secret's name and resume the role of hard-ass, one in which I've found myself quite a bit lately. "That's the date."

"That's a Sunday, though," she says, as if it hadn't occurred to me before now.

"Yeah. I know. I've looked at a calendar a few times recently."

"That means we'll only have a couple of hours to decorate between the late service in the morning and the wedding in the afternoon."

"*Late* afternoon. Nearly evening. It's plenty of time. We'll have lots of helping hands." Too many, in my opinion, but that's not worth getting into right now.

"And how are you going to keep Brice from seeing you before the ceremony if you're sitting out in the congregation that morning?" I can tell by her tone of voice that she thinks she has me on this one.

"We're not worried about stupid superstitions like—"

"Peyton!"

"We're not! But anyway, it's a moot point, because I won't be at church that morning. I'll be too busy packing and—"

"You're going to skip church? Does Brice know this?"

After counting to five and taking a very deep breath, I answer, "Yes, Mother. I have his permission."

Actually, the conversation with Brice went like this:

Me: *"I won't be at church on the morning of our wedding."*

Him: [intent on taping a frayed wire on the small lavaliere microphone he wears every Sunday] *"Yeah. I kind of figured. Makes sense."*

[End of discussion.]

Mom snipes, "You don't have to be snide."

"You don't have to treat me like I'm an idiot kid who can't think for herself," I fire back. "The wedding date is October twenty-first. We know it falls on a Sunday. There's plenty of time to decorate the church. I won't let Brice see me before the ceremony, even though it's a dumb tradition. Did I miss anything?"

Grudgingly, she replies, "No. I don't think so. But with

so little time, I can't promise you the perfect place for the reception."

Sigh. "I don't care," I say bravely. Not even a disappointed Princess Bear is going to make me back down on this point.

"Well, at least let us serve beef tenderloin at the reception. I know a caterer that can cut us a really good deal. I just think it'll look chintzy if we don't have a meal. Beef tenderloin isn't too fancy for your no frills policy, is it?" she asks with a side of extra snark.

Not for mine, but probably for my husband's-to-be. Life's about compromise, though, so I say, "Fine. Whatever. On the twenty-first. Of October. That's next month."

"Yeah, yeah. Sure. Okay, I'll call the caterer first thing in the morning." Then, as if she's breaking bad news to me, "It's probably too late to call them tonight."

You think? It was too late for her to be calling *me*.

We say our goodnights, but I'm awake now. And I need to touch a cow.

Despite the ungodly hour, I immediately dial Brice's number after hanging up with my wedding planner.

I wait through the sounds that signify he's dropped the phone and is having trouble relocating it. When he answers groggily, I announce without preamble, "I need to touch a cow."

Silence, then, "Pardon me?"

"I need to touch a cow. Tonight."

"O…kay… But it's—"

"Please. I need this. You. Me. Cows. Be here in twenty."

I end the call and then redial when I realize I need to tell him, "'Here' is my place. In case you didn't know. Bye."

Nineteen minutes later, I'm waiting next to my door with my purse when my doorbell rings. I swing the door open to the hallway to reveal my hubby-to-be, rubbing his eyes and yawning.

I'd have to be a real jerk not to feel a little guilty, so I say, "Aw, you really *were* sleeping."

"Yep," he replies, blinking hard. "I tend to be when it's the middle of the night, and I have an early morning meeting with your dad and the other church elders the next day, but let's go touch some cows."

As we're driving away from the heart of Chicago, the highway lights intermittently backlight his profile. Neither one of us says a word, until he pulls his red Jeep onto the shoulder near the spot where we stopped months ago on an impromptu road trip that eventually led to our first kiss.

There's not an udder in sight.

"Oh, man! Where are the cows?" I whine, jumping down from the SUV and searching the dim pastures.

Brice hangs back, leaning against his vehicle while I climb on the fence to make myself taller.

"Must be in for the night," he mutters. "And before you make me drive all over northern Illinois and into Wisconsin, that's probably going to be the case everywhere. It's nearly 1:30 in the morning."

I hop down from the fence and put my back to it, wrapping my arms through the rails. "No, I won't make you do that. It just would have been nice to touch one tonight. I needed it."

There's something about a cow that's calming. Until one tries to lick you with its long, sticky, purple tongue. But their general demeanor is one of patience and complacence and ease. They seem content with life, content with people telling them what to do: go here, eat this, graze there, come here. I guess it helps that they're not big thinkers. But neither am I, so why can't my life be as simple as theirs?

Why can't I be just as happy with everyone else taking control of my life?

Crossing his arms over his chest, Brice looks down at his feet. "So, what's up?"

The darkness out here away from the city is dense. The Jeep's headlights and taillights are the only illumination except for a tiny sliver of moon that darts in and out of the clouds. I know he can't see my eyes from where he's standing, so I have no choice but to speak.

"You're going to be mad."

When he doesn't say anything, I take the initiative. "It's just… our wedding's going to be a *little* fancier than we originally discussed." I think about that for a second and backtrack. "Actually, a lot, come to think of it."

"Peyton."

Quickly, I say, "I know that a wedding isn't the same thing as a marriage."

Nodding, he jams his hands in his pockets and continues to study his running shoes, but he says nothing to my statement.

"And I know the wedding doesn't set the tone for the marriage." I think about it for a second. "It really means nothing, except for two little words."

His head snaps up. "Actually, it's a very important ceremony in our culture and as part of our faith. It's a way for the bride and groom to express their love and devotion to one another, a way of *publicly* committing, in front of God and everyone, that they will always put each other first, after Him, and their love will never waver." Slowly, he walks over and stands next to me, leaning on the fence, gazing out into the dark field.

"Okay. What you said." I chuckle at his intellectual

analysis while stepping up onto the lowest fence rail to bring my face up to the same level as his.

He half-smiles. "I just don't want to send the wrong message to the rest of the church. We're talking about budget cuts and financial restructuring, and I think that if my wedding—*our* wedding—is some kind of celebration of all things material, they'll be understandably put off by that."

"But it's my mom and dad's money. Not yours or mine or ours or the church's. My parents'. And they want to do it. For us." I examine his closed-off face while he keeps his eyes on the empty pasture in front of us. "And anyway, it's not going to be a 'celebration of all things material.' We have some tasteful ideas." I ignore the little voice in my head that's taunting me about the petit fours and continue resolutely, "They're just pricey. Some of them." Still holding to the rails, I lean over and kiss his temple.

He blinks. "If that's what you want…" I'm surprised by the amusement in his eyes when he turns his head to look at me. "You know, I'm not trying to be a killjoy."

He's normally a happy-go-lucky, fun-loving guy, so I safely tease, "Yeah, it comes naturally."

"Lately, yes. And I'm sorry."

"Why are you apologizing to me?" I turn around so my back is to the pasture. "I'm the one who woke you up in the middle of the night and dragged you out here to talk about wedding shit. I feel so caught in the middle, though! I know what you want, and I know what Mom wants, and they're nowhere close to being the same thing, so it's—"

"I bet they're closer than you think." When I shake my head and smirk at how disparate their visions are, he stands in front of and leans into me. "We both want you to be happy. Period. So which wedding do you want? It's your choice. I'm showing up, no matter what."

I laugh, but really I want to cry with relief, so I keep my head down. "Really?"

"Heck yeah! You're not getting rid of me that easily."

Through my eyelashes, I check his eyes for sincerity before saying, "Okay. 'Cause I kind of want the princess wedding."

Trapping me between the hard metal fence rails and his firm chest, he nuzzles my neck and mumbles against it, "Done."

"You know what I really want?" I ask, closing my eyes and shivering at the feel of his warm breath against my throat. "I want this wedding to be over. All this planning is driving me crazy. And all this *waiting* is making me irritable."

He laughs and straightens. I open my eyes and look up into his face as he says, "I've been really crabby, too. I snapped at Marilyn the other day. But somehow I ended up the one nearly in tears. I've been a mess."

The thought of him in a showdown with the church secretary makes me smirk. But my mouth is quickly covered by his. I let go of the rails and twine my metal-chilled fingers in his hair. When our lips separate ever-so-slightly, I say, "I love you."

Breathlessly, he replies, "I love you, too," and goes right back to kissing me.

Eyes closed, hands roaming, tongues seeking, bodies aching, we're startled out of our own little make-out bubble by a squawk from above. "Move it along, you two!" a state trooper commands through his megaphone before shining a huge spotlight on us.

Brice freezes and turns to look over his shoulder. "Absolutely, officer," he calls back respectfully while I hide my face against his chest and laugh. We scramble up the slope to the shoulder of the road and scamper into the Jeep, giggling and blushing like teenagers.

Once inside, I say, "Take me home, Reverend Naughty."

He turns the key in the ignition and waves out the window to the trooper, who's pulling around us and back onto the road. "I refuse to apologize for kissing the bride."

HERE COMES THE BRIDE

*S*ix weeks later, when he kisses me in front of God and a packed church, I'm overjoyed—and frankly, flabbergasted—by the exuberant response from the congregation. First of all, Lutherans don't cheer in church. Second, it stands to reason that they'd be happier seeing their pastor marry someone like Justine Heidecker, the church's youth director. Or, if not someone that specific, a woman who knows how to make a casserole or knit a blanket. Sure, these people have known me my whole life, so at least I'm familiar to them (the evil they know?), which is part of the problem, in a way. They know my whole sordid history. But, today at least, it seems they've put aside all that. I guess they figure it could be worse. He *could* be marrying a non-Lutheran.

"Wow," Brice says, smiling into my eyes as he pulls back from the kiss.

"Yeah." I'm too shy to look out at everyone yet. This is the first time we've kissed in front of anyone outside of our families (unless you count the state trooper, which I don't, really), much less before what seems like the entire Messiah Lutheran congregation. As a matter of fact, I've gone out of my way for almost a year to make sure we haven't. So, it feels unnatural to give myself permission to do it now.

That doesn't mean it didn't feel good, though.

"I present to you, for the first time, the Reverend and Mrs. Northam," Vince announces, which gets everyone, including Brice, even more excited.

My brand new husband (that's a heady thought) hugs me and turns us to face the congregation almost all in one motion while I concentrate on staying on my feet. Laughing, I hold onto him for dear life and hope he doesn't trip on my dress and bring us both down.

After setting me down and letting go of me, he spins to hug his friend, Vince, a Lutheran pastor I met in person for the first time two days ago but who has become one of my favorite people during the past few months, as he's conducted our pre-marital counseling via Skype. It's obvious why he and Brice became such good friends when Brice was a prison chaplain in Florida and attended Vince's church. They could be brothers, personality-wise. The biggest difference I've noticed is that Brice tends to be more cerebral, while Vince is sort of like the Labrador retriever that wants to lick you all day. He throws the word "love" around like some people use the word "the." He... well... *loves* it.

Now, as I hug him, he says, "I love you guys! Congratulations!"

Brice grabs my hand and kisses it as we face the still-standing and clapping guests and head back up the aisle. After a couple of stops to hug his mom, my parents, and my seven-year-old niece, Sadie, who will not be ignored another second, we make our way to the spot where Brice usually stands to greet people after church. Again, it feels strange to be standing here with him.

Before we're mobbed, he leans down and kisses me again. "I love you," he murmurs through his grin.

After returning the sentiment and the smile, I say, "This is kind of crazy."

"You are beautiful."

I blush. "Well, thanks. Mitzi did my makeup and Jen did my hair," I give credit to my two best friends. "And the dress... Well, I hate to say Mom was right, but—"

"It has nothing to do with any of that. You're just... beautiful."

Over the years, I've had guys tell me that I'm pretty or "hot" (when they're drunk and trying to get somewhere with me) or cute, but Brice is the first man other than my father to ever call me "beautiful." And it's not the same when your dad's only saying it so you'll hurry up and get in the car when you're late for church or school (as in, "You're beautiful. Now, let's go!"). It's not the first time Brice has said it to me, but it still catches me off-guard when he does, even now, on our wedding day. For some reason, when he says it, it seems to encompass more than what everyone else can see.

"Oh."

Before I can respond more appropriately than that, Vince finishes his announcement about the reception and invitation to the guests to join us there following pictures. And that's the last time we have a minute alone for several more hours.

I wake up first. My internal compass immediately lets me know my body's not oriented at all the way it would be if I were in my own bed in my apartment. The disorientation lasts mere seconds, but it brings along with it a strange feeling of déjà vu. Instead of the shame I've sometimes felt in the past when waking up next to someone in an unfamiliar bed, though, I'm filled with an extreme sense of satisfaction and joy. It's been a long time since I've had that feeling. Last night—or more accurately, early this morning—was the first time in a long time that I experienced a *lot* of things.

I roll over gingerly, careful not to wake him up, and thankful that it's light enough in the room that I can see his face. I just want to look at him for a minute and convince myself this is really happening. And remember what happened last night.

When we got to the parsonage after the reception, we were both giddy. Part of that had to do with all the champagne and beer we'd drunk, but—for me, at least—some of it was down to nerves. I was surprised by how nervous I was, actually. It's not like I'm a virgin. As a matter of fact, I don't think I was as nervous back then as I was last night. I knew this wasn't going to feel the same as some lust-induced fumbling around on the sofa that happened to lead to something more. It was going to be so much more meaningful, and I *knew* it, so I had the jitters about it.

Having a slightly out-of-body experience, I stood inside the front door in my wedding dress and watched Brice take off his shoes and tie. *Good idea,* I remember thinking, sliding off my own shoes and detaching my veil from my hair. Then I merely stood there some more. Even though there was no mistaking what was about to happen, I wasn't quite sure how to get there.

Brice didn't seem to know what to do, either, so I didn't feel bad. Smiling shyly at me, he said, "Uh, welcome home." He held out his hand to me.

I took it, and thought involuntarily, *Everyone knows we're having sex tonight.* That made me blush and giggle like an idiot, but before he could ask me what my problem was, I pressed myself against him and kissed him—hard—on the mouth. You gotta start somewhere. I figured that was as good a place as any.

He eagerly kissed me back, surprising and delighting me when he bent down and scooped me off the floor.

"Oh!" I laughed, hanging onto his shoulders.

As soon as I was situated in his arms, he continued kissing me as he carried me down the hallway to his—*our*—bedroom. Once inside the room, he stopped walking, but he didn't stop kissing me, nor did he set me down. We stayed lip-locked for a while, until he dropped one of his arms so that I could slide down it and land on my feet.

"Let's get you out of that dress," he said as if he were suggesting we get a snack.

I smiled at his earnestness but didn't tease him about it, for once. "Good idea. It's going to take a while. Lots of buttons." I turned to show him, and he groaned.

"Oh. I thought it was a zip-up," he said, his face falling.

"Nope." I backed up to him. "Get those fingers movin'."

Starting at my neck, he methodically began the task of undoing all the tiny seed-pearl buttons, but about halfway down my back, I noticed his pace quickening, becoming almost frantic by the time he hit the last one at the small of my back.

He breathed, "Done," and at the same time, I pulled on the ends of my sleeves and shrugged out of the top of the dress, letting it fall around my legs. I stepped gingerly away from it, but he practically kicked it clear of us and lunged for me.

A girl who cared more would have warned him to be careful with her dress.

I was glad to be free of it.

Before any more of my clothing came off, we worked on his tux, which had a lot of annoying, unnecessary buttons, too. Stripped down to our skivvies, we fell onto the bed, both of us tugging his t-shirt over his head, then unhooking my bra, peeling off my pantyhose, yanking down panties and boxer-briefs, until *finally*... we were together as God had made us.

That's when he abruptly stopped. Out of breath, he said, "Wait."

"What? No, no more waiting," I panted back. It had been the longest nine months of my life.

He kissed my shoulder. "No, but we have to go kinda... slow."

"Oh. Right." The last thing I wanted to do was break the record for fastest consummation. And I didn't want to make him feel self-conscious, either, so I smiled reassuringly. "Okay. I'm not going anywhere."

His face relaxed. "True."

So we took it slowly. And it was wonderful.

And private. (Sorry.)

When it was over, and we had recovered, he pulled me up against him and said, "Nothing is ever like you imagine it's going to be."

"Oh? That was pretty close for me." Minus the violins, choir of angels, and beam of sunlight from Heaven. But I was eighty percent sure those things weren't really going to happen, so it wasn't too much of a disappointment when they didn't.

He grinned. "I didn't say it wasn't as good as I imagined. Just different."

It begged the question, *What* was *he expecting?* But his private smile let me know he probably wasn't going to give me the answer to that, so I didn't frustrate myself by asking.

I was suddenly too sleepy to talk, anyway. My day had started before sunrise, and it was way after midnight by that point. And it hadn't been just a normal day of doing everyday things. It was busy and frantic—and sometimes boring and annoying—and exhausting.

He, however, seemed wide awake. And cuddly. And talkative.

Rubbing my shoulder, he said, "I'm so excited to go on our honeymoon."

"Mmm," I agreed as enthusiastically as possible in my ultra-relaxed state. "It's going to be fun."

"I've never been on a cruise before. I used to see the ships in port and think I'd like to go on one someday. With someone. I love the ocean."

"Never been."

"Never?"

"Nope."

"That's incredible. How did I not know this?"

Unable to keep my eyes open, I smiled and replied enigmatically, "I'm mysterious that way. Still lots for you to learn. Anyway, it can't be that much different than Lake Michigan."

His laugh rumbled against my ear, which I had pressed up against his chest. "It's a lot different." I fell asleep to the sound of his voice as he enumerated all the differences and waxed poetic about the power of the sea.

I'm not sure how long it took him to fall asleep, but now it's just after seven, and my five hours of rest have done me a world of good. I wonder how much longer he's going to want to sleep. We don't have to leave for the airport until this afternoon, so there's no rush to get up, although we do have to swing by my apartment and pick up my bags on the way. In the meantime, I don't mind openly staring at him and thinking about how extraordinary and surreal it is to be his wife.

Exactly a year ago, I was also lying in an unfamiliar bed. And the first person I saw when I woke up was the same man currently with me. Only in that case, the bed was in a hospital. And my friend and pastor, Brice, was sitting next to it, waiting for me to wake up after having just given birth to a beautiful, perfect, sweet, and dead baby girl, a baby girl whose father didn't—and still doesn't—know she existed. To say it was the worst day of my life would be a comical understatement. But he was there to hold my hand and to listen to my hurt and angry ramblings. He felt my pain as if it were his own.

It seems like forever ago. Other than a headstone in a nearby cemetery, there's no physical evidence that it even happened. My body has resumed its former shape and size; I didn't even get stretch marks. For a long time, it was easy for me to just put it out of my mind. Too easy. I didn't want to remember, anyway. Secret was a big part of a very painful time in my life, a time during which I lied to nearly everyone I loved, and lived in alternating states of denial, sadness, regret, and defensiveness.

One person hung in there with me.

And again, one year later, he's the first person I see. Only this time, I'm not waking up from what seems like a nightmare; I'm waking up from what feels like the best dream I've ever had. And if not for Secret, none of this may have come to be.

Thank you, baby girl.

The tears that have collected in the corner of my eye while considering the events of the past year finally overflow with a soft *plonk* onto the pillow under my head. I blot at them with the back of my hand and sniffle as quietly as possible.

Fortunately, my nearly silent crying doesn't seem to be bothering Brice. He sleeps on peacefully, his lips parted slightly, his dark hair contrasting against the white pillow, his bare shoulder gently rising and falling, his eyelashes resting on his cheeks. I sigh affectionately, thinking, *That's* my *new husband. Mine. All mine. Minemineminemineminemineminemine.*

Without warning, his eyes fly open.

"Oh, shit!" I involuntarily whisper, bringing my hand up to my mouth.

He gasps, too, shrinking further onto his side of the bed by rolling onto his back. He brings his arm up and rests his forearm against his forehead.

"Peyton."

"Brice!"

"You startled me."

"Me?"

Moving his arm from his forehead, he places his hand on my shoulder and says, "Yes. I woke up, and you were… so close. And staring at me."

"Do you always wake up like someone coming back from the dead?" I ask, trying to keep the edge from my voice. I'm more embarrassed at being caught staring at him than I'm upset at being startled.

He smiles, rolls back toward me, and pulls me closer. "I don't know. There hasn't been anyone to observe and report in many years."

"You were sound asleep, and then your eyes popped open." I demonstrate. "It was creepy."

"Maybe I felt someone two inches from my face, staring at me."

Grudgingly, I say, "Point taken."

"How long have you been awake?"

I nestle against him. "Not long. Just long enough to think about how lucky I am to have you."

"So a few hours, then?"

"Exactly."

He kisses the top of my head, then the crest of my ear, then my shoulder and down my arm to my elbow, which he gives a silly little lick. When I throw my head back and laugh, he chuckles before continuing down to my fingertips, which he nibbles. Returning to my face, he kisses my lips quickly and then goes in deeper. I rest my arms on his shoulders, leaning harder and harder until he's on his back and I'm half on top of him.

I break off the kiss and suggest, "Maybe we should just dry hump, for old time's sake?"

"Never again," he answers. "Promise me."

The seriousness in his dark blue eyes is funnier than my original joke. He looks sincerely worried. I trail a finger down his chest. "You really *do* have a lot to learn about me, still, if you think I'll ever be satisfied with that again, Reverend Randy."

The clouds scatter from his face as a grin breaks through. "Good. Now, we only have five hours before we have to leave for the airport, so chop-chop."

He doesn't have to tell me twice.

3

THE HONEYMOONERS

*T*hree days of bliss. That's how I'd describe our honeymoon cruise so far. Unfortunately, it's a seven-day cruise, and we're already on day five.

I'll wait while you do the math.

The first three days were smooth sailing, literally. Brice was right about the ocean being so much more than Lake Michigan could ever be. It's not just about the scale of it, either. It's the smell and the feel and the power that are the most compelling. Once we got checked in and settled, we spent most of our first afternoon on the ship's deck, staring out at the water, breathing in the salty air. I couldn't get enough of it.

I couldn't get enough of Brice, either. And the feeling was mutual. So we eventually went below-deck and spent some time in our suite. A lot of time. Until it was time to go to dinner.

Our first night was a "formal night," so we were expected to dress up and socialize with some of the other passengers as we ate at a large table for ten. Brice was in his element. I was not. Everyone wanted to know details about our lives that I didn't want to talk about while on this break away from it all. And when they found out Brice is a Lutheran Pastor in Chicago and that we're newlyweds, it got particularly annoying. For the first time, I looked and acted the part of a proper pastor's wife: seen but not heard. I smiled patiently and let him do most of the talking, since he seemed perfectly happy to do so. By the end of the meal, they were referring to our family members like they knew them, based on stories Brice told about the wedding and the reception.

Afterwards, when we were alone again, staring out at the shiny, moonlit water he asked, "Are you okay? You're so quiet."

I assured him I was fine, but that's when I realized with dread what the real problem was: I didn't want to share him. With anyone. Ever. Potentially problematic.

In spite of this niggling knowledge, I made a self-deprecating joke about being a loner. But when he suggested we dine alone for the duration of the cruise, I declined, knowing how much he enjoys meeting new people and hearing their stories, and I decided to view our dinners with the other passengers as training for my new life. That strategy seemed to work. I made the most of our alone time, and we kept to ourselves except for those couple of hours each evening.

On the fourth day (one of our two "fun days at sea"), I went out to our small balcony first thing in the morning, as was becoming my routine while I waited for Brice to shower, and was amazed at the size of the swells around us. I had thought the boat was moving a little more than usual, but when you're honeymooners, it's hard to tell when the bed is really moving under you or if it just feels like it is.

Transfixed, I stared at the waves until Brice joined me with an awed, "Wow," next to my ear.

I turned my head to reply, but as soon as I did so, the seesawing horizon line went in and out of focus, and nausea like I haven't felt since I was pregnant slammed against my diaphragm.

I barely made it to the swaying toilet in our en suite bathroom. Brice, innocently following me to see what was the matter, barely made it to the bathroom sink when he heard me retching.

He recovered first and hurried to the boat's pharmacy, where he bought every seasickness remedy they carried. I spent the rest of that day trying all of them, to no avail, while we sailed through heavy thunderstorms. Brice lay on the bed next to me, rubbing my back and reading while listening to his MP3 player, which was blasting pop music into his ears at a volume that would make it impossible to hear me each time I ran to the bathroom. I eventually had nothing left to offer the porcelain gods, although that didn't mean the nausea left me alone. No, it's my BFF, as long as I'm awake.

Still feeling sick this morning, I encourage him to go to breakfast without me. Despite the fact that they don't seem to be working, I wear the seasickness wrist bands and sit, eyes closed, on the balcony, where the fresh air is supposed to help allay the nearly constant nausea. I don't care that it's drizzling and that I'm getting soaked. It's a warm rain, and there's no lightning, so the fact that I feel ten times better out here than I did cooped up in our cabin all day yesterday greatly outweighs the discomfort of getting drenched.

Brice returns to our suite and joins me on the balcony, where he squints against the rain and says, "You're not the only one on the boat who's suffering. The dining areas are pretty empty this morning. Only a hearty handful of us seem to be up to the task of eating."

"Great. Is that supposed to make me feel better?"

"I guess not."

Immediately, I feel bad for snapping at him. I crack an eye and say, "Sorry. I'm just so… miserable."

"I know," he replies in his typical understanding fashion. "Good news, though: we're sailing into calmer waters and docking in Grand Turk in just a couple of hours, so hopefully you'll be feeling better before too long."

Opening both eyes, I whine, "It just sucks that every time you hear me get sick, it makes you sick."

"Well, that's hardly your fault. Don't worry about me. I'm fine. I'm just so sorry you're not feeling well."

"If I feel better later, I'll have sex with you."

He laughs loudly. "Okay. Something else to pray about, I guess."

I smile faintly.

Cheerfully, he adds, "Anyway, this is good practice for when you're expecting our little ones."

I simply grunt at him to let him know this is not a good time to talk about the football team he wants to sire. The number of our future children seems to get larger every time we discuss it. When we were dating, the typical Brice Northam Kid Plan went something like this: "Being an only child is lonely, so I'd like to have at least two." Then, when we were engaged, it progressed to: "Three kids makes for a nice, cozy family." Then on the plane to catch the boat: "On second thought, someone always seems to be left out when there are three kids; look at Sadie, for example. Even numbers are better. So, four or six children probably would be better."

I quickly changed the subject before he got into the type

of numbers that would qualify us for our own reality TV show.

At this precise moment, I can't even fathom having one child, much less something that could be aptly described as a "brood."

Fortunately, he gets the hint from my near-silence on the topic. "In the meantime, I brought you some toast and orange juice. It's inside, where it's dry. You wanna try to get something down before we dock? You haven't eaten anything in more than twenty-four hours."

"There's no way. Just come get me when we dock. I'll eat when we're on dry land."

I barely resist the urge to kiss the white sand on the beach at Grand Turk. After an hour of lying under an umbrella, I'm ready to try to eat something. An hour after eating, I wake up from a refreshing nap and consider going into the water for a swim. But for the moment, I'm content to watch the sun sparkle on the turquoise water and the waves build and break on the sugary sand.

Looking up from his paperback on the history of Turks and Caicos, Brice notices I'm awake. He rests the book on his leg and smiles at me. "Hey! How're you feeling?"

"Really good," I answer, thrilled that it's the truth. I swing my legs over the side of my lounger, arch my back, and stretch my arms overhead. "I was just thinking about cooling off in the water."

"Sounds great." He marks his place and sets his book aside. Standing, he holds his hand out to me. "Let's go."

Hands linked, we wade out past the breakers and into deeper water. When I'm up to my chin, I hop onto Brice's back and let him carry me to depths that lap gently at his shoulders. He comes to a stop in the crystal clear water and bends his knees to dunk himself under. I tread, lifting my chin to keep my head dry, and when he reemerges in front of me, I cling to him again. Face-to-face now, we bob in the gentle surf.

I wipe away some water about to drip from his hair and forehead into his eyes, wrap my legs around his waist, and say, "This feels good."

"Yes, it sure does. It's good to see your smile again. And the sun."

"It's good to feel human again."

"Who knew you were so delicate?" he says, kissing my nose.

"Yeah, that's me. A delicate flower."

"It would figure that we'd be witness to two of the fifteen days of rain per year they get in this area."

"Did you learn that in your little book?"

Proudly, he answers, "As a matter of fact, I did."

"Fascinating." I kiss his lips to soften the sarcasm.

After the kiss, he smirks. "I've learned something else the past couple of days."

"Shrimp cocktail tastes terrible the second time around?"

"That, too. No, I've learned that I'm going to have to get over this sympathetic puking thing before we start our family. I won't be much help to you if I can't even be around you. And I want to give the mother of my babies as much TLC as possible." He nuzzles my neck. "When the time comes, that is."

"Huh-huh. Yeah." I'm relieved at that tack-on, but I'm still concerned about all the baby-making talk today. I suddenly feel like I'm on the clock.

I can dismiss the pregnancy-pressure from church members (Mrs. Hanson asked me *in the receiving line at our wedding* when we were planning to start our family) and even family members, because their timetables don't matter. Brice's timetable does. But mine should, too, damn it! And I'd like to be married for a little while before we introduce the stress of pregnancy and childbirth and parenthood. At least, longer than a week.

Again, my strategy is to ignore the conversation and hope it'll go away. I press my chest harder against his, adding distraction to that plan.

Sliding his hands under my thighs, he rubs his thumbs along my bathing suit line. "I just can't wait. It's going to be so exciting."

When he lifts his head and checks to see that I'm in agreement with him, I can't quite arrange my face into the correct expression quickly enough. His smile fades. "What's wrong? Do you feel sick again?" He pushes me away and holds me at arms' length, like I'm an infant he's worried is about to chuck up an entire bottle.

I shake my head, reeling him into me again. "No. I… Well, I think it's so cute how anxious you are to be a dad."

"But…? I sense a 'but' here."

"Let's just enjoy the honeymoon." I attach a "Maybe," so it sounds less like a criticism.

"Oh." He blinks, but he keeps smiling, albeit tightly. "I *am* enjoying it. Immensely. But that doesn't mean I'm not looking forward to the rest of our life."

Feeling terrible that I may have hurt his feelings, I touch one of the wrinkles on his furrowed brow. "And there's nothing wrong with that," I say. "I'm looking forward to it, too. But we have lots of time for all that. And only a few more days of this." I motion to the sea, sun, and sky around us and then rub his suddenly tense shoulders. "I want to savor this and think about nothing else."

Reluctantly, he mutters, "Fair enough."

To try to make up for what he's obviously perceived to be a rebuke, I ask, "Do you still want to go check out that lighthouse?" I originally wasn't thrilled at the prospect, but now I feel like it's the least I can do for him.

"Nah, we don't have to, if you'd rather relax."

"It's right over there," I point to the structure over his shoulder. "I really don't mind. It'll be interesting."

"Really?" His eyes brighten. "Because I read that it was actually built in London, England, and shipped to the island and then reassembled and—"

I put my wet, salty fingertips on his lips and laugh. "Don't ruin it for me. I want to read all the signs at the landmark."

He narrows his eyes at my teasing but laughs with me. Finally, he says, "I know I'm a dork, but I find that kind of stuff fascinating."

"You're a sexy dork. *My* sexy dork." I punctuate that with a kiss on the tip of his nose, followed by a wet, salty one on his lips.

Breathing slightly more heavily, he suggests, "Maybe before we visit the lighthouse, we can go back to the boat for a little while?"

It's hard not to feel smug about my effect on him.

4

BACK TO REALITY

*I*f someone gave me the choice between being seasick for the rest of my life or as sad as I feel at the end of our honeymoon on the plane back to cold, blustery Chicago, I'd choose seasick. At least that would mean I'd be on a cruise for the rest of my life and wouldn't have to return to reality.

Okay, maybe I'm exaggerating a little bit, but not by much. I'm really dreading stepping off this plane at O'Hare and ending what was without a doubt the best week of my life, thirty hours of seasickness and all.

Either Brice isn't feeling the same way I am or he's doing a much better job of hiding it. He actually has a half-smile on his lips as he sits there, scratching notes in the small, leather-bound journal he carries with him nearly everywhere he goes. I've always kind of wondered about that thing. He's hardly ever without it; usually, it rides around in his back pocket (although he kept it in our room on the ship). He tells me he jots down prayers, prayer requests, and sermon ideas, as well as inspirational quotes he hears on TV and radio or sees on other churches' signs.

I crane my neck to get a peek of what he could possibly be writing now and can hardly believe it. It's an outline for a sermon! He can't even wait to get home to get back to work.

Well! I guess he's had enough of me and is ready to move on, no looking back.

Obviously feeling my eyes on him, he suddenly looks up, but I quickly avert my face, staring out the window at the gunmetal gray clouds, so he can't see how visibly upset I am. I feel silly, for one thing. For another thing, what's the point of him knowing? It's good that he likes his life and is glad to be on the way home, where people call him at all hours of the day and night or constantly seek out his advice or complain to him about everything from the music selection for the services to the amount of money spent (or not) on the church property's landscaping. That's where he's in his element. I could tell he was a bit at sea this past week with no one to depend on him for any of their spiritual needs.

I, on the other hand, loved it. He could focus all of his attention on *me*. Now, how selfish is that? But I deserved it, damn it! I've been competing with four hundred other people for his attention for almost a year now, and it gets old after a while. I can't even recall how many times I've had to rearrange my plans around someone who's landed in the hospital or had a falling out with a family member or had a baby or *died*.

Before you go judging me for begrudging these people the care and support of their pastor, I'd like to point out that I've *never* complained to him about any of these instances, because I know it goes with the territory, and I know he does the best he can at balancing his personal life with his professional obligations. I'm just saying it was nice to be on a boat in the middle of an ocean—even on the pukey days—with no email or cell phones, and no way for people to get in touch with us to interrupt his personal time, no matter how worthy the cause.

Anyway, my melancholy is not completely about the obligations that come with being married to Reverend Responsibility, either. If I were to be honest with myself, I'm also not looking forward to going back to my own job at Smart Art. While I typically enjoy it, especially now that I've been promoted to Artist Liaison, it's still work, and I often put in ten- or twelve-hour days of hand-holding and ego-stroking at the gallery. At least now, though, I won't be coming home to an empty apartment at the end of the day. I'll have someone with whom to share my triumphs and frustrations. *That* will be a definite improvement.

Finally, at that thought, there's a lightening in my chest and on my shoulders. It won't be all bad. He's right; we have a great life ahead of us. Quiet evenings. Late nights. Later mornings. Inside jokes. Romantic dinners. Fun Saturday outings and day trips. It's something to look forward to, for sure.

I reach over and grab his left hand. He squeezes my fingers but continues scrawling in his journal without a moment's glance at me.

That's okay, though. I mean, I'm not *that* needy.

Am I?

Surely not.

Would it be nice if he'd at least wait until tomorrow to start ignoring me? Sure. But, to be fair, he's not really ignoring me. He's obviously inspired by something and needs to put his thoughts to paper so he doesn't forget them. I get that. This is just another instance of something coming up in his line of work at an inconvenient time. It's nothing personal, I'm sure (sort of).

I'm also sure I'd better get over being such a spoiled brat

if this is going to work. Not that there's an option of it *not* working. It *has* to work. And we have to figure out how to make it work. And by "we," I mean, "I." Because I knew what I was signing up for, and I may be able to get away with not knowing how to cook or knit or sew or play piano or sing or have a normal conversation, but I *will* need to learn how to put other people's needs before my own. Maybe not all the time, but enough that it will have to become second nature. Like it is for Brice.

How hard can it be?

∾

"Jared's coming over for dinner tomorrow night," Brice says as he checks his email on his phone while we wait for our stuff in baggage claim.

I flinch at this announcement. I know I didn't invite the future vicar for dinner the night after arriving home from a week's vacation (a.k.a., our *honeymoon*). That would be insane. And while I've doubted my sanity on many occasions in the past, I haven't done anything crazy like that in at least three months.

When I tell him Jared must be mistaken, he replies. "No, *I* invited him. I figured it'd be no big deal. It's just Jared."

Just Jared. Right. Jared Laszewski, the fourth-year seminarian from Concordia in St. Louis, who will be Messiah's vicar (a pastoral intern of sorts) starting in mid-December, is twenty-six going on fifteen. Wide-eyed, fresh-faced, energetic, idealistic, and—honestly—cringe-worthily naïve, it wore me out just being in his presence for a few hours when he came to visit the Messiah campus at the end of the summer as part of his vicariate application. But Brice claimed to see a lot of himself in the guy (which made me glad I didn't meet *him* until he had matured a little bit, because if he was anything like this Jared joker, that would have been a deal-breaker), and since he's the one who's going to have to work with him on a daily basis for a year, who was I to say anything?

Plus, it's not that I don't like Jared. For one thing, I don't know him well enough to have a real opinion of him. He was pretty nervous the time I met him, so that probably accounted for some of his gooberish behavior. But he seems like a nice guy. It's just that a little of him goes a *long* way. And I'm not sure that I want to experience even a little of him tomorrow after a long day at work.

Channeling the peace that passes all understanding, I smile tightly. "But we both have to go back to work tomorrow. And you know it'll be crazy; we'll be buried. I probably won't get home until 7:00, at the earliest."

Still scrolling through emails (which puts the onus of keeping a lookout for our luggage on me, I'd like to point out), he seems unconcerned. "I told him I'd pick him up from his hotel right after leaving Messiah for the day, around five. We'll wait for you. I'm sure there'll be plenty for us to talk about while we wait."

I see one of my three bags slide down the chute and onto the metal carousel, but I say skeptically before chasing it down, "You're going to leave the church by five tomorrow?"

He doesn't have a chance to answer, because I dart away from him to claim my suitcase. He's close behind me, pocketing his phone as he finally decides to pay attention to the matter at hand.

Reaching around me to lift the bag before I can get a handle on it, he says, "I'll go through my emails tonight so I can get a head start on the day; then I'll go in a little early tomorrow morning, before everyone else gets there, so I can get some stuff done while it's still quiet. I'll be at the house with Jared by 6:00," is his bold prediction, "with plenty of time to whip up something simple for dinner."

I guess as long as he doesn't expect anything more from me than to show up and pretend to be interested in what they're talking about, I can't really complain. The latter part of that assignment may be tricky, but I think I can handle it. I've had a lot of practice this past week.

"If you say so."

"I do," he says on a groan while hoisting suitcases #2 and #3 and setting them next to me. "Just a second, and I'll strap those two together." Minutes later he hefts his one suitcase and duffel bag from the carousel and delivers on his promise. Then he puts me in charge of guarding everything while he goes to find a trolley.

I follow his head until it's swallowed by the crush of people and then again when he bobs back into view. As he loads the bags onto the cart, he confirms, "Now, your brother is picking us up right out front, correct? And he knows what time to be here?"

If I didn't know better, I'd say Reverend Easygoing was worried about something. "I gave him all the information. But you know Jason. We'll probably have to wait a little while."

"Oh." He looks supremely annoyed by that. And when we do, indeed, have to stand on the cold sidewalk outside the terminal, watching for my mom's minivan (which I had to work very hard to get Jason to agree to drive, even after I told him how much luggage we had), he sighs more than once before saying, "Our plane landed twenty minutes late. Where *is* he?"

I already have my phone to my ear to call for a status update, but I can't help asking, "What's your rush?"

Refusing to look at me, he says, "I told the elders I'd be at their meeting about that foreclosure property we're thinking of flipping for a rental."

"You told them this, when?" I jab at the disconnect button on my phone when Jason's voicemail picks up.

"Before we ever left. I figured we'd be home by now."

"You committed to going to a church meeting the *day* we got home from our honeymoon?" I'm not doing such a good job of remaining serene anymore.

"It'll be, like, fifteen minutes. Tops."

My response to that is to cross my arms over my chest and purse my lips. We both know that nothing involving the board of elders takes "fifteen minutes, tops." My dad's opening prayer can last that long. Okay, maybe that's a slight exaggeration, but not by much.

Jason's arrival saves either of us from saying anything else on the topic for the moment. Unfortunately, that means I have to stew about it while Brice pretends like nothing's wrong and sunnily answers Jason's questions about the cruise as they load the van. We climb in and hang on tight while Jason navigates the roads circling the airport to get us to the highway.

When we're finally making progress toward home on the expressway, my brother asks, "Everything okay with you over there, Sis?"

"I'm tired," I answer shortly, but then I can't help but passive-aggressively add, "And I get to spend our first night home alone. I'm really excited about that."

"You're not going to be home alone all night," Brice responds from the backseat.

"We'll see."

"You won't! I'll make it quick."

"Unless you decide to pop into your office 'to return a few emails,' and the phone rings. Or one of the elders corners you after the meeting and wants to show you pictures of his new grandson. Or—"

"You're being ridiculous."

That stings, since I don't think I am. History supports my concerns. I know how easily "a few minutes" turns into a few hours for him when he steps foot into the church building. If it's not someone calling or stopping by to chat, it's his getting distracted and finding something that he feels needs to be done, which leads to something else that needs seeing to, which leads to three other things "that'll just take a minute." I've witnessed this firsthand. It's what makes him so good at what he does.

Jason snickers. "Whoa," he mutters under his breath.

"It's okay," I yield magnanimously. "Never mind."

"No, I'm sorry," Brice quickly says. "That was uncalled for."

"Whatever."

I don't want to hear his apology, no matter how heartfelt it is. What I want to hear is that he won't go to that stupid meeting tonight and leave me at home to unpack by myself. But after my not-so-gracious half-rejection of his attempt to make amends, not another word comes from the backseat.

To his credit, Jason doesn't make any smart-ass remarks. But I know he's thinking about a dozen of them, probably chief among them the same thing that's weighing heavily on my mind: *well, the honeymoon's officially over.*

Whether he's making a point or things just happened to

work out that way, Brice is away from the house for almost thirty minutes *exactly*. I didn't even get all my bags unpacked in the time he was gone.

"That was quick!" I don't mind admitting when I'm wrong, especially in cases where I benefit from it.

He tosses his duffel on the bed and unzips it. "I told—" My sharp look stops him from finishing that thought, but he quickly redirects with, "—um, *the guys* that I was on a tight schedule."

Short leash, more like it. I wait while my hair-trigger temper recovers from the "I-told-you-so," close call. As sweetly as possible, I say, "Thank you."

He shrugs. "I realized it *was* sort of insensitive to rush out the door as soon as we got home."

Don't say "der!" Be classy. Be generous. Channel the perfect pastor's wife.

"You just want to make everyone happy," I say, putting the best construction on it.

"Exactly. I really didn't think it was a big deal, and after being gone for nine days—"

"You got married and went on your honeymoon!" I can't help but laugh at his fierce—and in this case, illogical —work ethic.

He grins sheepishly. "I know, but—"

"No! Just stop. Now *you're* being ridiculous." I say it with a smile, because I don't want to get into a fight on our first night home, but I *do* want him to know what a big mistake he made saying that, especially in front of my little brother.

His shoulders slump as he shakes his head. "I never should have said that to you."

"Damn right. Ranks right up there with the time you said you were a fruit inspector, and I was a bruised apple."

Now he's laughing. "I *never* made that exact comparison!"

I poke my tongue out between my grinning lips. "Close enough."

"You're a grudge-holder."

"Knowledge is power, buddy. You should keep that in mind every time you consider saying something that might piss me off." I touch my fingertip to my chin. "*'Hmm... is it really worth it to make this point?'*"

Jutting out his chin, he stands with his hands on his hips and blinks while he taps his foot and tries not to smile at my dopey impersonation of his voice. "You are *not* giving me the sort of respect you should give your husband, woman."

Nonchalantly continuing to separate white from colored clothing into two piles of dirty laundry on the floor, I say casually, "What do you expect? I'm a bad apple."

The panties I'm currently holding become an ineffectual weapon as he pounces and grabs me around the waist.

5

UNWANTED VISITORS

*S*even days of backlog is always fun, so my first day back to work has been as big of a nightmare as I imagined it would be—only now with a twist that I wasn't expecting.

When the call comes through, I immediately recognize his number on my caller ID and want to dive under my desk to hide from him, as if he can see me through the phone. Instead I swallow audibly and pick up the phone. Trying to sound as confident and positive as possible, I chirp, "Smart Art, this is Peyton speaking!"

"Oh. Peyton." I can practically hear his sneer down the line. "I was hoping to speak directly to Marshall."

Stefan Svadjlenka: New York-based artist with an ego the size of Alaska (that's three times bigger than Texas, in case you didn't know, and a *lot* colder) and who delights in making my life miserable. And oh, yeah, Secret's father.

Not that *he* knows that. Good grief! Just thinking about the possibility of him ever finding out that our disaster of a one-night stand resulted in a baby gives me heart palpitations.

"Marshall's away on business…" (a.k.a., "a trip to Italy with his boyfriend that the gallery owner will write off on his taxes, since he'll be visiting some art galleries while over there") "…for the next two weeks. But I'd be glad to help you, Stefan, in the meantime."

I guess lying is somewhat like riding a bike. I haven't done it in a while, but lookit there! I still know how to do it well.

Now that I think about it, I should have been expecting to hear from the snake (although it's unfortunate it had to be my very first day back), because I've almost tricked myself into forgetting that I ever made the mistake of sleeping with him. Not that I regret it, as a whole. A lot of good came out of it, obviously. At least that's what I've reminded myself every single day since getting to know Brice, when good *did* start to come of it. Before then, it pretty much gave me nothing but shame and heartache. And all the symptoms from a Pepto-Bismol commercial. Plus, eventually, more heartache.

Anyway, it's only fitting that he should call when everything seems to have smoothed out in my life, and my tan hasn't even faded from my honeymoon. I mean, Heaven forbid I get to bask in any kind of happiness without him sticking his pointy little nose into things.

Normally, he makes his assistant, an equally snobby, unpleasant woman, deal with me, but it would figure that I'd have the pleasure of working with him directly today, when I'm swamped with emails and voicemail messages and mini-crises that have happened while I was away and that Marshall decided could wait until my return.

"I guess you'll have to do," Stefan says now with a sigh. "I'm being audited by the IRS, so I need detailed financial statements and records, and while Drex was a colorful guy and didn't balk at fulfilling some of the most inane requests (God knows I tried to find his limit), he wasn't much of a records-keeper, so I'm having a hell of a time putting my hands on some of my sales receipts."

At the mention of my ex-boyfriend, I can't help but smile. I must admit, I miss him. Or at least I miss the Drex I knew before he found out about what happened between Stefan and me, dumped my ass on Christmas Eve, and refused to speak to me ever again. And I'm silently blessing him for putting his former boss in a sticky situation with the federal government. Now *that's* karma, even though I don't really believe in it (that's what I tell Brice, anyway).

Trying—and failing—to keep the smile from my voice, I say, "Oh, that's too bad. Fortunately, I can easily send you copies of all the sales receipts from the pieces we've sold here at Smart Art." I don't add that Marshall wouldn't have been the right person to contact about that, anyway. As far as I'm concerned, Stefan can bypass me anytime, and I'll count myself lucky. "How would you like me to get that information to you?"

"Immediately," he snaps. "I've already spent too much time searching and calling galleries—"

"No, I mean, would you like me to fax you the copies or ship them overnight or email them…?" I trail off before I give him so many options that his low-functioning brain short-circuits.

Even more impatiently, he replies, "I don't know what my fax number is! Or if I even have a fax machine. Does anyone have one of those anymore? Just email the copies to me. Or not. Wait! Ship them to me overnight, I guess. They're going to want hard copies, and I don't have time to print and copy a bunch of fucking receipts."

His ugliness doesn't make me feel a bit shy about asking,

"Why are you doing all this, anyway? Where's your assistant?"

He pauses. "If you must know—and not that it's any of your damn business—she quit. The day I found out about this audit, as a matter of fact. She won't be getting a reference from me, that's for sure. And if I'd known what a shitty job Drex had done at keeping track of my sales, I wouldn't have given him one, either."

The last I heard (or read on Facebook, actually), Drex was waiting tables. I'm pretty sure he didn't need Stefan's stinky reference to get that job. But maybe by now he's making a living with his painting. I hope so. I really want him to be happy and successful, despite how things ended between the two of us.

That's why my stomach clenches when Stefan says, "I guess I'm going to have to call up the moron and try to piece together where to find the numbers to my private patrons."

"Good luck with that," I mutter hollowly, wishing it was appropriate—or even possible—for me to somehow get in touch with Drex to warn him about such an awful call. Impulsively, I add on, "Tell him that Peyton Stratford—I mean, Northam—I mean, Stratford—says hi."

As soon as it's out, I regret it. Not only would it be mean-spirited for Drex to find out about my marriage to Brice from Stefan, of all people, but I don't want Stefan to know anything about my personal life.

However, I have to say it's somewhat gratifying when Stefan's quiet for a beat or two following my stumbling through my last name (it's really hard to get used to calling myself anything other than Stratford). Then he has to go and ruin it by saying, "Hmph! *If* I can get ahold of him, I hardly think talking about *you* will put him in a generous mood. But it's good to know you're still as narcissistic as ever. Your new husband sure has his work cut out for him. I guess it's true that there *is* someone for everyone."

He's a client. He's a client. He's a client. He's a major *client,* I remind myself so I don't say something I'll regret.

Brightly, I say, "So, okay, then! I'll overnight those records to you. You should have them first thing tomorrow morning. If you have any problems…" *other than the obvious ones related to your being a miserable bastard* "…just give me a call. It was *so good* talking to you, Stefan." *You remind me how truly lucky and blessed I am to be virtually free of you.*

Before he can say anything else to further ruin my day, I hang up on him. I don't move or do anything but think about him for a long time afterwards, either. Damn him.

I should have said, *"Yes, I'm sure that gives you a lot of hope, Stefan,"* or *"My husband tells me every day how much he loves me, and I don't think he considers it 'work,'"* or *"Pleasing a woman is a lot of work for someone like you. Maybe you should get that checked out,"* or, simply, *"Fuck you, Stefan."*

Of course, it took me the rest of the workday to think of those comebacks, so that would have been a long, awkward phone call, with him sitting there waiting for me to deliver my insult. Even those are lame. And hardly becoming of someone in my new role.

Cursing is just something I can't seem to quit doing, no matter how many times I see Brice cringe when I say something profane. I know he hates it; I know it stresses him out when he considers the possibility of my doing it in front of someone from church, especially one of the kids in the youth group, and I know I should try harder to stop. But it's therapeutic. And I have decent control of my mouth in certain social situations. As I've told him a hundred times, he really has nothing to worry about.

When I arrive home from work, and I walk through the door connecting the garage to the kitchen to see him bent over, removing what appears to be a large glass casserole dish of enchiladas from the oven, the first thing I say to him is, "Please, tell me there's a special place in Hell for fuck-faces like Stefan. Please."

"Peyton." He sighs and closes the oven door with his knee before setting the dish on top of the stove.

"I know it's not true. But just humor me. I need to believe it's true." While he slides the oven mitts from his hands, I step out of my high heels and slink over to him, rubbing suggestively against his arm and cupping one of his butt cheeks in my hand. "Say it. I'll make it worth your while." I add a silly little growl for emphasis.

The sound of a throat clearing behind me makes me squeak, grab Brice's upper arm with both hands, and hide my face against his shoulder.

"Jared's joining us for dinner tonight, remember?" my husband calmly states. I peek up at him, but his head's turned as he looks out the window into our tiny backyard. Other than the twitch in the corner of his right eye, he doesn't give any indication of what he's thinking or feeling, but that little twitch is enough for me to know he's pissed off.

"Oh, right," I reply meekly, letting go of him and turning toward the new vicar with a smile. "Jared! Hey! Uh…" My face feels like it could burst into flames at any second.

The baby-faced, bespectacled future pastor is probably —if it's possible—redder than I am, leaving no doubt that he heard every filthy word (and sound) and saw every lewd gesture.

"Hi, Peyton. How're things?" he asks pleasantly, looking everywhere but at me.

"Dandy. And what brings you to town again?"

He defers with a nod to Brice, who answers, "I thought it would be a good idea for him to visit a couple of months before his actual vicariate starts, you know, in a low-pressure situation, so he could get to know the congregants."

Well, he just got to know me in a big way, so mission frickin' accomplished, Reverend Stratego.

"What a nice idea," I purr. I bend over to pick up my shoes and hold them up. "Well! I'm, uh, just going to put these away and change my clothes before dinner. I'll be right back."

In our bedroom, I seriously consider crawling into bed and staying there. For the rest of my life. But no sooner have I stepped from my dress and shed my pantyhose than the bedroom door opens a crack, and Brice slips through it.

At the stony look on his face, I cover my eyes and flaming cheeks with my hands. "I. Am. So. Sorry," I muffle, standing in the middle of the room in my bra and panties. "I totally forgot he was coming to dinner, and there was no car in the driveway or parked at the curb—"

"He doesn't have a car. I'm driving him around everywhere."

"I know! I'm just telling you how I could make such an embarrassing blunder." I cross to the closet and pull out the baggiest, most unflattering sweats I own. "He probably thinks I'm the foulest, nastiest—"

"I'm sure he's heard worse."

"At truck stops, maybe! And not from a pastor's wife.

Oh, my gosh! How am I going to go out there and face him the rest of the night?"

I poke my head through my shirt to reveal my husband working his mouth from side to side in an attempt not to laugh.

"It's not funny!" I hiss.

He shakes his head and rubs the back of his neck. "No, it's not. I know. But this was bound to happen someday. I'm thankful it was in front of him, not Mrs. Hanson or one of the elders."

"Brice!" I pluck a pair of balled-up socks from the dresser and toss them at his head. He catches them, holding them out to me in his upturned palm. "Go out there and tell him I don't feel well. Or something."

"No."

"Please!" I snatch the socks from him. "I've had such a horrible day, and now this!"

"Uh-uh. I'm sorry you had a bad day, but your potty mouth got you into this particular mess; now, you figure out how to get out of it."

I can't believe this! He's using one of the most mortifying experiences of my adult life (and that's saying something) as a teachable moment? I hop on one foot and then the other as I put on my socks. "I *have* figured it out; you're going to let me hide in here the rest of the night."

"Nope." He's completely serious. "We have a guest. Plus, I left the church early, even though I still had a lot left to do, to make dinner, so you're going to come out there and eat it."

I lift my chin. "Don't talk to me like I'm a child."

"Stop acting like one, then." At my indignant grunt, he says, "You think I'm not embarrassed by what just happened? And it's not even *my* fault. But I can't hide back here for the rest of the night. So neither can you."

"You could have clued me in sooner that he was sitting right there at the breakfast bar. He was in my blind spot!"

"I was too stunned to say or do anything!"

When I simply shake my head while I try not to cry as a result of the hopeless humiliation I'm feeling, he softens, crosses the room, and hugs me. "Come on. It's not that bad. I mean, it's *bad*, but he's a nice guy. He's probably just as embarrassed as we are. We should go out there and pretend it never happened. I'm sure that's what he wants, too."

I nod pitifully. "Okay."

"All right!" He grasps my shoulders and straightens his arms, looking down at me. "And do you think you've learned your lesson about dropping the f-bomb?"

"Probably not," I say, to which he laughs and gives me a playful shake. I let my head loll. When he stops shaking me, I shrug. "Sorry, but I'm just being honest."

He sighs, turns, and opens the bedroom door, which he holds open while gesturing for me to go ahead of him. "Ladies—or something like that—first," he mutters as I pass by.

6

SHIPS IN THE NIGHT

I wake up alone—again—and turn my head toward the empty pillow next to mine. I shift my eyes to the clock on Brice's bedside table and make a note of the time: 5:30. That's half an hour earlier than I woke up yesterday after rolling over and running into nothing but cool sheets. And an hour earlier than my alarm, which is obviously set way too late if I want to share any part of my morning with my husband.

The house is silent. I can feel its emptiness. Years of living alone have made me all-too-familiar with that feeling. It's dense and palpable. It's also something I thought I'd left behind.

When *was* the last time I saw my husband outside of church? The past week has felt like an eternity.

Let's see… On his day off, Saturday morning, we took a walk at the park, where he was promptly called to the bedside of one of our oldest members, who slipped away shortly after he arrived, and said prayers with her family. When he got home in the early evening, I kept him company while he did his ironing for the week (we've already agreed it will be best for his wardrobe if I keep a safe distance from the iron), but he wanted to put the finishing touches on his sermon for the next morning, which kept him up much later than I was able to last, so I went to bed and didn't even wake up when he joined me.

Sunday, he was up and at church before I was awake, so the first time I saw him that day was when everyone else saw him, in front of the congregation, doing his pastor thing. Between services, he disappeared to lead his teen Sunday school class, while I found myself cornered by Tracy Plucker and her mother, Beverly, who wanted me to join their prayer shawl knitting circle. ("Oh, I can teach you how to knit! I taught Tracy when she was four years old; surely, I can teach you!") Then my own mother and sister wanted to firm up plans for a spa day. After much hemming and hawing on my part, we finally decided to go on a Saturday when I was pretty sure Brice had a wedding to perform and wouldn't have the day off, anyway. Satisfied with that, the two of them left the church, and I rushed to the vestry, hoping I could make it before the start of the second service. If the organ prelude was any indication, I'd be cutting it close.

When I slipped into the tiny room, Brice was looking into the mirror, straightening his vestments after saying his pre-service prayers and before stepping into the sanctuary. I got no more than "Good morning," out when he said, "Hey, we've been invited to dinner at the Williamses' at 4:00. I'll pick you up at the house at 3:45." Then he looked at his watch, made a noise, kissed my forehead, and left me standing there, wondering, *Who eats dinner at 4:00?* and *What the hell just happened?*

The next time I saw him alone was in the car on the way to the Williamses, but I suddenly couldn't think of any of the things I'd wanted to tell him all day, so I sat mutely looking out the window at the houses as they became larger and larger and further apart the closer we drove to what can only be described as the Williams *Estate*, complete with horse stables, tennis courts, ponds with fountains, and *two* swimming pools.

As skeptical as I was about eating dinner so early, I would have preferred that to what really happened, which was that we arrived and socialized for *three hours* before dinner was served at 7:00, by which time I felt light-headed with hunger since I hadn't eaten lunch, as I thought I was going to be expected to eat an absurdly early dinner. When the meal finally happened, it was a two-hour affair, consisting of a menu of all of my least-favorite foods, including veal (why do wealthy people insist on eating baby animals?), eggplant, some sort of bean-and-cabbage salad that I was *still* burping three days later, and something else that Brice and I never did figure out but that we both politely ate and which ended up being the most tolerable thing on my plate.

By the time we got home after 10:30, I was gassy, tired, and suffering from the Sunday night blues as I dreaded the work week ahead. I was *not* in the mood for intercourse of any kind.

That being said, if I had known it was the last time I'd see my husband in days, I may have put forth a better effort. But probably not. I really was miserable. And on the sexy scale of one to ten—with "one" being ninety-year-old Mrs. Hanson and "ten" being that model in nothing but her undies and a diamond necklace on the billboard on my way to work—I was a zero that night. (At least Mrs. Hanson has that cute-old-lady thing going for her.)

Monday is usually his other day off, but he was up before me (jogging, he told me when I called him on my lunch break so I could apologize for being such a downer the night before) and still wasn't back before I had to leave for work. Then *I* worked late only to come home to an empty house with a note on the counter: "With Jared at the batting cages."

Up with the birds on Tuesday, he spent most of the day prepping for and presiding over the funeral for the church member who passed away on Saturday. Then he made his normal rounds at the nursing homes and hospitals before working late to catch up on things that he'd normally do on Tuesday if not for the funeral.

I have no idea what his schedule was like on Wednesday. We played phone tag all day but none of his messages were informative. He did finally call at about 6:30, but it was right before he was heading into confirmation class, so he couldn't talk long. Then he warned me not to wait up, because he hadn't even started on his sermon, so his goal was to get a rough draft finished after confirmation class, and he had no idea how long that was going to take.

Now it's Thursday. I know he's been around the house, because I see the evidence—dirty clothes in the hamper, dishes in the dishwasher that aren't mine, nerdy books scattered on end tables, an impression in the mattress and pillow where he's presumably in bed each night (at least for a couple of hours)—but I haven't caught him in the act of being home since Sunday.

And if this week were an anomaly, I'd shrug and chalk it up to one of those insane weeks that comes along now and then. But this is how our life has been for *months*. I thought once the Christmas season was over, things would slow down. It's March, so, I guess not. There's always something —or someone—to fill the time. For him, anyway. As for me, I'm lonely.

It's time to call the girls.

~

"Nip it in the bud, girl," Jen's reflection tells me that evening. We're lined up on three recumbent bikes in front of a mirrored wall in the fitness center at Mitzi's apartment complex. "You've been married less than six months, and he's already spending all that time outside the house? You should still be unable to get enough of each other!"

Pedaling listlessly, Mitzi looks at me as if I've just described a fatal disease I've contracted when she asks, "Isn't there anything you can do?"

I shrug. "It's not like he can help it. Stuff has to get done."

"If he works late in his office, maybe you can go there and sit on the couch and read a book," she suggests brightly. "At least then you'd be in the same room."

I consider it. "That would be okay, once in a while. But he's usually busy. I don't want to be a distraction. Or clingy."

Jen presses some buttons on her bike controls and pedals more furiously. "Get over that! He obviously doesn't get 'subtle.'"

Now I gulp and try to make it sound like a joke when I say, "Maybe he just doesn't want to spend time with me. Maybe he's sick of me." To hide any real emotion that may sneak through, I pretend to adjust the position of the seat on the exercise equipment.

Mitzi clucks, "No way! I *know* that's not the case."

"How? Do you two actually have conversations? Because if so, I'm jealous."

"No! What makes you think that?"

"She was kidding, you idiot," Jen snaps, leaning forward to look around me at Mitzi. "I swear, sometimes you are such a ditz."

Mitzi laughs at herself. "Oh! I get it now. Sorry."

I reach over and pat her shoulder. "It's okay. Apparently, I *am* too subtle."

"Let's hope Brice is smarter than Mitzi, then," says the only one of us still pedaling her bike. She ignores this fact when she continues, "Anyway, I think you're on the right track with working out. You're getting a little… chubby."

"What?" I whip my head up to look at myself in the mirror. "Do you really think so?"

"Yes," she answers at the same time Mitzi says, "No!"

Which one is it? Am I letting myself go already? And would that even matter to him?

Mitzi speaks up. "Brice isn't shallow."

"That we *know* of," Jen qualifies. "Peyton's never given him a reason to say anything that would give it away. Until now. Look at her face. It's definitely rounder."

The three of us study my face until I say, "This is stupid. I know what it is! I got a new haircut."

"Fire that hairstylist," Jen mutters.

"I think it's cute," Mitzi says soothingly. "Don't listen to her. You look fine."

Fine? Is that really how I'd like to be described? And not as in, "That girl is *fine*," but as in, "Just fine."

While I'm analyzing the degrees of "fine," Jen points out, "I mean, look at Brice. He jogs every day; he's one of the only men I know who eats vegetables other than potatoes; he drinks *milk*. He's the poster child for clean living! It's not fair for someone who takes such good care of himself to be saddled with a frumpy couch-potato wife."

"Hey!"

"No offense. And you're not there… yet. That's what I'm saying. It's good you're here at the gym."

I pump my legs and get the bike wheel moving at a good clip for the first time since sitting down.

"I can't believe you're letting her get in your head," Mitzi says, rolling her eyes. "Even I know better than to do that."

Jen wipes at her face with a towel. "Hey, when you land a hot husband, it's hard work to keep him interested. At least Peyton's already landed him. We're not even there yet. And you never will be, Mitzi, if you don't learn a little self-control and trade Ding Dongs for dumbbells."

"Good grief!" I cry between huffs and puffs. "You're particularly mean tonight."

"I haven't been laid in a long-ass time, Peyton. It starts to wear on a girl."

Oh, I remember all too well. But a newly married woman saying that is like someone preaching about that "one time" when you were "really cold and hungry" to a crowd of homeless people while walking past them to get into a restaurant with an all-you-can-eat buffet. So I keep my mouth shut while she and Mitzi compete to see which one has gone the longest since her last sexual encounter. Mitzi wins with three years but then quickly changes the subject when Jen goes over the top with her laughter and exclamations of disbelief.

"So, where is Brice tonight, while you're here with us?"

I shrug. "Some meeting. I probably won't see him until tomorrow night, if then."

Friday is his busiest day. He has breakfast with a bunch of other area Lutheran pastors; finishing touches on the order of service, weekly bulletin, sermon, and—if applicable—children's message; rounds at the hospitals and nursing homes that he doesn't visit on Tuesdays; and any other business that comes up unexpectedly.

"I rarely see him on Fridays." It comes out like an admission, as if I'm confessing that I seldom shave my armpits.

"Unacceptable," Jen says. "You should ambush him at the meeting."

"No!" Mitzi says. "That's not fair. He's just doing his job. Get up early enough tomorrow morning so that you guys can have a heart-to-heart."

An argument isn't my preferred way to start the day (especially at o'dark-thirty), but I know she's right. I can't go on like this much longer. And for all I know, something's come up to preclude his spending Saturday with me. If I wait for him to come to me, we could go months without spending any quality time together.

After I left the gym, I decided I couldn't even wait until morning, so I camped out on the sofa and waited for Brice. First I folded about a week's worth of laundry. Then I watched some TV. Then I read a book. Then I did some pencil sketches of a person withering away and dying on a sofa while waiting for her husband to come home.

At about midnight, I decided to rest my eyes.

7

REGROUPING

I wake up this morning underneath a blanket. The house is silent, as usual. Also as usual, I know I'm the only one home.

"Motherfucker!" I shout at the ceiling as I kick free of the blanket and jump from the couch, ignoring the sharp pain in my neck while I scramble for my cell phone to see what time it is. 6:50. Super! In addition to failing to catch my husband at home (the man is an effing ninja, I'm now convinced), I've also overslept.

I get ready in record time (thank God for dry shampoo), and now I'm just sitting in my freezing car at the park, waiting for Brice to finish his jog. Like a common stalker, I've been forced to anticipate his schedule, and it's pissing me off. When we said "I do," I didn't realize I was agreeing to be roommates with the Reverend Crouching Tiger (or is he Hidden Dragon?).

I'm definitely going to be late for work, but I don't care. I'll skip lunch. Or something. This is important! When he finally appears at the trailhead, he glances at me, looks away, and then does a double-take. Squinting, he bends slightly at the waist to see through my windshield. After confirming for himself that it really is his wife, sitting alone in a car in a parking lot at a public park at 7:30 a.m., he smiles uncertainly and waves. The closer he gets to me, though, the more worried he looks.

I step out of the car and hunker down into my coat as a strong gust of wind slams into me.

"What's wrong?" he asks immediately, looking torn between hurrying to me and hanging back in case I have bad news that he'd rather not hear.

"I haven't seen you since Sunday," I say. "Seems pretty wrong to me."

"Oh." He stops in front of me, smiles, and puts his hands on his hips. He's still slightly out-of-breath from running, his cheeks are rosy from the cold and exertion, and it suddenly hits me how much I've missed him.

Emotionally, I take two steps to close the gap between us and throw my arms around his shoulders, burying my face in his sweaty, scruffy neck.

It takes him a second, but he eventually returns my hug, hesitantly at first but then matching my intensity. "Hey."

In a choked rush, I blurt, "You're never home, and you spend more time with Jared than me, and we haven't been married that long, but I think maybe you're sick of me already, or maybe it's because I've gotten kind of chubby lately, but really I haven't—it's the way this new haircut frames my face, I think—and you know how I hate working out, but I'll do it if you want me to, and I'll even get up with you and run at 5:30, because at least then we'll see each other at least once a day, and I've tried to be understanding and get my own life, but hanging out with Mitzi and Jen and my family just isn't the same as being with you, and—and I miss you!"

He laughs nervously while trying to peel me off him. When I won't let go, he gives up and says with me still attached to his neck, "I've been home. A little. But you've been at work or asleep."

"That doesn't count, then."

"Okay..."

"Why don't you wake me up when you come home?" Now I separate from him just enough to look into his face. It's obvious that he thinks I've lost my mind.

His arm obscures his face as he wipes sweat from his forehead with the shoulder of his sweatshirt sleeve. "I don't know. I know how much you enjoy sleeping. And you always look so peaceful."

"Does it sound 'peaceful,' having nightmares about the rest of my life being like this?"

He lowers his arm and smiles down at me. "Aww, hon!"

"Don't 'hon' me! And don't look at your watch!" I add when he pulls back his sleeve to check the time.

"It's just that I have breakfast with—never mind. You're right." He widens his eyes and sniffs. "I'm sorry. I didn't realize you were so worried. I just thought we were both particularly busy this week."

"Yeah, busy being single again. Actually, I saw you more when we were dating than I do now. And we *live* together!" This realization feels like a kick to the gut.

He thinks about it and laughs. "Wow. You may be right."

"You used to go out of your way to be with me." I say it so softly that it's almost lost in the wind.

He sighs and seems to catch himself right before rolling his eyes. "Uh..." he begins before apparently thinking better of it. Then, "Hmm..." goes nowhere, too. Finally, he says, "You know what it is? I don't *have* to go out of my way to be with you anymore." He seems relieved to have come up with this explanation. "Yeah. I know you're going to be waiting for me at home——"

I disengage myself from him and give him some room to breathe. "So that's why you never come home?"

"There you go again with 'never.'"

"You're never home when I am."

Closing one eye, he observes, "As far as I can tell, that's only half my fault. I don't get upset that you're not home when I am, because I know you're working."

I clench my teeth. "Don't get cute."

He grins. "What? I can only be responsible for my own schedule."

"Exactly! But my work hours are set, so you know exactly when I'll be home and when I'll be at work."

"And that must be nice for you, but I don't have that same luxury. What do you want me to do?"

We square off, our cold breaths colliding.

After I realize he's not going to say anything else until I answer what I thought was a rhetorical question, I admit sullenly, "I don't know." Then I brainstorm, "But maybe you can go back to going out of your way to spend time with me."

"Why don't *you* go out of *your* way to spend time with *me*?"

His half-serious question throws me off guard and puts me on the defensive.

"Oh. Uh, I mean, well… What do you mean?"

He shoves his hands into the pouch on the front of his hoodie and jogs in place. "During the week, you act like you're on a set of rails that runs from home to work and that you're not allowed to veer off the track."

"I have a routine," I mumble.

"Yeah, well, work me in."

"Okay—Hey! Wait a minute!" He blinks innocently at me. "You're the one who's up before dawn and doesn't come home until after midnight, but *I'm* the one who's not making time for us?"

"You have more time to work with than I do. I mean, why don't you drop in on me in my office, like you used to? Or come with me when I visit people in the hospital or at nursing homes? Or, I don't know, *call* me or text me, just to say hello?"

"I never know what you're doing. I don't want to interrupt something important or bother you."

"If I'm doing something that important, then I don't have my phone with me. And I'm never doing something so important in my office that I wouldn't want a visit from you."

Smooth talker! In spite of myself, I blush and look down at my feet.

He stops jogging, pulls me to him, and rubs my back.

Sullenly, I ask what I've been wondering all week: "What's the point in having Jared around if you're not going to give him some of your stuff to do so that you can get more than four hours of sleep a night?"

"That's a whole other topic. Anyway." He pushes me away and nods toward my car. "Shouldn't you be getting to work?"

"Yes," I grudgingly acknowledge, "but this conversation isn't over!"

"It's not?" he mutters and then straightens and smiles brightly at me. "I mean, okay. We'll talk more later."

"You'll be home when I get home from work?" I press.

He winces. "It'll be close."

"Brice." I backpedal toward my car while he backs in the opposite direction, inching toward home.

"Tonight doesn't happen to be one of your late Fridays, does it?"

"No, it doesn't."

"Oh, man!" he laments theatrically. "Because I'd definitely be home in time if that were the case."

My butt hits my cold car door, but I remain facing him. "Well, it's not, so… Do you at least have tomorrow off?"

He perks up. "Yeah! Remember, we're going to your parents' house for Jason's birthday?"

Oh, shit.

While I process that reminder, he trots back over to me and pecks me on the lips and then returns for a longer kiss, which almost erases my worries about what may happen at tomorrow's Stratford family gathering and the last-minute birthday present shopping that I might as well do tonight after work if Brice is going to be home late.

"You. Me. Tonight?" he murmurs against my mouth.

I nod eagerly. "Oh, yes, please."

Ironically enough, I was thrilled when I drove by the church on my way home from getting Jason's birthday present after work and saw Brice's Jeep still parked there. All day, I've been thinking about what he said this morning, and I cooked up several plans for this evening, depending on whether he's home before or after me. My favorite plan requires him to arrive home after me, so I zoom into the garage, almost clipping the bottom of the door with the roof of my car in my impatience for it to open all the way. The overhead door has barely come to a rest before I hop from the vehicle, grab my bags, and run into the house, hitting the button to bring it down again. I figure that will buy me at least ten or fifteen seconds when Brice does get home.

Inside, I toss the bag that contains Jason's birthday gift onto the floor in the kitchen and race with the other bags to our bedroom, where I strip out of my work clothes, scrunch them into a ball, and toss them onto the floor on my side of the closet. Naked, I start pulling things from the bags: candles, a lighter, edible massage oils, bra and panties, and a baby-doll nightie land on the bed, some of the heavier items nearly bouncing off the other side. I gather my materials and start arranging candles on the dressers and bedside tables. As soon as they're positioned where I want them, I light each one and then slide the lighter into my bedside table drawer. I turn off the bedroom light.

In the flickering glow of the candles, I use my teeth to remove price tags from the lingerie, praying that it fits and that I don't have to return it. I don't have time to be cautious or worry about La Perla's return policy. I do, however, force myself to slow down as I put on the pricey negligée, careful not to rip the delicate seams or snag the silky material as it floats over my head and comes to rest on my shoulders before sliding against my breasts and cascading over my hips.

This is nice. Why didn't I think of this before? I must be the most unimaginative, most boring bride in the history of newlywed-dom. I guess it's just never been necessary. But just because something's not necessary doesn't mean it shouldn't happen. This should have happened months ago. Maybe then, when we overslept on Christmas Day and Brice was faced with the choice of opening presents or opening me, he would have picked me, and it wouldn't have mattered that his mom was in the room next door or that he was excited for us to exchange our first Christmas gifts as a married couple. Honestly, the necklace was nice, but I would have rather stayed in bed.

All trussed up like a centerfold, I dig through my purse and find my MP3 player, which I plug into its docking station on my dresser and set to repeat-play the romantic list of songs I compiled at work. (I really didn't do anything work-related today. I'll be the first to admit it, just not to Marshall.) When Van Morrison's smooth voice fills the room, I turn down the volume so that he's a soundtrack, not a concert, and head for the bed. There, I stash the bottles of massage oil under my pillow for easy access later, plump the pillows, and—with the help of the mirror on the dresser—arrange myself in the most flattering position I can manage, refusing to dwell on any "chubby" thoughts.

I eventually settle on lying on my side, facing the bedroom door, with my head propped on my right hand. Now, I just need to wait. And not move.

Four songs play. Pins and needles besiege my right hand. But I don't lose hope. He said he'd be home around the time I'd get home if I had to work a late Friday. He's only ten minutes past due, according to that estimate. And if something serious had come up, he'd have texted me or called me. So, it's gotta be any minute now.

My patience pays off two songs later when I hear the garage door buzz to life. I give myself one more check in the mirror to make sure everything's still in place. Then I hit "send" on the text I've had waiting on my phone on the bedside table.

I want you in the bedroom.

No sooner does my phone chirp to confirm that the message has been sent than I hear Brice talking and laughing on his way from the garage into the kitchen. "Yeah, that's one thing I learned early on, for sure—"

I roll my eyes, thinking he's on the phone. But my stomach drops when I hear a different laugh, one that's unfortunately become too familiar lately.

Brice says to Jared, "Ah! There's a text from Peyton right now. That's weird. Her car's in the garage, so I thought she was home. Maybe she walked to Cozzoni's to grab some dinner."

They come farther into the house. I hear the coat closet squeak open and closed just a few feet away from our bedroom door in the hallway. While dread builds in the pit of my stomach, Brice reads aloud in a monotone, "'I want you in the—'" Fortunately, he stops before the last word, which causes him to cough furiously and choke, "Oh!"

"You okay, man?" Jared asks.

"Fine! Just—" More coughing, becoming louder as he steps closer to our room, while, resigned, I slide from the bed and pull my bathrobe from its hook on the door. "Spit. Went down. The wrong pipe." Choke, choke, choke. "Uh, I'll be right back."

By the time he slips through the door, I'm engulfed in the oversized terrycloth robe, blowing out the last candle, and turning off the music.

I don't have to turn around to know exactly the look on his face (guilt, mixed with chagrin, mixed with feigned innocence) when he says, still a little choked up, "What's up?"

"Absolutely nothing," I answer dully, keeping my back to him.

"Oh. I, uh, didn't realize—"

"Just forget it. I'll be dressed and out there in a minute." I snag a pair of jeans and a t-shirt from my dresser and place them precisely on the bed. I look up at him and give him an icy smile.

Hand still on the doorknob, as if braced for a hasty exit, he says quietly, obviously so the vicar can't hear, "It's just that when we talked this morning, I thought 'tonight' meant later than this. And Jared's so far away from home, you know, and well, lonely——"

Sadly, I know how the Alaskan native feels. But I don't say that. I just stare at my husband, marveling at the irony that one of the things I love most about him—his caring, sympathetic nature—is currently causing me so much distress.

"I said forget it. I misunderstood you this morning, that's all. I should have known better." The disappointment is like an anvil sitting on my chest, making it hard for me to breathe. And the way he's standing there looking at me doesn't make it any easier.

"He and I aren't doing anything special, so I can tell him I have to take a rain check," he offers desperately when I shrug out of the robe to reveal what I'm wearing underneath it.

Struggling to pull the nightie over my head, I quickly answer, "Nope. *We're* not doing anything special tonight, either. So, let's go hang out with Jared. Again." He steps forward to offer me some assistance, but I shrug him off. "Really?" I ask impatiently as I finally break free and throw the scrap of silk away from me. I take pity on him when I see how wretched he looks. "I'm just disappointed. I'll get over it."

I remove the scrap of lace that qualifies as panties and slide out of the demi bra before stepping into a pair of boring cotton panties and expertly doing up the hooks on my plain full-coverage bra, spinning it around my torso, threading my arms through the straps, and tugging it into position.

"Not as disappointed as I am."

As soon as I've buttoned and zipped up my jeans and pulled my shirt over my head, I walk past him and pat his cheek. "Some other time, I guess."

"Another time just a few hours from now?" he asks hopefully.

I shake my head. "I don't think so."

He's going to have to learn this lesson the hard way.

8

MISCONCEPTIONS

"*J*ason didn't tell me his brother-in-law is a minister! I've always sort of had a thing for clergymen," Dusty, my brother's new boyfriend, gushes after Brice and I have been introduced to him.

Brice laughs easily. "The ministry is interesting to you, huh? What do you do for a living?"

Retaking his seat on the couch, crossing his legs, and sitting ramrod straight, he answers, "I'm a sales rep at the insurance company where Jason works. And I didn't say the ministry was interesting. I said I was interested in *ministers*! Especially tall drinks of water like you." Quickly, he turns to my brother, who's clicking away at an email on his phone, "No offense, babe."

Jason snorts something noncommittal. I wouldn't put it past him to ask someone like Dusty to pose as his boyfriend, just to make my dad's blood pressure skyrocket.

When my brother came out of the closet a little over a year ago, it came as a surprise to me, until I thought about it for half a second, and then everything sort of started falling into place. I had about a week of "aha!" moments related to our childhood and his dating history, and then I felt like an idiot for never seeing it before.

It's not like I'm a stranger to other sexual orientations. In my line of work, a heterosexual woman like myself is actually quite the minority. My boss and roughly sixty-percent of my clients are openly gay (or lesbian, bi-sexual, or transgender). It's so commonplace in my life that it has ceased to be an issue for me. For the most part, I file it under the category, "Irrelevant."

But when it became about my brother, it was all too relevant. And I was really conflicted about his coming out. I felt like the majority of people at church—with the Christian community as a whole backing them—would think—if not say out loud—that I should love him less for being him, or they'd fall back on something trite like, "Love the sinner, hate the sin," and I just couldn't agree with either take on it. I had so many questions. How can love be a sin? Why would God make someone gay, if that's not exactly how He intended them to be?

Brice typically avoids this debate at all costs. I've seen him fake a bathroom emergency at a party when someone asked his "professional" opinion on the "issue." But when I was really struggling with my feelings about Jason, he opened up to me and summed up his viewpoint this way: "I believe it's nature, not nurture, and God doesn't make mistakes, so I don't know. It's definitely one of the things I'll be asking about when I get to Heaven." I loved him for admitting he doesn't know or understand everything and giving me permission to accept the same of myself.

Now, I glance over his shoulder at the person in the room who would never admit or accept such a thing and see exactly what I expect: my dad looks like he's about to explode.

I say as moderately as possible, "It's really nice to meet you, Dusty. I wish I could say I've heard a lot about you, but Jason's pretty tight-lipped that way."

Dusty giggles. "Oh, he's tight-lipped all right!"

Oh, gosh. I couldn't be tenser if my muscles were made of rusty metal. My family, already prone to ugly scenes, may not survive Mr. Dusty. Or Dusty may not survive my family. Either way, I feel responsible for keeping the peace. That's my job, after all, in my family. I took a short break from it last year, and things got really nasty, so I've accepted that it's the way things run best.

Thankfully, I have a husband who's even better at the skill than I am.

Brice returns to an earlier topic. "So you sell insurance, huh? I like to think that I work in insurance, too. At least, that's how most people treat faith anymore. It's a backup plan; you know, a way to cover your bases. That's why there are so many of these amalgamations of faith nowadays. You take what you like from Eastern religions, add a dash of the easy parts of Christianity, and make sure you don't believe that Hell exists, and you get a good idea of what most people would say they ascribe to."

Dusty taps his chin, looks up at the ceiling, and grins. "Guilty!" he trills. Then he flourishes his hand and taps Brice on the knee. "Good looking *and* smart. You're a lucky woman, Peyton."

Lord. If we're going to get into a philosophical/religious discussion, I'm out of here. And I'm sure as hell not going to sit here and watch another man shamelessly hit on my husband. Smiling my agreement, I announce that I'm going to check on things in the kitchen, even though it's public knowledge that I couldn't care less what generally happens in that room, and excuse myself.

As soon as I push through the swinging door, Mom and Nicole crack up.

Clueless, I ask, "What?"

My sister recovers first. "How do you like Jason's boyfriend?" she asks.

"Oh. He's… animated."

"And he has the hots for your husband," Mom adds with a snicker. "We've been eavesdropping since you got here."

"Yeah, well, Dad's about to stroke out in there, so maybe someone should get a handle on things."

This information makes them laugh even harder. Nicole holds onto Mom with one hand and onto her lady parts with the other. "Oh, I'm going to pee!" she announces without making a move toward the bathroom.

"What am I missing?" I don't expect to get an answer, so it's no disappointed when I don't. The enormous open bottle of wine on the counter at my mom's elbow probably explains a lot.

I ignore the two of them and peruse the food on the counter. It's a meat-fest, starting with a lunch meat tray, continuing down the line with bratwurst, and ending with brisket. A lonely cold veggie tray sits at the end of the counter. I eat a piece of broccoli, just so I can say I did.

"So, where are the kids?" I ask Nicole. I'm particularly interested in what my niece, Sadie, is up to. We're always best buddies at functions like these. Kindred spirits, I guess you'd say. She has a unique perspective on things, and I find myself able to relate to what she says, usually. I don't know what it says about me that I identify more with a seven-year-old (nearly eight years old, but still…) than the adults in my family. I try not to analyze it too much.

Nicole levels a glare at me. "Who cares where the kids

are? They're playing. Somewhere. We want to hear more about what you think of Dusty."

Now I'm suspicious. "Why? He's flamboyant. So what? As long as Jason's happy—"

This sets off another round of hysterical giggles, but before I can demand they tell me what's going on, Brice steps into the kitchen.

"Ladies," he says with a charming smile. "There's just too much fun going on in here." He hugs me around the waist from behind. "What's so funny? Oooh! Brisket!"

"Your new boyfriend's cute," Mom splutters nearly unintelligibly.

He deepens his voice and says smarmily, "What can I say, ladies? When you've got it, you've got it."

"That doesn't make you uncomfortable?" Nicole asks, smirking behind her wineglass.

He laughs. "Nah."

The two of them look disappointed. Then Nicole queries more hopefully, "What's Dad doing? What shade of red would you say his face is?"

Thinking about it for a second, he answers, "When I left to come in here, I'd describe it as maroon. Why?"

When the laughter subsides this time, Mom informs us proudly, "Dusty's a plant."

"I knew it!" I yell.

Brice raises his eyebrows.

"Shhh!" Nicole admonishes me before revealing, "Lonnie lasted two minutes in the same room with him before he decided playing Barbies with Sadie would be more fun." She looks up at Brice. "And we thought *you* would totally freak out—"

"You don't know him well *at all*, then," I say.

She sticks out her tongue at me.

Mom says, "I can't believe your dad's still out there! I thought for sure he would have found something to do in the garage by now. I'm pretty impressed with his fortitude."

I twine my fingers through Brice's, which are resting on my waist. "So, who is this 'Dusty' guy? Is that even his real name? And why are you torturing Dad?"

"His real name's Dustin, and he's really Jason's boyfriend, but he's nothing like that. I'm trying to teach your father a lesson," Mom says, pouring herself the last of the wine from the bottle. "When Jason said he was bringing a boyfriend, your dad threw a fit. Not at Jason, but *I* had to listen to it. I knew from stories Jason's told me about Dustin that he's a fun guy, with a really good sense of humor, so I asked your brother if he thought he'd be up to playing a little trick on your father. I told him I wanted Dustin to act outrageously to try to get a reaction from your father. Jason and Dustin have been working on the material for weeks. Although the stuff about the clergyman fetish was my idea," she adds proudly.

"Nice touch," Brice says. "But why is that odd?"

She giggles at him. "Anyway, before we eat, we'll let him in on the truth. I just want him to see that it's wrong to judge someone before you ever get to know them."

From the other room, we hear "Dusty" squeal, "Oh my gawd! Is this a picture of you, sweet-cheeks, when you were in high school?" He growls like a large cat. "My, my, my. Those football pants fit you quite nicely."

I close my eyes and shake my head. "You'd better end this sooner, rather than later, Mom, before you end up at the hospital with Dad. Dustin's a little too good."

Like a little kid, she snaps her finger while moving her arm in a swooping motion. "Darn. It's been so much fun, though. Just a few more minutes. I think Brice was a good influence on your dad."

The concept of Dad following Brice's lead on anything makes me laugh.

"It could happen," he mumbles defensively. "I believe in miracles."

Mom sighs. "Okay, okay. I'm going!"

After she leaves, Nicole smiles at us while uncorking another bottle of white wine. "Look at you two. So cute. Can't keep your hands off each other. Still! How's married life treating you, anyway? You guys settling into a routine?"

Crossing to the fridge, Brice makes affirmative noises while getting a beer. He holds a bottle up at me, like a question, but I shake my head and say, "No thanks." In answer to Nicole's question, I grin cheekily at my husband and say, "Well, some-one's never home, and when he is, he has a little shadow named Jared with him. I guess you can call that a routine. Of sorts."

Brice beams back at me and in the same teasing tone says, "And someone else refuses to stop taking her birth control, so what's the point in being alone?"

My mouth drops open.

Nicole cracks up. "Brice! You're a goof! 'What's the point?' Trust me. Savor these kid-free days."

He twists the top off his beer and lifts one shoulder in a half-shrug. "I don't want to be kid-free for too much longer and risk being old parents, that's all." Two long pulls of his drink, and then he says around a burp, "I want to be young enough to enjoy my kids."

"We're young!" I've finally recovered enough to respond to part of his shocking disclosure.

"You're younger than I am," he points out as if it's news to me.

"So what?"

"So, you think you have all the time in the world, because you're still in your twenties, but I'm starting to feel... older."

"You're still a baby," Nicole dismisses his concern while swirling the wine in her glass and sniffing it. "What are you, thirty-one?"

"Nearly thirty-three."

"Oh. That's right. You're a year older than me."

"Yeah, and you already have three children."

She waves this observation away. "Whatever. You're a baby," she reiterates.

"Whatever," he parrots irritably. "The point is, I'm ready to *have* a baby."

"Good luck with that," I say drily. "God didn't equip you correctly for it."

He smirks at me. "You know what I mean. I'm ready to start our family."

"Well, I'm not!" Frustration and defensiveness work together to make the declaration fierier than I intended. A lot fierier.

Nicole's smile fades, and she sloshes wine onto her hand at my outburst. "Shit," she mutters.

To Brice's belligerent expression, I repeat more quietly, "I'm not. Okay? And I'm not comfortable talking about it here."

He shrugs as if to tell me he doesn't care one way or the other.

"Didn't mean to start a fight, guys!" Nicole chuckles nervously. "C'mon! You two are much cuter when you're all cuddly."

"Cuddling? What's the point?" I spat, pushing away

from the counter. "Come get me when it's time to eat. I'm going to play Barbies with Sadie and Lonnie."

~

Barbie angrily stalks around her plastic "mansion," her hair swinging furiously behind her. She paces from her dining room, where she kicks a few chairs for good measure, to her kitchen, where she stands in front of the open refrigerator, looking for something suitably unhealthy to eat, to her bedroom, where she flops on the bed, to her bathroom, where she sits in the empty bathtub with all of her clothes on.

Lonnie left to take a call right after I arrived in the basement, so it's just the two of us.

Sadie giggles at my antics. "Auntie Peyton! What's your Barbie doing?"

"Decompressing," I answer.

"What's that?"

I smile down at her. "It's kind of like when your mom gets mad at you, so you go to your room and cry and pout about it."

She nods knowingly. "I usually just sit on my bed, though. And think about being a princess who's allowed to do whatever she wants."

"Sounds nice." I take Barbie from the bathtub and sit her on her bed. I can't help but laugh at her posture, straight-legged and with her arms permanently bent at right angles. "She doesn't look very comfortable, does she?" I consult my niece. After laying her flat on her back, I say, "There. She's staring at the ceiling, imagining what it's like to be a princess. What do you think she's thinking about?"

Immediately, the seven-year-old supplies, "Riding horses. And eating candy."

"At the same time?" I picture Barbie on her steed, eating an enormous lollipop. "Sounds… hairy. Do you think she has a Prince Charming?"

With a wrinkle of her nose, she answers, "No. Boys are gross. 'Cept Uncle Brice, I mean. He's nice and funny and sneaks me the kind of bubble gum my mom doesn't let me have."

I make a disgusted noise. Yeah, he's hilarious. Especially when he brings up something super-duper private in front of my sister, who will directly report it to my mother, who will naturally take his side, because she's one of the people who won't shut up about when we're going to have kids.

Anyway, since when has he even been bent out of shape about my still taking birth control? He's said something about it *once* since we've been married. When I set my rectangular packet of pills on the edge of the sink on our first night of the cruise, he said glibly, "I guess you won't be needing those anymore." That was supposed to serve as a serious conversation on family planning? I was supposed to take from that that he wanted me to throw them away? Has he been stewing about it since then? I take them on the advice of my doctor for a host of reasons other than for preventing pregnancy. Otherwise, I wouldn't have had to take them before we got married, considering we never did anything that would make such a thing possible.

I didn't even explain that much to him at the time, though, because I thought he was kidding. We'd been married less than forty-eight hours! We didn't need any more digits than the ones on our hands to count the number of times we'd made love. I sure as hell wasn't thinking about adding a crying, puking person to our party. Much less a baby.

I mean, am I crazy? The fact that I totally agree with Nicole supports that hypothesis, but I think she's right that we should enjoy our kid-free days. That doesn't mean I don't want them—someday. But I feel like we'll regret it if we rush into parenthood, and we'll end up looking back on this first year—or two—and wish we'd taken the opportunity to spend time alone and do things you just can't do when you're lugging around seventeen tons of toys and diapers and bottles. We'll also wistfully think of all the sleep and uninterrupted sex we could have had (or *should* have had, if someone wasn't so hell-bent on packing 26-hours of work in a 24-hour day).

Plus, I'm not even used to being a wife yet! And he wants to add being a mother to that? I have no idea how to take care of someone completely dependent on me. I've never had so much as a goldfish since I've been out in the world on my own. When I was expecting Secret, I planned to take a bunch of parenting classes, but I didn't get around to it before she died, so I'm still as clueless now as I was then. And this time around, I may not be facing single motherhood in name, but I may as well be, considering how much Brice is away from the house. No thanks! A *lot* has to change before I'll be willing to say we're truly ready for such a huge lifestyle change.

Unless Jared's willing to be our nanny.

"I don't want us to be old parents."

What a lame argument! Is he going to want us to join a shuffleboard team and move to a retirement home at fifty? I mean, I guess age is a legitimate concern for someone whose parents *were* a lot more mature than his peers' parents. But it's hardly a legitimate concern coming from someone who's a mere thirty-two years old. Maybe if he ate like I do and sat behind a desk all day, I'd take him a little more seriously. But he's healthy, active, and comes from fairly hearty stock: one parent lived to be almost eighty and another is still kicking at seventy-four.

That must be it, though. His dad's death is still so raw for him. His mortality is close to the surface. And I suppose he's worried about how long his mom's going to live (although Mary has more pep than I do most days... Maybe I shouldn't be broadcasting that). I understand that he wants her to see her grandchildren; that's something he never could give his dad. But we can't live our lives with everyone else's schedules and priorities in mind.

And those aren't even the *biggest* reservations I have. Those are merely logistical. Those things are within our control and are rectifiable. Knowing that my mom and his mom and the entire Messiah congregation and Brice want me to pop out babies like a human Pez dispenser doesn't change one very important thing: I've recently failed at this baby-making thing. And it's terrifying to try again with so many people watching.

"Auntie Peyton!"

I snap out of my trance. "Huh?"

"I said, 'I think Uncle Brice is pretty handsome, too,'" she repeats what obviously didn't get the reaction from me that she was expecting.

Chuckling, I pull her up against me for a hug and sniff her baby shampoo-scented hair. "It's a good thing he is some days. Otherwise, he'd be in big trouble."

"Why?"

"Never mind. Let's go see if everyone else is ready to eat. I'm hungry."

~

The rest of the day went surprisingly well. When Sadie and I rejoined the rest of the family, Dad had just found out that he'd been tricked, and Dustin came out to play.

The first thing he said to me (without a hint of a lisp) was, "Sorry I hit on your husband. I was totally kidding. Not that he's not worthy. But you know what I mean. I would *never* act like that to a married man. In front of his wife, anyway."

After he stopped acting so over-the-top, he even looked different to me: a lot less like a male figure skater and more like a preppy male model. It was interesting to observe him and Jason together as a couple and even more interesting to find out that Dustin—bookish, clean-cut, smart Dustin—is Jason's type. I don't spend much time considering what his type is, but if I did, Dustin wouldn't be it.

Dad was so relieved that "Dusty" was a plant that he was practically giddy the rest of the day; Lonnie was just glad he didn't have to hide anymore (although considering the sort of legislation his conservative senator father has historically supported, he may want to keep a few secret spots in mind for a quick getaway, if necessary); and Brice seemed happy that everyone else was happy (and that I wasn't pouting or making a big deal about what he said in the kitchen).

As a matter of fact, when the focus returned to Jason and the reason we were gathered—his birthday—everything smoothed out, and I think I can honestly say it was the most pleasant family get-together I've been a part of since... well, since I've been an adult.

I'm still musing about this and basking in the rare feel-good afterglow of the party when one of the things Brice said at Mom and Dad's echoes back at me while I'm brushing my teeth and taking my birth control pill before bed. *"What's the point?"*

I stare at the plastic case in my hand and let it sink in what he really meant. He thinks there's no point having sex with me if it's not going to possibly result in a baby. Ouch.

And what?

This is in direct opposition to something he said to me before we even had our first kiss. I distinctly remember (because it made my stomach flip—in a good way) that he said it was "dismal" to think about sex within the bounds of marriage as being solely for the sake of procreation. So what's caused the change of heart? Am I not good enough? Is he bored? Is something wrong? Do I do something (or not do something) that bothers him?

I have to know.

He's sitting on the couch, his sock-clad feet propped on the edge of the coffee table, his lap serving as a desk, his head bent over a pad of paper, and a college basketball game playing on the TV in front of him. I watch him from the hallway for a while, aware that he has no idea I'm back here. Every once in a while, he looks up and watches the game for a few seconds, but his attention always goes back to the paper in his lap.

I'm curious about what he's writing (although I'm not sure I want to ask and risk drawing him into a long, intellectual conversation about something like female archetypes in the New Testament), considering he told me this afternoon on the way to Jason's party that he was finished with his sermon for tomorrow, and Jared's taking a crack at his first sermon next Sunday, God help us all. Whatever it is, though, he's in the zone. I almost feel bad interrupting him. Almost.

I sit on the sofa cushion next to him and pull my knees up to my chest. As unobtrusively as possible, I peek at the paper. It's a grocery list. Just goes to show you that some people look smart no matter what they're doing.

He bestows on me an encouraging smile, complete with dimple, so I don't feel too tentative about coming right out and asking, "Do you really think that you're wasting your *seed* when you have sex with me?"

Geez. That didn't come out at all like I'd hoped. I sound so stupid! And pathetic. And old-fashioned. Seed? Really? Who says that? I do, apparently.

I can tell by the way he's working his mouth back and forth and clamping his lips together and flaring his nostrils that he, too, thinks my question is utterly moronic.

He clicks his pen a few times, taps it on his pad of paper, and finally says, "Hmm… I'm not sure I ever said that." He coughs, but it doesn't sufficiently cover his laugh, so he tries again by clearing his throat.

"Okay, I know I didn't say it right. And I wasn't trying to quote you." I take a deep breath and push on, despite my embarrassment. "It's just… when you said there was no point, that's what meant, right? You meant, what's the point in having sex with me. Is it that much of a chore?" I preemptively look away, not able to face an affirmative answer to my question.

Now he doesn't even try to hide his laughter. "Oh, wow."

"You said it! And Nicole was a witness!"

"Peyton. Look at me."

"No. Just answer my question." I stare at the giants on the TV screen and hear their squeaky shoes without really seeing or listening. I'm only interested in hearing one thing.

He sighs. "I can't believe I'm even having this conversation," he mutters.

"You started it with your 'what's the point' comment in my parents' kitchen." Still, I avoid his eye contact.

Putting his feet on the floor, he leans forward to set the grocery list on the coffee table and rubs his face. "I misspoke, okay? Of course, it's not a chore; I don't think it's a waste of... whatever; and I know there's a point."

"Which is?" I finally get the nerve to look over at him.

Readily, he supplies, "Well, to foster a sense of closeness and intimacy between a husband and wife, for one thing."

"That sounds like a very pastoral answer you tell couples you're counseling. Did you say that to Lonnie and Nicole?"

With a look of infinite patience, he answers, "You know I can't tell you that. Or if that was even one of their problems." When I roll my eyes, he continues, "The point is, it's a very important part of a marriage, no matter what the goal is."

"Why did you say that then? Especially in front of Nicole, of all people. The whole family will know by Easter, and everyone will be giving us these pitying looks, like, 'Oh, the poor dears. Having problems in the bedroom already,' and taking bets on how soon it'll be before you're divorcing me, because you only married me for my uterus—"

He clamps a hand over my mouth. "Stop. Please." When I lick his palm, he gives me a warning look but keeps his hand in place. "Just stop. I'm going to tell you something right now that you may not believe, but it's the truth." After a deep breath, he confesses, "I said what I said at your parents', because I'm sick of you blaming me for everything in our marriage that isn't what you expected it to be. I said it out of spite, and I said it to get a reaction from you. I lost my temper. Period. The fact that your sister happened to be there was unfortunate."

I pry his hand off. He lets me. "So you didn't mean any of it?"

His eyes shift to his lap. "Weeelll… I wouldn't say that. I meant some of it. Like all things said in the heat of the moment, there was some truth behind it."

"Like what?"

He puts my face between his hands and kisses my lips. "I do want to start our family as soon as possible."

I clench my jaw and sigh.

"So that little packet of pills in the medicine cabinet *does* tend to taunt me." Quickly, he adds, "I know you must have your reasons, and I trust you, so I pray about it and hope that you'll be ready soon, and one day I'll open the door, and the packet will be gone."

"You'll find out when I'm ready from *me*, not from the medicine cabinet."

"Whatever. You know what I mean." He takes up the grocery list again. "Now help me figure out what I'm forgetting. We have zero food in this house."

"Who cares?" I shift to my knees and suck on his earlobe.

He inhales sharply but replies, "I care. I like food."

"I know something you like more. I think. Maybe."

Grinning, he affirms, "Oh, I do."

"Why don't you take five minutes to finish your silly shopping list, and then meet me in our bedroom—you know, it's the room down the hall with our bed in it?—for something really tasty?" I whisper into his ear.

He shivers. "Will it be covered in something silky?"

"If that's what you want. Eep!" I squeak when he surprises me by dropping his pen and paper and picking me up while at the same time attacking my mouth. I laugh against his lips. "Or we can skip those parts."

"Let's. Some other time, though. Please."

"You got it."

Now *this* is how it's supposed to be.

9

THE OTHER WOMAN

*W*ell, isn't that a sight? It actually takes my breath away. I bite down on my lower lip and breathe through stinging nostrils while Brice takes the sleeping infant and cradles him like a football as he holds him over the baptismal font. He baptizes the baby in the name of the Father, Son, and Holy Spirit while I choke down tears.

Baptisms always get me. Always have. But especially the ones I've witnessed these past couple of years. And especially the ones I've seen Brice perform. He takes such delight in them, and he always gets emotional. It's touching to watch. And contagious. There's rarely a dry eye in the house by the time he's finished.

Today's sacrament is especially meaningful for him, since he's baptizing his godson, Isaiah. I focus on that tiny black-haired head in Brice's hand and try to block out every negative thought I've ever had toward Justine Heidecker, the proud new mother standing at her pastor's side.

She deserves this. I know she does. The youth director's probably wanted to be a mom since she was old enough to hold a doll. But she's single and so busy with the church youth group that I don't think she ever takes the time to date. Or she has no prospects. I guess it doesn't matter why she's single—voluntary or not. The point is, she wanted to be a mom. So, she decided to adopt. Good for her. I appreciate a woman who knows what she wants and goes for it.

Anyway, let's face it, adoption is so much more "Christian" than going the artificial insemination route. I mean, this way, she's doing a good deed *and* getting a baby, and it doesn't look as obvious that she's given up on God ever presenting her life mate to her (I'm pretty sure I married the one she had her eye on, anyway).

Of course, she went through a *Lutheran* adoption service, too. Not that there's anything wrong with that. On the contrary, it's so right. Because she's Justine. She always does everything right. And now, after nearly a year of waiting that must have seemed interminable to her (almost as interminable as her abstinence pledge has been), she has a beautiful son.

And she looks so happy. That's really all that matters. I'm happy for her. Now she can show us all what it really means to be a perfect Christian mother.

Okay, so it was a little weird that she asked Brice as an individual—and not us as a couple—to be Isaiah's sponsor. After I thought about it, though, I wasn't too offended by that. Brice did a lot to help her through the adoption process. I didn't do anything, really, except sacrifice time with my husband every time she had an "urgent" question or needed him to sign a reference or help her fill out an application. Sure, it's a little unconventional for your pastor to be your kid's godfather. But who better to act as your child's intercessor with God and show him the teachings of

Christ than a pastor? It's actually quite smart, especially if you don't have any real friends.

Oh, gosh. I'm awful. What am I doing? Why am I thinking all these terrible things? What did she ever do to me, besides try to prove at every turn how superior she is to me in every way, especially when it comes to her faith and her dedication to the church? All that should mean nothing during this beautiful moment. She's my sister in Christ. Her triumphs are mine; I should be exalting in this joyous occasion in her life, not smirking at what I perceive to be her transparent attempts to put the best spin on her human nature.

I try to concentrate as Brice tells us that we should take Isaiah's baptism as an opportunity to remember our own baptismal vows. Then he reminds us that it's our responsibility as a church family to help Isaiah know Christ, making sure he has everything he needs to flourish spiritually. Finally, he tells us to bow our heads to pray.

Just before I do, I see something that makes my head jerk up, my eyes pop wide, and my spine stiffen against the wooden pew.

Uhhhhhhhhhhhhhh…

Justine has threaded her right arm through the crook of Brice's left elbow while he says the prayer over the newly baptized baby. Maybe it's an innocent gesture; lots of people hold hands or link arms or otherwise touch each other when they're praying together. But the territorial, insecure part of me that can't seem to adjust to the fact that she's no longer my competition—if she ever was—doesn't have to like it.

During the never-ending prayer (my husband's having one of those days where he seems to really like the sound of his voice, I've noticed), I can't take my eyes off the two of them. They look so much like a couple! Dark-haired Isaiah could pass for Brice's son, at least from this distance, and Justine looks completely comfortable up there next to my husband. It's like a living recreation of some kind of Hallmark figurine. I think its title would be, "Toothache." As a matter of fact, I kind of want to march up there and dump the baptismal font over Justine's head. It would be a shame to wake up that sweet baby, though. It's not his fault his mom is a husband-coveting hussy.

"Amen! Everyone, please join me in welcoming Isaiah Brice Heidecker to—"

WHAT? I don't even hear the rest of what Brice says. The clapping of the congregation around me seems muffled, too, as I process what I've just heard.

You have to be fucking kidding me. Yes, I just thought the f-word during church. You bet your ass I did. Oh my gosh. Oh my gosh. Oh my gosh.

Mom pats my shoulder as if she's congratulating me on how awesome it is that another woman gave her son my husband's name. I don't care that it's just a middle name. Middle names are important! That's the name you use when you hate your first name, because your parents named you after dear Uncle Nemo. That's the name parents use to address their kids when they mean business. And damn it, that was supposed to be *my* first son's middle name (I'm not a big fan of "Juniors," and it would be too confusing to have two Brices in the house, but it's a perfect middle name—I have already given this a *lot* of thought).

Now Brice kisses his godson on the forehead and passes him back to Justine. Both of them are misty-eyed, but he manages to choke out, "Now, for our next hymn," before giving Justine a hug and Isaiah one more pat on the head and sending them back to their pew, which is, fortunately (for her), on the other side of the sanctuary from where I'm sitting. He sits down in his chair while the hymn starts, takes a sip of water, and opens his own hymnal.

While everyone else is singing about writing Isaiah Brice's name in the Book of Heaven, I'm writing Justine Heidecker's name a little higher on my shit list. She's crossed the line, big-time. I don't know who she thinks she is or what she thinks she's doing, but she'd better watch her step or she and I are going to have a throw-down at her next cutesy youth group hoedown or whatever. Someone can hold her baby for her while I pummel her face.

I push the cool backs of my hands up against my hot cheeks as the song ends. Good grief. What is *wrong* with me? I'm thinking more like a cast member of *Jersey Shore* than a child of God!

But I mean it.

"That was a cute trick Justine played today," I say as casually as my temper will allow when Brice gets home, hours later.

He pauses with his hand in the coat closet, where he's hanging up his jacket. Eventually, he says, "I don't follow. Did I miss something?"

"Isaiah's middle name. I find it interesting that she waited until you guys were up there in front of everyone to drop that bomb."

Closing the closet door, he turns to me and asks ultra-innocently, "Oh, you didn't know? I'm pretty sure I told you."

Yep, he still sucks at lying.

"Nope. Must have slipped your mind. Or you knew I would *freak out*." I tap my foot, waiting for an explanation.

Brow furrowed, he replies, "I had no idea you would

care. I think it's a nice gesture. What's for dinner?" He edges past me and goes into the kitchen, where he opens the fridge, freezer, and several cupboards before saying, "We never have any food."

I follow him. "You eat a lot. And stop changing the subject."

He leans against the counter and crosses his arms over his chest. I try to ignore the fact that he's wearing my favorite V-neck sweater, which clings quite fetchingly to his broad chest. I will not be distracted.

"Hon, I really don't understand why you're upset. If it were anyone but Justine, you wouldn't care," he theorizes.

"That's *our* son's middle name!"

Looking around himself, he says, "Our son? Really. I didn't realize we had one." Now a cupboard he's already searched also gets another look. He grabs a can of soup and pops the top open. Before I can scold him for missing the point, he adds, "Anyway, with a name as awesome as mine, who says *everyone* can't use it?"

"She did that on purpose."

While pouring the soup into a bowl and putting the bowl in the microwave, he states, "Most people are pretty purposeful when they choose a name for their child, so I'll have to agree with you on that one." He licks soup off his thumb and punches the numbers on the keypad. Then he stands with his back to me as he watches his dinner spin and drops, "You're being overly sensitive."

Overly sensitive. I think that's closely related to "ridiculous." And I'm neither.

"She's hot for you. Always has been."

"Oh, for crying out loud!"

"She has! Just because you refuse to see it doesn't mean it's not true."

He drops his head back and stares up at the ceiling. "I'm not saying it's never been the case, but it's not anymore. And, anyway, it doesn't matter."

I hop onto the counter and sit with my legs dangling. "Which one is it, Brice? She doesn't lust after you, or it doesn't matter that she does?"

Beep... beep... beeeeeep!

After retrieving his soup, he turns to get a spoon, but my legs are blocking the drawer. "Excuse me."

I don't move.

"Please. I'm hungry."

Recognizing that I've pushed him to the edge of his patience (which is a lot shorter when he's hungry), I scoot down the counter enough that he can open the drawer and pull out a spoon.

"Thank you," he mutters, carrying his bowl to the breakfast bar and straddling one of the wooden stools. He curls over his dinner and after a quick, silent prayer, begins eating.

I guess I'm not going to get an answer to my question. I already know the answer, anyway. He knows it, too.

"Listen, I trust you," I say now. "And I know it doesn't matter to *you* how she feels about you. And it wouldn't matter to me, as long as she understood her place and didn't cross the line."

His response to that is to blow on a spoonful of soup and look at me through his lashes.

"The way she touches you and looks at you and names her kid after you... That's inappropriate."

He dips his spoon for more, keeping his eyes down on the bowl when he says, "Sounds like you need to have a frank, loving talk with her, preferably without profanity."

"Ha! Very funny."

"I'm serious. Especially about the profanity."

"I'd prefer it if you'd tell her to back off," I declare, but he shakes his head.

"I haven't noticed all these things that you have. If she were to challenge me and ask me to name specifics, I wouldn't be able to do so. But you seem to have a plethora of examples." Slurp, slurp.

"You don't want me to talk to Justine about this, trust me."

"Pray about it."

"That's your answer to everything."

He laughs. "Pretty much. It's a proven strategy."

I hate when he gets flippant like this. He knows I'm right, but he just doesn't want to deal with it. He'd rather pretend she's not panting and drooling all over him and having fantasies about being his perfect wife with their perfect baby and cooking his perfect meals and knitting his perfect... socks... and spending every waking minute at the church doing... churchy things. And he knows it would be so much better if he were the one to say something to her about it.

Sounding like a peer of Sadie's, I say, "*You* pray about it. Because if I end up needing to have a 'frank, loving' conversation with Justine, she's going to need your prayers."

"Now, now..."

I hop down from the counter. "I'm serious, Brice. I've had some time to cool down, so you don't understand how angry I was during church when you so sweetly and emotionally said that baby's full name. Or when she put her hand through your arm during the prayer."

"Sounds like the devil was hard at work on you." He lifts the bowl to his mouth and tilts it to drink the broth at the bottom.

I hold my hand out for the empty bowl, rinse it and the dirty spoon, and put them in the dishwasher. "Yeah. And that's what I'm going to say when I punch her smug face: 'The devil made me do it.'"

"This is not attractive behavior," he informs me, but he's smiling. He stands and comes around the breakfast bar so he's standing in front of me. He puts his hands on my shoulders and squeezes gently. "Do me a favor. Be a little more charitable and understanding. Put yourself in her place and think about how it feels to be her. She's not being malicious. She's just being Justine. And you have *nothing* to worry about." He kisses my forehead. "Now. I don't want to talk about church or work or Justine or anything else that puts that little line between your eyes."

Walking into his chest, I try to relax into his hug. Sniffing his warm, clean smell helps.

He rubs my shoulder blades with his thumbs. "I do want to hear more about these names you've chosen for our children. This is an encouraging sign."

10

UNLIKELY MENTOR

*S*ome days it still feels like we're playing house, and I can't believe this is really my life. I wake up to the sound of Brice singing incongruous pop songs the shower (this morning, he had moves like a Rolling Stone. I particularly like hearing what he decides to substitute for the profanity in songs. Most of the time, he says, "Beep!" but sometimes I'm treated to some very creative replacements, like blowing raspberries, armpit farts, or actual word swaps. My favorite is "Chicago," in place of "shit"), go to a job that I can do in my sleep most days, come home to a tidy house and oftentimes a hot meal (both courtesy of my husband), fold laundry in front of primetime TV, go to bed, get up and do it all over again. If it weren't such a pleasant life, the routine of it might drive me crazy, and I'd say we were in a rut. But it *is* pleasant. And relaxing. And drama-free, which is a new way of life for me.

So today, when I come home from work to an unexpectedly empty house for the first time in weeks, I get a bad feeling that the drama-free streak has ended, and something must be brewing at church that's keeping Brice later than usual.

Per our new agreement, I walk the block from the parsonage to the church to find out what's delaying him. This is our solution to his pathological workaholism: I'm allowed to call him or drop by his office when he starts to fall into fifteen-hour workday patterns. I usually give him two or three long days before I hold him to our arrangement. I don't want to be a nag, after all. And sometimes, I have to admit, I enjoy the solitude. I think it helps, too, if it's my decision to be alone.

Tonight, I don't want to be.

The first surprise I encounter when I enter the church office is that Marilyn is still behind her desk. And the phones are ringing persistently.

Cautiously cheery, I say, "Hey! I wasn't expecting to see you here so late."

She rolls her eyes and takes off her reading glasses, letting them dangle from the chain around her neck. In a near whisper, she says, "Jared strikes again," while nodding her head toward Brice's closed office door.

I cringe, wondering what it is this time. It's been one thing after another since he started his vicariate just before Christmas. He's supposed to be making Brice's job easier, but his youthful exuberance and inexperience have actually resulted in a lot more work. Brice has tried to gently advise him to tone down his over-the-top energy, which—while sincere—rubs a lot of people the wrong way and makes them uncomfortable at best and downright angry in other cases.

For example, parents are a little (okay, a *lot*) sensitive about how much a pastor (or vicar/pastor-in-training) touches their children, especially their teenaged children.

Especially when the vicar is the object of several of those female teenagers' crushes. So, Brice had to have a heart-to-heart with Jared about boundaries when some parents observed what they considered to be "excessive contact." It was perfectly innocent, of course, and Jared was horrified that his back pats and silly hugs were misconstrued. Crisis was averted with Brice's swift intervention. He smoothed the parents' ruffled feathers and took over assisting with some of the youth activities for a while (I'm sure that was just fine with Justine) until things settled down.

The next issue arose when Jared repeatedly called someone by the wrong name—at the man's own funeral. The family was understandably upset; Jared was suitably apologetic; Brice was characteristically diplomatic. He explained to the family that Jared was new to the church and to the profession, and he appreciated their understanding, since—after all—pastors have to learn how to be pastors, too. Fortunately, it was one of the families who thinks Brice can do no wrong and would probably walk across hot coals if he told them it would increase their chances of getting into Heaven, so Jared was rescued again.

Next, a series of unfortunate, ticky-tack events—while petty—kept Brice in non-stop public relations mode from Christmas until Easter: Jared greeted several members with, "Happy Holidays!" on Christmas Day, taking the "Christ" out of "Christmas" (yeah, Lutherans aren't down with political correctness when it comes to our Savior's birthday); he got a case of the giggles during his first sermon when he slipped and said, "love thy enemas," instead of "love thy enemies" (come on! You'd have to be a robot not to laugh at that one, though); he called a baby boy a "she" throughout the baby's baptism; he was late for one of the midday Lenten services that he was leading in Brice's place (he overslept and missed his bus); and he kiddingly called one of the Sunday school students a loser when the young boy had a hard time finding any of the plastic eggs at the church Easter egg hunt.

Unfortunately, I can relate a little too well to Jared and his propensity for doing and saying the wrong things. To be fair, part of it is that people seem to be looking for things to bitch about. Apparently, Brice has a gene that allows him to know exactly how to react to any given situation. But I don't have that gene, and neither does Jared. For now. Brice seems to think that he'll develop more common sense and grace with experience. He's probably hoping I will, too. So far, it's not happening. However, I'm learning to speak less. Jared doesn't have that benefit. He has to learn how to speak and behave *correctly*.

Hoping I'm not interrupting some unprecedented butt-chewing, I knock softly on Brice's door and open it just enough to poke my head through. Playing dumb, I say, "Hey, guys. Who wants to walk over to Cozzoni's for dinner? My treat."

Jared looks like a death row inmate who's just received a stay of execution. Brice rubs his face and digs at his eyes with his fingers.

"Hey, Peyton!" the vicar greets me. "I screwed up again."

I fully enter the room and close the door behind me. "Uh-oh," I reply as if it's the first I'm hearing about it. Lightly, I say, "You should probably try to stop doing that."

He laughs ruefully. "I know Pastor wishes I would. I don't do it on purpose, you know."

I sit down next to him on the couch and pat his knee. "Yeah, I know. What'd you do this time?" I glance at Brice, who's watching the two of us with his hands on top of his head while he swivels in his chair behind his desk. His expression is unreadable, but I figure if he wanted me to butt out, he'd interrupt and ask me to excuse the two of them.

Jared pushes his glasses up on his nose. "It's so stupid—"

"It usually is," I say.

Chuckling, he sheepishly nods. "Yeah. I have a talent for that, I guess. Anyway, I really honked some people off hard-core this time. But really, I was just making a suggestion for improving things around here."

Uh-oh. One of the hardest, fastest rules in the Lutheran Church (particularly *this* one): no changes allowed.

"I may have mentioned that things may run more efficiently if we reduce the number of elders and rely more on congregation-wide voters' meetings. You know, cut out the middlemen."

I keep my face pointed in the direction of Jared's and regulate my reaction while keeping an eye on Brice through my peripheral vision.

Rocking subtly, Brice prods, "What words did you use, though, Jared, while describing the Board of Elders? Not just middlemen, which would have been bad enough, but…"

He gulps and blushes. "I may have used the phrase 'Mafioso middlemen.'"

I grit my teeth. "Wow."

"It slipped out!" he eagerly explains.

"Who'd you say it to?" Brice asks in a way that makes it clear he already knows the answer and is dragging it out of Jared for my benefit.

After biting the inside of his cheek, the vicar looks directly and apologetically at me. "Uh, I said it to your dad. I'm sorry!"

I close my eyes just a beat longer than a blink and take a deep breath. "Oh. Well. That was probably unfortunate. He's not really receptive to constructive criticism."

"'Mafioso' isn't very constructive, either," Brice states the obvious.

"I'm sorry, Pastor," Jared says for what I can tell isn't the first, second, or twentieth time.

Brice leans forward and places his palms flat on his desk. "As I said before, there's really no point in apologizing to me. I don't disagree with your assessment."

When the vicar looks sharply at me, I wave dismissively so he knows this isn't news to me, nor am I offended by my husband's statement.

Brice continues, "Unfortunately, we have to be more diplomatic. You know how there are certain topics—such as religion and politics—that you avoid in most social situations?"

Jared nods.

"Well, in religious settings—especially Lutheran settings —the taboo topics are a little more specific. We let the Synod do the dirty work and make the decisions when it comes to the issues of…" He ticks them off on his fingers. "…the ordination of women, open or closed communion, new hymnals and liturgy, and anything related to Church government, including—but not limited to—governing bodies, such as the Board of Elders, Board of Trustees, etcetera."

"But—"

Brice holds up a finger. "Bup! I'm not finished."

Chastened, Jared falls back against into the sofa but jiggles one knee anxiously as his mentor explains, "Now. Lucky you. By the time you've been ordained and called to your own church, it will be time for another Synodical

Convention of the Lutheran Church Missouri Synod. It's good fun. And *that*, my friend, is where you will be in your element. Because you can debate doctrine and policy all day long. With the big boys."

"Okay, debating is one thing, but what about some results?" He pushes his glasses higher on his nose. "I don't want to talk about giving women the right to be ordained; I want to make it happen! I don't want to discuss *why* it's right to open communion to everyone who believes, regardless of whether they have a confirmation certificate that says they do; I want it to be policy, because it's right! You know what I'm saying? There's too much conversation and not enough action."

"Whoa, Elvis," I mutter as a way to get a word in and re-route the discussion. "Can we get back to the original issue here? What's with the ringing phones out there?" I point to the closed door, through which we can still hear the insistent trilling.

Brice stands up and stretches. "That would be the other elders trying to call me to convince me not to reduce their numbers. Your dad kind of has them in a panic (imagine that). If they knew the Church charter as well as they should, they'd know they have nothing to worry about from me; I don't have the authority to do anything like that without their consent. But I'm going to let them think I'm that powerful for a little longer." He crosses to the door, opens it, and stands with his hands braced on the doorframe.

"Marilyn. Go home," he sings in a loud, silly basso profundo, not even waiting for her to end her current phone call. "That's what voicemail's for," he says in a normal speaking voice.

Recovering from her startle, she quickly gets rid of her

caller and silences her phone with the push of a button. "Are you sure?"

He nods. "Yes. I'm leaving, too. I'll call everyone personally tomorrow."

She slides open her drawer and jangles her keys. "If you say so, Pastor."

"I do. For what it's worth. Have a nice night."

"I think mine'll be better than yours," she mutters, to which he laughs.

Spinning to face Jared and me, he says, "Now, I seem to remember there was a dinner invitation on the table. No offense, but I think I'll be going alone with my wife."

Jared jumps from the couch and runs a hand through his hair. "No offense taken, Sir. None at all. I hope you and Mrs. Northam have a great evening. I'm going to go home and crash. After eating some of Mrs. Hanson's chicken and dumplings."

"Sounds prudent," Brice wearily approves of his plan to retreat to his room at the elderly woman's house. "We'll revisit this tomorrow and come up with a solution to this problem. Try not to worry about it. It'll all work out."

Who's he trying to convince?

During dinner at Cozzoni's, I let him eat his calzone in peace. The fact that he chose such an unhealthy entrée is telling; he's seeking the kind of comfort that can only come from grease and garlic and a lot of meat and cheese. But when he wipes his mouth after swallowing the last bite and draining the last of his beer, I say, "We've gotta do something about Jared."

He groans with the beer bottle still in his mouth. Setting

it down with a thunk, he begs, "Please. Don't make me think about him anymore tonight. Let's talk about something less stressful. For example, your irrational dislike of Justine is much more cheerful subject."

I narrow my eyes at him. "First of all, that's not funny. Second of all, it's like you can read my mind sometimes. Spooky."

When he tilts his head questioningly, I explain, "Because I was just thinking, what does Jared need?"

"A zipper for his mouth?" Brice supplies.

I laugh. "Yes. But since that's not really anatomically possible, let's move onto the second thing he needs: a distraction. A life. A girlfriend. A Justine."

"Not gonna happen."

"Why not? They're perfect for each other!"

He puts his elbows on the table and leans closer to me. "You think I haven't already thought of this? Trust me. I've tried."

The mental picture of Reverend Cupid makes me giggle. "Really? You tried to set them up?"

He balks at my incredulousness. "Yeah!" Then he makes a disgusted face. "But that whole thing with the parents getting all touchy—no pun intended—killed whatever chance there was. If there was one. Jared's a lot younger than Justine, you know."

I roll my eyes. "She's going to have to stop being so picky about things like that. They're all too young for her."

"Not nice."

"Fine. So, not Justine. How about Tracy Plucker?"

He seems to take a second to consider before saying, "She's not available."

Sensing some juicy gossip, I pounce. "What? Tracy Plucker has a boyfriend?" I can't picture the meek kindergarten teacher looking a guy directly in the eye, much less spending enough time with him to date him.

"She and Michael Yserman are sort of a thing. But you can't tell anyone that."

I cock an eyebrow. "What is this, high school? Why the subterfuge?"

A straw paper on the table between us is suddenly very interesting. "She would prefer that her mother not know."

"The Mother Plucker?"

"Peyton."

I cover my smile with the back of my hand. "Sorry." I laugh, though, when he can't hide his own smile. "Anyway, that's interesting."

"And confidential. I'm just telling you that much so you'll know how important it is not to spread it around."

I glare at him. "Since when do I tell anyone anything? Secret-keeping is my specialty, remember?" As intriguing as Tracy's not-so-rebellious rebellion is, I go back to thinking about Jared. After a few minutes of neither of us saying anything, I concede, "Well, maybe a woman isn't the answer. He'd end up doing something stupid and not being discreet about it, probably, and it'd just be another headache for you."

"Good point."

I remember how it was for us. We didn't necessarily sneak around, but we had self-imposed curfews and never traveled overnight anywhere without "chaperones." And don't forget The Rules. I got so sick of the ever-growing list of things that were off-limits to us but commonplace for just about every other couple on the planet. I'm sure Jared wouldn't be under such an intense microscope, but he would still be expected to behave appropriately, something that's a definite problem for him. He seems squeaky-clean enough, but lust makes people do uncharacteristic things. I should know.

Suddenly Brice perks up. "You know what? I think a woman *is* the answer."

"Who?" I ask, wracking my brain for someone at Messiah who's single and the right age.

He grins and points, his finger and thumb in the shape of a gun. "You."

I toss the straw paper at him. "Hardy-har. Very funny."

"I'm serious." He widens his eyes. "I think you're the perfect role-model for our young friend. He seems to listen to you and respect your opinion. He's also comfortable enough to confide in you and admit when he's done something stupid."

"I don't like this idea. At all."

"Why not?" He tilts his head and grabs my closest hand. "You'd be doing me a huge favor, keeping him out of trouble."

I snatch my hand away. "I'm not a babysitter!"

"No, I don't mean it that way."

"Yes, you do!"

Rubbing the back of his neck, he clarifies, "I was thinking more like just taking him under your wing and being a good example to him. You know, when I'm too busy to keep track of him."

"Babysitting."

"If you insist on calling it that, then yes."

I cross my arms over my chest. "Let's say I agree to do this—and I am *not* agreeing to it yet. How are you going to get him to spend time with me without coming right out and telling him that he needs constant supervision?"

Looking levelly at me, he replies, "Oh, I'm going to come right out and tell him he needs constant supervision, believe me. There'll be no question that this is what's going on. After everything he's said and done the past few months, I don't think I need to be delicate about it."

"Why are you punishing me?"

He laughs. "I'm not! If you don't want to do it, I understand. But I think it would be good for him. And you, too, maybe."

I don't even want to know what that's supposed to mean.

"I think you're crazy," I state. "If he can't learn tact and class from you, then he can't learn it from anyone. And he sure as hell isn't going to learn it from me. I may teach him a few new words, but not how to be a good pastor."

Now he looks alarmed. "Uh, I've got the pastor thing covered. Like I said, he'll still be with me most of the time, but I think it'll be helpful for him to have someone to vent to. Someone who's not his boss. Someone who's not going to raise their eyebrows when he calls our elders 'Mafioso,' but who will give him a heads-up that saying something like that to the wrong person—ahem, Kent Stratford—is a *really* bad idea. Then he can get nonsense like that out of his system."

"Yeah, I would have advised him against saying that."

"Exactly! And he would have listened to you. Just like the kids in the youth group listen to you more than they listen to Justine or me. We're just dorks. But you're cool."

I sigh. "Shut up. I'll do it, okay? Stop kissing my ass. It's giving me a headache."

"That's not what you said last night."

My mouth drops open.

My husband is *not* a dirty talker, not even in the privacy of our bedroom, much less in a public place, where he may be overheard. He doesn't even get half of the "That's what she said" jokes I mumble at the innocent things he says. Or maybe he's been feigning innocence all these months.

He cracks up. "I just wanted to say something like that once. Your reaction was so worth it." Standing, he picks up the check and offers me his hand.

As he pays for our dinner and then as we walk through the chilly, dark, quiet neighborhood toward home, I find myself peeking at him from the corner of my eye, studying him, as if I'm seeing him for the first time.

11

THE ODD COUPLE

"*W*ho's Stefan?" Jared says nonchalantly while rearranging the tiny wooden Scrabble tiles on his letter rack.

I nearly knock over my tray at his question. "Uh…" Biting my lower lip, I pretend I'm concentrating too hard on my letters to answer.

He looks up abruptly at my reaction. "Oh! I mean, if it's too personal, or whatever… I mean, I don't mean to pry. It's none of my business. But that one day when you came home from work, and I was here for dinner, you seemed really upset at him. I've never seen you like that before."

Actually, I was really hoping he'd forgotten all about that incident. The fact that he not only recalls it but remembers it well enough to know the name of the person whom I called a—what was it again? Oh, yeah, a "fuck-face"— means that he hasn't forgotten anything about it. Including the suggestive things I said to my husband while trying to coerce him into saying something borderline blasphemous. But whatever. I should be used to people having embarrassing dirt on me by now.

I smile reassuringly at him while frantically trying to decide how much to tell him. Eventually, I just blurt, "He's a guy I work with who I was also..." I trail off and blush. "Romantically involved with" isn't at all accurate or truthful, so I somehow can't make myself say those words to guileless, trusting Jared, who's blinking at me expectantly, his face a blank. "Well, you get the idea," I toss out there, hoping he finally will.

I can see the exact second he does. His brown eyes widen, and all the color drains from his face before shooting back up into it.

"Ah," is all he says, though, before intently studying his letters again.

"Yeah. Not one of my finer moments. Your turn."

"Huh?" he says, his head snapping up to reveal something close to panic in his eyes.

"It's your turn. In the game," I clarify.

He giggles at himself. "Oh. Gosh. I thought you were saying it was my turn to share. And I..." There's sweat on his upper lip now, and his hands are shaking as he plucks some tiles from his rack and places them haphazardly on the board. He spends an inordinate amount of time making sure each square is nestled perfectly in its place. "Anyway, I don't have any stories like that."

"Okay."

"I don't!"

Laughing, I tell him, "I believe you! Sheesh!"

"Why? You think there's no way I could have any secrets?"

"No..."

"Because I've had girlfriends, you know."

"I'm sure you have."

"I have!"

I record the score from his word, play my next word, and record my own score before saying, "Jared. I don't care."

"Oh."

The dull way he says it makes me qualify, "I mean, if you want to talk about it, fine. But I'm not going to think any less of you, even if you tell me you were the biggest man whore at one time in your life."

"Well, I wasn't!"

I sigh. "That was just an example. Calm down. The point is, I try not to throw stones from the front porch of my glass house."

He stands up from the kitchen table and takes his glass to the sink, where he refills it with water and powers it down. At this rate, this is going to be the longest game of Scrabble in the history of the game.

I cross my arms over my chest, lean back in my chair, and watch him while he fills his glass yet again and sips with his back to me. It's clear by the set of his shoulders that he's tense and uncomfortable.

He was the one to start the conversation, but it seems like he's waiting for me to end it, so I'm about to do just that and change the subject when he turns to me and says, "And Pastor knows about you and Stefan?"

I nod. "All about it."

"Everything?"

"Everything. It's sort of an important part of my life. Plus, he was... part of the aftermath."

"Pastor was?"

Good gravy. Now I'm not worried about my pride as much as I'm afraid his head's going to pop off. Before he strokes out—or drowns himself one glass of water at a time —I summarize as matter-of-factly as possible, "Shortly after my encounter with Stefan, I found out I was pregnant. I went to Brice—my pastor—for advice."

"*That's* how you two met?"

"No. We met when he first became Pastor at Messiah. But we got to know each other—and became friends—after I went to him for help."

"Oh." He sets his glass on the counter behind him and rests his hand on the side of his face while trying to process what I've told him. "I just always assumed… I don't know. I guess I thought you two had a more *conventional* courtship." Suddenly, he drops his hand. "Wait a minute. You said you were pregnant. But where's the baby? Did you…?" His eyes widen even further. He blushes. "Oh… Never mind. It's none of my business. I get it. You went to him for 'advice.' I see. Okay. That's unexpected advice, though. I mean, I can't imagine him giving you *that* advice."

As amusing as it is to watch him stutter and fumble through his ridiculous assumption that Brice—of all people—would recommend an abortion to me (to *anyone*), I can't let him think that for even one more second. "I had a baby. She was stillborn. Several months premature. And at that time, Brice and I were still just friends. He was there for me. He was the only one who was willing to be honest with me, even when I didn't want him to be."

His face softens. "Oh, man. I'm sorry about your baby. That must have been tough."

"It was. Still is, some days, when I think about her. But life has gone on. Positive things have come from it. God uses all things for good, blah, blah, blah."

He laughs at my unorthodox homily. "Yes, He does. I'm surprised that Pastor hasn't told me any of this. Well, maybe I'm not surprised, but still… It's fascinating to learn people's backstories, you know?"

Especially a juicy backstory like ours. Instead of saying that, though, I simply nod and point to the board game. "Are we going to play this or not?"

~

Hours later, while Brice takes Jared home, I soak in a hot bathtub nearly overflowing with fragrant bubbles. My first night of babysitting the vicar may have gotten him out of my husband's hair for a few hours, but what transpired probably wasn't what Brice had in mind. I'm not sure he wanted one of the only private details of our life laid out for one of the people with whom he works most closely, someone who's supposed to look up to him and respect him.

Lying back in the tub, I close my eyes and try not to worry too much about it. I mean, it's not *really* a secret anymore. Do I want to take out a billboard that I had a one-night stand two years ago? No. Is it one of the most shameful things I've ever done? Yes. Am I ashamed of Secret? Hell no. And I don't think Jared's going to repeat what I told him, anyway, considering that's Rule Number One in his future line of work. In any case, more people than I realize probably know, thanks to the Messiah Lutheran rumor mill, which is one of the most efficient systems of communication in the world. The only detail I told Jared this evening that he couldn't have gleaned from a five-minute conversation with any one of the elders is the name of Secret's father and his relationship to me. Everything else is pretty much common knowledge. And on the verge of becoming ancient history to everyone but me.

Just as I'm dozing off, the sound of the garage door vibrates to my ears through the now-tepid water. It takes massive effort, but I lift my heavy limbs from the water and emerge onto the fuzzy bath mat, where I pat myself dry and wrap up in my warm, fluffy robe. When I open the door to the bathroom, I nearly collide with Brice in the hallway.

"Oops. Sorry!" I say, laughing as I clutch at his arm to avoid falling backwards into the bathroom.

"Hey." He wraps an arm around my back and pulls me against him. "I thought you'd be in bed already."

"Headed that way. Kicking Jared's butt at Scrabble was exhausting."

Leaning down slightly, he kisses my lips. "He didn't stand a chance. You have that stinkin' Scrabble dictionary memorized, don't you?"

"No!" I deny but laugh at his observation, because I nearly do.

"Mmm-hmm," he replies skeptically as he follows me into the bedroom. He sits on the foot of the bed, takes off his shoes and collar, and untucks and unbuttons his shirt. He looks as tired as I feel.

"Long day?" I ask, making small talk in an attempt to both stall and figure out if Jared told him what we talked about.

He sighs. "They all are, aren't they?"

"I guess so. It'll get better in the summer, though, right? Maybe after Vacation Bible School we can take a week off and go visit your mom on our way to or from someplace fun," I suggest, stepping into a pair of panties and pulling a t-shirt over my head.

His unconvincing, "Maybe…" makes me look sharply at him. "You *will* take some time off this summer, right?"

"I'll try." He drops his pants, kicks them free of his feet, and sits back down on the bed in his t-shirt and underwear.

I know it's the best answer he can give me, so I don't push. Instead, I scoop up his dirty clothes and carry them to the hamper on my way to hanging up my bathrobe on its hook. By the time I turn around to face him again, he's flopped onto his back, his legs still hanging off the edge of the bed as he stares at the motionless ceiling fan above our bed.

I lie next to him and grab his hand. "So, I told Jared about Secret and… stuff."

We turn our heads at the same time to look at each other.

"And stuff?" he asks.

"Yeah. You know… stuff. I mean, nothing too detailed, of course, but he remembered my tirade from the day after we got back from our honeymoon and asked me about it, so… When in doubt, tell the truth, right?" I utter one of his favorite maxims.

He smiles crookedly. "Aw! You're learning!"

"Shut up." I rise up on one elbow and roll over on top of him. Looking down into his face, I ask seriously, "So you're not mad that I told him?"

"Why would I be mad?"

"I could see why you wouldn't want him to know all that. You know, if you're embarrassed that I… used to be like that."

Chuckling, he assures me, "I'm not."

"I don't want my past to reflect poorly on you. It's not your fault."

He sighs.

"I mean it!"

"I know. And I appreciate that. But you don't need to worry about that. Your life experiences made you who you are, and I love that person. If you're comfortable with Jared knowing, then that's your call." He reaches around me and strokes my lower back with his thumbs.

I grin. "Good answer."

"Well, I mean it."

"I know you do."

"Anyone who claims never to have done something despite knowing in their heart that it was wrong is a liar. And that's just as wrong."

"Well..." This is one ideological issue that we tend to disagree about (however good-naturedly).

"A sin is a sin," he claims.

"Hmm... Still not so sure about that one, Reverend Redemption. I don't think lying is as bad as a one-night stand; nor is a one-night stand as serious as murder."

"You're starting to sound a little Catholic."

His funny face, complete with wrinkled nose, makes me laugh. "Well, we can't have that," I tease. "What would Martin Luther say?"

With a straight face, he answers, "He would say you should submit to your husband and know that in these matters he is wise and learned."

"I say we should stop discussing this." I press my lips to his and run my hand up his t-shirt and against his ribs.

When we break apart after several minutes, he murmurs, "What were we talking about?"

"Nothing important," I assert. "Right now, I think talking is completely worthless, anyway."

He grins and flips me underneath him. "That's something I can agree with wholeheartedly."

CONTENTMENT AND PEACE

I'm so sick of being sick. What started as a mild spring allergy attack has evolved into a sinus infection that two types of antibiotics haven't been able to kick. I even gave it to Brice. Of course, Reverend Resilient was better before he was even finished with his first and only round of antibiotics (and complained about having to continue taking them until they were gone, as directed by his doctor), so I'm suffering alone again. I go nowhere without a box of tissues. A box. Not one of those wimpy travel packs that fits in a dainty purse. A box. And when a sneezing fit hits, I'm like a volcano.

Heading into my third week of this nonsense, the last thing I want to do is play another game of Scrabble with Jared on a Friday night while Brice does whatever Brice does when he gets some precious time away from the vicar. Don't get me wrong; I've really come to like Jared. He's a nice guy. And I feel bad for him that he's so far away from home and that his only friend is a snot-spewing, cynical pastor's wife who, more often than not, hangs out with him out of a sense of obligation, not because she wants to.

Tonight is a perfect example. But when he gave me an out ("If you don't feel well enough, I understand. I'll just go back to the church and check with Pastor to see if there's anything I can do to help with last-minute Sunday preps"), I knew that would result in a grouchy husband later, so I quickly pasted a smile on my face and mumbled through my congestion, "Doh, I'b fide. Cumb od id," while stepping back from the door so he could enter the house.

When every one of my plays in our Scrabble game relates to illness, he pushes aside his letter rack. "You know, we don't always have to play Scrabble."

"We don't?" I ask stupidly, unable to think of any other thing we could do. This game is kind of the fallback in my family. Even in the tensest of times, when we have nothing to say to each other, we can pull out the Scrabble board.

Truth is, since our first night in together, when I told him about Stefan and Secret, I don't really know what to say to him. He's never brought it up again, and it's not like I catch him staring at me in a way that would make me think he's judging me or wondering what other secrets I have lurking in my past, but we kind of summed up the biggest event in my life on that evening, so now I'm out of conversation fodder. I'm just here in case he needs a sympathetic ear or wants to ask me for advice. When he doesn't need those services (which is admittedly rare), I'm at a loss with him.

He clears the board and puts the letter tiles in their velvet pouch. "No. We don't. Your heart's not in it tonight anyway. Your highest-scoring word was 'mucus.' Although, I must say, nicely played on that triple word score spot."

I laugh at myself. "I'm a little preoccupied. And tired."

"Let's watch some TV then."

He and Brice usually watch sports when it's just the two

of them, so I immediately suggest, "There's a hockey game on, I think."

Plopping down onto the couch, he takes up the remote and punches in some numbers. Instead of a bunch of brutes in helmets, jerseys, and skates, though, a home improvement show pops up on the screen. Thinking he's accidentally pressed the wrong buttons, I don't let myself get too excited.

"I think the game's on a lower channel. Not sure of the number. You'll just have to scan."

He leans back into his corner of the sofa and sets down the remote on the arm next to his hand. "I'd rather watch this." Quickly checking with me, he adds, "Unless you'd like to watch hockey."

I blink. "No. Not really. This is good."

Brice hates this stuff. When he does submit to watching it with me, he keeps a running commentary about how much money everything costs and how it must be nice to have professional carpenters and electricians and plumbers on staff to make everything look easy. Every time I think, *Oh, what a good idea!* he ruins it for me by pointing out something that they've finessed through the magic of TV, until I finally change it to the History Channel or ESPN and resign myself to learning about the Dead Sea scrolls or watching overgrown children with outsized egos take out their steroid-fueled aggression on each other.

It's gotten to the point that even when I tune in to interior design or home improvement shows alone, I find myself skeptically wondering what they're editing out that would make it impossible for me to get the same result. He's ruined the entire genre for me.

Now when the room on this show goes from dingy white to vibrant red seemingly in the span of a commercial break, I wait for Jared to say, "How many production assistants worked overnight to paint umpteen coats on those walls?" but he doesn't.

Instead, he simply says, "Wow. That looks so much better. It's amazing what a little color can do."

I relax into the couch cushions. "Right? I'd love to have a red kitchen like that. Or a yellow bedroom."

"Do it," he says distractedly, his eyes glued to the show.

"It's a lot of work to put into a house that isn't ours," I say, echoing what Brice told me the one time I mentioned that the parsonage might be a little bland for my taste. He also told me that a parsonage isn't supposed to have personality.

It's not outdated, just... blah. And it's wrong to complain about it, since it was renovated with new everything when Brice became the pastor here a few years ago. The trustees simply went a little safe with the color scheme (white and tan), and he hasn't done anything to personalize it, since he doesn't care about things like that, and he's never home, anyway.

"We could have a painting party," Jared suggests. "Get the youth group involved. It'd be done in no time flat. Cost: a few pizzas, sodas, and paint supplies. I bet you could do the kitchen and your bedroom *and* the bathroom for less than 200 bucks."

"Nice idea."

"But?"

"I don't think Brice is going to want to mess with it." I honk into a tissue.

"Do it on a Sunday afternoon, then. He won't have to be involved at all. He'll come home from work that night and BAM! It'll be done." He grins over at me. "Where there's a will, there's a way."

"Do you ever take no for an answer?"

His grin becomes even broader. "Nope. Well, there have been a few occasions, but for the most part, I try to find ways to make things work. I'm a can-do guy. I TCB."

"TCB?"

"Take care of business." He sits up straighter. "When someone gives me a 'can't' or a 'no,' I like to give them three ways to make it happen, anyway."

Cautiously, I break it to him. "Some people might call that 'obnoxious.'"

He laughs. "I know. But sometimes there's no good reason for naysayers. They just say no, because they like to burst people's bubbles. That ticks me off."

"You'd better get used to it, if you're going to be a pastor. You get ten no's for every yes. It's a study in patience."

He snorts dismissively. "There's a difference between patience and complacency. You have to at least ask for things."

Now I bristle, sensing some criticism being leveled at my husband. "You also have to pick your battles. There are too many of them to fight them all. And if you try, you'll only alienate your congregants and exhaust yourself."

Unfortunately, it doesn't sound that eloquent, since none of my n's or m's come out sounding like the right letters, but he gets the point and hastily revises, "I mean, I'm not saying that's how Pastor is. I'm finding out just how difficult he has it. He deals with some tough cookies."

"Like my dad?"

Smiling guiltily, he says, "I wasn't going to name names, but yeah. Like your dad. And when you try to keep everyone happy, nothing gets done."

"Things get done. It just takes a little longer, and it takes some finessing. Finessing. A skill you need to work on, by the way." I nudge him so he knows I'm not being mean-spirited.

He sighs. "I know, I know. But I'm never going to be like Pastor. I'm just not built that way. I need to be the pastor of a church with a young, energetic congregation who will appreciate what I can bring to the table."

Gently, I remind him, "Yeah, but that's not how it works. *They* call *you*. And the church that calls you may not be a perfect fit for your personality. *You're* going to have to adjust. Or you'll be miserable."

He nods, but I can tell he thinks he'll be the exception to the rule. He thinks it won't happen to him; he'll charm all the little old ladies and the crotchety elders and the mocking teens in the youth group, and everyone will bend to his whims, because he'll be young and enthusiastic and full of good ideas. I'd try to convince him otherwise, but I think this is one of those lessons he has to learn for himself. And Jared seems like the type of guy who needs to learn most lessons the hard way. Still, he may learn all this during his vicariate. Goodness knows he's getting plenty of opportunities.

Pointing to the TV, I say, "So what about this kitchen/dining room makeover? Do you think it's possible to do something like that in two days?"

He turns his attention back to the show. "All things are possible through God, right? And I'm sure they have a few other tricks up their sleeves, but that doesn't mean the show's not fun to watch. You can still get a lot of good ideas from it."

"That's what I always say."

"That's something you could definitely do *easily* in this living room to give it a little personality."

"A parsonage isn't supposed to have personality," I mumble dully, which makes him snort and laugh.

"That's a load of hooey."

What's the advice I gave him, though? Pick your battles. And so I shall. I have to save my demands for things that really count.

What really counts tonight: a sandwich and a head massage (your priorities shift remarkably when you don't feel good).

Sitting on the floor in front of the couch at Brice's feet, I munch on the salami, pepperoni, ham, turkey, and provolone sandwich while he kneads his fingers against my scalp. He has surprisingly strong fingers for someone who works mostly with his brain for a living.

"Mmmm," I say about both the sandwich and the massage. I'm not sure which one I'm enjoying more. My head is so full of snot that it's pulsating like a zit. The pressure makes my eyes bulge in their sockets. But I'm ravenous. So even though I can't really taste much, and it kind of hurts to chew, I'd say the sandwich is winning. The only thing that would make it better is...

"Banana peppers."

"Hmm?" Brice asks, keeping his eyes on his sermon notes.

"Do we have any banana peppers?"

"No. You ate them all the other night while we watched *The Mentalist.*"

"Damn. Oh, well. Probably couldn't taste 'em anyway."

"So I just wasted three pounds of meat on that sandwich?"

I chew and swallow a huge mouthful of said meat. "No. It's still nourishing my body, even if I can't taste it."

"Water and crackers would have done just as well, then." He turns the page on his notes with one hand and then goes back to digging his fingertips into my skull.

Closing my eyes, I say, "No, because I know what it's *supposed* to taste like. Just keep rubbing."

"Yes, my bride."

While he resumes reading, I resume eating, feeling warm and safe and happy, despite my stuffy head. I just feel so content. Like I'm wrapped in a fleece blanket. Oh, wait. I am. But still. The feeling goes deeper than that. I can't stop smiling. And I don't know what the difference is. I mean, I've been relatively happy for a long time, but this is more than that. I can't even describe it. It's an all-consuming sense of gladness and serenity. And it's so remarkable, because I've never felt this way before.

Stuffing the final bite (okay, more like two bites) into my mouth, I can't wait for my mouth to be empty before I announce, "I'm so happy!"

He chuckles. "I'm glad you feel better."

My manners take over, so I finish chewing, then say, "Oh, I don't. Not really. I still feel like ass. Although I think these new antibiotics are finally working. I'm not as drippy."

"Lovely."

I stand, giving him a rest from his massaging duties. Tossing my paper plate in the recycling bin in the kitchen, I say loudly enough for him to hear me in the other room, "Have you ever felt like things are exactly the way they should be, and like there's a warm spot of sunlight that just follows you around everywhere you go, keeping you warm and safe and peaceful?"

There's a long pause and then, "Yeah. I have. It's a good feeling."

"The best feeling." Suddenly I'm exhausted from all the joy flooding my system. "I think I'm going to go to bed now," I inform him on my way through the living room.

He looks up sharply from his notes. "What?" After a look at his watch, he says, "But it's only 6:30!"

"Yeah, I know, but I'm tired. And there's church tomorrow. And stuff…" I trail off, too exhausted to itemize all the reasons such an early bedtime is necessary. Instead, I let a huge yawn say it all.

With an affectionate smile, he lets me know, "Well, I'm going to be a while yet."

I step forward and give the top of his head a kiss. "I don't expect you to escort me. I'll see you in the morning."

If I had enough breath to spare, I'd whistle as I get ready for bed. Instead, I sort of bob to the beat of an internal soundtrack, a tune with a poppy beat and sunny notes. I use the toilet, brush my teeth, and wash my face, and then I shake an antibiotic capsule from its bottle and poke my birth control pill through the foil pack, tossing both of them down with one glass of water.

"Aaaah!" I say to my reflection, giving myself a toothy smile.

Closing the pill pack, I notice that next week is the final row of tiny pills. Must remember to tell Brice that my "bye" week (his clever way of describing my period in sports talk without conjuring graphic mental images) is approaching.

"Doo-doo-doo, boppity-bop-bop-boo," I sing in my raspy voice, which is flat and squeaky at the best of times and downright scary tonight. It's so bad that I laugh at myself while putting on a warm pair of flannel pajamas and pulling back the covers on the bed to slide in.

I'm just settling against the cool sheets after turning off the light when the bedroom door opens, light spilling across my face from the hallway. I squint through the beam.

"Are you okay?" Brice's silhouette asks after a few seconds.

His out-of-the-blue question makes me unsure of myself and what the right answer is. "Yes?" I answer.

To my disappointment, he comes into the room and sits on the side of the bed, draping one arm over the hill of my hip and rump. I really just want to go to sleep. This bed has never felt so good.

"Everything's fine at work?"

"Yes!"

"And Jared, he's not annoying you too much, is he? Or saying things that make you worry about the next stupid stunt he's going to pull?"

I slide my hands under my cheek and wiggle my shoulders and hips as a way of hinting that I mean business about this sleep thing. "No. He's fine. Am I supposed to report back to you everything he says so *you* can be worried?"

He stiffens. "Why? Has he said something?"

I sigh. "No. Like I told you, we mostly talked about redecorating last night. Relax."

In the scant light from the hallway, I can see that he's anything but. The wrinkles in his forehead would make a Shar-Pei jealous.

"What's wrong with you?" he finally asks.

"I told you—"

"Yeah, I know, but something's not right. Is it the antibiotics you're on? Do they make you feel strange?"

"No."

"It's just... I know you. And—don't take this the wrong way, but—you're never this happy."

What other way am I supposed to take it than the way that would offend?

When I'm at a loss, he rushes on, "You know what I mean."

That bubble of joy in my chest has a tiny pinhole in it, courtesy of Reverend Meanie.

"Oh, I see. You mean, you knew when you married me that I was prone to pessimism and downheartedness, but you were okay with that? You love me *in spite of* it? So when I'm happy and dare to show it, there must be something wrong?"

"I told you not to take it the wrong way, but at least this reaction is a bit more typical of you." He plucks self-consciously at the blanket covering my hip. "Are you acting happy to hide something from me?"

"What? No!"

"Your happiness seems over the top. Like fake happiness."

I close my eyes and grit my teeth. "Until about three minutes ago, it was completely sincere. Now, you'll be glad to know I'm a little less happy, because I really want to go to sleep, and you're asking me these bizarre questions and looking for trouble where there is none, which is—frankly—usually my job."

"That's what I'm saying!"

"Go away."

At first, he says nothing and doesn't move, but when I keep my eyes closed and make it clear that I won't be continuing this conversation, he says, "Okay. I'm sorry. I— I thought I should check."

"Goodnight. I love you," I say, as dismissively as possible.

With that slight statement of forgiveness from me, he

leans down and presses his lips to mine. "I love you, too," he whispers. "So much."

Those two added words and the heartfelt way he says them wake up my libido like it's a hibernating animal that suddenly feels the need to be on high alert. My eyes fly open. Before he can straighten, I put my arms around his neck and pull him down to the bed.

"Stay here for a while," I invite him suggestively.

"But you said you were—"

"I'm not anymore." I tug at his long-sleeved t-shirt. "Come on. You can get back to work in a little while."

"I'm not worried about that," he assures me, undressing himself as quickly as possible.

I wiggle out of the pajamas I so recently and gleefully put on and hold up the edge of the covers so he can come on in. I'm giving myself whiplash with my mood swings, so I can only imagine how he's feeling. However, he's not complaining right at this moment.

I suddenly just *need* this. Like an exclamation point on the "Woo-hoo!" that has been my day. And aren't I blessed to have a husband who's ready and willing to provide it at a moment's notice? I think I am. The joy bubble is re-inflating in direct proportion to—

Well, there's no need to be vulgar and graphic about it. Suffice it to say, my happiness soundtrack is playing louder than ever.

13

TOO HAPPY

*W*hat *is* wrong with me? Because something's definitely not right. It's not just about my uncharacteristic contentment, either. I called my mom the other day, just to talk. I was *nice* to Justine when she stopped by Brice's office (ostensibly to talk about plans for an end-of-the-school-year lock-in for the youth group but really to show off Isaiah and flirt with my husband). I volunteered to call church members to solicit item donations for a rummage sale. I attended a voters' meeting, without being specifically asked by my husband to do so. If I didn't know better, I'd say I was—gulp—growing up and taking owner-ship in this thing called my grown-up pastor's wife's life.

No. That can't be it. This is just some strange phenomenon, like Christmas spirit, that has taken hold of me for reasons that are too subtle for me to put my finger on but that have a definite impetus.

Maybe it was that documentary I recently watched on PBS about the people in a small Ohio town who decided to institute a city-wide policy of goodwill to see how it affected their quality of life. It had some amazing results (hence, the documentary), and I was pretty impressed by the idea, but I didn't walk away from it saying, *I'm totally going to do that!* As a matter of fact, I seem to remember thinking, *That would never work around here.* But maybe it made a bigger impact than I thought.

Also, come to think of it, once I finally got rid of that ridiculous sinus infection, I was astounded by the amount of energy I had. I'd forgotten what it felt like to be well. And it was like I couldn't sit still. I had to burn the energy somehow.

But surely I'm not going to sustain this. I value my free time way too much to fill it up with good works, no matter how worthy they are and how unwilling other people seem to be to step up and do them. What happened to my strict "Not My Problem" policy?

What's happening to *me*?

I know better than to ask Reverend Philanthropy. He'll get all ooey-gooey-eyed and start gushing about the psychological and physiological benefits of goodwill, volunteerism, and an overall generous spirit. He'll say something to lead me to believe he's been worried that I haven't been more charitable heretofore and that his prayers are being answered, because I'm finally understanding my role in the church, blah, blah, blah. Then I'll get all defensive and feel the need to rebel against doing what may be expected of me, even if it's something I don't mind doing and even *want* to do. No, nothing good can come from consulting him for a possible explanation for this shift in attitude and behavior.

I must say, though, that I'm setting precedents here. People are taking notice and asking me to do more and more things, thanks to my sudden, frequent use of the word, "yes."

I guess I'll just have to deal with those consequences,

though, because for now, "yes" is my new favorite word. It feels good.

So it feels relatively foreign for me to whisper, "No," as panic grabs hold of my internal organs and jiggles them around. "Uh-uh. Nuh-uh. *Nonononono*. Oh, hell no."

"It's just a pimple," Brice startles me by saying sleepily behind me in the bedroom, where he's still in bed.

I toss the totally empty rectangular case in the trash next to the toilet in the tiny half-bath and say lightly, "Yeah, I know. Sorry. Didn't mean to wake you up. You know how much I hate them."

He grumbles something about how early it is while turning over onto his stomach and burying his face in his pillow.

Normally, I'd apologize again for waking him up so early. Well, not really. I don't think I've ever been out of bed before him. But a staggering thought woke me from a deep sleep and had me up like a spitball through a straw. And right now I'm too busy doing math to repeat my apologies for waking him up. This math is hard. It's biological. It's terrifying.

When I keep getting the same answer, I stagger back toward the bed and sink to the edge of it—or where I thought the edge of it was. What actually happens is that I miss the mattress by a good three inches and land flat on my ass with an "Ooof!" onto the floor.

Brice rises up on his elbows and peers over the side of the bed at me. Laughing, his hair sticking up in all directions, he says, "Did you just fall down?" When I don't answer, he sobers and asks, "What's wrong? Are you okay?" He scrambles onto his knees, kicking at the sheets and comforter as he tries to untangle his legs and get to me.

"I'm fine," I tell him before he does damage to himself. "At least, I'm not hurt."

"What happened?" he asks, as he finally pulls his feet free. He sits on my side of the bed, looking down on me as I remain seated on the carpet with my legs straight out in front of me, my posture making me feel a lot like one of Sadie's Barbie dolls. He rubs his eyes fiercely with his knuckles and yawns.

Well, there's no use denying it; he's going to find out eventually, and he'll be hurt if he finds out I didn't tell him as soon as I knew. If I weren't such a klutz, I may have been able to buy myself some time, but I've drawn his attention to me in a huge way by doing my best Three Stooges imper- sonation. (I wonder which one I'd be. Moe, most likely.)

"I'm totally pregnant," I tell him matter-of-factly, nervous-laughing like I've just told him I peed my pants when I fell down (which has happened in front of him before, unfortunately).

That definitely wasn't what he was expecting. He freezes mid-eye rub and yanks his hands away from his face. "You'd better not be kidding," he warns severely.

I don't appreciate his drill-sergeant tone. "I'm not! I hardly think that's something to joke about!"

"How do you know?" he asks, grasping me by the elbow and pulling me up onto the bed next to him.

I swallow hard and try not to think of what I'm really saying as I say it. It's better to just disconnect. "I, uh— Well, I missed my period this month."

"When did you figure that out?"

He's staring so intensely at me that it's making me blush. "Just now. I woke up with this picture in my head of an empty birth control pill packet. I must have been distracted when I took the last one last week. But when you take the last pill, you're supposed to be on the last day or two of your period, and I wasn't. I mean, I haven't had anything… going on… down there."

"Oh. Wow."

"Sorry. I'm not trying to overshare on the lady talk." I'm too freaked out right now, though, to worry about his sensitivity regarding talk about bodily functions.

"No, that's not what I meant. I mean, 'Wow!'" He pulls me up against his chest and squeezes me so hard that I exhale audibly. He loosens his embrace exponentially. "Oh, man. Sorry. I just… Oh. I…" He pulls back more and kisses me, but either his aim is bad or he has a sudden affection for my left eye.

I wipe the saliva away and blink. "Yeah. I've just been so busy lately. And the weeks are flying by."

"Did you have a period last month?"

I stare into space before admitting guiltily, "I don't know. Oh, gosh. I don't think so. But I was sick! And taking medic — Oh."

Shit.

A snippet from a conversation from a long time ago (another life, it seems) bounces around in my otherwise-blank brain.

"And these stupid antibiotics are going to ruin my weekend with Neco, because everyone knows that antibiotics don't play well with birth control, and Neco hates using condoms."

Neco. He was a douche of the highest order, but Jen fancied herself in love with him. That's not the point, though. What was the point again? Oh, yeah: "…*everyone* knows antibiotics don't play well with birth control." Everyone. Even stupid college girls who don't know better than to insist their grubby man-whore, walking-STD boyfriends wear condoms, no matter what other methods of birth control they're using.

"It was the antibiotics," I mumble now.

"The antibiotics got you pregnant? And I thought it may have had something to do with me."

I ignore him and explain, "The antibiotics decreased the effectiveness of my birth control."

"Oh, darn."

"Did you know that could happen?" I force my eyes to focus so I can glare menacingly at him.

He holds his hands up defensively. "No! How would I know that?"

"Everyone knows that."

"Well, I had no reason to know that." He thinks about it for a second. "I did know a woman at my church in Kansas who had three little boys and got pregnant again when her anti-seizure medication interacted with her birth control, but…" He taps his chin and smiles. "That was an interesting situation, actually. She came to me, upset about having another baby, but when it was all said and done, it turned out to be a huge blessing, because she gave birth to a girl who was then a bone marrow match for one of her older sons, who was diagnosed with leukemia shortly after the baby girl was born. The last I heard, they were all doing really well."

I take a deep breath and count to three, then five, then ten. I do *not* want a sermon right now about blessings in disguise. Somehow I've managed to hide from him, though, that I'm on the edge. Or that I'm not as thrilled as he is.

Suddenly he lets go of me and lunges backward to reach for his phone on his bedside table. "I can't wait to tell Mom."

Argghhhhhhh!

I haven't even been able to tell myself in a way that is believable and makes sense. I sure as hell don't want to tell anyone else yet.

"Um, wait!" I practically shout as he presses at the buttons on the touchscreen of his phone.

He barely pauses to say, "I know, you're worried about telling people too soon. But it's just my mom. She'll want to know. You should call your parents, too!"

"No, I don't think so."

He puts the phone on speaker and holds it between us so we can both talk to her. When I hear Mary's phone begin to ring, I stab at the button to disconnect the call. The phone falls silent.

"Why'd you do that?" His smile fades.

Near tears, I say, "Just wait, okay? Can I have five minutes to—"

I'm interrupted by his phone ringing in his hand. He announces unnecessarily to me, "Mom," even though I can see her name flashing on the screen. "What do you want me to do?"

I sigh. "Answer it. But don't tell her yet. Please!"

He looks like a little boy who's just been told he's not allowed to go trick-or-treating, but he says sulkily, "Fine," before answering the call. "Hey, Mom!... Oh, I must have pocket-dialed you. Sorry.... Yeah, I know it's early.... No, everything's fine. Really fine. Great." Now he grins, and I can see it in his eyes but can do nothing about it when he makes the decision and says, "Peyton's pregnant!... I know! We're super-excited, too.... No, we just found out.... Oh, it's still really early, but we didn't want you to have to wait to hear the news with everyone else.... Yeah, she's right here." He holds the phone out to me. "She wants to talk to the new mommy."

I shoot daggers—no, more like cruise missiles—at him with my eyes.

He innocently pushes the phone closer to me.

I snatch it from his big hand and hold it to my ear. "Hey, Mary…. Yep, big surprise!"

It's semi-official now. I've peed on a stick, and it gave me two lines (although my heart skipped hopefully when one was sort of lighter than the other, until I read in the instructions that it was common but still meant, "knocked up"). I say semi-official, however, because I won't quite believe it's happening until a certified doctor gives me the verdict—I mean, sentence—I mean, news.

It's not like I'm devastated by the idea. That would be wrong and selfish. Okay, so it's not happening on my preferred timeline. Big whoop. So I wanted more time (much more time) alone with my husband before we had kids. Again, not a good enough reason to be upset. So I'm terrified that something will go wrong.

Okay. I can't think about that. I have to stay focused on reality and what *is*, not what could be.

Plus, this irrational happiness still has control over me most of the time (when I don't think about Secret or how sad it is that I had no one with whom to share the excitement of her impending arrival). And after hearing the elation in Mary's voice on the phone, I couldn't even work up a good snit about Brice going against my express wishes and telling her. Between the tears of joy in her voice and the ones in his eyes, I found myself getting caught up in the moment.

But that moment ended. And after I threatened my

husband with his life if he did that with anyone else before we both agreed to tell people, I informed him I was going to a drugstore in a neighborhood away from the church so I wouldn't run the risk of bumping into anyone we know while buying a pregnancy test, which I should have taken before he said anything to anyone, even his Mom, I scolded him.

He just grinned at me and pulled me back onto the bed with him.

Thirty minutes later, I left for the drugstore.

The thing is, I don't *feel* pregnant. And I know how it feels. That is, I know how awful it feels. And this doesn't feel like that. I'm not tired, I'm not weepy, I'm not pukey, I'm not ready to kill people at the slightest provocation, I'm not scary, I'm not zitty, and I'm not spacey. Something must be wrong.

That's what I kept telling Brice as I urged him each day to check his schedule to figure out the best time for us to go to our first doctor's appointment. I don't want to do any of this alone this time around. I had enough of that before. But he'd come home every night with the same response: "Oh, man! I forgot to check again! Just schedule something, and I'll work around it." And I would have taken him up on it, only I knew it wouldn't end well. Finally, he wised up and brought home his entire desk calendar (only he would still use a desk blotter calendar when he has a computer and an iPhone at his disposal). When he walked through the door that night with the two-foot-wide pad tucked under his arm, I cracked up. He slapped it onto the kitchen table and said, "Here. Let's look at our options so you can relax a little bit."

He's right. I *am* tense. I need Dr. Walsh to look up there and say, "Yep. There it is. Alive and... alive." I need her to tell me what all the books say, that I may not have any of the same symptoms I had the first time, that every pregnancy is different, and that just because I don't have any negative symptoms, that doesn't necessarily mean there's something wrong.

In other words, you don't have to feel like shit to be pregnant.

But I simply can't imagine a pregnancy without puke.

Brice can. He dreams of it, prays about it, and gives thanks for it. When I mention—at least three times a day—how odd I think it is that I'm not sick all the time, he shakes his head and asks, "Why can't you just be thankful? Why question something like that?"

I don't tell him this, but I question it because I don't believe in things that are too good to be true. Even the seemingly new me who's the poster child for "happy" still wonders, what's the catch? There's always a price. Okay, so I don't have morning sickness (yet); what's going to be the trade-off? Will I gain 100 pounds, because I'm always hungry? Then Brice'll have to push me around on a hand cart and tie my shoes for me and help me off the couch, where I'll spend most of my time, because I can't move.

I need reassurance, that's all. I really don't want to screw this up.

So after we wait in the exam room for the doctor for twenty torturous minutes, I'll be the first to admit that I'm a little impatient when she asks me just about every question the nurse already asked when we first got here. "What was the date of your last period?" "What are some of the symptoms—if any—you're having?" "Did you take a home pregnancy test prior to coming here?"

My leg jiggling, I say with a smile to take the edge off, "I think the nurse made all these notes already." I point to the computer mounted to the wall. "In there."

Dr. Walsh, familiar with my brusque exam-room style from the last time I came to see her fairly regularly, barely looks up from the paper file in her lap. "I'm sure she did."

What's the point in having a chart if no one's going to refer to it? I'm just about to ask when Brice puts his hand on my knee and squeezes. My paper gown rustles.

He clears his throat. "Uh, I'm sort of new to this. I mean, I realize you and Peyton know each other and have a history, but…"

She looks up fully now and flashes him a big smile, like it's the first time she's even noticed he's in the room. "Yes. The first-time dads are pretty easy to spot. Because they're here." She laughs at her own joke. When he humors her with a polite chuckle, she says, "Anyway, if you have any questions, don't be afraid to come right out and ask. There are no silly ones. After all, it's your baby."

He uncrosses and re-crosses his legs and cranes his neck as if his clerical collar is too tight. "Okay. I was just wondering, what's going to happen here today?"

She pats the exam table and answers, "Peyton's gonna get up here—now's fine." I eagerly follow her directions. "And I'm going to have a quick feel and look around, see what we've got. Then, based on the information you've given me and what I see and feel, we'll calculate a due date, set up some future appointments on a monthly, then semi-monthly, then weekly basis, as we get closer to your due date, and answer any questions you have."

She raises the stirrups and guides my heels into them. Then she nonchalantly does some prep work that clearly makes Brice uncomfortable—snapping on the latex gloves, squirting some lubricant on the speculum (why are guys such babies when it comes to things like this?)—before settling on a low, rolling stool between my knees and murmuring warnings about "cold" and "pressure."

I stare at the ceiling, trying not to read too much into it when she seems to be taking a while down there. It's not like you want your doctor to rush something like this, anyway. I preach patience to myself and think about what a cute dad Brice is going to be. I picture him holding our little boy—or girl—on his hip while greeting everyone at the doors after church on Sundays. Or chasing him or her in the park. Or tossing him or her a ball. Or taking a nap on the couch with a baby on his chest. Oh, that's a particularly sweet image.

Finally, Dr. Walsh removes the speculum, wheels back, peels off her gloves, and announces, "You're not pregnant."

14

JUST KIDDING!

"What?" Brice and I ask together. His voice is a lot higher than mine.

She gently asks me, "How many periods have you missed?"

"Two!"

"What's been going on in your life lately? Anything stressful? Have you been sick?"

My mortification makes it even harder to keep from blowing up about having to answer that, since I specifically told the nurse all about the sinus infection and the antibiotics. "Yes! I had a sinus infection for, like, a month!"

Brice pipes up. "But she took one of those home thingies. I saw her. I mean, I didn't watch her do it, but I saw the result. It was positive. Positively."

The doctor smiles comfortingly while helping me to a sitting position. "I believe you. Both of you. This happens a lot, believe it or not." I'm a little worried that she means *If you can believe there are that many idiots out there*, but I try to take her words at face value as I nod earnestly. I want to believe her.

She continues, "We actually got a positive hit from the urine sample you provided this morning, but there were some other markers that we test for that made me suspect you received a false positive from the home test. I wanted to do a thorough exam, though, to make sure. And to check for some possible problems, which I didn't see, by the way, before you start worrying about that."

"Oh."

Rolling up her sleeves, she washes her hands and says over her shoulder, "So, tell me what's up. How long have you two been married? What's life like right now? Have you been trying to conceive?"

Brice points to me as if to say, *You're on!*

At least these questions aren't the same ones I've already answered for someone else. Unfortunately, I can't give complete answers with him in the room. I gloss over everything with, "We've been married for seven whole months. Life is... busy. Very. And no, we haven't been trying. I was actually on birth control, remember?"

"Okay. So, why do I get the feeling this is a disappointment? You guys look disappointed." Then she nods to Brice. "Well, you do, anyway. You look like this is the worst news you've ever heard."

He attempts a smile. "I'd be lying if I said I wasn't disappointed. I just... I thought we were going to have a baby. I really want one, but I guess... Well, not yet."

His heroic efforts to be cheerful and to fight the tightness in his throat make me feel fiercely proud. And sad. He's fine until he glances up at me, but then his eyes well up.

His smile wobbles and falls before he says, "So, anyway..." and can't go on.

Oh, shit. What am I supposed to do here? I feel so bad for him! And I want to do something to comfort him, but

I'm sitting here in a backless paper smock and stuff is sort of oozing out of me still. And... Oh, screw it! I hop down from the exam table and kneel down in front of him, painfully (and coldly) aware that my back and butt are completely exposed to the doctor. But whatever. She just got up close and personal with my lady parts, so it's silly to worry about her looking at something that could be shown on network television (but hopefully *never* will be).

Grabbing his hands, I say, "Hey. I'm so sorry."

He looks up sharply from our joined hands in his lap. His eyes are suddenly clear and dry. (How do guys do that?)

"What? No! It's not your fault."

Before I can say anything else, Dr. Walsh cuts in. "Listen, you guys. Unless you have questions, I'm going to leave you alone." At the door, she adds, "Peyton, everything looks fine. My advice, if you want to keep trying, is for you to get plenty of rest, exercise, eat right, and if you're not pregnant in a couple of months, and your cycle's not back on schedule, call me. I bet you I'll see you two back here very soon, with a very different result, though."

After she exits, Brice stands and pulls me up by the hand. He retrieves my clothes from where I placed them earlier in one of the other chairs in the room, then hands me some tissues so I can clean up before getting dressed. It's obvious that he doesn't want to talk, but I can't stand the silence.

"I feel like an idiot," I say. "And before you go on and on about how it's okay and you're not mad at me, I already know. I'm not fishing for absolution. But I feel terrible that you got your hopes up and..." Now *I* puddle up. "I should be feeling relieved, but I'm not!" It's the first time I've come out and admitted to him that I wasn't pleased to find myself unexpectedly pregnant for the second time in my life.

I jam my legs into my black pants, which I pull roughly over my hips and fumble with the zipper and buttons. After struggling with the tight inside button, I give up and roughly yank down on the hem of my long shirt. Brice looks on in silence.

Angrily, I grumble to his confused expression, "I wasn't ready. I said, '*Nonononono*,' when I figured out what had happened. I missed the bed and hit the floor! That's how much I didn't want it to be true. But now I feel almost as bad as I did when Secret died. About a completely imaginary baby! That's insane."

"It wasn't imaginary to us." Rocking on his heels with his hands in his pants pockets, he hypothesizes, "And, deep down, you obviously really *did* want a baby."

"No, Brice! I really didn't! Really, really, really. I can't string enough really's together for it to be sufficiently emphatic. I know you can't fathom that, but it's true!"

He rubs the back of his neck and glances nervously at the door.

"I don't care if anyone hears," I lie, suddenly very self-conscious about how loudly I've been talking. A little lower, I say, "But I started getting used to the idea. And it's made you so happy. And *I've* been happy, too. All I have to do is picture you with our kids, and I forget everything else. I'm not worried or scared or dreadful about losing sleep. I was excited for you—and eventually for myself. And now... now, I'm just an empty vessel. Again. Only this time, there was never a baby, and I was too dumb to know the difference."

Handing my purse to me, he says, "Hey! The only way the doctor knew was to poke around up there, so 'dumb' had nothing to do with it."

"This time," I sniffle, and smile miserably.

He laughs. "Yeah."

I grab some more tissues and blot at my eyes. "How many people have you told?"

I ask it so bluntly and suddenly that he readily falls into my trap and answers, "Just a few—I mean, Mom. That's it."

I sniffle and roll my eyes. "Why do you even attempt to lie? You're so bad at it. Who did you tell?"

Again he starts with, "Mom. And I may have mentioned something about it to Jared. And then Justine and Marilyn guessed, and I couldn't lie!"

I can't help but laugh at him. "Yes, you could."

"You just said how horrible I am at it. They would have known the truth, and they would have known I was lying, so what's the point?"

Exiting the exam room, I try not to think that all the nurses and doctors are staring at us as we walk down the hallways and back out through the waiting room and into the sunny, warm spring day. Next to my car, I say, "Well, the point would have been that you wouldn't have to tell everyone, 'Just kidding!' which is what you're going to have to do now. And they're going to know I'm an idiot who couldn't tell the difference between *whatever* is going on with me and being pregnant."

He shakes his head. "I'll just tell them it was all a late April Fool's joke."

I kiss his lips. "You are such a doofus if you think you can pull that off."

"Well, not to my mom. I don't lie to her. Never could, anyway."

"Doofus."

∿

Since it became obvious that telling Jared, Justine, and Marilyn was almost as an effective way of telling everyone at Messiah about our "pregnancy" as announcing it in the middle of a sermon, I agreed with Brice that he could disabuse the congregation of this knowledge in an actual sermon.

This is a major departure from my usual stance on this issue. We've had more arguments on this topic than on any other so far in our relationship. I hate how he turns everything that happens to us into a sermon. Nothing is private. And I find myself weighing my words around him, because I don't want to have to eat them a few Sundays down the road in front of hundreds of other people.

The typical disagreement goes something like this:

"What are you writing down?"

"Sermon idea."

"Oh, shit! What did I just say? Whatever it was, please, don't write a sermon about it! Not everything we say and do has to be a lesson for the masses!"

"My life experiences are a source of inspiration. What else am I going to use? I don't call people out by name or—"

"You mention me by name all the time! It's embarrassing! Especially when you say stuff like, 'When you live with someone who has a potty mouth, like my wife…'"

"Nobody takes me seriously when I say those things. That's why it's funny. They all think I'm joking."

"My family knows you're not kidding. Jared knows. And it's humiliating."

"That makes it even funnier; some people in the congregation are in on the joke. Anyway, if it's so embarrassing, maybe you should stop being such a potty mouth."

"Even if you never mention a name or specific relation, people will always try to figure out who you're talking about. And sometimes their incorrect assumptions are worse than the truth."

"I can't be responsible for what people choose to assume. The only solution to that is to name names. Do you want me to mention names, or not?"

"I want you to stop using those sorts of stories altogether."

"Not going to happen."

I have yet to win this argument. I'm starting to resign myself to the fact that I never will.

But in this case, it's appropriate for him to address the elephant in the pew. And this time, he ran the exact wording past me when he finalized the message, and I approved it, something along the lines of, "You can be given all the evidence that something is one way, but don't be surprised when it turns out to be something else entirely. Maybe not even something you can put a name to." Then he went on to say that we were disappointed that things weren't what they appeared to be and tied that in with a message about life in general and how God often turns things upside down just when we think we have everything figured out. At least, that's how he practiced it.

I can't attest to the faithfulness of his delivery to his rehearsal, however, because I didn't attend services today.

Call it shame, call it embarrassment, call it whatever you want, but I didn't want to see those pitying looks. I didn't want to watch as each person took a mental trip through my history and remembered another heartbreak that involved a real pregnancy and a baby who wasn't meant to grow up. I didn't want to put them at ease with a mea culpa shoulder shrug and a blithe, "Better luck next time," or "We won't be buying that brand of home pregnancy test again. Ha ha ha."

So I stayed home and caught up on all my favorite shows that were at risk of being deleted by our full-to-bursting DVR. I knew the minute church was over, though, because my phone jumped to life on the sofa arm next to my head. I took the calls from my mom and sister (I guess I felt I owed them at least that much, since they never heard "the news" straight from me to begin with). Mom said, "If your doctor's not worried, then you shouldn't be." Nicole said, "Oh, darn. You'll just have to keep trying. Good thing it's so much fun."

Then I turned off my phone.

I haven't even talked to Mary since we found out. I already know what she's going to say, anyway: "Well, kid, I was forty-two when I had Brice, so you're not off the hook yet."

They all mean well. And their words are comforting, in their own way. But I don't need comfort; I need amnesia. Like a stage performer who trips and falls on her face in front of a packed house, I need to get up, dust myself off, and deliver my next line. And then do it all again the next night. Only, that actor has the benefit of being in front of a whole new audience in subsequent performances. So, I gave myself permission to hide backstage in my dressing room for just a little while.

The doorbell is the next thing to interrupt my TV marathon. I'm tempted to ignore it, but I figure someone might get worried if they can't reach me by phone *and* I don't answer the door. It would be just like one of the ladies from the Lutheran Women's Missionary League, delivering a casserole or pie, to call the police from our front porch rather than simply find Brice and "worry him" to come check on me.

However, there's no food waiting for me on the porch when I open the door.

Hands in his pockets, Jared grins and says, "Hey!" a little too cheerfully. "I tried to call, but…"

"I turned off my phone."

"Oh. Right." Without warning, he steps forward and gives me a bear hug.

After a few seconds, when it's obvious he isn't going to let go anytime soon, I halfheartedly return the hug. Patting his shoulder, I eventually say, "Okay. And scene," when it moves past awkward and into downright weird. I gently but firmly push away from him.

He smiles sheepishly. "Sorry. I can't stop thinking about how upset you must be, considering how disappointed Pastor seems. I mean, it must be, like, a hundred times worse for you—"

"I'm fine."

Stepping past me without an invitation into the house, he crosses the living room to one of the sofas and sits down, leaning back as if he's here for the duration. "That's what I thought you'd say, but you don't have to play tough with me."

I remain standing by the front door, leaning against the wall. "I'm not. I really am fine."

"But you didn't want to come to church today?"

"Nope. Not a big fan of everyone staring and feeling sorry for me. Or giving me their lame advice," I explain shortly.

He laughs. "All righty then."

"I'm just being honest."

"Nothing wrong with that, I guess," he allows. After

fidgeting on the couch for a few seconds and avoiding my eye contact, he ventures "If *I* can be honest for a second, I have to say, you don't look 'fine.' I mean, no offense! Obviously. But when I'm upset, I don't get dressed, and I mope around the house and watch TV and avoid people. Kind of like what you're doing today."

I can't imagine him doing any of those things, ever, but nevertheless, I say, "I do this more often than you think. And I'm not upset. I'm just having a lazy day."

"Okay," he says way too easily in a tone and manner that suggest he's humoring me and doesn't believe me for a second. "But you know, it's nothing to be embarrassed about. Everyone makes mistakes. Trust me; I make a *ton*. But you know that."

"Jared, no offense, but the whole point of not going to church today was so I could be alone. And since you're here, I'm not. Alone, that is. Which kind of defeats the purpose of my staying home." At the slackening in his face, I quickly add, "I know I can tell you that and not hurt your feelings, because you'll understand that it's nothing personal, right?"

He pops up from the couch, nodding like his head's on a very loose spring. "Absolutely! Yes! I'm sorry for barging in. Of course, it makes sense that you don't want company. Just thought I'd check. Because, I dunno…" He pushes his glasses up on his nose and blinks rapidly. "I was sort of surprised you weren't there today with Pastor. Show of solidarity and all."

He moves toward the door while I try to keep my temper in check at the reproach I'm sensing in his last sentence.

"Brice understands why I didn't want to be there today. It's deeper than just this incident."

"Totally. I get that," he gushes. "Yeah. Plus, he's always

more concerned about how others are feeling, anyway. He wouldn't want you to be uncomfortable. Maybe it was even easier for him to deliver the message, knowing that you weren't there."

"Maybe." I wonder if that means Brice veered from the script a little and revealed more than I would have liked.

"I'm sure of it. He probably doesn't like to get emotional in front of you, anyway. I know *I* wouldn't."

My stomach drops. "He got emotional during the sermon?"

Jared's eyes widen. His mouth opens and closes twice before he finally answers, "Oh. Well, you know how he is sometimes. It was just the usual. I mean, nobody made a big deal about it. It's not like he broke down sobbing. But unlike me, he's okay with getting choked up in front of everyone. I'd die a thousand deaths if that happened to me. I'd rather say, 'enemas' instead of 'enemies' a hundred times than even think about crying up there." He tilts his head and asks, "By the way, *does* it bother you when he does that?"

I shake my head mutely, staring off into space. But it would have bothered me in this case, obviously. I'm suddenly infinitely gladder that I wasn't there.

"Anyway," Jared continues cluelessly. "I'm glad you're okay. I feel sort of responsible for you guys having to say anything at all, because I might have told one or two people what I thought was your good news after Pastor told me. But he never said not to tell anyone, so I didn't realize it was a secret or anything. And when Justine said something about it to me, I thought for sure it wasn't a secret, so I told a few more people. And… I dunno. I'm a moron sometimes. I was just so excited for you guys. Because you seem like you're going to be great parents. You remind me a lot of my parents, who are awesome, by the way. I really miss them.

Although, I think they're okay without me. But you and Pastor will be fun parents. Well, maybe you more than Pastor. But he'll be very understanding and nice. Probably fun, too, now that I think about it and how he acts around all the kids at church. Anyway, I'm sorry if I told too many people. That's what I'm trying to say."

During this verbal diarrhea, I merely stare at him. Part of me (a part of me way, way, way deep down) wants to laugh at the absolute ridiculousness of his rambling. But that part is being held down by the much-bigger, really sad part of me that just wants him to leave so I can sit on the couch alone and cry.

Eventually, he takes a breath and gives me an opening to say something, but when I don't take it, he opens the front door. "Okay, then. Well, I'll leave you alone now. I promised Pastor I'd help him brainstorm a theme for Vacation Bible School, and I haven't even started thinking about it. I'd like to take at least twenty good ideas to him later on, and it'll take at least an hour to think of that many."

He pats my shoulder and steps onto the porch. "See you later!"

"Bye," I mumble like a shell shock victim.

I watch him speed-walk toward the church with his head down and hands in his pockets, but as soon as he makes it across the street, I close the door, stumble to the couch, and collapse into the sort of crying typically reserved for deep grief and spoiled children.

I don't even know why I'm crying. At least, that's what I tell myself.

∾

Brice walks through the door a little after six and plops

down next to me on the couch. My eyes are bleary from weeping and watching so much TV, but it's dim enough in the room that he probably can't tell. If he can, he's not rubbing it in.

Even though I feel like my eyeballs are about to fall from their sockets, I agree to sit through the Cubs game with him. Baseball isn't really TV-watching, anyway. It's more like blank staring, occasionally interrupted by blinks and short stretches of attention when something semi-exciting happens, like a home run or a stolen base or a bad strike call.

We watch an hour of the game without saying anything to each other before I ask during a commercial about car insurance, "So, how'd it go?"

He answers simply and sincerely, "Everyone was very nice."

That's when I'm nearly overwhelmed with the guilt I've been fighting all day. I can't believe I made him face it alone. He's not supposed to have to do anything alone anymore. I'm supposed to be there with him, no matter how difficult it is. I bet he wishes he had had the option of lying on the couch all day in his pajamas, watching TV and hiding from everyone. But he's so much braver than I am. He knows what to say and how to act.

He also knows to tell me "everyone was very nice," because that's mostly the truth, and I don't need to hear about the people whose discomfort with the situation caused them to say unintentionally insensitive things like, "Next time you won't tell everyone so soon," or "Let's hope this isn't a sign of things to come." Because I know there were those people. I've known them my whole life. "Tactful" and "subtle" are not listed on their social resumes.

I want to tell him I'm sorry for letting him do the hard

work alone, but the commercial break ends, and we go back to vacantly staring at the screen. He puts his arm around me. I list against his chest. Propped against each other, we fall asleep to the sound of the ball slapping into gloves and cracking against bats.

15

NOT TRYING

Since the beginning of my sex life, the number one rule of the game has been, "Keep the sperm away from the egg." The methods have differed, depending on the partner, the situation, and the relationship. Casual: condom; committed or long-term: pill; drunken: prayer. Some methods work better than others. Some methods are more madness than method. But at least there was some sort of security in the consistency with which I tried to exert some sort of control over my reproductive rights.

Not trying to *not* get pregnant (not to be confused with "trying to get pregnant") sort of feels like flipping around on a trapeze without a net. It should be fun (the trapeze part), but I keep looking down (the no-net part). And just when I think I don't need no stinkin' net, my sweaty hand slips on that bar, and I think, *Holy shit! Where's the net?*

But the point of "not trying" is "not caring." We're supposed to delude ourselves into thinking that "whatever will be will be." Well, I've always hated that stupid song (I mean, talk about stating the obvious!), and after weeks (technically, months now) of "not trying," I'm beginning to hate that, too, in all its forms.

Nobody could ever accuse me of being an overachiever, but even I recognize that it's counterproductive to approach something—be it fishing, fitness, painting a picture, or having a baby—by consciously *not trying* to do it. All you can think about is how you're not supposed to be trying, but that makes you try harder. And when it doesn't work, it's so frustrating!

When I mention the oxymoronicness of it all to Brice this morning after another session of "not trying," he contemplates my gripe while tying his running shoes and says, "I guess you have to just think of it more like a happy accident. Like buying a lottery ticket."

"No. You consciously buy a lottery ticket in the hopes of winning. Bad analogy."

He braces his elbows on his knees and gives it another go. "Okay, more like when you narrowly miss being in a car accident. You weren't *trying* to *not* get in the accident; it just worked out that way."

"Are you comparing baby-making to a car wreck?"

"I'm beginning to compare this conversation to one."

"Okay, then." It's hurting my brain, anyway.

"C'mon. Time for our morning walk," he says, pulling on my foot and yanking the covers away from me. "You heard the doctor. Rest. Exercise. Good food."

"Sounds like a lot of trying to me," I mutter, but I haul myself out of bed and submit to the routine nonetheless.

Once at the park across the street from the church, I ask him, "Are you actually going to walk with me this morning, or are you going to run laps around me?"

"I'll stay back here on the slow track," he says, pretending it's a huge sacrifice. He hip checks me.

"Ow. You have a bony butt."

"You're a grumpy bug this morning," he accuses in a tone that implies he's getting great amusement from it.

Instead of instantly objecting to his assessment, I think about it and say, "Yeah. I kind of am." It surprises me. I thought I'd fallen out of the habit.

"Tell Pastor what's on your mind," he says in an ingratiating voice, leaning down toward me and placing his hand on the back of my neck.

"Ew! That's creepy. Stop."

"Mwahahaha!"

"I've changed my mind. You should just jog on ahead." I push on his shoulder to try to prod him ahead of me on the gravel trail.

"Nope. You're stuck with me." He wraps his arms around my shoulders and crab-walks next to me before lifting my feet from the path and carrying me several feet.

When he sets me down, I move to the edge of the footpath and ask, "What's wrong with you?"

"What's wrong with *you*?" He grins.

"Stop smiling at me like a goober."

"I don't think you're a goober."

"No, *you* are. Smiling like one."

"Ohhh…"

I roll my eyes. "You're just doing things to annoy me."

"It's so easy today. Seriously, tell me what's wrong." He edges closer to me and grips my hand.

When I'm sure he's simply going to hold it like a normal husband would, I relax. "I dunno. It's hot outside, for one thing. I mean, it's not even seven o'clock, and it's all sticky and gross out here!"

"This is the day the Lord has made. Let us rejoice and be glad in it."

I glare over at him. "Seriously?"

"Just a gentle reminder."

Again, I roll my eyes. He knows I hate it when he preaches to me. I shouldn't have to weigh everything I say to make sure it's Christian-y enough.

"Anyway," I defend myself. "It's not just the weather." But I stop, worried that I'll invite another sermon if I tell him what else is bothering me.

"Okay…" he trails off uncertainly when I don't expound. "I can't help you if you don't tell me what it is." The sun makes both of us squint as we make a turn that has us facing due east.

I shade my eyes with my hand, annoyed that I didn't bring any sunglasses. Stupid sun! "Why do you always assume you can do something to help, anyway? I don't need you to fix everything."

He chooses not to say anything to that outburst. Another one of his specialties: *not* fighting. I find myself having a lot of arguments with myself and then feeling crazy when I realize I'm providing the responses to my statements ("You've come home late every day this week. And I know you're going to say that it's not your fault, but you need to learn how to say no to people. I don't care that you're uncomfortable with that; some of these people take advantage of your good nature. And I'm not buying it that they do it unconsciously. They know exactly what they're doing. And don't give me that 'benefit of the doubt' nonsense. That's what they're counting on"). One night I went on for ten minutes before he looked up from the mail he was sifting through and said, "What are you even talking about?"

So today, I don't anticipate his side of the conversation. I walk silently next to him. If he really wants to know, he'll tell me something to make me certain he's not going to give me a "Pastor" answer to everything I say.

Eventually, he says, "I'm a guy. We fix things. Or try to. And usually end up making it worse. But you know what I mean. If you want me to simply listen, then just say so."

It takes me a while to decide to reveal what's bothering me. In the meantime, he waits patiently but walks faster so that I'm forced to pick up my pace, too, and I'm slightly out of breath when I ask, "Aren't you sort of worried that, you know, we've been— Can I just call it 'trying'? It's stupid to pretend otherwise."

"Call it whatever you want."

"Aren't you worried that we've been trying for months, and... nothing?"

"Nope," he immediately answers, smiling down at me. "Plus, it's only been two months. That's hardly a long time. I can see where *you* would be worried, though."

"What's that supposed to mean?"

"You're less patient than I am and tend to worry more."

"You mean I have less *faith* than you do. Why don't you just say what you mean?"

He scratches his nose. "Ah. I didn't say that."

"Well, it's obvious that you would have more faith than me. You're a pastor."

My assertion makes him laugh loudly.

"So? We don't have a monopoly on faith. And just because you voice your worries more than I do doesn't mean you believe any less than I do that God will take care of them."

"That's right." He's sort of stolen my thunder by defending me for me.

"I know."

"Yeah, you know everything."

Chuckling, he says, "Wow. Maybe you should have just stayed in bed."

I gulp down tears. "I'm sorry."

"You're forgiven. Just saying…"

"No, I'm being a bitch. You're right. I'm just so frustrated!" Now I stop walking and point at him. "I only want you to listen when I say this next thing; no fixing, no preaching!"

He shuffles to a stop and wipes his forehead on his shoulder. "Okay. Go."

"I don't understand why God seems so intent on making things difficult for me. When I don't want a baby, I get pregnant (or think I am); when I do want a baby, nothing." He opens his mouth, but I rush ahead. "I know it hasn't been long at all, and I'm not saying I'm *worried* or that I'm panicking or anything like that. But I'm *wondering.* Why?" I lift my hair off my forehead and fan my face. "It gets really old after a while. Just *once* I'd like things to happen easily and seamlessly the way I want them to happen. Just once. And I want to pick what it is. I don't want to waste my one opportunity—if I even get that—on something silly like hitting all green lights on the way to work. I want it to be something big, something meaningful."

My mention of work makes me suddenly aware of the time, so I start walking again with swift, choppy strides. Brice quickly catches up.

"Am I still just listening?" he asks.

"You are if you're going to say something that'll piss me off."

Walking backwards in front of me, he says, "Judging by everything else so far this morning, I'd say I have a pretty good chance of making you angry, no matter what I say."

"Proceed," I allow through gritted teeth.

He does, reciting the lyrics from a popular song comparing someone to a firework as if it's high poetry.

I try to keep from smiling, but my lips have a mind of their own. "Has anyone ever suggested to you that you may be obsessed with Katy Perry? Just a little?"

He ignores me and continues saying the lyrics over my protests until he gets to the chorus, which he belts out like a Broadway singer, eyes closed and arms outstretched.

"Oh, my gosh," I mutter, looking around to see if anyone else is witnessing this.

My chagrin only makes him sing louder and add hand motions.

"Brice, shut up! People are staring."

He opens his eyes and looks around. "Who? I don't see anyone else."

"Well, if there *were* other people here, they'd be staring. You're scaring the ducks."

"I didn't even get to the 'boom, boom, boom' part. It's my favorite."

"Too bad. Save it for the shower." But my scowl's officially gone. I defy anyone to stay grumpy after her husband serenades her, even if it is with a song meant to console self-hating teens.

"Actually, I was sort of being serious," he says, walking next to me and facing forward once more. "The song has a decent message: there's a reason for everything. Even if you think it's trite, it's true."

I loop my arm through his. "I know it's true. That doesn't mean I have to like it."

"Yeah. Well, what if you hadn't gotten pregnant when you *didn't* want to? Would you have ever gotten to know me as more than the dorky guy who stands up in front of everyone every Sunday and annoys the crap out of your dad?"

I laugh at his apt description. "No. Who wants to know that guy? Even if he's super-duper cute."

At the end of the trail, we turn and head for home. "Aw, shucks," he mumbles. "Anyway, you had to go through some awful stuff, but would you change any of it?"

"Nope. Well, maybe I'd take Stefan out of the picture and replace him with someone a little less... douchey."

We trot across the street at a break in the traffic, which is starting to pick up as the time inches nearer to rush hour. On the other side, he stops with me under a tree next to the church parking lot.

"My taste in guys has definitely improved." I go up on my tiptoes and kiss his nose.

He cups my rear end and draws me closer to him. "Let's just hope it doesn't keep evolving, or I'm in trouble." Leaning down, he kisses me languidly.

A car door slamming nearby makes both of us jump. Marilyn waves across the parking lot at us. "Hey, you two!" she calls playfully.

Brice straightens, removes his hands from my butt, and half-steps away from me. "Morning, Marilyn," he greets her with a sheepish salute. I merely wave with one hand while blotting at my mouth with the other.

"Don't mind me," she insists, bustling toward the church doors.

I giggle, feeling like a teenager who's just been caught making out with her boyfriend next to her locker in the school hallway. Brice watches his secretary as she unlocks the church door and slips inside. Then he nods toward our house and says, "First one there gets first dibs on the shower." He takes off running.

I follow at a leisurely pace, enjoying the view.

He's crazy if he thinks I'm going to a) run; b) wait to take my shower.

16

CHANGE OF PLANS

"*S*o that's when I said, 'I know you're not really a cop; you're an alien from another planet. I've always wanted to have sex with an alien. Let's go back to your spaceship and do it.'"

"Mm-hm. That's nice."

"You are *so* not listening to me!" Jen slaps her hands on my desk. I startle.

"What?" I look away from my computer monitor and blink at her. "Yes, I am. He's a cop who likes to do freaky things."

She narrows her eyes at me. "No. That's not what I said. I made up a bunch of shit to try to get your attention."

"Oh. So, he's not a cop?"

Sighing, she answers, "Yes, he is. Just… never mind. I can tell you're obviously distracted by something and not interested in hearing about my stupid love life. Although God knows how many hours of your stories I've sat through over the years."

"I'm sorry! No, you're right. I'm listening." I prop my

chin on my hands and widen my eyes. "Really. Tell me again."

She starts over while we wait for Mitzi to meet us for our monthly girls' night out. And I listen a little more this time, but my mind keeps straying to the email that landed in my inbox two seconds after she arrived.

We need to talk. Will call you this weekend.
—Stefan

I'd like to be optimistic (or stupid) enough to believe this has something to do with work or his IRS audit or his entry into a rehab program that requires him to make amends with people he's treated poorly in the past. But I know otherwise. I know the day of reckoning has arrived. I can sense it in the same way you can sense when someone's looking at you or thinking about you. It's giving me chills.

I just never thought this day would come. I really thought I'd gotten away with it. Now I need to prepare myself for what I know I deserve.

Way back then, I knew that I should have told him, even though I had all kinds of justifications for not doing so at the time. Chief among them: I was simply too scared. Close second: he's so horrible! I wanted to pretend like nothing ever happened between us, and I wasn't going to let a tiny detail like having his baby prevent me from doing so. Plus, at first *nobody* knew. And then by the time everyone else did and things started to settle down, it seemed silly to bring in a whole new layer of drama by telling *him*. And since nobody really challenged my decision to keep it from him, it was easier to stay quiet.

Then she didn't make it. That made things more and

less complicated at the same time. Less complicated, because there was nothing more to hide from him; more complicated, because I knew if I did the right thing, I'd have to tell him two really hard things instead of just one. I lied to myself and said it was better for everyone involved to let it go.

I *couldn't* talk about it for a long time anyway. And then, when I could, I didn't really want to, because life seemed to go just a little (okay, a lot) more smoothly when everyone, including me, pretended she never existed. But you can only ignore something—or someone—that important for so long.

It didn't happen quickly (and I think it's still happening in some ways), but I've come to terms with Secret and her role in my life. I thank God every day that He worked through her to bring about some positive changes, not just for me but also for my family and Brice. Like I told him on our walk: no regrets.

Not even Stefan. The more I think about it, the more I realize that God even had a plan there. He made sure that Secret's father was so repugnant that I wouldn't want anything to do with him. And that opened the door to Brice, whom He had intended for me all along. So as much as I cringe at the memory of the person I was, the kind of person who would have a one-nighter with the kind of person like Stefan, it happened for a reason and couldn't have happened any other way if things were to work out the way they did.

"And… she's gone again! I never thought I'd say this, but I can't wait until Mitzi gets here, so we can get to the restaurant, and you'll tell us what's going on." Jen loops her purse strap over her shoulder and stands.

I look regretfully up at her.

She glowers at me. "Don't give me that look. I know that look."

"It's just that—"

"No! We barely see each other anymore, and now, on our one night out a month—which is pathetic, by the way—you give me *that* look."

Before I can defend myself, Mitzi breezes through the gallery door, strikes a pose, and warbles, "Ladies' night!"

Jen calls out to her, "Yeah, except we're about to be dumped."

"What? No!" Mitzi rushes to my desk and stands next to Jen. They both look down on me with disapproval.

"Listen," I tell them, straightening up my workspace and tossing out some old sticky-notes and dried-up pens so I don't have to look my friends in the eye. "Something just came up. Just. Like, right when Jen got here."

"Don't tell me. You're ovulating," Jen snipes.

I freeze. I was going to tell them everything. I was going to show them the email and tell them what I think is going to happen and ask for their advice and tell them what I've always planned to do if this situation arose and if I think it's still a viable option. But now? No way.

Mitzi smacks Jen's arm and hisses at her, "Not nice!"

Sadness settles in my chest when I realize we're just not the same as we used to be. It was always "friends before men," between the three of us, no matter what was going on. Foolishly, I hadn't thought marriage was going to change that. But I didn't take into consideration that Brice wouldn't be just another man. *He's* my best friend. Best-best friend. There's no question about it. There's nothing they can say or do to compete for that spot. And I refuse to apologize for that, either. They feel like I've put them on the back burner, and they're right; because that's where they belong in my life. For once, I have my priorities sorted correctly.

I swallow, then take a deep breath before looking up at her and saying levelly, "No, but I still can't go out tonight. Sorry." The only person I want to be with is my husband. I can't get home fast enough to tell him about the email from Stefan.

As is characteristic of her personality, Mitzi looks disappointed but says supportively, "Sure thing, sweetie. I hope everything's okay."

I smile tightly. "It'll be fine. I just won't be very good company tonight." Saying this, I appeal to Jen for forgiveness with my eyes. No matter how necessary this cancellation is, I still don't want to hurt anyone's feelings.

She rolls her eyes. "Whatever. You know, someday you're going to turn to us for something, and we're not going to be here. We'll have gotten sick of waiting for you to fit us into your happy married life whenever it's convenient for you." With that, she stalks away from me, yanks open the gallery door, and disappears into the sea of people walking past on the sidewalk.

With a shaky smile, Mitzi reassures me, "She'll be okay. I'll go out with her and pay for all her drinks and listen to her stories about her new boyfriend—apparently, he's a hot cop—and by the time she gets over her hangover tomorrow, she'll have forgotten all about being mad at you."

"Thanks." I stand up and gather my things. "I'll call you both this weekend."

"I know you will," she replies, giving my arm a pat. "Take care."

After I lock up the gallery, she heads one way, following in the direction that Jen went, and I go the opposite way, toward the vast parking garage, my car, and home.

〜

Brice understands the gravity of this. I can tell by the pinched way he's holding his mouth and the wrinkles on his forehead and the fact that he hasn't eaten any of the steamed broccoli on his dinner plate before he pushes it away and asks, "How do you want to handle this?"

I'm relieved that he's not trying to downplay it or step in and take care of it for me. Those are two reactions that would set my teeth on edge more than they already are. After all, I'm not telling him so that he can reassure me it's no big deal; nor am I telling him so he can fix it. I'm telling him because he's my husband, and he needs to know, and I want him to know.

"Oh…" I trace patterns on the kitchen table with my pinkie. "I'm sure I'll handle it with my usual grace and class," I joke.

He puts his elbows on the table and extends one arm to me. Grabbing my hand, he asks, "On the freak-out scale of one to ten, where are you sitting?"

"An eight," I answer after a pause. "I mean, I've been dreading this—and avoiding it—for two years. Longer. Since I got that first positive pregnancy test result. I've thought of a million scenarios and reactions and responses. I can't believe it's actually going to happen. Something in me still believes it's *not* going to happen. I mean, a *phone call?* Really?"

"Not how I would do it. But it's sort of comforting that that guy and I never do anything the same way," he says with a half-smile.

"Not *anything*," I confirm, squeezing his hand. "Anyway, I guess I'm just going to answer his call and his questions as honestly as I can and be prepared for him to be his usual ugly self."

Brice pushes back his chair, takes his plate to the sink, and says with his back to me, "He better not be."

"He will be, though. It's the only way he knows how to be."

Unless he's trying to get you into bed. Then he's only mildly obnoxious, but he's generous with the drinks and easy on the eyes, so it evens out. Sort of. When you have low self-esteem and haven't been laid in a really long time.

After churning up his uneaten broccoli in the garbage disposal, Brice puts his rinsed plate in the dishwasher, closes the door, and leans up against it, his arms bent behind him at right angles as he grips the edge of the counter. "No, I mean, he *will* be respectful, or he will get zero answers."

"I should have told him before now. He deserves to know."

"And that's why you've put up with his nonsense for as long as you have, this misplaced sense of guilt you have at keeping information from him that would have had no impact on his life, because he is the way he is. But it would have impacted *your* life—negatively—for him to know; he would have made you miserable, because he's sick and gets off on making people miserable. He would have had a huge stake in your life. *Our* lives. Especially if Secret had lived."

"But she didn't."

"No, she didn't." He looks down at his knees. "She didn't. And just imagine the havoc he would have wreaked if he had been in the picture when she died."

I think about how exponentially worse it would have been to deal with Stefan in those weeks and months following Secret's death. He would have made me feel like it was my fault, like something I did or didn't do had caused her to die, even though Dr. Walsh said that wasn't the case, as far as she and the pediatrician could tell. But they never could figure out why her heart stopped beating. It just... stopped. And I never truly believed there wasn't something I could have done better. He would have twisted that knife every single chance he had, when I was at my most vulnerable and fragile.

Still, it surprises me and brings tears to my eyes when Brice says, "You made the right decision." He looks up at me, but I look away. Then he maintains, "You were right."

"I don't think I was right about anything back then. I was a careless, selfish reactionist who consistently made bad choices. Who's to say not telling him wasn't just another bad choice?"

Now he walks behind me and puts his hands on my shoulders. Rubbing gently, he states emphatically, "You were absolutely right to limit his involvement in your life. He's toxic."

"And scary."

And he knows it. He knows the power he has over people.

"Well, he's not allowed to be scary on this phone call tomorrow. He has no rights or privileges where you're concerned."

Staring into space, lulled by the shoulder rub, I slur, "He said he'd call this weekend, not necessarily tomorrow."

"Oh. Well, whatever. Whenever. You don't have to take his grief." With that, he gives me a final pat between my shoulder blades and announces, "Plus, we're not going to sit around waiting for his call."

"We're not?" I swivel in the chair and look up into his face.

He shakes his head. "Nope. Summer's more than halfway gone, and what do we have to show for it?"

"A burned-up lawn?"

"Exactly. That's it. I don't even have tan lines from mowing the lawn. I say it's time for some fun. Let's get up early tomorrow and go do something fun."

I clap my hands. "Yes! Can we go to that one place where we went off-roading that one time and… almost had a lot of fun?"

He laughs. "If you want to. But I kind of got the impression that you didn't enjoy the off-roading part of the experience."

He has a point there, but I liked the setting and the seclusion, and I'd like to have a chance to finish what we started in the back of the Jeep before I had an uncharacteristic crisis of conscience. Now, there'd be no crisis, just…

"I kind of had something else in mind, though," he divulges.

"Really?" I reply suggestively, wiggling my eyebrows.

Ignoring—or not picking up on—my tone, he says innocently, "Yeah. I mean, off-roading is sort of something I like to do in the fall or spring. It's so hot in the summer."

Hot and steamy.

Noticing the dreamy look in my eyes, he quickly says, "But if that's what you really want to do…"

"What's your other idea?" I ask. Although I have a feeling he's not headed down the same track as I am (the only track I really have), it'd be silly to decide before knowing all my options.

"Well!" He pulls out the chair next to mine and sits knee-to-knee with me. "I was thinking, have you ever been to a waterpark?"

Sure he's kidding, I laugh and slap his knee and answer sarcastically, "Yeah, let's do that."

His shoulders droop. "Oh. You don't like waterparks?"

"I *did*, when I was a kid. Is that really your other idea?"

Looking embarrassed, he answers, "Well, yeah."

"Nuh-uh."

"Yes! I've never been, and Sadie was talking about how her big brothers got to go with some friends a few weeks ago, but she wasn't invited, so, I thought we could take her." When I say nothing, his posture becomes ramrod straight. "Never mind. Off-roading it is."

Aware that I've hurt his feelings, even if I'm not sure why, I say, "Hey, if you want to take Sadie to a waterpark, that's fine. It'll be fun. But what if Stefan calls while she's with us?"'

Brice looks so excited one second and disappointed the next that I don't even wait for an answer. "You know what? Who cares? If he does, I'll call him back after we take her home."

Hope lights up his face. "Really?"

"Yeah!" I stand up and push my chair under the table with a loud squeak. "It's a really sweet idea. And if Sadie's not available on such short notice, then we'll think of something else."

"Or we can still go," he says in a rush, also standing. "I mean, I've *never* been. Ever. But I've always wanted to go. I'd feel less silly if we had Sadie with us. But I still want to go, no matter what."

"You poor, sheltered man."

"Plus," he adds, "I asked Jared to oversee some stuff around the church for me, and I'd prefer to be out of contact for the day, so I can just answer his five hundred questions all at once at the end of the day, instead of getting calls every five minutes."

I nod approvingly at that plan and turn to leave the kitchen. "I'll call Nicole as soon as I change my clothes."

On my way down the hallway to our room, I yell over my shoulder, "And then you'd better head to the nearest store to buy out their entire stock of SPF 50, because you, my man, are *white*."

17

WET AND WILD

J'm interested to see if Brice can keep his swim trunks from falling off. When he left Sadie and me at the base of the waterpark's biggest, steepest slide, which he'd pointed out from afar in the parking lot as his first target, I'd advised him to triple-knot the drawstring on his plaid board shorts, but I don't think he realized I was serious. Unfortunately, though, I know from experience how quickly these waterslides can denude a person in front of hundreds of strangers.

I was sixteen. The last of my baby fat had finally melted away during the previous school year, thanks in some part to my earning a spot on my high school volleyball team. Oh, and a short stint with what I guess would technically be called an eating disorder but that I had called a strict "diet," if anyone ever asked why I never ate. I did eat, though. When my parents were watching. It was during the other twelve hours of the day that I avoided food altogether.

Anyway, I came to this same park with a group of friends—and my first serious boyfriend, Ben—and wore my very first bikini. I was really proud of myself and the second looks I got from men of all ages. Cocky and high on this first taste of sexual power, I confidently waited my turn at this slide, never thinking that a two-piece bathing suit would behave differently than the modest one-piece suits I was used to wearing. So it didn't occur to me to double-check the knots around my neck and back.

I plunged down the slide, suddenly scared shitless at the experience, but still too much of a bikini virgin to worry about what would happen when the laws of physics had their way with me at the bottom of the slide. And did they ever!

I felt my bottoms dropping as soon as I started to float to the surface, so I grabbed hold of them and pulled them up before standing. But it wasn't until I was on my feet, my torso exposed, that I realized anything was amiss with my bikini top. The knot around my back had come undone, and the swirling water at the bottom of the slide had spun the top around my neck so that the bra cups weren't even hanging in front anymore.

As soon as the air hit my breasts, I knew something was extremely wrong, but I couldn't pull up my bottoms and fix my top and move away from the bottom of the slide at the same time. I provided the passersby and bystanders—including my boyfriend—a good ten seconds of wet, naked booby action before I could get everything sorted out. For a split second, it was embarrassing. But for the most part it was thrilling, considering how many whistles my performance received.

Ben didn't look at any other girls the rest of the time we spent in the park. And he spent a lot of time and energy in the upcoming weeks trying to get another glimpse like the one he got that day. I eventually gave it to him, but his recip-rocating show-and-tell wasn't as impressive, so I decided shortly thereafter that I wanted to see other people. Literally.

Thinking about this now as I stand down here next to the pool where it all happened, I suddenly feel old. Not in a bad way, though. More like someone completely different from that girl, as if I'm seeing a movie in my mind of her experience, instead of recalling a memory. Not only are my bikini days long gone (my "diet" didn't last much longer than my relationship with Ben, because I woke up one day and remembered that I liked food—a lot), but so is that girl. She just doesn't exist anymore. She was fun, in her own way. But she was also dumb. Not IQ-wise, but in just about every other way.

Brice has been in line for close to ten minutes now, but since the line snakes around the back of the slide, out of our view, I have no idea how close he is to his turn. After each new person splashes into the pool in front of us, I blink away the water and look up to see the next victim, only to be disappointed when it's not my husband.

"Come on," I mutter, squinting into the sun and shifting from one foot to another.

Sadie apes my behavior and asks with exasperation, "Where's Uncle Brice?"

"I don't know. He should be up any minute now. Then we can do whatever *you* want."

She grins. "I wanna go into the big wave pool and ride on an inner tube."

"Sounds good to me. I'll share a tube with you."

Shrugging, she says a little too casually, "Or I can share one with Uncle Brice."

I take my eyes off the slide platform to look down at her, surprised at how stung I am that she'd rather ride with him than me. I've always been her favorite, since the very first time I held her in the hospital and she finally calmed down after hours of crying. (At the silence, a nurse actually poked her head into the room to make sure Nicole hadn't smothered her with a pillow.)

Seemingly oblivious to my hurt and shock, she keeps her eyes pinned to where she expects to see her uncle at any second and asks, "How come I'm allowed to call him 'Uncle Brice,' but all the other kids at church are s'posed to call him 'Pastor'? Grady got real mad at me and said I was calling him the wrong name."

I go back to watching for him. "Well, I guess you can call him 'Pastor' at church and 'Uncle Brice' when we're not at church, but that's kind of confusing, I think. Grady just needs to get over it."

She giggles at that sassy reply. "That's what Mommy says Grandma needs to do all the time."

Oh-ho! So, the favored daughter doesn't think everything her idol does and says is perfect? I learn so much when I hang out with my niece. I'd love to know more, but if I let on that she's said something potentially interesting, she'll bull up, so I file it away for later. I'll just ask Nicole myself what she and Mom don't see eye-to-eye on.

"Oh! There he is!" I point excitedly when I spy him towering behind the two people ahead of him in line. He grins and waves down to us.

Sadie stands on her tiptoes, craning to see, so I pick her up and hold her as high as I can up against the front of me to give her a little more height. Her warm shoulder nudges against my cheek.

Now he's on deck, waiting for the person in front of him to clear the bottom of the slide so he can get the signal from the lifeguard to go. He sits at the top and holds onto the handles that he's supposed to use to propel himself down the water-filled ramp that will guide him into the steeper chute.

"How come you can't see Uncle Brice's muscles when he's at church?" my niece asks while we watch him. "He has good muscles."

I try not to laugh, because I can't say I blame the girl for noticing. The abs had me at "hello," too. Of course, at the time I blamed my attraction on overactive hormones. I don't know what Sadie's excuse is.

To answer her question, I say, "Because all of his muscles are covered up by his clothes and his robes."

"Here he comes," Sadie announces with foreboding, like she's worried this might be the final fun thing he lives to do.

He crosses his feet at the ankles, pushes off, and lies back with his arms crossed over his chest. When he hits the drop-off, he seems to be going faster than the other people before him were going, so I wince at the plummet I know he just experienced in his belly. As he swooshes his way down the plastic chute and plunges into the wading pool at the bottom, I ready my hand to slap over Sadie's eyes in case his shorts don't make the journey to the surface with him. But they're hanging tough when he stands and whips the water away from his face, which is covered with a grin.

Brice swims to the steps that lead to the observation patio, where Sadie and I, giggling, are waiting for him.

"Did you see that?" he asks, wringing water from his trunks.

"Uh, yeah. I thought for a second that you were going to go airborne."

"Me too! It was awesome!"

Sadie wiggles from my grasp, lands on her feet, and grabs his hand. "C'mon! We're going to the wave pool next.

Auntie Peyton says you have to hold me with you in an inner tube so I don't drown."

Why, that little liar!

Of course, Brice falls for it. As they head off in the direction of the huge pool, leaving me in their wake, I hear him say, "She's absolutely right. Those waves are big. Bigger than the ones in the ocean by Grand Turk. Remember those pictures we showed you?"

Wow. I feel a little like a third wheel. But in a good way. They look so cute together, hands linked, as they rush to the next fun thing on their list, anxious to do it all but slightly overwhelmed by the choices. The twenty-five-year age difference doesn't matter. They're both just a couple of kids having an experience that they'll never forget.

They do me the honor of waiting for me at the inner tube check-out counter. Brice hands me a bright yellow rubber donut with blue handles and then takes one for himself and his tube-mate. Holding their flotation device under one arm, he keeps a grip on Sadie's right hand as we wade into the chlorinated, slope-floored pool. When the water reaches his waist, he sets the inner tube on the undulating surface and hops onto it, settling his butt into the middle. I lift Sadie into his lap and push them toward the deeper water and the bigger waves before boarding my own watercraft and paddling after them.

In the deep end, it's so crowded with other tubers that nobody really moves. Rather, we all bump against each other in the sun while we ride the gentle—but surprisingly large—machine-made waves. To ensure we don't get separated, I keep hold of one of the handles on their tube, close my eyes, and listen contentedly to their conversation and Sadie's intermittent giggling.

"What should we do next?" Brice asks her.

"I wanna go on a slide. But not that real big one you went on. That's too scary."

"You're not tall enough to go on that one. I checked."

"Good. I hope I'm never tall enough."

He chuckles at that one. "Well, I'm pretty sure you will be someday. Doesn't mean you have to go on it, though."

"Good. I'm not gonna."

"Okay. Hmmm… What about that twisty one over there? It's not really steep. And you could probably ride down it with your aunt—"

"Or you!"

"Or me. Sure."

I smile to myself as I try to remember how old I was the first time I had a crush on a grown man (who wasn't someone famous). I was probably about Sadie's age. Who was it?

I barely keep from laughing out loud when I recall that it was one of my dad's co-workers. I met him at the company picnic and thought he was the most handsome man I'd ever seen. He was blond and tan and had dazzling white teeth that sparkled when he laughed, which was often. He volunteered to help with the pony ride line. I rode that stinky pony about thirty times. His name was— Oh, what was it? Craig! Craig Tennant.

After that day, I'd listen for his name at the dinner table and perk up any time he was mentioned. It didn't matter that I had no idea what Dad was talking about. I'd picture Craig as the hero at work, always saving the day (whatever that meant at an engineering firm) and getting pats on the back from his co-workers, like Dad, while he laughed and flashed those pretty teeth.

But he wasn't with the company for very long, and it wasn't until years later that I flippantly admitted to my family at some get-together after I'd had a few too many that I'd had a crush on him. When everyone stopped laughing, I defended myself with, "I was a little kid! And he was cute. And nice."

Mom, Dad, and Jason said together, "And gay."

Well, at least Sadie's world will never be rocked by a revelation like that. And who can blame her for having a little bit of a crush on her uncle? First of all, it just proves once again how alike we are. We even have the same taste in men. Second, he's been a true hero in her life. He helped save her parents' marriage and married me, her favorite (okay, her only) aunt, making me the happiest she's ever known me to be. Plus, he's a strong, positive male role model who makes her feel like she matters.

At home, her parents lavish most of their attention on her gregarious, high-maintenance older brothers. Lonnie knows all about boy stuff, but he's admittedly at a loss when it comes to interacting with his daughter. He's thanked us on more than one occasion for picking up the slack. Nicole… well, I think Nicole has viewed Sadie as competition from Day One. And it's rankled that her daughter is more like me than like her. I'm sure that's one of her worst nightmares come true, no matter how well we tend to get along. She's told me that her daughter is "tiring," so I know she enjoys the frequent breaks we offer.

Today's outing is a perfect example of our efforts to give Sadie some individual attention. She's used to me doing it— our sleepovers, shopping trips, and makeover days have created some of my favorite memories (and I hope hers, too) —but I think it means even more to her that a father figure like Brice enjoys spending time with her. And I encourage their bonding, because I know how important this interaction will be to her in a few years, when she starts dating.

She'll be much better off comparing potential mates to Brice than her own father, who's had his challenges with staying faithful (although I hope her knowledge of that is limited). I want her to see how husbands and fathers should really behave, so she'll accept nothing less someday.

Plus, it gives Brice a chance to flex those paternal muscles that he's so eager to use.

"Auntie Peyton!"

I flinch from my doze when water splashes on my face. Sadie helpfully points at her uncle, whose wet hand, hovering inches from my face, corroborates her claim.

"I tried to tell you," she says.

I reward her loyalty by kicking my feet fast and hard so that I drench the two of them (and myself, in the process). I continue this, amidst their laughing protests, until a fun-allergic lifeguard blows her whistle at me and points before shaking her head as a warning.

Wiping water from his face, Brice laughs and says, "Ha! You got in trouble!"

"Shut up."

"Ummmm!" Sadie covers her mouth and points at me.

Brice mimics her.

"Are you goody-goodies going to float around here all day, or are we actually going to do something fun?" I ask, hopping down from my tube and towing it toward the "beach," flashing a grin at the two of them over my shoulder when my feet hit bottom and I see they're right on my heels.

It's time for the waterpark expert to show these novices how it's done.

∾

I'm in the company of two worn-out passengers on the drive home. I think I may have discovered Brice's kryptonite: chlorine. He's reclined in the passenger seat, elbows akimbo with his hands behind his head while he snores. Snores! This is a first. I half-turn to laugh about it with Sadie, but she's passed out, too.

Amateurs!

Of course, I'm not immune to the fatigue brought on by all the sun and water and walking today, but I volunteered to drive when my slightly crispy husband (there's not enough sunscreen on the planet) sighed at the prospect of doing it himself. I knew he had to be exhausted in order to hint around that I should drive. And in his defense, he'd spent most of the day toting Sadie around. She's fairly small for her age, but she's still an eight-year-old girl who weighs about sixty pounds. He carried her in deep water; he carted her when she couldn't keep up with his long strides as we practically ran from one ride to the next; and he held her to give her legs a rest while we waited in seemingly endless lines. The only time he got a rest was when we took a break to eat lunch. Even then, she was right next to him on the picnic table bench, swinging her legs happily and munching on her corn dog as they plotted their next adventure.

As I exit the highway to get to my sister's house in the 'burbs, my cell phone rings from inside my purse at Brice's feet. It's my generic ringtone, which I reserve for work-related calls so I can screen them more easily on the weekend (let's just be honest).

"Shoot!" I mutter, at being unable to reach my phone and at the sinking feeling in my stomach that it's most likely Stefan. Oh, well. It's not like I can talk to him right now, anyway, with Sadie right there in the backseat. I'll be home within the hour and will just call him—or whomever—back.

Although, if I pull over and return his call now, I can do so without getting Brice involved. From the sounds of things over there, nothing short of a car accident is going to wake him up.

Just one street away from my sister's, I pull over in front of a house with impeccable landscaping and a prominent garage about twice the size of the entire parsonage. I put the Jeep in park but leave it running, the radio playing at the same volume as when we were on the road. Carefully, I reach over into the passenger side floorboard, startling when Brice's hairy leg twitches suddenly as I'm lifting my purse slowly toward me. A quick look at his face confirms he's still asleep. His snores stop temporarily when he closes his mouth but start back up again seconds later.

I pull my purse to my chest, slowly squeeze the door handle to release the latch, slip out of the driver's seat, and rapidly push the door closed just enough that the interior light goes off and the "open door" chime quiets before waking anyone up. I walk around to the back of the vehicle and lean against the tailgate while I dig my phone out from underneath receipts, tampons, lip gloss tubes, my wallet, and three packages of gum with only one piece left in each of them. After locating the phone, I check the call log and see that it was, indeed, Stefan's promised/threatened call that I missed. He's left a voicemail message, but I'll only be delaying the inevitable by listening to it, so what's the point?

I look at the blazing sky and take a deep breath. Okay. Here goes.

Stefan's snobby reply greets me only two rings after I hit the button to dial the last number to call me. "Where are you?"

"Uh, taking my niece home," I answer, before considering that it's none of his business.

"Oh. I don't care. I don't know why I asked. So, can you do it?"

This call is less than ten seconds old, but I'm lost. "Depends on what you're talking about," I say cautiously. I can't seem to reconcile how his question relates to Secret. What does he want me to *do*?

"Please tell me you at least took the trouble to listen to my message before calling me," he snaps. "You know how much I hate repeating myself."

"I'm sorry. I just pulled over and called you right back."

"Am I supposed to be grateful for that?"

I sigh. "Nope. Simply informed. So, I can hang up with you and listen to your message and call you back, or you can repeat yourself."

Petulantly, he answers, "I'm not sure I like your sarcastic tone, but I'll just tell you what I said in my message. I want to do a Chicago show. Soon. Like within the month."

"A show?"

"Yes, a show."

"A show?"

"Yes! Hello! You know, one of those things that you promote, and then one night, I put my paintings on display at Marshall's gallery, and people can come in and meet me and buy my work and commission me to do other work? A *show*."

"And that's it?" I check before I allow myself to feel too overjoyed.

"What the fuck is the matter with you? What else could I possibly want from *you*? Now, can you do it or not?"

Overwhelming relief has me blurting, "Yes!" while on the verge of tears. Then I tone it down and try to steady my quivering voice as I add, "I mean, I think we can probably work something out."

"Well, I need you to do better than your usual 'proba-bly.' I need a definite answer."

His rudeness brings me back to Earth in a hurry. So he doesn't know about Secret, and I'm not going to have to deal with him in my life in that capacity, but I still have to deal with him, period.

Coldly, I say, "If you had simply said all of this in your email yesterday, I could have given you a definite answer. However, all I can give you right now is a 'probably' and get back to you on Monday."

"Typical bumbling bullshit. You know, Marshall wouldn't survive a month in New York City, considering the incompetent people he chooses to help him run his gallery."

My hackles rising, I chuckle ruefully. "Stefan, I find it hard to believe that anyone else would be able to give you an answer in a similar situation."

"It's not my fault you have a dull imagination and don't have a concept of how *professional* art dealers work. I'm trying to run a business here. I'm trying to set up my sched-ule, and I was giving you and Marshall the benefit of getting first pick at a date for a show."

"And we sincerely appreciate that." I meant for it to come out with a less sarcastic tone so he'd have no ammuni-tion against me, but I didn't quite achieve the genuineness I was aiming for.

"Never mind, then."

My heart pounds. I can tell by his tone of voice that he's gearing up for one of his tantrums. And I know that the calmer I am and the less I react to his fit, the angrier it'll make him. I also know I'm risking my job by calling his bluff, but I can't help myself. I close my eyes and pinch the bridge of my nose.

"That's your choice," I state pleasantly, channeling my inner robot.

"Just go fuck yourself! Stupid, fat whore!" His shrieking is so loud that I have to hold the phone away from my ear. "You are worthless! Fucking worthless!"

Suddenly, my phone is being yanked from my hand. I jump and whirl, ready to defend myself. But I immediately see it's only my husband who's mugging me.

"What are you?"

He ignores my confused half-question as he puts the phone to his ear. His nostrils flared, the edges of his lips white, he growls into the device, "I don't know who you think you are, but this conversation is over." With that, he jabs at the button to end the call and takes my phone with him back to the passenger side of the SUV, where he yanks open the door and flops into the front seat.

Dread of a new sort building in my belly, I walk around the Jeep and get behind the wheel. Sadie's still sound asleep in the backseat, but I don't want to talk about this until we're alone. Brice seems to be on the same page. He jerks his seat into an upright position, clutching my phone so tightly that his knuckles are white. I hope he doesn't break it. Marshall just bought that for me. I'd have to pay for a replacement.

When we pull into Nicole's driveway, he pockets the phone, exits the vehicle, opens the back door, unbuckles Sadie, and carries her to the front door, all in scary silence and without a glance at me.

Why do I have the feeling *I'm* in trouble?

18

ALPHA MALE

I tried to extend our visit at Nicole's as much as possible, knowing that as soon as we got in the car to go home, we'd have to talk about what just happened with Stefan.

Unfortunately, Brice wasn't about to be easily distracted. He was curt, just short of rude (because he doesn't do "rude"), and he kept edging me toward the front door. Physically nudging me at first and then grabbing my elbow and steering me, he had us saying, "Hello," "We had fun," "See you tomorrow at church," and "Goodbye," in less than five minutes. Then he practically raced me to the Jeep to claim the driver's seat.

Before he had even backed out of the driveway or I had my seatbelt fastened, he was off. "What a piece of work! I can't believe he had the— the *stones* to talk to you like that!"

"But—"

"I know he *always* talks to you like that, and I'd rather not be told that, because it makes me think seriously un-Christian thoughts. And if he thinks he's going to have the privilege of saying a word to you ever again if he insists on talking to you like that, he has another think coming."

"Yes, but—"

"The utter disrespect, the… the callous disregard for you as a person! I doubt he would speak to an animal as profanely and obscenely as he spoke to you, someone who has time and again shown tremendous patience with his vulgarity and ugliness, someone who had the decency to go through with a pregnancy that resulted from a horrible experience with a horrible person such as himself, someone who endured unspeakable pain as a result of going through with that pregnancy! And he has the audacity to verbally abuse you? He should be bowing down in front of you and kissing your feet and asking what he can do to make amends for every despicable thing he's ever said, thought, or done to you!"

"You shouldn't have hung up on him," I state quietly from my side of the car.

"What? I wish I could do more than that. I have half a mind to get on a plane to New York and wring his neck."

"Can I have my phone back?"

"Not if you're going to call him back."

"I'm not."

When he takes his hand from the steering wheel to dig my phone out of his pocket, I see how badly he's shaking.

"Brice. Calm down. Or pull over."

"I'm fine." He puts his trembling hand to his forehead and rubs at his hairline. "I mean, I'm *not* fine. I'm not at all okay with what he said to you, but I'm fine to drive."

"His call wasn't even about Secret."

His hand drops. So does his jaw. After a beat, he asks, "Then why was he screaming at you?"

I'm not sure if the real reason will make him angrier or

if he'll find it mildly funny and be as relieved as I am that Stefan still doesn't know. "I couldn't tell him for sure if I had any show openings in the next month."

"Tell me you're kidding."

Okay, so I guess we're going with Option A.

I shrug my shoulders up around my ears. "I'm kidding…?"

When all my statement gets is silence and then a strange whispering/murmuring sound, I look over to see what's going on. His lips are moving, and he's rocking slightly in his seat while gripping the steering wheel with both white-knuckled hands.

"What are you doing? Putting a hex on him?"

"Worse. Praying."

"For Pete's sake," I mutter; then louder: "I, for one, am thrilled that he's still only yelling at me about petty work shit. That's why I was perfectly content to stand there with my phone held away from my ear and wait for him to tire himself out. He's like a spoiled child who throws temper tantrums."

"And who spoiled him? You and Marshall and every other person in his life who's ever allowed him to act that way."

"So this is *my* fault?"

"Partly, yes."

I knew I wasn't imagining the anger directed at me earlier. "How interesting."

"And what's the deal with you stopping on a strange, random street to sneak out of the car to call him? For all you knew, that conversation was going to be *that* conversation. And you thought you'd just go it alone?" He merges onto the highway and accelerates.

"Yes! I 'went it alone' a lot before you were ever a part

of my life, and in particular when everything happened with *him*, so I thought it would be appropriate to handle it myself." I toss my phone into my purse and hold the bag primly in my lap. "I know how to handle Stefan. And it's not by hanging up on him."

"You mean, you know how to let Stefan walk all over you?"

"He may think that, but—"

"He thinks it because it's true! How can you let someone speak to you that way? You are a child of God. You are worth too much to allow yourself to be—"

"They're just words."

"Not when they're spoken to my wife!"

"I'm not your possession!" I smack the dashboard for emphasis.

He finishes passing a semi and drifts back into the slow lane. After a deep breath, he says, "I didn't mean to imply that you are."

"You imply that I am when you confiscate my phone, tell off and then hang up on one of my biggest clients, and then lecture me about how to do my job."

"Your job should not involve being verbally abused by a small-minded jerk."

"Well, it does! As a matter of fact, it involves being verbally abused by several small-minded jerks on a daily basis. Is he the worst of them? Definitely. But I'm good at what I do, because I don't take it personally, and I keep the peace. I've kind of been doing that my whole damn life, in case you just tuned in." I actually *harrumph* while crossing my arms over my chest.

Sullenly, he states, "I thought he was yelling at you about Secret."

Still pissed off, I shout, "So what if he was, Brice? So

what? I'm not an effing damsel in distress who needs you to come untie me from the railroad tracks!"

"I know."

"No, you don't. You still see me as that pathetic, scared, confused, messed-up person who came into your office with a heavy burden on her shoulders that she just couldn't carry alone anymore. That hasn't been me for a long time."

He reaches his right hand over the center console and curls his fingers around mine. "I'm sorry," he says miserably. "I'm protective, not possessive, I promise."

"Well, stop wasting your energy! Especially on Stefan. I learned a long time ago that he's just not worth it." When he doesn't have anything to say to that, I stare out my window and fume.

After a few minutes, he says quietly, "You know, he really deserves our pity."

"I wouldn't go that far."

"I would. As a matter of fact, he deserves our prayers. Imagine being so unhappy, so *wretched*, that your feelings for yourself manifest themselves in that sort of behavior towards other people. He needs Jesus," he says completely seriously, while I try not to laugh at the understatement of the century.

"He needs an exorcism," I mutter.

My stomach growls loudly, as if it's seconding my observation.

Brice looks sharply at me. "Was that you?" A slow smile spreads across his face.

"Yes," I grouch. "Hurry up and get me home. I'm starving."

∾

A soft, warm kiss lands on the back of my neck.

"'Bye' week," I mumble sleepily.

"Oh, man! Really? Already?"

I don't know why I'm lying. It was out before I was even fully awake and could consider the wisdom (or foolishness) of it.

Instead of compounding the fib, I merely stare straight ahead and think it through to its logical, awful conclusion: when I *am* on my period next week (or the week after. Things are still a little irregular now that I don't have those handy pills to keep things in check), how am I going to explain that? Too tired to figure it out right now. I just know that I'm not in the mood, and I definitely don't want to give him the real reason.

Truth is, I'm still miffed at him for hanging up on Stefan. Not necessarily because it made me look like a weak woman whose husband comes to her rescue at the slightest hint of trouble (although that's up there on the list), but because it's caused some major headaches in my work week so far.

I spent the first half hour of my Monday in Marshall's office, explaining why he had received a call from an irate Stefan on Saturday night. After my succinct explanation, which ended with, "I just didn't have the show calendar in front of me, so I couldn't give him the definitive answer he wanted," Marshall leveled a look at me over his bifocals and said, "I'm sure there's an app for that. Figure it out and make sure this never happens again."

Fair enough. I spent much of my morning doing just that. When the show calendar was successfully uploaded to my phone, I took a big swallow of pride and called Stefan to try to make amends while also scheduling his show. I got his voicemail, left a sugary-sweet message, and braced myself for an indeterminate period of the silent treatment followed by the inevitable verbally abusive call.

It's Wednesday, and I still haven't heard back from him.

Now, I get to look forward to the possibility that he's already scheduled all his shows for this month, and I'll have to answer to Marshall for that, since sales are bleak. We could really use a decent show from someone like Stefan, who's one of our biggest sellers.

However, if I admit that I don't want to have sex with Brice because of that stupid phone call, I'll only be confirming my penchant for grudge-holding. I can't help that it's the case, though. Faking my enthusiasm for a morning quickie would be just as wrong as the grudge-holding.

Now I feel super-guilty when he remains cuddled up against my back and says softly against my hair, "Sorry. I know you must be bummed. I'm bummed, too."

Oh, shit. I forgot that my "bye" week (when it's for real) is a major disappointment on the baby-making front.

I gulp. "Yeah, well... Isn't everyone always telling us how fun it is to try?"

"That's the spirit," he says proudly, pecking my shoulder blade, rolling over, and getting out of bed.

I am the worst wife ever. Well, maybe not as bad as that woman who cut off her husband's penis. Or someone who's been convicted of killing her husband. But pretty bad. He's so sweet and trusting and concerned with my feelings. And how do I repay him? With lies. Because I'm a little irritated at him. And just so I don't have to be "bothered." What a bitch! I don't deserve him.

A loud sob breaks painfully from my chest as the tears flood in. I try to cover it with a cough and sniffle, but to no avail.

"Oh, hon." He crawls across the mattress and kneels at my back.

Quickly, I kick my legs over the side of the bed, sit up, and swipe at my face. "I'm fine."

"It's okay."

"I know." I know how *un*-okay it is.

He grasps my upper arms and kisses the side of my neck. Lips still in contact with my skin, he whispers, "Hey. Shhhh…"

Disgusted with myself, I shrug him off and lurch to my feet. He sits back on his heels, his palms resting on his knees as he stares at me.

"What's going on?" he asks.

"Nothing. I'm just emotional." Because I'm *pre*-menstrual, but I can't tell *him* that, because according to what I told him two minutes ago, I'm supposed to be past that. Oh, and I hate myself. Can't tell him that, either.

"Some people try for *years* to conceive. We've been at it for mere months. I'm not worried. Please don't be worried." The pleading look in his eyes is killing me.

"Please stop staring at me."

"I'm not star— Okay." He puts his hands defensively in front of himself, dismounts the bed, and goes across the hall into the bathroom to start the shower.

Good. No walk today. I'm so not in the mood for that, either.

Just when I think I'm off the hook for the morning, he comes back into the bedroom while I'm sifting through my closet for something to wear.

Hands behind his back, he looks reticent when he asks, "This may sound like a stupid question, but are you *sure* it's *that* week?"

My hand freezes on the plastic hanger I was sliding

along the metal bar. *Busted.* The hook breaks off with a snap as I put just a little too much weight on it while trying to figure out how to get out of this one.

"I've noticed some… things lately," he states.

"'Things'?"

Oh, shit. He's observed there are no feminine product wrappers in the trash. Or something. Reverend Sherlock Effing Holmes!

He blushes. "Yeah. Just stuff. Like, well, stuff." Rushing on, he suggests, "Maybe you should take a test this morning." When I just stare at him, he explains, "You may think you're… you know… but it could be spotting. That's what the books say, anyway."

Finally realizing the "things" he's alluding to have nothing to do with my lies, lies, lies, I narrow my eyes. "You think I'm moody and weepy and maybe even a little thicker around the middle." I say this third thing, because *I* noticed my bathing suit was tighter around my legs at the waterpark.

"Not that last one. But the other two things. Maybe. Maybe it's worth a check." Now he brings his hand out from behind his back. He's holding a home pregnancy test.

I sigh.

He taps the box against his soft gray t-shirt-covered chest. "What can it hurt?"

Oh, I don't know. Getting a negative response could push me over the edge on this already shit-tastic week. Plus, *I* know that it's probably too early to take a test and expect an accurate result. But my big, fat lying mouth has talked me into a pretty tight corner, so I shrug, walk toward him, take the box, and resign myself to kissing fifteen bucks (no, twenty—I got the Cadillac of tests last time in an effort to avoid another false result) goodbye for the pleasure of getting a negative response.

I turn and disappear into the half-bath connected to our bedroom. A couple of minutes later, I cap the urine-soaked stick, prop it on top of the toilet tank, and open the bathroom door, expecting to see Brice on the other side, anxiously waiting. He, however, has gone about his morning routine. I hear him singing "Mr. Brightside" in the shower. I wish he wouldn't get his hopes up. Moody and weepy and paunchy is typical monthly activity for me, which he should know by now.

Anyway, I'm too hungry all the time to be pregnant. If history has taught us anything it's that Peyton + Hungry = No Bun in Oven. That should have been the tip-off last time, no matter how many peed-on sticks said otherwise.

That thought leads me to wonder how unacceptable it would be for me to eat Cheetos for breakfast. Maybe Brice will leave the house first this morning, and then I'll be able to do just that without his judgmental oversight. Unlike him, I can't eat the same thing every morning. Raisin bran every single day? Really? Sometimes he mixes it up and eats plain bran flakes. Or if he's really feeling frisky, he'll go with granola. But four out of five of his work days start with the raisin bran. Bo-ring!

Bodes well for me, though. I mean, if he can eat the same cereal every morning for however many years, seems like sticking with one woman for the rest of his life may not be too tall an order.

In the middle of my musings about where I fall on the metaphorical spectrum between plain bran flakes and granola, Brice saunters into the bedroom in a towel and raises his eyebrows expectantly at me on the way to his closet.

"Well?" he asks, pulling out his standard black shirt and

black pants and tossing them, still on their hangers, on the bed.

I blink at him and almost answer, "Raisin bran," before I realize he's inquiring about the pregnancy test, which I've already dismissed and have left for forgotten on the back of the toilet. "Oh. That. Haven't checked yet."

He laughs at my absent-mindedness and steps into the tiny bathroom to see for himself.

"Oh."

I roll my eyes at the predictable result.

Then I hear him rustling in the trash before he asks, "Where's the box?"

"It's plus or minus. Do you really need the instructions?"

How ambiguous can it be? I know he's just looking for a loophole so he doesn't have to accept an answer he doesn't like. I've pored over my share of home pregnancy test inserts for the very same reason (although I was always looking for the opposite answer).

"Well, when you've been burned once like we have…"

"This is a completely different brand," I say, finally deciding on an outfit and tossing it on the bed next to Brice's clothes.

"That's reassuring," he says in a strange, distracted voice. "But I still want to be sure." His voice cracks on the last word.

"Stop torturing yourself. You're not worried; I'm not worried. Sure, we just wasted a twenty-dollar test, but there are bigger tragedies in life."

"Yeah, well…"

"I'm gonna hop in the shower."

"Wait!"

"Oh, shit. Are you wearing the last towel?" I can't remember the last time I did laundry. It hasn't been this week, that's for sure. I cross the bedroom, planning to whip the towel off his body to take it with me to the shower. He meets me at the bathroom doorway, the pregnancy test pinched between his thumb and forefinger.

I wrinkle my nose, about to criticize him for touching something I've so recently peed on, when my eyes fall on the purple plus sign in the results window.

"Now, don't get too excited," he warns, his enormous grin revealing that he's definitely not heeding his own advice, "but this is a pretty awesome sight."

I put my fingers to my lips, which I squeeze together into a duckbill while I look back and forth from the test to his face as I refuse to allow myself to hope that it's true.

He looks at the test and back to me. "Huh? What do you say we both take the day off, buy about a dozen more of these, and see if this is a fluke?"

I love his enthusiasm.

19

SECRET SNIFFERS

*A*fter a very long week's wait, Dr. Walsh confirmed what the twelve home pregnancy tests had already told us (I should have known to take Brice literally when he said "a dozen," but I still laughed when he came home from the pharmacy with that bag full of tests): we're expecting a baby in early April.

Confessing to Brice about the "bye" week fib could have put a damper on things (I had to immediately come clean when he started worrying—yes, *worrying*—about my reported "spotting" and wanted to call Dr. Walsh about it right away), but he was so happy about the positive tests that he barely blinked when I told him. He did say, "You never have to lie to me about something like that. Just say, 'Go away.'"

I blanched at the word "lie," even though it was completely accurate. Plus, before I could feel too ashamed, he was hugging and kissing me, and I knew I was absolved. For everything, ever. I think I have perpetual amnesty, thanks to this little person hanging out with me for the next thirty-three weeks (or so). Feels pretty nice.

Of course, I've had to temper his excitement a little. Okay, a lot. I threatened to confiscate *his* phone (see how *he* likes it) if he even thought about telling anyone for five more weeks. Even our families. He protested, playing the "Mom will be so hurt" card, but I stood firm. No repeats of what happened a few months ago allowed.

"What if something happens?" I asked. "Remember those hideous, pitying looks?" I don't have to think back too far to remember them, either. As of just a couple weeks ago, I was still getting doleful stares from Jared and Justine when they thought I wasn't paying attention. Buh-rother. I can't imagine how they'd act if I actually had a miscarriage or— Well, I can't think about that.

"If that's God's will, then we'll need the support of our families and our church family," he argued.

"And we'll have it. Then. From the people who *need* to know."

"How can people pray for us *now*, though, if they don't know *now*?" he argued.

Even though I knew it was an illogical answer, I said, "Your prayers count for ten of theirs, so I think we're covered. Don't. Tell. Anyone. I'm begging you."

Mercifully, I think I could ask Brice to do anything right now (except, possibly, renounce God), and he'd do it. I'm exercising extreme discipline not to take advantage of that. His dedication is adorable, though. For now. I can see where the frequent phone calls when we're apart and hyper-attention to every sound I make when we're together may get old, but for now, I'm ashamed to admit that I'm enjoying it. I'm not actively seeking it, mind you (that would be obnoxious), but if he's offering… Hey, I'd be an idiot to refuse to be spoiled. I've never had that before. I just want to get a taste of what it's like. Then, when I've had enough, I'll tell him to stand down.

As far as not telling anyone until we've hit that magic twelfth week, it's not like people aren't going to figure it out before then. Doesn't he realize how obvious it will be once I start running for the bathroom in the middle of conversations and wearing that slightly green-tinged, chagrined expression 24/7 and puffing up like a sodium addict? Granted, his mom won't have the benefit of seeing those huge clues, but it's going to be apparent to everyone else who sees me regularly that something's different. They were slow to catch on when I was expecting Secret, but "pregnant" was the last thing they thought to look for in perpetually single me. Or they were in denial. This time, they'll be all over it.

Anyway, Brice has reluctantly promised to keep his mouth closed for now. I'm still considering following him around everywhere to make sure he keeps that promise.

Unfortunately, it's not what he *says* but what he *does* that's most telling. He watches me constantly and touches me a lot and doesn't let me carry anything. He even tried to commandeer my purse the other day as we were walking out of the church together. I snatched it back from him and told him to get a grip—on reality. If we could just live in a cocoon and never go out in public together, it'd be a lot easier to keep this particular secret. But, obviously, our lifestyle doesn't permit that.

I'm particularly concerned about my family finding out too soon. Mom's instituted Sunday dinner with the whole family, because "That's what's wrong with our society; we don't put enough focus on the family." I've tried to hide behind Brice's schedule ("He works on Sundays"), but she's conveniently set the time for when he should be finished at the church: 6:30 p.m. And since there's food involved, he now makes it a priority to finish work on time on Sundays.

It's not that I don't want to spend time with my family. But one evening *every* weekend is a little much. I know we're going to reach our family-time threshold before too long, and something ugly's going to happen at one of these dinners. That's just how we operate.

For now, though, things are okay. It's been three weeks with nary a cross word spoken, except for that time Jason made a crack about my dad's golf game, something which Dad takes very seriously and doesn't have much of a sense of humor about. That was tense. But I stepped in, as usual, and smoothed things over by complimenting the food—or something equally inane—and the conversation rebooted.

Tonight, I'm trying to keep relaxed while worrying about things like, *Why isn't the smell of this food making me sick? Does that mean something's wrong with the baby?* and pretending like I don't have a care in the world, like everything's normal. We still have a little less than a month before we make an official announcement, so I'm also paranoid about saying or doing something to alert the media— er, my family, who's probably about ten times worse than any paparazzi.

Teetotaling, the usual giveaway, isn't an issue, since I gave up alcohol when we started trying to conceive (or *not* trying, whichever we eventually agreed to call it). Everyone's finally used to remembering not to offer me anything to drink. As Jason likes to say, "Good. More for us!" And since I haven't had a minute of nausea this entire pregnancy (welcome, but weird), there are no food aversions or frequent trips to the bathroom to hide.

The opposite is actually the case: I have to hold myself back from eating so much that everyone stares. Especially

Nicole. My stick-bug sister has always looked down her nose at my appetite. My *normal* appetite, I'd like to add. It's not like I've ever entered one of those hot dog eating contests (ah, *there's* my old friend, Queasy!) or that I can sit down with an entire half-gallon of ice cream (although right now, it'd probably be possible). If I ate the way I wanted to eat right now, she'd definitely make a comment. So I take moderate helpings of mouth-watering ham, homemade mashed potatoes and mac-n-cheese, creamed spinach, and green beans. Then I force myself to chew everything really well and eat slowly so that I'm not finished before everyone else.

To my frustration, I'm still finished before everyone else, since they all take second helpings. Except for Nicole, of course. But she's the slowest eater in America, I'm convinced. So, I sit, sipping my water and trying not to stare at each forkful that goes from Jason's plate to his mouth as my half-full stomach gurgles unhappily.

While Jason goes into more detail about why Dustin's not joining us this evening (family vacation in the Galapagos Islands with his parents and siblings), Brice sets his fork down and leans to his left, closer to me. Quietly, he asks, "Are you still hungry? Eat some more."

I shake my head briskly and mumble back, "I'm full."

Having witnessed me eat three times what I just did and then polish off an ice-cream-topped brownie just the other night, he checks, "You feeling okay?"

"Fine." Nicole and Mom are starting to pay attention to us, so I smile tightly and nod at his plate. "Never mind."

"Everything okay over there?" Mom inquires from across the table as soon as Jason stops talking.

Great. Thanks, Reverend Subtle. I nudge him in the ribs. He jerks away from me and goes back to eating with a tiny smile on his lips.

"Fine," he answers for both of us when I say nothing. "Food's great."

That's enough to divert her attention from me. She goes into a long, convoluted story about finding a new recipe for the green beans in a magazine in the dentist's waiting room and going to great lengths to rip it from the publication without being caught. All but two of us laugh at her story.

I'm only half-listening while I hold Nicole's steady eye contact. I will not blink first. It may seem like it, but I know I'm not see-through, nor does she have X-ray vision, so there's no way she can know for sure what's going on. For all she knows, I'm on a diet. And if my husband would just play it cool (I realize I'm asking a lot of someone who doesn't know much about the concept), everything would be fine.

My oldest nephew, Caleb, pulls his mom's attention away from me when he asks if he and his younger brother, Everett, can be excused from the table to go outside, which prompts Sadie to put in her request, too, which starts an argument when the boys tell her she can't play with them, because she's too little (actually, that's what Everett says, but Caleb mutters, "lame," under his breath, either too quietly for his parents to hear or they don't care).

After much simultaneous talking, Nicole snaps, "Sadie, just go play with your Barbies like you always do, and leave your brothers alone."

The boys crash out the front door, hurling insults at each other. Sadie stomps toward the basement, sniffling, but I grab her elbow on her way past and whisper next to her head, "I'll be there in just a few minutes, so save me the pretty Barbie."

After she's gone, Nicole turns to Brice and me. "You two really want a piece of that?"

I merely shrug, as if I don't think about it constantly, but Brice enthusiastically replies, "Yep!"

Lonnie chuckles knowingly. "Just wait. Life as you know it will cease to exist."

"I know. Can't wait," Brice states.

Mock-offended, I turn to him. "Gee, thanks."

He wipes his mouth, laughing into his napkin. "I didn't mean it that way, Miss Sensitive. I just mean that it's going to be fun." Resting an arm along my shoulders, he pulls me toward him in a half-hug. I fall against him limply as I silently will him to stop talking. My subliminal begging seems to work. But then he brings his other hand over and rests it tenderly on my belly.

Nicole's eyes widen. My hand twitches with the urge to pick his hand up by the pinkie and move it back to his own lap, but I know that will only look more obvious.

A sly smile touching her lips, my older sister asks, "So, when are you guys due?"

All movement at the table ceases. Dad stops mid-chew. Jason looks at us over the rim of his wineglass, which is tipped toward his face, but still unattached to his lips. Mom's head tilts expectantly. Lonnie merely stares, his arms resting on either side of his empty plate. We look like a Thanks-giving diorama in a natural history museum of the future.

My non-answer is, "Whatever, Nicole."

Brice murmurs, "Peyton."

I look up at him warningly.

Mom gasps, as if she's been holding her breath. "You guys! Is it true?"

Brice's smile couldn't look guiltier, and it's all the answer they need. Pandemonium breaks out around the table. Dad makes the kind of happy noises I haven't heard him make since… ever. Mom starts crying. Nicole shouts, "I knew it!" Jason and Lonnie come around the table to clap Brice on the shoulder and shake his hand, which he offers to each of them in turn after accidentally hitting me in the back of the head when he removes his arm from my shoulders.

"Ow," I grumble, largely ignored, as I observe the chaos around me.

Eventually, Jason breaks away from Brice, bends over, and gives me a hug from behind, placing his chin on my shoulder and saying near my ear, "Way to go, Sis."

His simple approval surprises me and brings tears to my eyes. "Oh. Thanks."

Mom's voice cuts through the melee. "Ahem. You guys never answered Nicole's question, though. When's the landing date?"

I dab at the corners of my eyes with my index fingers. "April fifth. Give or take two weeks."

"Or more," Nicole warns gleefully. "I thought Everett was never going to come out!"

"Don't tell her that!" Mom reproaches, but I can tell she secretly approves of the scare tactic. She loves horror stories like that.

"I was there, Mom," I remind her. "I was about to reach up there and pull him out myself." To Nicole, I say, "You were so cranky!"

"Just you wait. You'll understand when you get to that last month."

Her unintentional gaffe tweaks a nerve, maybe *because* my first baby is so forgotten that my family makes comments like that all the time. It surprises me how much it hurts, though, and how much the knowledge that I never made it to the last month with Secret weighs on my mind.

I shake it off. This is no time to be hyper-sensitive. Instead, I smile at her and say, "I'm sure you'll be right there to say, 'I told you so.'"

"You better believe it. Now, where are you two going to register? You know what? Before you do that, you have to come by my house and look through all the stuff I still have. It's all covered in plastic in the basement, so it's like new. I'd love to get it out of my way."

Mom dismisses my sister's baby gear talk with a double-handed wave. "Never mind all that. Names. What are the names you guys are discussing?"

"Uh, none yet," I lie. "I thought we'd wait until we find out if we're having a boy or girl."

Brice smiles mildly at me. "Unless we decide to keep that a surprise. We've thought about that, right?"

"Keep the name or the sex a surprise?" Mom clarifies, looking terrified of either prospect.

I shrug. "Maybe both." I can't resist goading her.

Picking up on this, Brice nods earnestly. "Yeah. There just aren't enough surprises in life. Plus, how can you name a kid before you know what he or she looks like? The name has to fit the personality."

"Newborns don't have personalities! And they'll fit whatever name you give them. We need to know if we're buying dresses or rompers with trucks on them. And we have to get things monogrammed!"

Dad steps in. "Peg, leave the poor kids alone. You're gonna give yourself a migraine."

Jason pats my shoulder and goes back to his chair. He, Lonnie, and Nicole start talking about how vicious the "date, time, and weight" pool got when Nicole was expecting Sadie, the first granddaughter on either side of the family.

Mom chimes in with, "But I won!"

Dad argues, "Uh, I don't think so! I was closest on date and weight, so *I* won."

I look at Brice, sigh, roll my eyes, and laugh at them.

He winces and whispers, "Sorry."

I shrug and say, "Whatever," in a way that makes it clear I'm not mad. As a matter of fact, I'm sort of relieved.

Maybe now I can relax.

LOSING SLEEP

*S*leep has never eluded me before, so this prenatal insomnia is a new experience. Of course, I'll take sleeplessness over nausea any day, but lying awake all night is maddening in its own way. It's a long time to think. Lots of thoughts. Scary thoughts. Pleasant ones, too. But mostly scary. There's something about the darkness and the silence that breeds doubt and fear.

And hunger. There's been more than one occasion that my growling stomach has woken up Brice. He's been a good sport about it (he *better* be), but he's also taken to encouraging me to eat before bed to prevent the midnight hungries. It doesn't matter, though. Eight hours is a long time to go between meals when you're me. It's not a big deal when those hours are filled with sleep. But when I'm just lying here, staring at the inside of my eyelids (or the ceiling or Brice's back or chest), the hours drag, and my metabolism doesn't quite get to that dormant, hibernating state that it would reach if I could only sleep deeply, instead of this annoying on-and-off dozing I do on a nightly basis.

Actually, it's more like doze and jerk, wake and starve, growl and ache, toss and turn, repeat.

Tonight, especially, there's no hope of sleep. Tomorrow's Stefan's show. I didn't get it scheduled for the end of August, but the third Friday in September was close enough to keep me off Marshall's shit list. In the past, I scheduled vacation days around Stefan's visits to town, If Marshall ever caught onto that, he never pointed it out; if Stefan caught onto it, well… I don't care if he did. But in my new position as Artist Liaison, I can't do that. When we have shows, it's my job to be there to take care of the artist to his or her liking. Some artists are easy to please. Others… not so much. One guess which category Stefan falls into.

In my head, I can't stop going over the lists and lists of Stefan's demands. Some of them are the same as always: five 20-ounce bottles of New York tap water; one bottle (same exact style as water bottles) of straight vodka; a padded, swiveling, high-backed stool (40 inches tall, all-black) with a good vantage point of the entire gallery and near (but not directly under) an air conditioning vent; and gallery thermostat set to precisely 71 degrees. But he has some different "requests" this time around that I want to make sure I don't forget: paintings arranged in reverse alphabetical order by title; all easels and displays draped in white crushed velvet cloths; and a host of last-minute preps that I'm blanking on now, in the middle of the night, but that I have written down on a list at work *and* in my purse.

If I didn't know him better, I'd think he was trying to make this show particularly difficult and stressful for me. But that's a paranoid notion. He tries to make *every* show particularly difficult and stressful. I'm pretty sure he lies awake at night coming up with new and creative ways to make *me* lie awake, worrying, the night before his shows. I'll be damned if he'll ever get the slightest bit of satisfaction from that knowledge, though.

I've already vetoed Brice's repeated requests, pleas, threats, and promises to attend the show with me. I told him there was no way I was going to do my job with a body-guard lingering in the background. Since he's a grown man with his own transportation, however, there's nothing I can do to stop him from showing up anyway. I just have to hope he honors my wishes. I don't want to make my human body pillow sleep on the couch for a night.

He shifts under me now in his sleep. Worried that my right leg, which is draped over his waist, is bothering him, I slide it slightly lower so it's twined with his. He twitches and grunts, but when I look up at his face, it's obvious he's still sleeping. Must be nice.

I flop onto my back to rid my left hand of pins and needles, turn my head, and note the time on the clock. Three-forty-seven. Only two hours and forty-three minutes until the alarm rescues me from this Hell. Because this is what Hell is like, I've decided. Forget flames and demons. It's full of beds, but you're unable to get a wink of sleep. And add extreme hunger to that, just to make it really fun. And a—

CHARLEY HORSE!!!

"Oh, *fuckfuckfuckfuck*," I whisper, rolling onto my right side and pushing on the bedside table to give me some leverage for sitting up, while my right leg screams at me but proves itself completely useless in the matter of mobility.

"What's wrong?" Brice turns on his light and sits up sleepily. When he sees me trying frantically to get out of bed, he becomes wide awake. "What's the matter? What's happening?"

I finally manage to gasp, "Charley horse!" just so he'll

know it's nothing serious, but I can hardly speak for the pain.

"Well, don't try to walk on it; you'll fall down and hurt yourself." He flips the covers back and jumps from the bed, practically running around the foot of it to get to me. He kneels in front of me and says, "Put your foot up on my shoulder."

It sounds like a ridiculous ploy, but if it makes the pain go away, I'll stand on my head and put my foot in his mouth.

When I comply, he grasps it and my ankle, pushing my toes up toward my knee. Then he rubs my calf. After a few cycles of this treatment, he asks, "Better?" as the muscle slowly unclenches and softens under his hand.

I nod, my face relaxing by degrees, so he lowers my leg, which I can already tell is going to be sore as hell tomorrow.

Catching my breath, I tell him, "I got these all the time when I was pregnant with Secret, but this is the first one I've had in a long time. I've forgotten how terrible they are."

He winces. "I used to cramp up when I'd run cross-country in high school. Awful. Hold tight. I'll be right back."

He springs up and jogs from the room, down the hall. I hear him opening and closing a cupboard in the kitchen and running the kitchen tap before he returns to the room with a large glass of water, which he hands over to me. "Here. Drink this."

I do, although I know it's just going to make me pee in thirty minutes. After downing half of it, I give him a grateful smile. "Thanks."

"Anytime," he smiles sexily back at me before returning to bed. He pulls the covers up to his chest and turns out his light.

I set the water glass on my bedside table. When I burrow

under the covers and up against him, he asks, "Have you slept at all tonight?"

"Nope."

"That's not good, hon."

"Nope."

"Anything I can do to help?"

I know better than to mention Stefan's name to him, much less in our bed, so I stick with the reliable, "Nope." Then I check, "Does it bother you when I use you as a body pillow?"

I can hear the smile in his voice when he replies, "Nope."

"Are you sure? Because sometimes it helps me sleep, but I can't imagine it's the most comfortable thing for you."

"I love it."

"Okay, now."

He laughs. "Too far?"

"You're a sucky liar, remember?"

"I'm pretty proud of that." He strokes my hair. "Anyway, if it helps you sleep, cuddle away."

"Thanks."

"You bet."

Suddenly, I'm very content. And very sleepy.

Oh, gosh. If I could just put my head down on my desk and sleep for fifteen minutes, I would be so grateful. Just a cat nap. That's all I need. What would it hurt? Okay, my co-workers would think I've lost my mind. Big deal. And I'm still not ready to tell Marshall about being pregnant (he's going to go into freak-out maternity leave planning mode as soon as I do), so if he asks me what's wrong, I'll have to gloss over it. I guess it's not worth it. But it really might be worth it. Dealing with Stefan while feeling like this could get me fired.

Desperate, I limp off to the bathroom during my lunch hour, go into one of the stalls, close the door on it, sit on the commode, and lean against the wall. Just to rest my eyes, that's all. Five minutes. It's for the greater good, I tell myself.

I jolt awake when there's a knocking close to my temple. My legs are straight out in front of me, my feet resting at old angles to each other as they stick out from under the stall door.

"Uh, Peyton? Is that you in there?" comes the voice of Deirdre, one of the part-time clerks. "Are you okay?"

I clear my throat, but my voice still sounds froggy and groggy when I reply, "Yeah, I'm fine. Just… fine."

Standing brings on vertigo, one of my faithful companions lately. Before gaining my equilibrium, I bounce against the stall walls like a pinball, finally grasping onto the tiny metal door handle while my vision clears. I emerge to face a bemused co-worker.

She's all of twenty-two and has the sort of complexion that hints at a very healthy sleep schedule, diet, and exercise regimen. I don't know her (or any other of the part-time clerks) very well, but she strikes me as the type of person who pops out of bed every morning, tosses on whatever's handy (and makes it look trendy), brushes her teeth, musses her purposely messy hair, and sings along to the radio all the way to work. I've never seen her in a bad mood. Ever. I sort of hate her.

"Rough night last night?" she quips.

I'm distracted from answering her by a dripping on my leggings, down the middle of my (still sore) calf. "What the…?" I mutter, looking first up at the ceiling and then around me. The more I move, the more droplets dance around me in an arc, landing on the tiled floor.

Deirdre steps away from me. "Um, looks like maybe your top got kinda… wet."

Sure enough, when I clutch at the hem of my tunic top, my fingers brush against soggy fabric. My heart goes into my throat, and I feel like I'm going to pass out until I confirm it's not blood, but toilet water. Relief lasts about ten seconds. Then it hits me that I've been sitting with the edge of my top soaking in the toilet for who knows how long.

"Aw, shit," I whine, blushing and sweating when I realize I'm going to cry about it.

Deirdre looks almost as embarrassed as I do.

My chin wobbling, I try to reassure her (and myself), "I'm okay," as I go over to the hand dryer and hit the button. Holding my top under the nozzle, I try to explain through my pent-up tears, "I'm just tired. Really tired. And stressed out. This show…"

Probably all in an effort to avert her eyes from the mess that is me, she inspects her perfect makeup-free pores in the nearest mirror. "Yeah, Stefan's kind of a dick. But he's hot."

I can't help but snort. "Oh, gosh. Don't even go there."

"Why? Did *you*?"

I half-turn to look at her, relieved to see she's just fishing for information. "Uh, no!" I lie, with a laugh that sounds demented since it's mixed with my leftover tears. "And neither should you." I hate how I sound like a dried-up old prune when I say it.

She runs a finger along her eyebrow. "Oh, is it against the rules, or something? No fraternizing with the contributors?" Her tone tells me that she doesn't really give a rip about the rules.

"No, not technically."

"Then, what's it to you? I thought you were married."

Not to sound snobby, but this is why I'm not close to any of what we call the "shop front" workers. They're all a bunch of irreverent, spoiled-rich-kid fine arts majors with entitlement issues. And to them, I'm just the "old chick," who... "What does she do, anyway?"

I keep this place running, that's what I do, Deirdre, so stop looking at me like I'm a pathetic idiot who passed out in the bathroom with her shirt in the toilet.

Now I say to her, "Yes. I'm married."

"Yeah!" It's coming to her now. "Aren't you married to a preacher, or something?"

"A pastor, yes."

"Preacher, pastor. Same thing."

"Not really, but—"

"Does he know you were out partying last night and had to come to work hungover?" she half-teases.

"I'm not—" I begin but think better of it when I realize I don't have a better explanation that I'm willing to give. "I was with him," I say truthfully. "So, yes. He knows I'm not feeling very well today."

She raises an eyebrow. "Wow. That's one progressive preacher."

My teeth squeak as I grit them while fighting the urge to correct her. Instead, I hit the dryer button for the third time, thankful that my top is almost dry, and smile tightly. "We're Lutheran," I say, as if that explains everything.

I can tell this means nothing to her (*I'm* not even sure what I meant). But she pretends to know (because she knows *everything*) as she returns my smile and nods.

Also, it's unclear why she's in here, unless she used the bathroom while I was passed out, but surely I would have heard the flush. I wasn't *that* out of it, was I? What time is it, anyway? How long have I been in here?

"Are you sure you're okay?" she asks, looking skeptical.

I catch a glimpse of myself in the mirror and see why she might still be wondering. I look crazed, with my smudged makeup and under-eye circles and creased face.

After I insist that I am, she leaves me alone, but not without a backwards glance at me as she pushes open the bathroom door.

Great. At best, I go bar-hopping with my "preacher" husband and show up to work hungover on show dates. At worst, I'm a druggie who shoots up in bathroom stalls and then passes out.

A few minutes later, when I return to my desk after washing up and fixing my makeup, I'm not at all surprised when my phone rings and it's Marshall, summoning me to his office. I bet Deirdre couldn't walk her perky butt in there fast enough to report what she thinks she saw in the bathroom.

I hang up my phone, sigh, and make my way down the hall to Marshall's office. When I poke my head around the doorframe, I expect to see him giving me one of his signature "looks" over his bifocals before asking me bluntly what the hell's going on. What I don't expect to see is Stefan sitting in one of the purple plush chairs in front of his desk.

He half-turns to look me up and down, rolls his eyes, and says, "Finally! If you'd walk faster, you might burn a few calories."

SHOWDOWN

"Have a seat, Peyton," Marshall says in a neutral tone, gesturing to the chair next to (too close to) the one that's holding Stefan, who's facing forward again, sitting with his legs crossed, his foot bouncing, his face pinched in its usual *Something stinks in here* expression.

Unfortunately, he might actually be smelling me. I checked before I left the bathroom to make sure my top didn't smell like a toilet, but maybe it does.

I finger my hem self-consciously and look shiftily back and forth between the two men. "What's up?" I try for the carefree and casual approach as I remain standing.

"We just wanted to have a word before tonight's show about Mr. Svadjlenka's current level of customer service, make sure we're all on the same page," Marshall says soothingly. When Stefan turns to look smugly at me, Marshall widens his eyes over the artist's head and nods toward the chair. Then he winks at me.

I take a seat, somehow managing not to roll my eyes or sigh. This is the part of my job that I truly hate: butt-kissing. Too bad it comprises more than half of my typical day.

Ignoring the hormone headache that's threatening to blow the top of my head off, I pleasantly inform the two of them, "Not everything is set up for tonight's show just yet—I have a few last-minute things to do, like arranging the food when the caterers get here—but is there something besides the things we've already discussed that you'd like me to take care of?"

I turn to Stefan and force myself to blink innocently into his unshaven face. If he had any friends, they'd tell him he doesn't look trendy or sexy like that and should leave that scruffy look to guys like Drex, who know a thing or two about sex appeal.

Elbows rested on the arms of his chair and hands folded serenely across his lap, he returns my steady gaze and answers, "I haven't had a chance to look around out there. I'm more interested in talking about the treatment I've received in the past."

"Oh?"

He's going to have to spell it out. I'm not going to retroactively—not to mention, blindly—apologize for *anything*, even if I'm pretty sure I know to what he's referring.

"Yes." He gestures toward my boss. "As I was just telling Marshall, I was terribly shocked when someone—I'm assuming it was your husband—was very rude and hung up on me when I called to try to schedule this show."

Well, add this to the limited list of things that nauseate me: Stefan's Little Mr. Innocent act.

I glance at Marshall, who gives me the "just-humor-him" nod.

Taking a deep, bracing, stomach-steadying breath, I say, "I'm sorry you were offended…" then louder and more forcefully when he looks a little too smug at my apology, "…

when my husband put you in line after you *verbally abused* me—"

His expression sours. "My business was not with your husband, Sweet Cheeks."

"Please do not call me that." Just had a vivid and stomach-turning flashback to *that* night. He knows it, too. He used that sarcastic term of endearment on purpose. I can see it in his cold, dead, Viking eyes.

"Okay, folks," Marshall implores, clapping his hands once. "Let's keep it professional and civil."

I refuse to be lumped in with that Nordic ass and rebuked for being "unprofessional" when I'm being the absolute definition of it. After all, I haven't slapped him yet or stormed out of here.

I hold up a hand. "Excuse me, but I *am*." I stand up and look down at my client. "Stefan, I am sorry I could not accommodate your request during your original call to schedule this show. But that does not give you the right to scream obscenities at me so loudly that someone—who just happened to be my husband—could hear you from several feet away. Now, if you'll excuse me, I have things to do to get ready for your show."

I turn toward the door but only make it a couple of steps before he booms, "I'm not finished!"

I whirl on my heel, gratified to see how put off Marshall is by the yelling. I tilt my head and make a face that says, "*See what I mean? This is what I deal with.*"

Marshall's face says, "*Wow.*"

Oblivious to our silent conversation, Stefan continues, "I don't appreciate the sarcastic, condescending way you insist upon talking to me. Like I'm a *child.*" He pulls back his chin indignantly. "But I'm *not* your child, am I?"

I blink at his rhetorical question. Something in his icy

blue eyes alerts my brain (and my feet) to run as far away from him as possible. So I do. Well, not run, because I don't do that. But I walk very swiftly away from that office, not even sure why I'm suddenly so terrified of him. I just know I am and that my fear is justified.

Unfortunately, it's futile to flee. I mean, where am I going to go? I can't just run from the building (and my job). I really do have work to do to finish preparing for the show. Plus, Stefan's following me.

"That's right, Peyton," he sing-songs gleefully behind me. "I know! Drex told me everything."

Freezing in my tracks in the middle of the gallery, wedged between two white-velvet-draped cubes, I allow that statement to sink in while keeping my back to him.

Deirdre and Jetson stop their work, centering Stefan's paintings on top of the cubes, to gawk at me.

I'd play dumb, but that would just prompt him to be more explicit, so I slowly turn to face him and simply say, "I'm sorry you had to find out that way."

He narrows his eyes. "So it's true?"

Hmm... thought we'd already established that. To prevent my admitting to something that I didn't do—there's enough to admit to that I *did* do—I suggest, "Let's go somewhere more private and talk about this." I have no idea where in this open-plan store would be more private, but the middle of the street would be preferable to me at this moment. At least none of my co-workers are out there.

He replies obstinately, "No. The only thing I have to be ashamed of is that I slept with you. And apparently knocked you up."

Deirdre covers her mouth and giggles.

Stefan turns on her. "It's not funny, girlie, and I suggest you and your little boyfriend here make yourselves scarce before I have your boss fire you for being you. And ugly," he adds after looking Jetson up and down.

The two of them leave the sales floor, but I know they're hovering out-of-sight, continuing to listen. Hell, I would.

Returning his attention to me, he says, "And you. You're sorry I had to find out from Drex? How else was I supposed to find out? You were never going to tell me, obviously."

I can't feel my extremities, and my lips are strangely numb, like I've had too much to drink, but it doesn't seem to be affecting my speech when I say, "At this point, it doesn't really matter, does it?"

"It mattered at the time!"

While my ears ring, I take in the sight of Marshall hanging back, listening to everything. Oh, yeah. That guy. I'd almost forgotten about him.

When he catches my eye contact, he asks quietly, "What's he talking about?"

Matter-of-factly, I answer, "The baby I lost was Stefan's."

Stefan turns to Marshall. "Trust me, it was just one night."

Marshall shakes his head, obviously confused. "But you're—"

"Yeah, yeah. I know," he says, waving dismissively, "but I was going through a phase, trying new things."

Now I'm lost. At least, I hope I am. "What's that supposed to mean?" I ask, loathe to draw their attention to me again but really needing an answer to that question.

My boss informs me, "He's gay."

"Since when?" I squeak two octaves higher than my normal voice while sidling up to and sitting down gracelessly on one of the cubes. The velvet slides against the slick surface underneath it, almost dumping me onto the ground.

I recover at the last second and perch on the corner of the display.

Casually inspecting his fingernails, Stefan answers, "Oh, since forever. Like I said, I was just kind of bored and thought I'd see what all the fuss is about vaginas. Still don't know what all the fuss is," he adds with a mutter.

I didn't think the nightmare that was that night could be any more horrendous. Shows how much I know.

Gay? Really? Oh, gosh. I don't feel very good. It's like Craig Tennant all over again. Only this time, I'm an adult and shouldn't be so clueless. How could I have never seen it? It's so obvious now that it's been pointed out to me. The way he carries himself; the things he says; his idiosyncrasies and quirks and mannerisms. He's probably one of the gayest men I've ever seen, now that my eyes have been opened to the fact.

And it all seems so much more regrettable and pointless, knowing that I slept with awful Stefan, and he doesn't even like sleeping with people with vaginas. Why me? Why *my* vagina?

He takes in my pale appearance and snorts. "I thought you knew!"

Dumbfounded, I shake my head. "No. Drex said you went on dates with women. I'm sure of it."

"I did. A few. It was a very confusing time." He snaps out of his reverie. "Back to you, though. *You* withheld information from me. You've had plenty of opportunity to tell me and chose not to."

I can't seem to think of any of the things I've planned to say to him at this moment. No apologies, no excuses, no defenses spring to mind. Thankfully, he's not really pausing to let me say my piece, anyway.

Deep breaths. That's what I need to concentrate on

right now: *not* passing out. I can't focus on what he's saying, but by the look on his face, it's just more vitriol. I get the idea.

"This is so stressful," I put my hand to my forehead and mumble in the middle of his diatribe about what a disgusting person I am. I close my eyes and start praying, my lips moving, but no sounds coming out.

"Are you even listening to me?" Stefan screeches. I open my eyes for a second, when his voice seems to be getting closer to me, and see him struggling against Marshall's attempts to shut him up and remove him from the room.

I cover my ears, squeeze my eyes closed more tightly, and pray for God to tell me what to do here. Or to at least bring me some semblance of peace.

That's when I pass out.

When I come to on the sofa in Marshall's office, I hear him and Stefan arguing about me, so I keep my eyes closed, hoping it was all a dream and that as long as I keep my eyes shut, it will stay the truth.

"…don't appreciate your using my gallery as a stage for your Jerry Springer tactics, Stefan! Just look at her! She's out fucking cold!" Then my boss's furious tone changes, and he says solicitously, "Reverend! Hi! Marshall Atwood here…." and my eyes fly open.

Oh, no. No, no, no!

"Yes, everything's fine, I think. No need to worry, but Peyton, well, she passed out here at work…. No, no. It's sort of difficult to describe what happened, but since you're her emergency contact…."

I scramble to a sitting position, thankful that my abs still work. "Psst!" I hiss at my boss while pointing at his phone, then dragging my finger across my throat.

He shakes his head and turns his back to me, plugging his free ear with his finger. "About five minutes. She just woke up, actually."

I jump from the couch and limp blindly across the office, fighting through vertigo. Blinking hard, I lunge for the spot where I think Marshall's arm should be and hit nothing but air. Bumping into a corner of his desk, I bounce off and fall sideways into one of the purple chairs.

"Oh my God!" Stefan says, laughing but not making any effort to help me or check if I'm hurt.

Marshall turns at the sound of the commotion and says into the phone while staring down at me, "You know, maybe that would be for the best.... Okay, we'll see you in a few minutes."

"No!" I howl as soon as I'm sure the call's been ended.

He grasps my elbow and helps me from the chair. "What's the matter with you?" he scolds. "Sit down on that sofa over there and don't move until your husband gets here. I won't be responsible for any bodily harm you do to yourself while flailing around like an idiot."

Stefan's doubled over at this point. "You're married to a minister?" he wheezes at me. "Well, that just takes the cake. Holy shit. Pun intended!"

"You! Shut up!" Marshall snaps at him. "And if I were you, I'd be invisible when her husband does arrive. He's going to want to know who's responsible for this, and I can't say I'll stop him from doing anything to you, if the spirit moves him. Go down the street and get yourself a coffee or something."

Stefan sobers immediately and goes into a pout. "But

I'm not finished asking Peyton my questions!" he protests. "I have a right to know some things!"

"Why don't you ask your buddy Drex? Seems like he knows plenty and doesn't mind blabbing his big mouth." Marshall points to his office door and beyond, toward the double-glass front door of the gallery. "Now, go!" He gets up to watch Stefan's exit but immediately returns to the sofa when he's sure the artist is gone.

Turning his knees toward me, he says, "Peyton, Peyton, Peyton. What am I going to do with you?"

"Uh…" I'm not sure if this is surreal because I may have a concussion, or if it's just legitimately surreal.

"Are you freaking out because your husband doesn't know about all this?"

I sigh and grumble into my lap, "He knows everything." Well, I guess not *everything*.

Marshall pats my arm. "What are you worried about, then? The couple of times I've met him, he seems like a nice, understanding guy. Perfect for someone like you."

I wish I could justifiably take offense to that, but I know exactly what he means, and he's right.

"So, you had a one-night stand with Stuffing."

My head snaps up. I haven't called him Drex's private name for him in ages.

"Yeah, I know about the nickname. And I could just kill that slimeball Drex for ratting you out. I thought he was a nice guy."

"Well—"

"No! You don't do that to someone you care—or cared —about. That's petty and disloyal and—and mean!" He scratches at his perfectly groomed, white beard. Then he curses under his breath and says, "Listen, Princess, I'd drop

Stefan Svadjlenka like the dog turd he is if I could. Trust me, I would, but—"

I blush. "Marshall, don't worry about it. It was my mistake, and now I'm living with it. I'd never ask you to do something like that. It's… Well, it is what it is."

"That's bullshit is what *that* is," he replies. "Now, let me finish. I can't afford to stop doing business with him, but that doesn't mean *you* have to do business with him, okay? From now on, I'll deal with him. You focus on our other artists."

The weight that lifts from my chest makes me more lightheaded than I felt right before I ate the sales floor. "Really?" I don't even pretend that I'm brave or strong enough *not* to take him up on his offer.

"Really. He's so ghastly to you. If I'd had any idea, I would have done something sooner. Why didn't you tell me?"

I'm not sure if he's talking about Stefan and Secret or Stefan in general or both, but the answers are all the same: "I just figured it was my problem, my responsibility to handle. And… I was afraid if you found out, I'd be… fired."

He shakes his head. "How long have you known me?"

"Seven years."

"Well, you obviously don't know me at all," he says sadly. "Otherwise, you wouldn't have worried a second about that. And if I'd had any idea how he talks to you, I would have nipped this in the bud like that." He snaps his fingers. "If for no other reason than that I don't want your husband mad at me."

That makes me laugh. "Brice? He's a teddy bear. And a pacifist. Usually." I can't even get him to kill spiders around the house. However, he might make an exception for Stefan.

"Uh-uh. He's scary, and I'm not talking about physically. I just said that stuff to Stefan, because I know he's a big pussy who lives in fear of breaking a nail and it would get him out of our faces for a while." He puts his hands together as if praying. "No, your husband has *God* on his side." He shivers. "You don't mess with that, no matter what you believe or don't believe."

"Oh, brother," I mutter, making a move to get up from the couch.

He holds me in place. "No way, sister. I promised the good Reverend that you'd sit tight 'til he gets here."

"What? I feel fine." I stop trying to rise, though. I'm too tired to win that fight. For the record, I say, "I sure as hell don't need my husband to come down here and take care of me. He can't make Stefan disappear or turn back time and make me less stupid, so there's nothing he can do to make me feel better."

"Bull. Shit." He holds my hand and pats it paternally. "You watch. As soon as he walks through that door, you're going to feel a million times better. And there's nothing wrong with that. Doesn't mean you're not capable of fighting your own battles. Just means that it always feels better when you know you don't have to go it alone."

I smile, glad to be given permission to be a little dependent, for once.

"It also helps to know that your husband can beat up your former baby-daddy, if he so chooses," he adds mischievously.

Amen!

~

The roses are back in my cheeks (Marshall's words, not mine) by the time Brice arrives. With Jared.

"Oh, geez. I didn't realize you were bringing backup," I

groan. "I passed out. Big deal. Not enough sleep plus light lunch plus…" I glance nervously at the vicar and my boss as I come to the end of the list of public reasons for my collapse, "Anyway, all that equals nosedive."

I take another long drink from the bottle of New York tap water I stole from Stefan's stash. "Check out this pretentiousness," I say lightly, pointing to the fancy plastic bottle. "You wouldn't believe how much this stuff costs. And it's literally tap water. From the New York Public Works Department."

Marshall gets up from the couch so Brice can sit next to me. While my husband sinks onto the cushions and studies my face, looking for—what? Bruising? Mismatched pupils? —*something*, I introduce Jared to Marshall and vice versa.

Jared gushes, "This place is so cool! And you guys are having a show tonight? Would I know the artist?"

The door chime sounds in the distance. Marshall and I both tense, but after he pokes his head through his office door to check who's arrived, he relaxes and announces, "Caterers are here." I move to get up, but he says, "No ma'am. I've got this. This is *my* artist's show, remember? Hey, Jared, wanna give me a hand with some tables? There are some free canapés in it for you."

The two of them leave, with Marshall closing the door behind him.

Gaaa! Alone with Reverend Intensity, I drop my head against the back of the sofa, waiting for the onslaught of questions. When he simply continues to stare at me, I laugh nervously and say, "So, you'll never believe what I found out today."

"Does it have something to do with your fainting?" he asks quietly.

"As a matter of fact, probably."

"Then I'm interested."

I give him the condensed, no-shouting, no-profanity, no-insults version of events, which takes all of about fifteen seconds and doesn't explain at all how I could have fainted, because it doesn't convey the intensity and trauma of the experience, but it does deliver the information about Stefan finding out about Secret from Drex and the not-so-shocking news about Stefan's sexuality and the welcome message that I don't have to work with Stefan ever again. Beginning tonight, apparently.

"Did you really faint?" he finally asks what feels like an eternity after I conclude my not-so-gripping tale.

"Yes!" I answer-laugh. "I really fainted. I also fell asleep in the bathroom earlier and let my shirt fall into the toilet, so it's been an eventful day."

Sitting sideways, facing me, his elbow against the back of the couch, he braces his head on his fingers and pinches the skin at his temple. "I don't think this is funny."

"It's a *little* funny. I mean, I literally fell asleep *in* the toilet. Then, because I don't want anyone here to know about *you know what* yet, I let the girl who discovered me in the bathroom believe that you and I were out late last night, partying, because we're Lutherans, and that's how we roll. But she kept calling you a preacher, which you know is my pet peeve, and then she said something about Stefan being a hot dick—I mean, a dick, yet hot—and I was like, 'Oh, don't go there,' but—"

"Peyton!" He doesn't say it loudly, but he says it forcefully enough to make me flinch.

"Sorry."

Eyes closed as if he's digging deep for patience, he states, "I don't need to know all that right now."

"Okay. But it's funny…"

Now he blinks hard and says dismissively, "Maybe it will be later. What I need to know right now is that you passed out—be it from lack of sleep or low blood sugar or stress or whatever—but that you weren't pushed or touched in any way by someone."

"Someone? You mean Stefan."

"Whomever."

Turning to face him and looking steadily into his eyes, I say, "I fainted. Period."

"Because I know, for whatever reason, that you're not telling me everything."

Now I look away.

"And while I'm not *okay* with that, I can accept it if I know you're not withholding something like *that* from me."

I pull his hand away from his forehead and hold both his hands in mine on the sliver of couch cushion between us. "Okay. I edited out some nasty language and gratuitous mudslinging for your benefit."

His nostrils flare.

"*But* I didn't change any of the events. I really did get overwhelmed by the situation—and lack of sleep, for sure—and lost consciousness. I don't feel sore anywhere, including my head, so I don't know if I hit anything on the way down. You'll have to ask Marshall about that. But nobody hit me. I promise. Okay?"

Nodding, he pulls me forward and wraps me in a nearly painful hug, with my head crammed up against his chest and my neck bent at an awkward angle. But as uncomfortable as it is, I let him hold on as long as he wants. He obviously needs this.

When he finally lets go, I ask, "So, what's the deal with bringing Jared? Is he part of your holy brute squad?"

He rolls his eyes at me. "He's here to drive your car

home, Heaven help him. If he hadn't been in my office, I would have brought Marilyn. So, no. No brute squad."

"Oh. Good. Because I don't think violence is cool or sexy, and I would have been really mad at you if you had come here with the plan of punching Stefan, or something like that."

Spine stiffening, he stands. "Where is the little potty mouth, anyway?"

I grab his hand and let him pull me up next to him. "Never mind. If Marshall's serious about running this show, I need to fill him in on a few things, and then I'd like to be chauffeured home, where I'm going to take a warm (not hot!) bath, eat a lot of food, and go to bed. Until Sunday."

"Am I involved in any part of this plan?" he asks, opening the office door.

"Uh, yeah! I can't sleep without my body pillow."

He rewards me by smiling for the first time since walking through the door. Marshall was so right. I *do* feel a million times better now.

22

THE DRUNK DIAL

The typical woman breathes regularly for the first time in months once she hits her second trimester of pregnancy. The risk of miscarriage is dramatically reduced, so she gets to tell everyone her good news (or stand by while her husband tells everyone—and I mean *everyone*, including strangers in the grocery store, where she's no longer allowed to go unaccompanied, in case she tries to lift something heavier than a can of coffee); morning sickness and other pesky first trimester symptoms generally disappear; her energy level increases; sex is great and not yet impeded by a ginormous belly; she has a cute little bump, not yet the aforementioned uncomfortable ginormous belly; and everyone tells her how wonderful she looks. It's an exciting time for the normal woman.

Of course, I'm not normal. No, my anxiety level has ramped up 300 percent since I hit Week Twelve. I carry two pregnancy books in my tote bag at all times and consult them constantly to make sure what I'm feeling or not feeling is normal and nothing to be worried about. When the books give me possibly conflicting or confusing answers, I call the doctor's office. When the books give me matching answers, I still call the doctor's office to make sure nothing's changed since their publication dates (hey, things change all the time!).

Was I this nervous when I was pregnant with Secret? No. And look where it got her. If there's a problem, I'm going to know right away this time. There had to have been signs last time that something was wrong, but I was just too clueless and complacent (and possibly apathetic) to detect them. If only I had been more vigilant... Well, this time, nothing's getting by me. I don't give a crap how many sighs I have to hear from Dr. Walsh's nurse. Okay, I care a little bit, but that's not going to stop me from calling.

Meanwhile, the biggest worry on Brice's mind: to know or not to know the baby's sex. Gosh! I wish that was all that kept me awake at night. And I wish he'd stop burdening me with his arguments for and against finding out. I've already told him I'll do whatever he wants to do. Frankly, I can't concern myself with something so petty. Being pregnant is serious, busy work.

Every single day, I have to eat right (no shellfish, lunch meat, alcohol, caffeine, or 7,000 other things) and get enough exercise (but not too much) and remember not to participate in dangerous activities (hot tubbing and horse-back riding and skiing) and stay away from cat litter (that's the easiest one, since we don't have a cat) and get plenty of sleep on my *left* side (not my back) and practice good posture (never one of my strengths) and take frequent breaks away from my desk (to prevent varicose veins) and keep my skin moisturized (to prevent stretch marks) and pee constantly (to prevent bladder infections, not to mention embarrassing accidents) and wear hideous, low-heeled shoes and take my prenatal vitamin and about a billion other things that I'm sure I'm either forgetting or screwing up.

But sure, Brice, let's pile another thing on my plate. I wish he'd just make the decision on his own and let me know what it's gonna be. I'm going to be focused on something much more important than reproductive parts on that ultrasound day. I'm going to be looking for a heartbeat.

Other than telling random strangers about the fetus growing inside me and his ever-growing pros and cons list about finding out the baby's sex before the delivery, I have to admit he's been a model dad-to-be. It may have something to do with the book I woke up to find him reading in bed late one night when he thought I was dead to the world (*My Crazy, Pregnant Wife!*) or maybe he's actually gotten some decent advice from veterans like Dad and Lonnie (doubtful) or maybe his seminary training or experience as a prison warden are applicable in unexpected ways or maybe this nurturing thing just comes naturally to him.

Whatever it is, it's working. I can grit my teeth and put up with a lot of repeated agonizing about "But how are we going to plan ahead for sex-specific things, if we don't find out?" when he's willing to drop everything to satisfy my food cravings or massage my lower back or rub lotion on my belly. It's a decent trade-off.

Of course, he has no idea how often between our monthly appointments I call the doctor to ask questions, nor does he know how I walk around in a constant state of worry (and I know that's not good for the baby, either, so spare me the lecture). What's the point in telling him everything I'm thinking and feeling at every minute? Then he'd have to speed-read his little secret book and upgrade to the one called *My Certifiably Insane Pregnant Wife!*

He'd also refer me to his favorite answer: prayer. As if I'm not doing that practically every waking minute already. Plus, if he hasn't thought of all these things himself, then I don't want to be the one to plant the seeds of worry. One of us worrying is enough. Let him concentrate on whether it's worth it to piss off everyone we know by waiting until delivery day to find out if we're having a Meirwen (girl) or a Jordan (boy). Or any of the other twenty names we've tossed around that all sound unisex to me, but that Brice is very particular about whether they're boy or girl names.

When I'm with him, I put on my happiest or most contented face and pretend like names and girl or boy parts and nursery colors are the heaviest things on my mind, too. He has to know otherwise, given what happened to Secret, but neither one of us is talking about it.

Today I'm in his office, baring my belly to him so we can laugh about how ridiculously plump it's grown seemingly overnight, when Jared comes through the open door.

"Oh! Sorry!" he says, quickly turning to leave when he sees what's going on.

Brice gives me one final pat and replies, "No, you're fine. Come on in."

I lower my shirt and perch on the edge of the desk. It's time for him to leave for the day, so I don't want to get too comfortable and give him the idea that he can linger over whatever it is he's doing (looks like he's already selecting songs for next Sunday's service—no Katy Perry, I notice). We're due at Mom's for Sunday dinner in half an hour.

Now he lightly asks Jared, "What'd you do this time?"

The vicar guiltily shuffles his feet. "Oh. You've already heard?"

Chagrined, Brice stops typing. "No. I was kidding. Seriously, Jared?"

He rubs the side of his nose. "This time, it wasn't really my fault."

"It's *never* your fault. Let me guess. It's Peyton's fault. Because she's been too busy lately to babysit you."

I cringe. Yikes. That was kind of harsh.

Jared seems to think so, too. He crosses his arms over his chest and pushes his glasses higher on his nose. "I don't need a babysitter, and even if I did, that wouldn't have prevented this problem, because it wasn't my fault!"

"Just tell me what happened so I can fix it and get on with my weekend."

"Forget it! I'll fix it myself. Not that it can be fixed."

"Do I even want to know what that means?" Brice mutters before stating more loudly, "You have to tell me what happened, even if it can't be fixed, as you claim."

When the pastor-in-training simply stares at his superior, I want so badly to step in, to make peace, but I know it's best if I keep my mouth closed. It would actually be best if I left the room and let them have it out without an audience, but I'm dying to know what Jared did and what Brice's reaction is going to be this time, so I keep a low profile.

Unfortunately, Jared hasn't forgotten about me. Looking from me to Brice, he says from the side of his mouth, "It's kind of confidential, if you know what I mean."

Damn.

My husband surprises me, though, by saying, "Peyton's a good secret keeper. Spill it, Laszewski."

He looks unsure but obeys. "Okay. So, you know how the ladies in the altar guild are supposed to put the non-alcoholic shot glasses in the very center of the Communion shot glass holder-thingy?"

"Yes…"

"Well, they screwed up this morning when they were preparing the Communion stuff—"

"No, no, no." Brice braces his elbows on his desk and puts his face in his hands.

"Yes, yes, yes! So, when I offered the cups to Mrs. Peretta, she took the wrong kind… for someone like her."

"Please tell me this is a joke."

Wincing, he holds up his phone and sets it on the edge of Brice's desk like it's a live grenade. "She just drunk-dialed me. I didn't recognize the number, so I let it go to voicemail. I saved it, if you want to listen to it."

I can't help but be thrilled when Brice *does* want to listen to it. I mean, it's horrible that an alcoholic would fall off the wagon due to a mistake like this. I can't help it, though, that I want to hear what it sounds like when a sixty-seven-year-old woman drunk-dials a twenty-six-year-old vicar.

"Vicar Leshefshki, I thought this uz your nummer. Hey! I gotta feelin' I took the wrong kinda Commun-Commun—glash this mornin' at shursh, cuz I came home'n wanned ta have a few drinks. I wish you'da been around, cuz I'd like ta get ta know ya little better. Keep meanin' ta ashk ya ta come over for dinner sometime. I useta have Pashtor Norfam over all the time, but he's married now an' awful busy. I think it's so shweet that he's gonna be a daddy. 'Dja hear 'bout tha time we all surprised him for his birthday? It was a good time. But I bet you know how ta have good times, too. Heh-heh."

Brice plops his head on his desk and beats his forehead on his blotter.

"Annaway, I guesh you're alread' busy or doin' somethin' fun that

young guys like you like ta do, if ya know what I mean. But if ya get this meshage an' don't have annathin' better ta do, swing on by my housh. My address is… It's… Well, it's in the shursh d'rect'ry. Or you can ask Pashtor for d'rections. Bye!"

I cover my mouth and pinch my nose as Brice turns his head on his desk and looks over at me. My eyes water. But I will not laugh. I know it's not funny. At all. But it sort of is, if you disregard the fact that someone who's been sober for more than two decades isn't any longer, thanks to one innocent mistake.

He groans and closes his eyes.

Jared hangs up on the automated voicemail lady, who wants to know what he wants to do with the message, and says to Brice, "So, what do you want to do?"

Eyes still closed, he replies, "I want to go to my in-laws' house and eat roast beef and mashed potatoes and dinner rolls." His mention of food makes my stomach growl loudly. "Exactly. Then I want to go home and fall asleep watching the second half of the Sunday night football game. That's what I want to do."

Looking worried, Jared points out, "But we have to do something about Mrs. Peretta, right? We can't just let her—"

"I know that, Jared!" he snaps, lifting his head from the desk and running a hand through his hair. "Obviously. We have to go to Mrs. Peretta's house, sober her up, and decide what we're going to do to help her stay that way, including getting in touch with her family and letting them know. *That's* going to be a fun phone call. Then tomorrow, you and I are going to call an emergency meeting of the altar guild, explain in general terms—meaning *no names*, Jared—what happened so that everyone understands the importance of paying attention to detail when preparing the Lord's table for Communion and training new people how to do it. And then we're going to pray that nobody else was affected by this colossal cluster-bomb."

"But you agree that this wasn't my fault, right? This time."

Readily, Brice acknowledges, "Amazingly, not your fault. But does it matter? It's all our faults, really. We're responsible for each other, and when something like this happens, we let people down in the worst way. We may not even ever know how many people we've let down in this case, unless they come forward. Do you think Mrs. Peretta's the only recovering alcoholic in the congregation who took the quote-unquote 'wrong' Communion today?"

Well, when he puts it that way, it kind of takes all the funny out of it.

I put a hand on his shoulder. "Do you want me to come with you?" I ask.

He shakes his head. "Uh, no. You can't know about this. You *don't* know about this."

"Right."

I can't un-know the flirting tone Mrs. Peretta used in her message to Jared, though. Oh, gosh. It's starting to be funny again. I clear my throat and think serious thoughts (a Republican White House, an ice cream shortage, the cancelation of *Modern Family*).

Miserably, Brice shrugs on his coat and says to me, "Tell everyone I said hi."

"I'll bring home some food for you," I offer lamely, pecking him on the lips.

He half-smiles. "Thanks."

In the parking lot, as he and Jared are getting into the Jeep, I hear the vicar say, "So, what's our strategy?" and almost laugh out loud. Mrs. Peretta's going to think she's died and gone to Heaven when those two show up on her doorstep. Their "strategy" will involve patience and lots of strong coffee.

23

GIRLS JUST WANNA HAVE FUN

*Y*eah, I'm an excellent secret keeper, but sometimes you need a good story to break the ice when you haven't been around your two best friends in weeks in the middle of one of the most important times in your life. So I've changed the names to protect the innocent—and the drunk—but I've just finished telling Mitzi and Jen about Mrs. Peretta and the Communion wine debacle as we finish our Mexican food feast, which is a precursor to some intense Christmas shopping.

I can tell Jen didn't really want to laugh at the story; she wanted to stay mad at me for my weeks of neglect and physical absence from her life. But when I told them how Brice described the widow's behavior when he and Jared arrived at her tiny house and how even he couldn't keep a straight face when he told me that she laid a wet one on Jared the minute he walked through her front door, her resolve crumbled, and she almost shot margarita from her nose.

"I gotta meet this Jared guy," she says, while mopping herself up. "He sounds like a spaz."

"He's not, really," I defend him. "He's just so young,

even for his age, and he acts and speaks before he thinks, so that's constantly getting him into trouble. But he's such a nice guy. Means well. Has a heart of platinum."

"And is a jewel-encrusted pain in Brice's ass, it sounds like," Jen adds.

"Pretty much. And I just haven't had the time or energy to spend as much time with him as I used to, so he's been finding other ways to keep busy, and that's usually not a good thing for him to do."

Turning to Mitzi, Jen says deceptively lightly, "Well, Mitz, we kind of know how that feels, right? Maybe we could take the good vicar out on the town and start a Peyton's Rejects Club."

To my surprise, Mitzi laughs. "Yeah! Well, she can't do anything fun anymore, anyway, since she's preggers, so we might as well hang out with someone who can keep up with us."

I laugh good-naturedly, even though their half-serious kidding hurts. Instead of getting all defensive and ruining our evening, though, I stick with the topic of Jared. "Yeah! Maybe you guys could go on a double date. You and Jared"—I point to Mitzi—"and you and Mr. Police-man"—I direct to Jen—"You *are* still seeing him, by the way, right? You were last week, when we talked on the phone."

She smiles quietly and plays with the ice in her drink. "Yes, I'm still seeing *plenty* of Mitch."

"Oooh! Sounds fun," I say.

"Yeah, especially the hanging out naked part," Mitzi adds, kicking Jen under the table.

"Yeah, that's what I meant." I watch the two of them give each other knowing looks and realize I'm missing an inside joke. "Wait. We're talking about sex, right?"

Mitzi giggles. "Nope. I mean, yeah, they do that, too, but Mitch likes to just *hang out* around the house. Naked."

I grab Jen's hand. "He's an exhibitionist?"

She shrugs me off. "Yeah. Well, sort of. I mean, he doesn't go to nudist colonies for the weekend or anything creepy like that. But he prefers not wearing clothes when he's at home."

"So now *you* prefer not wearing clothes when you're at home?" I question. That's the kind of chameleonic behavior she would have made fun of Mitzi for demonstrating in the not-so-distant past.

Coolly, she replies, "When I'm with Mitch, yeah. Not when I'm home alone. But I feel silly when he's walking around in the buff, and I'm fully clothed."

"Can't you compromise and wear underwear?"

She shoots me a dirty look. "Just because you're not comfortable with your body doesn't mean those of us who *are* comfortable are weird."

"I tried it the other day," Mitzi says. "It was weird. No offense, Jen," she quickly tacks on. "It's just not for me. I couldn't figure out how to *arrange* myself! And I was alone. I can't even imagine if someone else was sitting there with me, seeing *all that*."

I laugh and ask her, "What were you doing during this naked time? Not ironing, I hope. That could be dangerous."

She shrugs. "Just watching TV. With all the blinds closed, of course."

"Der," Jen intones, draining the rest of her margarita. "Listen. It's not like Mitch and I sit around discussing politics or watching PBS in the nude. We're usually *doing* things. And then we don't put our clothes back on when we we're finished, so we'll get something to eat."

"You *eat* naked?" I say, a little more loudly than I intend.

Two older women at the next table turn to look at us and then titter to each other.

Taking a deep breath, Jen answers patiently, "Yes. All the time. What's the big deal?"

"But your boobs! And his… stuff! And…" I can't finish for laughing.

Mitzi pipes up, "I have a theory that it's because he's a cop, so he has to wear so much stuff all day long—you know, all the parts of his uniform—so when he comes home, he just wants to be free. It's kind of a more extreme version of me taking off my bra and pantyhose as soon as I get through my front door."

"It has nothing to do with his job," Jen snaps. "He just likes to be naked. And I do too. You're just a couple of prudes."

"Hey, at least I tried it!" Mitzi objects.

They both look at me. I laugh all over again as I try to imagine Brice and me chillin' in our birthday suits. Given some of his favorite lounging positions and my unladylike postures, it wouldn't be a pretty sight. Plus, as often as people just "pop by for a visit," we'd have to be crazy to attempt it. I blush at the idea of Jared—or anyone—catching a glimpse of us through the windows on either side of the front door.

"Prude!" the two of them accuse in unison while pointing at me.

"Whatever." I dismiss their chants while fanning myself with my napkin. "Brice and I aren't prudes. But we have to be ready for visitors at any time."

Jen abruptly stops chanting to ask, "When was the last time you two had sex somewhere other than your bed? Or any bed?"

Damn. I was going to say the bed in the guest room at

his mom's. Hmmm… There was the cruise. Still on a bed, though.

Mitzi giggles. "Ohhh! You can't remember!"

"Or it's never happened, more like," Jen observes.

"Shut up."

"Good grief!" she grins. "At least tell me it's not all missionary position. You don't have to take that so literally, you know. God will understand if you mix it up a little."

I blot sweat from my upper lip and say, "We were supposed to go off-roading earlier this fall—you know, that place where things got a little *intense* before we were married?—and I was really looking forward to recreating that scenario, only minus the guilt. But then we found out I'm pregnant, and—"

"So? You act like there's crime tape across your cooter because you have a pea in the pod," Jen charges.

"No, I don't! I'll have you know that we still have sex—a lot—now that I'm pregnant."

"Missionary bed sex," she mutters, nudging me so I'll know she's teasing.

"Well, so what? It's still good. It still *counts.*"

"What happened to the girl who used to tell us stories that had us questioning physics and anatomy as we knew them? Remember Chad?" She pokes me in the shoulder.

Mitzi says dreamily, "Yeah, you were my hero."

"I vaguely remember Chad, yes," I quip. He was a tool, but he had quite the tool. The mature me says, "That's just it, though. Half the time I was drunk out of my mind when I would do those crazy things. Plus, I was a whole lot younger and a lot more limber. And so was Chad."

Tsking, Mitzi says, "You act like you and Brice are eighty years old."

I don't want to admit it, but sometimes it *feels* like we are.

We like what we like, and it's satisfying, and if it's not broke, don't fix it. Or bend it in odd positions.

"Yeah!" Jen injects. "And I'm sorry, but I know your husband well enough to know that he can physically handle something a little more advanced than Remedial Sex 101."

"Oh, you do, do you?"

"I do. The man could be on the cover of *Men's Fitness* and no one would have a clue that a) he's a pastor and b) he has no imagination in the bedroom."

"Hey! Why is it his fault?" I take offense on his behalf.

"So, you admit that *you're* the prude then?"

When I merely grit my teeth after falling into her trap, she laughs evilly.

"You got married and forgot everything you knew about fun sex. Maybe you should take a page out of mine and Mitch's book and slink around the house naked for a couple of hours. See how that spices things up. I couldn't tell you the last time we had sex in a bed."

"Gross," Mitzi moans.

"You need every page in your book to help hide your naughty bits from the mailman peeking in the windows," I mutter.

That gets all of us laughing so hard that our server comes over and hands us our tickets as a gentle hint that we've lingered long enough over our now-empty plates.

As we're leaving the restaurant, Jen loops her arm through mine and says, "Well, at least I know what I'm getting you for Christmas this year."

Mitzi grabs my other arm, grins, and says, "Me, too."

I make a mental note to exchange gifts with them in a very private setting.

24

THE NUTCRACKER SEDUCTION

*W*e don't talk about sex. I mean, I think about it a lot, and we do have it often, and I talk about it with Mitzi and Jen, but Brice and I, we don't talk about sex. There's no *need* to talk about it. It would be like having an in-depth conversation about... steak. We both like it; there are several ways to have it, although we tend to have it the same way all the time; sometimes it's better than other times; and though we may vary the recipe, we usually have it the way we know we like it. What's there to talk about?

Here's where the comparison ends, though. Even though I think a conversation about steak would be silly, the thought of having that conversation wouldn't make me break out into a sweat.

I was a lot less sweaty before my best friends brought to light some issues that I've been trying to ignore.

You see, I know everything about him. And he knows a lot about me. Not just the good stuff, either; he knows a lot of the bad, too. He was around for some of the worst of it. And I've told him plenty more. Just not all. What's the point? I'm not keeping anything from him that would affect him or our marriage. He doesn't need to know about every stupid thing I've done while under the influence of alcohol, or worse. All that's in the past. Dredging it up isn't going to do anything but cause trouble. Plus, what I consider naughty is laughable in the eyes of most people nowadays. Unfortunately, it's not really as laughable in his eyes. It's all relative.

But I've sort of reinvented myself since being with him. Most of that new person is someone I like and would like to keep around. But I have to admit that there are parts of my old self—parts that he doesn't know because I've never introduced him to them—that I miss. To tell him this, though, I'll have to admit that I haven't really been myself around him for the past two-plus years.

I think it would be easier for me to prance around the house nude than broach that subject.

So, of course, I'm going to take the easy route.

Well, eas*ier*. It's not quite "easy" to strip down to nothing when you have a bulging belly and heavier-than-normal, achy jugs that require a herculean amount of support and then walk down the hall into the middle of the living room as if there's nothing unusual about your behavior.

Oh, gosh! The blinds! They're still slanted slightly open.

I duck back into the hallway and peek around the corner. Brice is prone on the couch with his eyes closed, a book lying face down on his chest as he listens to music. I know he's awake, because he's smiling, and his foot is swishing back and forth to the beat. "Pumped Up Kicks" isn't necessarily the song I would have chosen for my seduction routine, but if I waited for every part of this situation to be perfect—like, oh, I don't know, the blinds to be closed—I'd never do it.

However, I am *not* a prude. That's the whole point of this, isn't it? To show Brice who he really married. I'm not kinky or depraved, by any stretch, but I used to like a little variety in my repertoire. He'd never know it, based on the way I've always been with him, because I've gotten lazy. I've gotten used to letting him take control and do his sweet, tender thing, which is nice. Always nice. I don't want him to think I don't like it or that I'm criticizing his technique. But maybe he needs to get a glimpse of *my* techniques, the techniques of the woman who used to be Mitzi's "hero." Not that that's saying much. But still.

All right, Peyton. Showtime. Just go over there, pull the cord on those blinds to close them all the way, and do what needs to be done. Introduce the real you to your husband. The you who likes to be on top. The you who doesn't even necessarily need her partner to do anything to get the job done. Remember her? She was fun. I bet Brice would like her. A lot.

Shit. I'm starting to get really cold standing here in the hallway, giving myself this lame pep talk. Time to channel the topless sixteen-year-old girl at the waterpark and wield some sexual power.

Back straight, head high, I stride into the living room, cross to the window, and pull the blinds shut. The *zip* and *clack* makes Brice open his eyes in the middle of whistling along to the song. His puckered lips fall slack. Then he startles at my appearance. His book falls onto the floor.

"W-what's the matter? Is something wrong?"

Great start. He thinks I'm standing here naked to show him a boil on my ass, or something?

Still, I maintain my confident posture while I push him back onto the couch as he attempts to sit up. Despite feeling ridiculous and cold and… exposed, I kick his book out of my way and rub the length of my body against his as I lie down on top of him. My bump is a little too big now for me to lie on my stomach, so I have to shift so that

I'm more on my side with my butt against the back of the couch.

He laughs nervously. "Uh, what's going on?"

"*This* is going on," I answer stupidly in my normal voice. I never have been good at "husky," so I don't even bother trying to pull it off now.

"Okay." I'm relieved and thrilled when he kisses me and rubs his hands up and down my body. Then he whispers, "Let's go back to the bedroom."

With extreme control, I manage to keep the exasperation from my tone when I say, "No, I want to stay out here."

He rests a palm on my belly. "Really? Because this doesn't seem very comfortable. For you."

Unfortunately, he's right; this *isn't* very comfortable. But I'll be damned if I'm going to give up that easily.

"It's fine. Now, shhhhh…" I guide his hand lower and cover his lips with mine.

He breaks away with a loud sucking noise. "But what if someone comes over?"

"They won't."

"But what if?"

I sigh. "We'll be like normal people and pretend we're not home."

"The Jeep's in the driveway, because of all the baby stuff in the garage."

"We could be away in my car. Or out taking a walk."

"It's snowing like crazy out there! And we never take your car anywhere. Unless we want to get stranded and end up walking in a snowstorm."

"So? They don't know that. Whoever *they* are."

"And they'll be able to see us through that window by the front door."

"No, they won't. We'll lie here really still until they leave."

"They can still see us."

"Arggh!" I push against his chest and look down my straight arms at him. "Oh, my gosh. Never mind!" But I can't seem to get my legs un-wedged from between him and the couch.

He cups one of my breasts. "I don't want to 'never mind.' I'm just trying to be practical."

"Yeah, well, you've *practically* killed the mood, so…" I scissors-kick my legs to try to free them. During this flailing, one leg breaks loose unexpectedly, sending my knee crashing into his crotch. Hard.

"Gaa!" he groans, both of his hands flying to the affected area. "Oh, Chicago!"

Immediately contrite, I croon, "Sorry! Oh, shit." I stop moving on top of him and put my hands on either side of his maroon face. "Babe, I didn't mean to do that!"

He nods and rasps, "I know. Just. Need. To sit up."

I somehow manage to find the strength and muscle control to roll off him and land on my hands and knees on the floor in front of the couch. He swings his legs around, curls into a ball, and rocks quietly with his chin rested on his knees.

Stroking his hair, I repeat, "I'm so sorry," while kneeling next to his legs.

"I know," he mumbles through gritted teeth. He blinks rapidly.

After several cycles of this torturous dialogue, he straightens, puffing out his cheeks as he exhales slowly. Blinking the water from his eyes, he smiles sickly at me. "I think I'm okay now."

For about the thousandth time, I say, "I'm sorry. It was an accident."

"I hope so," he chuckles, averting his eyes from me.

That's when I remember I'm still stark naked. And I have no idea how to gracefully make that not true.

"Uh, I think I'll go put some clothes on now," I announce, springing up and jogging through the room and down the hall, trying not to worry about how unattractive it must look.

I pull on some maternity yoga pants and one of Brice's football jerseys and try to decide if I have the guts to just stay back here and pretend like none of that happened. I'm afraid that would seem even more peculiar, if that's possible. Plus, I really feel awful for hurting him. I'm not even mad at him anymore for ruining my fun. It wasn't really fun, anyway. It was awkward and stressful and contrived. Hell, maybe I'm *not* that girl anymore. Maybe I'm Missionary Molly, the prudish pastor's wife whose definition of sexy is keeping the lights on or having sex on top of the covers (but never both at the same time).

As I'm mourning my dearly departed mojo, Brice limps into the bedroom and gingerly sits down next to me on the side of the bed. He grabs my hand. "Hey, I'm sorry about… out there."

"No, *I'm* sorry! I'm the one who kneed you in the nuts." With my free hand, I brush away a tear that I didn't even realize had formed until it dropped onto my face and trickled down my nose.

"Well, that wouldn't have happened, maybe, if I'd shut up. About everything." Before I can agree, he rushes on, "But, you know, people sit on that couch."

I can't help but laugh. "Yeah. People do."

"No, I mean, like *people*. Church people and— and I don't know… People!"

I look into his earnest face. "I get it," I say, nodding understandingly. "It was stupid. I'm sorry."

"I'm just not comfortable expressing our love somewhere that feels like public property to me."

"But this is our home!" I object. "The walls and floors and roof may belong to the church, but that's *our* couch and this is *our* bed, and we *live* here and eat here and 'express our love' here, whatever that means."

"You know what I mean."

"Yeah. I know what you mean. Have sex. But you can't even bring yourself to say it. Is it that terrible?"

"What? No! I just don't like referring to it that way."

I snort.

"I'm serious! 'Having sex' is what college kids do in back rooms during keggers."

"No, that's 'fucking.'"

He winces. "Please."

"Hey, if you're going to get all technical, then let's be precise with our word choice."

"The point is, I make love to you. That's what I should have said earlier. I was tongue-tied. I'm all flustered by what just happened." He takes a deep breath. "What just happened?"

I'm sullen again. "I dunno. I was trying to have some fun, that's all. I used to be fun."

"I think you're fun."

I pick at the NFL logo on the jersey and mutter, "That's because you didn't know the old me. She was *more* fun."

He sighs. "I don't know what to say to that. What do you want me to say? And what brought this on, anyway? And stop doing that to my jersey." He pulls my hand away from the embroidered logo.

Keeping my eyes on my lap, I tell him a (very) small portion of the conversation at the Mexican restaurant, ending with, "Long story short, I've become a prude. I was horrified at the thought of Jen and Mitch eating naked. I was sickened when I found out Stefan is gay. And I tapped that. When did I become so stodgy and homophobic, anyway?"

"First of all, can we *not* talk about your 'tapping' anyone but me? I mean, I know you have, but… "

"Sorry."

"And having a concept of what's right and wrong *for you* doesn't make you stodgy and homophobic."

"Well, I couldn't tell you the last time I had sex some place other than a boring old bed, much less in some position other than man-on-top. I'm just chewy, old, pan-fried steak. No garnish, no sauce, no pizazz. Lying there on the plate, doing nothing."

"What are you talking about?" I can tell by his tone of voice and the look on his face that he's frantically trying to remember the chapter in *My Crazy, Pregnant Wife!* that warns about one's wife comparing herself to bland, unappetizing food, and he's coming up blank. That's how crazy I am: they don't even have a chapter crazy enough for me.

When I can't explain myself through my tears, he says, "I was with you all the way up until the steak part, so let's just forget about that and focus on something I understand."

I nod and wipe my nose on the back of my hand.

"You don't have to be swinging naked from the light fixtures to be fun. I mean, did you really feel *fun* when you were single like Jen and Mitzi?" I shrug, unwilling to admit that life wasn't that great back then. "Probably not," he answers for me. "You were living a fairly normal life with its fun moments, but it was still *life*. You're romanticizing it now, because *they* romanticize it to you: 'Yeah, we're single and free and fun!' but I bet a lot of times, they're lonely and wish they had a little less 'fun' and a lot more stability."

"I know," I sniffle, "but when I was single, I was the one they looked up to. We were in it together, but I was sort of the ringleader. Now, I'm just the boring, pregnant pastor's wife who sometimes tags along and makes them feel awkward about drinking too much."

He hands me a tissue from the bedside table next to him.

"You should see them!" I continue, pulling apart the plies of tissue. "They used to barely tolerate each other. I was their common bond, but otherwise, they wouldn't have ever hung out together. Now they have inside jokes just between the two of them, and sometimes they even agree with each other about stuff. Especially when they're saying how boring and lame I am. They definitely agree with each other about that."

He puts his arm around my shoulders and squeezes me up against him. "Hon, you are not boring. *This* is not boring."

I can't help but laugh at that.

"Do you really think your life is that dull? I mean, you have a busy career, and when you're not at work, you're at the church, helping out with something, and when you're not at the church, you're with your family—who could never be described as boring in a million years! And yes, you're a pastor's wife. You make that sound like it's a fate worse than death. I, for one, thank God every day that you are. And you're going to be a mother, which is exciting. Maybe not to them, but it is to us. I thought you were excited about it, anyway."

"I am!"

"Then who cares what their definition of 'exciting' is? Having my man parts shoved up into my stomach is not what I call 'fun' or 'exciting,' m'kay?" He kisses the top of my head while I crack up at that statement. When I stop laughing, he adds, "Anyway, think of what you have that they don't. You've got it figured out. You're no longer out there, wading through the quagmire that is dating and casual sex and trying to find someone whose weird habits— like letting it all hang out or singing pop tunes in the shower—"

"Or calling sex, 'expressing your love'?"

He laughs at himself. "Hey. I took that back, okay? C'mon. Haven't you busted my balls enough tonight?"

"I said I was sorry!"

Wrapping his arms around me again, he hugs me tightly. "I'm just giving you a hard time."

After a few minutes of sitting in his arms and thinking, I finally get up the nerve to admit, "I miss my friends. And I hate that they miss me, too, because they think I'm a totally different person." I break down completely now, hiding my face in my hands and sobbing.

"Oh, boy," he mutters, rubbing my back. "Come on, now. Don't get so upset. This is all just temporary, a blink of an eye in the big picture. You're all adjusting to your new roles in life and in your friendship. Things'll settle down once this becomes the new norm."

That makes me wail louder. The thought of this dynamic between the three of us being the new norm is unbearable.

"What'd I say?"

"Nothing," I reassure him, resolving to get control of

myself. I already hurt his feelings enough earlier by making him think being his wife isn't fun or good enough.

Plus, I don't want to dwell on this any longer. He's trying so hard to comfort me, but I'm inconsolable, and it's not his fault. We could be here all night, with him unintentionally digging the hole deeper and deeper.

I swipe under my eyes and take a deep breath. "It's fine. Things change, right? Most of the time for the better."

"Yeah. Exactly."

It's just so hard to know the difference between a change for the better and change for change's sake. And I can't keep track of which is which in my life anymore.

With my ear pressed against his heart, I contemplate that riddle, trying to sort one from the other.

After a while, Brice takes a breath, as if he's going to talk, but all that comes out is, "Hmm."

I wait for it, knowing he's pondering something and that he's trying to work it out in his mind before putting it to words.

Eventually, he asks, "So, when Jen and her boyfriend…?"

"Mitch," I supply, pushing away from his chest and looking up into his face.

"Yeah. So when Jen and Mitch dine *al fresco*…"

I roar at the description, but he talks over my laughter.

"Does the five-second rule apply if they drop something into their laps, or…?"

"Well, if they're practicing good table manners, they keep their napkins in their laps," I manage to sputter as I picture it.

Completely seriously, he shakes his head. "Even so… No, I'm sorry. That's just too weird. None of that has a place at the dinner table."

"That's what I said!"

Now he sounds uncharacteristically disdainful when he states, "I think some people try just a little too hard to be 'interesting.' I'd much rather have an intellectual discussion with my dinner than a side of… meatballs."

I fall backward onto the bed, laughing too hard to support myself in an upright position.

He half-turns and looks down at me. "I'm just saying…" Then, my giggles apparently contagious, he starts laughing, too.

If the people we know had any idea about some of the conversations in this house. Well, no one would accuse us of being boring.

25

GOODBYE, OLD FRIEND

"Come on, baby. Come on. You can do it. Come on! Do it! Come! On! You know what? You're a piece of shit, that's what you are. Thanks a lot for nothing!"

I bang the steering wheel of my little car and flop back into my seat, ignoring the stares of the other commuters as they speed past me while I sit on the shoulder with my hazards on.

"I'm done defending you," I tell it. "Next time Brice threatens to get rid of you, which is probably going to be today, when he has to come get me and drive me the rest of the way to work, you're gone. No more sentimentality. Gone. Scrap heap for you. You can't be trusted. You think I'm gonna trust you with my baby? No way. You'll strand us on the side of the road. Like this." A semi blows past, shaking the entire car.

"After everything I've done for you. Oil changes, tune ups, new tires, car washes. And this is how you repay me? So it's a little cold outside. Big frickin' whoop-dee-doo! If you'd start, you'd be a lot warmer."

Desperate now, I wheedle, "Come on. Prove me

wrong. Prove *Brice* wrong. *I* love you. He's really the one who doesn't trust you. But I think you're the best little car in the world. We've had such good times. Please, just start."

I twist the key in the ignition again and receive a sick coughing for my trouble.

"Shit. Those commercials about how long cars like you last are a bunch of lies. I thought I was going to get to pass you down to my children, like all those liars in the commercials, but no, you have to go and *die* on me."

At the word, "die," I choke, and my voice breaks.

"Damn you! Now, you're making me cry like a big, fat baby."

I take a deep breath and try to compose myself. I can't call Brice while I'm crying. Again. Last time that happened, he almost had a heart attack. And when he found out that I was upset about the lady at Subway being short with me when I changed my mind mid-order, he was pretty pissed. He tried to hide it, but I could tell by the way he was enunciating so precisely and not using any contractions ("It is going to be okay. Do not cry. You will feel better after you eat your sandwich") that he was trying to hide how annoyed he was. So I cried harder.

I'll be the first to admit that I'm a wet, hot mess lately. I cry because I'm happy; I cry because I'm sad; I cry when I'm worried (uh, all the time); I cry when I'm hungry (ditto); I cry when I'm embarrassed; I cry when I'm stressed or overwhelmed. It's exhausting for me and everyone around me. But it seems there's nothing I can do about it. I simply have to ride out the tears and explain, "I'm usually not like this. Just give me a minute, and I'll be fine." I've given up wearing eye makeup. Even waterproof is no match for my waterworks. They should bottle my tears (I have a never-ending supply, apparently) and market it as eye makeup remover.

"Bup-bup-bup-bup-bup," I babble while staring at the ceiling and waiting for this latest boo-hoo-fest to end. As long as I don't think about having to leave my friend on the side of the road like a sad, deserted puppy, I'll be okay.

Oh, my poor baby! I got this car as a high school graduation present. That was only eleven years ago. Okay, she was five years old when I got her, but still... Those damn commercials say... And I took good care of Lillibeth. (Yes, Lillibeth. That's her name.) But she's dead anyway.

"Waaaaaaaaaaaah!" I wail, draping myself over the steering wheel.

Now I'm going to have to get some unsightly minivan that makes me look and feel older than I am. Grocery baggers are going to start calling me "ma'am" and asking me if I need "help out." I'll never be carded again. Because I'll exude minivan-ness. "This lady," (yes, I'll be called "lady") "drives a minivan," the neon sign over my head will say. Worse, it'll be a white minivan. Like a big egg. A rolling symbol of my fertility.

"Why, Lillibeth?" I moan. "Why are you doing this to me? You're sentencing me to a life of sliding doors and rear hatches and DVD-players that swing down from the ceiling so my kids can rot their brains, even when we're on the go. Thanks a lot, Lillibeth. I thought we were friends."

Okay, anger dries up the tears. Unlikely and unexpected, but good to know.

"Dumb car. I hate you," I grumble while digging in my purse for my phone. I jab at the picture of Brice on the screen, wait through the rings, and say furiously when he answers, "My fucking car is fucking dead."

There's a pause (during which I'm sure he's closing his

eyes and counting to five, possibly pinching the bridge of his nose) and then, "Where are you?"

"On the side of the fucking interstate on my way to work."

"Okay. Calm down."

"I'm calm, all right? But it's shit-ass cold out here, and I'm late for work, and now I'm going to have to get a minivan."

He actually laughs. "What? Never mind. I'll be there in fifteen minutes. Stay in the car. Call a tow truck while you're waiting."

"I hope you're walking out the door while you're saying all this. I've already been sitting here for a while."

"Why?"

Sheepishly, I say, "I had to stop crying before I called you."

"Oh, Peyton. Marilyn, I'll be right back. Peyton's having car trouble."

Tragedy, trouble, what's the difference?

Still speaking to the secretary, he says, "If Kent gets here before I'm back, tell him everything's fine. I don't want him to worry." To me now, he directs, "You still there? You want to stay on the phone with me? I can call the tow truck later."

My sigh catches on a rogue sob, which undermines the strength I want to project when I say, "No, I'm okay. I'll call the truck. Just drive."

"You sure?"

"Yes!"

"Okay, I'll see you in a few."

"Wait! Why's my dad coming to meet with you?" I suddenly think to ask. But he's already gone.

Oh, well. Maybe it's better that I don't know. This morning's been stressful enough.

R.I.P., Lillibeth.

If she were a cartoon, she'd have black x's over her headlights, and there'd be a tongue sticking out from between her grille and front bumper. Since this is real life, though, the old girl's body *looks* pretty good. (Except for that butt-shaped dent on her hood, where one of my ex-boyfriends tried to do a *Dukes of Hazzard* move. And epically failed at it.) But *I* know she's dead, so she looks different to me. And sad.

I've tried to convince Brice to have the repair work done to get her up and running again (new engine and transmission), but he just laughed. Laughed. He said, "We could put a really big down payment on nice new car for that amount of money. Why would we invest that much in a sixteen-year-old vehicle?" I don't think he understands. I thought guys were supposed to form irrational attachments to inanimate objects like cars. Why isn't he normal?

One of the church members, Dion, owns a scrap yard and is supposed to be here any minute to come haul her off. I'm not sure I'll be able to watch, so I'm saying goodbye now. Goodbye to yet another part of my former self. There it goes, on the scrap heap. Superfluous.

Well, I'm not replacing Lillibeth with some lumbering daycare on wheels. I'm ready to stick to that decision when we go car shopping later today, too. (Yeah, I don't even get a day to mourn my car. "With our schedules, we need two vehicles," Reverend Practical informed me last night. "Vince McIntosh told me he could give us a good deal, so we'll start at his lot.")

I'm not interested if it has more than four doors or any doors that slide. Also, if it floats more than rolls, that's a deal-breaker. I want something that's called a "car." No vans, trucks, crossovers, SUVs, or wagons allowed. Front bucket seats, no benches (because this isn't a picnic). No hideaway or stow-n-go nonsense, either. If something can't fit in a normal trunk, I don't need to be lugging it from place-to-place, anyway.

These are my terms. Anyone who doesn't like them can suck it. And that includes the man I'm married to.

Before I get all choked up again, I trudge back into the house, stomping snow from my shoes onto the door mat.

Brice looks up from eating his bowl of raisin brain on the couch while keeping an eye out the front window for Dion. "Did you say your goodbyes?"

"I know you're not making fun of me."

He smiles innocently. "Never. Hey, I remember my first car."

"The kind you used your feet to move?" I tease.

Sticking his front teeth over his lower lip, he says, "Harrrrr! Funny."

"Sorry. Go on."

"What? Oh, that's all. I remember my first car."

I roll my eyes. "You are so good at this comforting and consoling thing. Has anyone ever told you that you should be a pastor or a counselor?"

After tilting the bowl and drinking the extra milk, he stands up and goes into the kitchen to put his dirty dishes in the dishwasher. I plop down at the kitchen table and rest my head in my hand.

"Aren't you just a little excited?" he asks. "I mean, you're getting a new car today! I'd be excited. New cars are fun."

"I like my old car."

"Your old car—even when it ran—had mystery stains on the seats, no air conditioning, a radio that rarely worked, a tape deck—a *tape deck*—that ate anything you put in it, manual windows and locks, a leaky moonroof, and it smelled like a Taco Bell." He crosses his arms over his chest. "Now tell me a new car isn't going to be better."

"You mean a Mom-mobile?"

"Ahh, I see."

"What do you see?" I challenge him, the guy who gets to drive whatever he likes.

He peeks around the breakfast bar to check the driveway, which still only holds Lillibeth. Assured that Dion's not waiting for him, he explains, "You're desperately hanging onto your youth, and you think keeping that car's going to do the trick."

"My youth was over before I even got that car. It has nothing to do with that. That car was fun. She zipped in and out of traffic; I could find a place to park her pretty much anywhere—"

"We'll get you a Mustang, then. Will that be *fun* enough for you?"

"Really?" I sit up a little straighter.

"No!" he laughs. "You have to get a car that can hold a baby's car seat."

"Mustangs look pretty roomy," I mutter.

"And you need a real trunk, one that can carry groceries and baby gear, all at once. And this new car also needs to be safe and practical."

Oh, here we go again with being practical. I'm beginning to hate that word almost as much as I hate the words "tween" and "webinar" and "interface."

"Why are you glaring at me like that?" he asks, checking out the front window again.

I shake my head. "You don't get it."

"Guess not." He tosses his hands up and lets them fall to his sides.

"You're a practical guy."

"Guilty."

"So 'practical' is a good thing to you."

"So far, you've got me pegged."

"Well, in case you just met me, I'm not practical. I don't like it. I think it's boring and claustrophobic and stifling and—"

"Got it. Okay, so you're balking at getting a new car that runs, has some cool features, and doesn't have a butt-dent in the hood, because it may be—gasp!—practical." He covers his mouth with his hand and widens his eyes.

"You can be such a dick sometimes."

He shoves his hands in his pockets and laughs.

"Seriously. You have everyone else fooled; they think you're so great and sweet and, 'Oh, Peyton, you're so lucky to be married to a guy like that!' but you deliberately miss the point so that you can make *your* point and prove how smart you are and how dumb and *impractical* and silly I am." I misjudge the amount of clearance I now need to give myself and scrape my belly on the edge of the kitchen table while standing up. "Ow."

"Watch it." Still grinning, he says, "Oh, come on. Don't be mad."

"At least when I'm mad, I'm not crying, so you should be thankful, you big asshole."

"Criminy, Peyton."

"Don't 'criminy, by-jiminy, okaley-dokaley,' me, okay?" I point at him. "I'm *not* going to drive a minivan!"

"Okay, fine!" He's not smiling or laughing anymore. "Nobody said you had to. Heaven forbid anyone *know* you're a mom or a wife or whatever you think is so shameful."

Gesturing to my belly, he jabs, "I hate to break it to you, but you're not hiding it well, no matter what car you're driving."

"Well, thanks!"

"It wasn't supposed to be an insult!"

"Somehow, it was, though. You're so talented that way."

"Are you listening to yourself?"

"Why should I? *You* never do. You just want to tell me your pat answers and get on with your day and hope that I'll get on with mine and stop being so high maintenance."

"You said it, not me."

"Screw you." Actually, it comes out more like, "Screw you-hoo-hoo-hoo-hoo," when the dam finally breaks.

Unmoved, he simply stares at me. Finally, after what feels like forever, he says quietly, "I guess I'm supposed to feel sorry for you, but I'm having a hard time mustering any sympathy. You're blowing something way out of proportion and then you accuse me of being everything from oblivious to duplicitous to uncaring to cruel, but I'm supposed to just chalk it up to hormones and go over there and comfort you now? Well, I'm sorry. I can't do it." A flash of sunlight reflecting from the driveway grabs his attention. "Anyway, Dion's here, so I couldn't, even if I wanted to. Maybe you should just go lie down before you make yourself sick."

With that, he yanks open the door to the garage so hard, I'm afraid it's going to come off its hinges and then slams it behind him as he jogs down the steps, calling, "Hey, Dion! Thanks for coming out to do this, buddy!"

"Hey, Dion! Thanks for coming out here and hauling away one of the last vestiges of my wife's former life. This piece of junk just doesn't belong here, in our new, perfect life."

I flip the bird at the closed door.

FLASHBACKS

I got a new car, but I'm not happy about it.

I'm actually *thrilled* about it. It's shiny and black has a bunch of gizmos and toys and smells good (Brice was right about Lillibeth smelling like Taco Bell). And I'm not so much of a brat that I haven't been able to admit to Brice that I like it. I kind of had to when he offered to trade me the Jeep for the new car, and I turned him down. I mean, the Jeep is *him*. It's sturdy and dependable. And carries stuff and lots of people. And it's square-ish. Plus, I don't want to put half my salary into a gas tank every week. No, the car is *mine*.

On the way home from the sales lot, I called him with my new hands-free, voice-activated system and told him I was sorry. It just seemed easier to say it over the phone (and I wanted to try out my new toy). I could see his outline in the Jeep behind me, but obviously, I couldn't see his face, so I was worried when he didn't say anything for a while. Then he said, "You worry me when you act like that."

Well, when Brice is worried, that's a problem. And the "when" implies that I do it a lot. I felt like an ass, but I just gulped and apologized again and resisted every urge to explain myself or make excuses. Plus, when he expressed his regrets for making light of something that meant a lot to me, it seemed tedious to say anything that might lead us right back to the middle of that atrocious argument, so I accepted his apology and tried to feel relieved that the whole thing was over.

I'm getting pretty good at pretending like everything I'm really worried about doesn't exist.

"Why haven't you scheduled that ultrasound yet?" Dr. Walsh asks me now. "My nurse has called you three times to try to set up a time, but you keep putting her off."

Brice raises his eyebrows at me and looks innocently at the doctor when she turns to him for an answer.

"What ultrasound?" he asks. When she merely blinks back at him, implying that he has proven her wrong about there not being any stupid questions, he flinches and says, "Oh! *That* one. Oh, yeah. It's about that time, isn't it?"

"Past time," the doctor says pointedly. "Four weeks past. I need to get a look at that baby. You know the drill. Get a weight check and check for cleft palate. Make sure our due date still looks accurate. Let you know if you're having a boy or girl, if that's what you want. Any of this ringing a bell?" Her tone is light, but I can tell she's annoyed with me.

I smile sickly. "Yeah. I know. But…" Time to throw Brice under the bus. "It's such a busy time of year at the church, and when your nurse calls, I'm always at work, so I can't check Brice's schedule, which is *really* busy right now."

"You already said that."

"Well, it's Christmas. You can imagine how crazy things get at a church at Christmastime." I laugh nervously. When she simply taps her foot and waits, pen poised, for me to give her a day and time, I turn to Brice, "Hon? I mean, do you have *any* free hours between now and the end of the year?"

"This *week*, Peyton," the doctor insists.

I widen my eyes and wince theatrically, trying to signal to him that it's okay if his schedule won't allow it. "Gosh. I don't know."

He eagerly answers, "Any time." I sigh and curse the fact that one year of marriage obviously isn't long enough to learn how to read each other's non-verbal cues. Hope tweaks my tummy, though, when he backtracks, "Well, not *any* time." Then he goes and ruins it by being cooperative again: "But my late mornings and early afternoons are usually open. Most of the stuff going on this time of year is in the evenings and on the weekends."

"The lab isn't open at those times, anyway," she reassures him drily. "Okay, then. Uh, let's see… Friday at ten?"

"Ooh," I hiss regretfully.

Dr. Walsh ignores me. "Friday at ten it is." She jots it down in the file without waiting for me to confirm that it's going to work for me and tosses the folder on the counter behind her. "Now, lie back so I can get a look."

I'm just glad they took my blood pressure *before* I found out I'd have to do that ultrasound in two days.

Don't even try to point out to me how ass-backwards it is that I worry all the time about what's going on in there and mercilessly harass the nurse on the phone (although since I've been dodging her ultrasound appointment calls, she hasn't heard from me in a while), but then when I have a chance to really see what's going on and get some peace of mind, I treat it like someone's asking me to schedule my own execution. I know it's weird; I know it's downright stupid. But I can't help it. I'm petrified about what they're going to find. Or not find.

Ultrasound day was my last day with Secret. I hate ultrasound day.

Just thinking about it now is making the walls close in on me. That stupid poster on the ceiling that's supposed to give me something to read and distract me from the knowledge that someone has her entire hand inside me is quickly coming closer to my nose. I turn my head to the side and close my eyes.

"Oops," Dr. Walsh misinterprets my squirming. "Sorry if that hurt. So, are you two going to find out on Friday what you're having, or are you going to wait until baby's birthday?"

I keep my eyes closed and focus on breathing through my nose.

Brice steps in. "Uh, I really want it to be a surprise, but I don't think I can wait until April. Right, hon?"

He may as well be consulting the wall.

In my head, I'm in that dark ultrasound room, naked from the waist down, draped in a warm sheet. The tech is rubbing that wand back and forth, back and forth, making tracks through the jelly on my giant belly. And there's silence. And black nothingness on the screen. She gives me a look that I'll never forget. That look that says, *"Damn, I hate days like this. I'm going to have to call my husband and make sure he has my gin and tonic waiting for me when I get home."* She picks up the phone to call the hospital and tell them, "We have another one of *those*." She hangs up and dials Dr. Walsh.

Today, Dr. Walsh says, "Peyton! Are you okay? Hey!"

I open my eyes and try to focus on her face, which is disturbingly close to mine and blurry. Am I becoming farsighted now, on top of everything else? I pant, feeling like my chest is about to explode, even though I can't get a full breath.

"What's wrong?" she asks. "What are you feeling?"

I can't even begin to tell her. She whips the stethoscope from around her neck, puts the ends in her ears, and presses the flat knob against my chest. She asks Brice to help her turn me onto my left side so the baby has optimal blood-flow, and she can listen to my heart through my back. After she's listened, and I remain mute, she opens the door to the room and shouts down the hall toward the nurses' station.

Brice leans over next to the exam table, his eyes full of worry and fear. His mouth is dry when he asks, "Hon, what's the matter?"

"Chest hurts," I finally manage at a near whisper.

Dr. Walsh is back, strapping a blood pressure cuff on my arm and doing a quick reading. After that one, she takes another. "Good grief. Your blood pressure's off the charts, Peyton. Is the baby moving?"

As if on cue, he/she kicks me hard in my ribs. "Yeah." And again. And again.

"A lot?" Then she can see the answer for herself. "Brice, we need to get her to the hospital *now*."

"Okay," he barely has time to reply as the room floods with nurses.

"An ambulance is on the way," one of them informs the doctor.

"She's stable for now," Dr. Walsh says. "Let's keep her on her side. Give her some oxygen." Someone slides an elastic band over my head and pushes a plastic mask against my mouth and nose. "She was fine! All of her vitals were normal. I did the pelvic exam, and she just… faded."

I close my eyes and grit my teeth.

"Uh-uh! Brice! Keep her awake over there."

He timidly taps my cheek. "Hey. Everything's fine. Stay awake, huh?"

There's no danger of my falling asleep in the midst of all this, but I nod and open my eyes so he knows I'm listening. A tear hisses onto the paper covering the exam table. I swallow back its friends that want to follow. Crying isn't going to help anything. I just wish I could stop crying about everything!

"Breathe, Peyton!" Dr. Walsh barks while continuing to obsessively monitor my vital signs. She tugs on my wrist and watches the clock as she takes my pulse. "How far away is the ambulance?" she asks a nurse who looks just old enough to be *playing* nurse.

"Two minutes," is the terse answer.

If I stop holding my breath, I won't be able to hold back the tears.

Dr. Walsh strains to see around me and finally says to Brice, "What's she doing? Is she holding her breath?"

He glances down and sees me, red-faced, blinking and swallowing. Quickly answering the doctor, he says, "Yes," then, "Uh, this is one of those times when it's okay to cry. Let it out. You have to breathe!"

So I do, even though I think they're going to end up regretting their request, because now I can't stop. I'm hysterical. I rip the oxygen mask off, because—ironically—I can't breathe with it up against my face. I push Brice away, because he's standing too close. I kick out at the nurses who are crowded around me. Even when they hold my arms and legs, I can't stop shaking. The tremors vibrate the exam table.

Shouting over my keening, Dr. Walsh says to Brice, "Okay, can you get her to stop crying?"

He looks helplessly back at her. "I haven't really figured out that trick yet."

I'm so loud that I don't even hear the siren when the

ambulance arrives at the building. I also don't hear a thing that Dr. Walsh tells the EMTs before they load me into the back of the impossibly confined emergency vehicle or feel the IV being inserted or understand a word of what the EMTs are saying to Brice or to each other. And then, I don't care. All is silence and blackness and peace.

I wake up to a dreadful feeling of déjà vu. Before I can take stock of myself, I observe the dim hospital room, hear a bleating baby, and see Brice sitting at my bedside with his head bowed and his hands folded. I clamp my eyes shut. No. Not again. Then I feel the kick against my pelvic bone. Keeping my eyes closed, I move my hands to my belly and explore the swell, receiving two more kicks as a reward.

"Thank you, God," I whisper. I want to cry, but for some reason I can't.

"Hey." I feel lips against my forehead and then on mine.

When I open my eyes, I'm greeted by a bloodshot, unshaven, rumpled husband. "Hey. What happened?" The events at the doctor's office come rushing back before he can answer, so I share, "It felt like I was having a panic attack. The worst panic attack in the world."

"Funny you should say that, because you were. Would have been good information to know at the time," he says with a weak smile, "but you weren't really communicating well." He retakes his seat and holds my hand.

"When I woke up, I thought—it was just like last time. For a minute, I thought the past two years had been a dream, and I was waking up again after—"

He nods. "Yeah. I was kind of worried about that."

I struggle to wet my chapped lips with a very dry tongue.

Just out of reach is a giant plastic container of water with a wide straw poking from the top. I nod at it. "Can I…?"

"What? Oh!" He hops up, grabs the mug, and holds it for me so I can suck through the straw.

"Thanks," I tell him after draining half the cup. Again, I'm struck by how calm I feel. As he turns away to put the cup down, I ask him, "Hey. Why do I feel so weird?"

He spins to look at me, tilts his head, and furrows his brow. "What do you mean?" I can see the worry building in his eyes.

"No, no. Not bad. Like, floaty and mellow."

His features relax as he nods. "Oh. That. I'm pretty sure you have a cocktail of happy juice in that IV." He nods to the bag hanging next to the bed. "You know, to keep Scary Peyton away."

I wish I could laugh, but all that comes out is a faint smile. No strong emotions allowed, apparently.

So now is the perfect time to tell him without fear of losing control, "I'm terrified of that ultrasound, Brice."

Scraping his lower lip with his teeth, he looks down at his feet. "I guess I don't have to ask why." He squeezes my hand supportively. "But it's something that has to be done."

"Really? What did women do before ultrasounds? We had babies just fine without them."

"Not really. I mean, there were a lot of surprises—and not the good kind—before ultrasound and amniocentesis and other diagnostic tools. Were healthy babies born? Yes. Lots of them. Do I think the health of our baby depends on this ultrasound? No."

"Exactly."

"But the doctor wants to know some things, and you have to be there. Obviously." He scoots closer to the bed, dropping the rail so he can put his hands on my belly.

"Whoop," he says, smiling, when he gets a "hello" nudge. Looking into my eyes, he continues, "He's going to be born the way God wants him to be born. But it'd be nice to know ahead of time if there's something that may need a little extra attention. Or if he's on track to weigh fourteen pounds by his due date and isn't going to fit through the birth canal."

"Okay, this happy juice isn't *that* happy. Please, don't say —Wait! What's all this 'he' and 'him' business?"

He rests his chin on the bump under the sheet but looks straight ahead, avoiding eye contact. "What if I told you that God knew it would be best if you were unconscious during the ultrasound?"

"Really? They did it while I was out?" I'm feeling a strange, watered-down mix of elation and disappointment at that news.

He turns his head so that his ear is up against the hill of my tummy, and he's looking at me. His expression is sheepish when he informs me, "They had to. Your blood pressure had really spiked, and the baby was showing signs of being in distress."

"God made me have a panic attack so I'd have to be hospitalized and sedated during the ultrasound?"

"He knows best."

I stroke his eyebrow. "You obviously have information, so spill it."

"No problems that they can see. Average size—no four-teen-pounder for you... this time." His teasing grin fades, and he sobers when he says, "He's beautiful."

Damn drugs. All I can do when he blinks furiously at the tears brought on by his declaration is smile and pat his head. This should be a priceless moment, but I'm emotionally hamstrung by whatever is dripping persistently into my veins. For the first time in months, I couldn't produce a tear if someone held a gun to my head.

"He is?" I whisper.

He nods and bites his lip but can't speak.

"Aww. How could you tell?"

Sniffing, he sits up and reaches behind him on the tiny table where the room phone is sitting on top of an envelope. "The pictures are really clear. Here. I had them print some out so you could see them when you woke up."

He puts the envelope in my hands, but before I open it to look at the pictures inside, I search his face and ask, "And you're sure he's going to be okay? I didn't hurt him, did I? I just— I couldn't breathe when I remembered how I felt that day when they told me about Secret."

His hand moves up to tuck a piece of hair behind my ear. "He's really okay. They just came in a little while ago and disconnected the fetal monitor, because they're sure he's fine. You're only still here so they can observe you overnight and monitor your blood pressure. It was still a little high the last time they checked it."

He nods toward the pictures. "Now, come on. You need to see those. You're going to crack up at some of his facial expressions."

"He has facial expressions? Maybe I should wait until I can actually feel something."

"We'll look at them again later," he promises, taking the envelope from me and sliding out the prints.

He perches on the edge of the bed and holds each one up for me, pointing out the less obvious features when I tilt the pictures and my head in confusion, trying to figure out what I'm seeing. At one particularly clear picture of the baby's face, he says, "And this is the one that has me convinced he already knows some of your favorite words and is thinking them after being poked and prodded for several minutes."

When we come to the end of the stack, we start over. And then again. We look through them three more times.

There aren't enough drugs in the world to dull this feeling.

CONFINEMENT

*I*t doesn't occur to me until we're in the car on the way home this morning and I see the date on my discharge papers that it's just two weeks before Christmas. And it's a Thursday.

I gasp. "Oh, no!"

Brice almost runs my precious new car off the road and then nearly overcorrects into the lane of oncoming traffic. "What? What's wrong?"

"Church last night. Who…? I mean, you weren't—"

His shoulders slump. "Oh. Jared took care of it." A touch irritably he says, "For crying out loud! I almost wrecked the car when you made that noise. You scared the doo-doo out of me."

"Sorry," I mumble. "I was worried that all that nonsense from yesterday screwed up the Advent service."

He reaches over and grabs my hand. "It wasn't 'nonsense.' It was a scary emergency. But I called Marilyn and Jared as soon as you were settled. You slept a long time." Unfortunately, he's gotten next to no sleep in the past twenty-four hours. Now he reminds me more gently, "Anyway, no worrying, remember? So, stop it."

That's right. Doctor's orders: no stress, no salt. The first one, I'm okay with; the second is going to suck. But she told me if I don't obey those rules and my blood pressure gets too high again, there'll be a lot more no's, including no work and no sex. Life really won't be worth living if it comes to that, so I will banish the worry and forsake the fast food and forbidden Cheetos breakfasts. I'll join Brice every morning at the table with a bowl of bran flakes, and we'll go on our walks in the sub-zero temperatures, and when I get the urge to worry about the baby, I'll look at his pictures and do kick counts and take deep breaths. I can do this.

As for other stress, I'll handle each instance as it presents itself and keep things in perspective. And remember the "no sex" threat. I think that ought to do it.

First test:

"I've gotta stop in at the church on the way home, check my messages and ask Jared how everything went last night."

I consciously unclench my teeth and open my hands from the fists they're forming. After a deep breath, I suggest, "Why don't you take me home first and run up to the church?"

"I'd rather not."

"You can leave me alone, you know. I'm not on suicide watch. I'm not going to binge on potato chips or pour a shaker of salt into my mouth as soon as I'm left unattended." I'm irritated, but not stressed. "I really just want to get in my own bed."

The stress level rises ever-so-slightly when he passes our street and continues on toward the church, but I close my eyes and breathe through my nose as he explains, "If you're with me, there's less chance of my getting stuck there for hours. Five minutes. That's all I need. If Jared's not in his office, then I'll just catch up with him on the phone later."

"Fine," I relent. It's not like I'm going to win the argument, anyway, so what's the point in risking my elevated blood pressure?

As we pull into Brice's reserved parking space, an enormous black SUV slides into the spot right next to us. When I look over, I'm dismayed to see Justine scrunch her shoulders up around her ears, grin, and finger-wave down at me. I limply return the greeting with a dull wave of my own.

"Mother-fu—"

"Now, now," Brice warns.

"Why is she always here?" I complain. "I think she's stalking you."

"The youth group Christmas party is tomorrow. She's probably getting stuff ready, decorating the gym. Don't *worry* about it." He gets out of the car, goes around the front, and opens my door while talking gibberish through the backseat window of Justine's monster truck. "Isaiah, buddy! What's kickin', chicken?" he asks his godson.

Justine whistles. "Nice car, guys! Is this the one you just bought from Vince?" She pulls the grinning, drooling baby from his car seat and readjusts his coat hood against the wind.

"Yeah," Brice speaks for both of us. "It's quite an upgrade. But we got a good deal. And the Jeep's paid off, so…"

Hurrying toward the warmth awaiting us inside the church, nobody says anything else until Brice holds the door open for us and snags Isaiah from Justine on her way past. "Oof! Chunky monkey! How many bananas are you eating now? Six, seven a day? Argh! My back!"

Justine giggles at his antics. I smile wanly. Okay, it's cute.

But I'm tired. And this is going to take a lot longer than five minutes if he's going to play with Isaiah while doing all the other things he wants to do. I don't mean to be selfish, but I'm just not in the mood to socialize. Why couldn't he drop me off at the house, like I asked? And then grow a pair and tell everyone that he wants to get home to be with me. He doesn't need me here to convey that.

My pulsating eyeballs are warning me that the old ticker is pumping it into overdrive. Hoping I don't look rude, but knowing I can't really care if I do, I walk ahead of the two of them, enter the church office, and sit in the nearest chair to wait and think serene thoughts.

Marilyn looks up from her computer and smiles when she sees it's me. "Why, hello, there. How're you feeling?"

"Tired."

She shoots a perturbed look at Justine, who's holding Brice hostage as she plays peek-a-boo with the baby in his arms. After a few minutes, Marilyn says over their giggles, "Pastor, everything's under control here. Why don't you take your wife home? I'll forward any urgent calls to your cell phone."

Handing Isaiah back to his mother, Brice says, "Oh. Yeah. Well, I wanted to have a word with Jared, check my emails…"

"You can do all of that from home," she replies firmly. "I'll send Jared over in a little while, after you've had some time to get Peyton settled."

He edges toward his office door. "She's fine. This'll only take a sec—"

His secretary stands up and moves in front of his door. Nodding at me, she says, "She's exhausted. Look at her." He does. I try not to look too pathetic, but I really am bushed.

Shamed by the older woman, he gives his office a last

longing look over her head and says, "All right. Yeah, Jared can either call me or come by the parsonage when he gets a minute. How'd the service go last night?"

"Fine. He did a nice job. And his prayers for the two— three—of you were discreet. Now, go home. You actually look worse for wear than your wife." I chuckle at her candor.

Justine stops her incessant babbling to Isaiah long enough to say, "What's this? I was home last night with Isaiah. He had a slight fever. I think he may be teething. What did I miss?"

Brice sighs. "Oh, we had a little scare yesterday and had to spend a night at the hospital."

"Oh, no!"

Her "gee whiz" tone is grating on my nerves. "Everything's fine. Nothing a little *rest* can't fix," I say firmly.

Brice grins. "Yeah. And we found out we're having a boy, so…"

Marilyn's and Justine's squeals (and Isaiah's resulting cries) drown out the rest of his sentence and the dirty look I shoot at him. I can't believe he just told them that. I mean, Marilyn, I don't mind (although I would have preferred my own mother knew before the church secretary), but Justine? Justine? Really? The thought that Justine Heidecker knows the sex of my baby before my sister and brother and parents and Brice's mother—that chafes.

This is not helping my blood pressure.

When Jared's drawn to the main office by the noise, I mumble on my way past him, "Can you let Brice know I went home?"

"What? I mean, sure," he answers uncertainly as he watches me leave.

I'll even let Brice drive the car home. I need the fresh air and exercise. It's only a block, anyway. Sure, there's still about six inches of snow on the ground, but the sidewalks are clear, and I'm wearing sensible shoes (for once), so I don't feel like I'm taking any undue chances with mine or the baby's safety. But I can't be held responsible for what I may say if I stay in that office.

I know part of my problem is that I'm exhausted. It's amazing how draining it is to be in a bed when that bed is in a hospital staffed with nurses and doctors who see it as their life mission to never give their patients a minute's rest. It seemed like every time I started to doze off, someone was at my side, taking my pulse, temperature, or blood pressure. I'd wake up enough to answer their questions, and by the time they were finished, I was nearly wide awake. They'd leave, and I'd try to get comfortable again, but usually, I found myself watching Brice doze fitfully on the room's vinyl loveseat and feeling guilty that he looked so uncomfortable.

It's more than just a physical tiredness, too. I'm weary. I'm worn out from being in an unfamiliar place and having people poke me and read into every simple answer I gave them. I'm pooped from the stress and excitement, even the good excitement of finding out we're having a son and really seeing him for the first time. And I'm already fatigued from the effort it's taking *not* to worry, *not* to stress, *not* to let things get to me. It's draining to go against one's nature every second of the day. I'd even go so far as to say it's stressful *not* to worry. At least, it is when you're me. Now I have to worry that I'm worrying too much.

I should just stay in bed for the next sixteen weeks. That would make things a lot easier. Although, then I'd start worrying about bedsores.

When I arrive home, I'm slightly out of breath but feeling pretty good about my decision to distance myself from the stressors at the church *and* get exercise at the same time. The decision seems more fortuitous the longer I'm home, too, because I have time to eat something, take a shower, call my mom, Nicole, and Jason to tell them the big news, choose a movie to watch, and settle on the couch before Brice gets home. I would have been sitting there forever, waiting for him. Ugh! This is so much better.

The car door slamming shut echoes in the garage, the garage door buzzes closed, and the kitchen door clicks open. Brice's shoes squeak on the kitchen floor, but I don't worry about the dirty melted snow he's probably tracking all over it (See? I *can* not worry, especially when it comes to housework).

I smile absently when I see him walk through the archway from the kitchen to the living room, but I don't take my eyes off the opening sequence of my movie (*Elf,* possibly the best Christmas movie ever).

"What the *Hello Kitty* were you *thinking?*" he yells. (Yes, yells. I am *not* exaggerating.)

The remote clatters out of my hand and thumps onto the floor when I jump a foot in response to the volume of his angry question.

All the blood drains from my head as my eyes snap to his face. "Huh?" I respond inarticulately. I don't even know how to react to his behavior. I can't remember a time he's ever done anything that comes close to the definition of *yelling* at me.

He snatches the remote from the floor and pauses my movie. "One minute, you're sitting there, and the next minute, I look over, and you're gone!"

I'm so confused. And a little scared.

"At the church?" I seek clarification. "That was like, almost an hour ago!"

"Yeah, because I've been looking for you!"

"What? I told Jared when I left to tell you that I was walking home. And anyway, why didn't you just call my cell phone?"

He produces my phone from his pocket. "You mean this? The phone you left in the car?"

"Oh." I hold out my hand for it, but he doesn't give it to me. Instead, he just stares at me. "What? I didn't do anything wrong! You're being ridiculous!" See how *he* likes being labeled that. "I'm going to punch Jared in the kidneys next time I see him. He can't even deliver a simple message." I hunker down under my fleece blanket and mutter, "That's not good, if he plans to be a pastor."

Brice sighs and runs his hand through his hair. "I didn't ask Jared until after I'd been looking for a while."

"Who says you needed to ask? To any normal person, it would have been obvious—once all the excitement died down—to inform you of what I said as I was leaving."

Dropping down into the recliner that neither of us ever sits in, he covers his eyes and explains, "He went back to his office before we stopped talking about the baby. I guess. I never saw him come into the office at all."

"Well, you were pretty distracted, what with all the screeching about your wonderful news."

He looks sharply up at me. "Are you kidding me? I spent the last forty-five minutes searching the church property, looking in every office, every bathroom stall, expecting to find you unconscious somewhere!"

I laugh but cover my mouth quickly when I see how much angrier it makes him. "I'm sorry. But you pass out in a toilet once, and you never live it down."

"This isn't funny, Peyton! I was worried!"

I lean over and yank the remote from him. "Stop yelling

at me. And stop worrying. It's bad for your health. If you had just thought for a second, it would have been logical where I went." I trace around the remote buttons with my fingers. "I told you I wanted to go home. I'm not a mental patient who needs round-the-clock care and supervision."

"But you just got out of the hospital."

"Yes! I did. Which is why I wanted to be at home, so I could take a shower and put on some clean clothes and eat something and get some real rest. Oh, and call my family to let them know that a) I'm okay; b) the baby's okay; and c) we're having a boy, before they heard all of it second-hand from someone at church, who heard it through the Justine Heidecker grapevine. I suggest you call your mother soon to let her know, too."

Incredulously, he squawks, "What are you talking about? I called both of our mothers yesterday right after the ultrasound and asked your mom to spread the word to your siblings. Everyone in our families already knows!"

I blink at him, trying to make this information make sense. "But I— I just talked to my mom, and she— she acted like it was news to her!" I only left messages for Nicole and Jason, though. "Wait a minute! You mean, they all knew before *I* did?"

"You were still sleeping."

"Brice! My mom probably thinks I've completely lost my mind after the conversation I just had with her. Why didn't she tell me she already knew?"

He looks guiltily at his hands. "I don't know. Maybe she didn't want to burst your bubble."

I slap the remote against the sofa cushion. The battery compartment cover flies off. "There would have been no bubble to burst if you'd just told me what you'd done!"

"I forgot," he mumbles defensively. "Okay? I forgot that

you were asleep when I made those calls. Yesterday's one big blur."

"Well, most of it is one big black hole for me, so you're gonna have to help me out a little bit. Shit!"

I'm annoyed (bordering on stressed), but he looks so pitiful in that stupid overstuffed chair that I decide to let him off the hook for botching the ultrasound results. And let's face it: he botched it. I mean, I know he must have been excited to share the news, and it would have been hard to wait until I woke up to tell me and *then* tell everyone else, but the man needs to learn some restraint in this department. The mom gets to be one of the first people to know. And by "first," I mean "before anyone else" (in case the word is ambiguous).

Going back to the original argument, I explain while putting the remote back together, "I didn't want to go anywhere near the church today. I didn't want to make nicey-nice talk with Justine and coo over Isaiah or ask Jared how things are going or even see Marilyn. I just wanted to be home." When he says nothing to that, I add, "I'm sorry you didn't get the message that I was leaving, but I'm not sorry I left. So, Jared eventually figured out you were looking for me and told you I went home?"

He nods sulkily. "Yeah, after I walked past his office about half-a-dozen times, he was like, 'Hey. Peyton wanted me to let you know she was going home.'"

I stifle my smile at his impersonation of Jared's voice.

Miserably, he repeats, "I really didn't see him come into the office at all when I was telling Justine and Marilyn about the baby, so I didn't think to ask him if he'd seen you."

"Well, next time you'll know to ask around before you start running all over the place, assuming I'm wandering the church grounds, disoriented and suffering from some sort of reduced-sodium-induced dementia. Or whatever."

"I love how I'm the bad guy here."

"Not bad, just clueless."

At that assessment, he gets up from the chair with an exaggerated sense of calm, walks down the hallway to the bathroom, and slams the door. The shower starts running. I shrug and hit "play" on my movie. I'm sure he'll be fine after a shower and some sleep. In the meantime, I'm going to hang out with Buddy the elf and not worry about it.

28

VOCATIONAL DOUBTS

I was wrong. Brice is *not* fine. He's had several sleeps and showers since the day we got home from the hospital, but he continues to be quiet and terse and morose. I don't know what to do. I'd apologize if I knew what I was apologizing for. But I'd feel stupid saying, "I'm sorry I called you clueless," because a) it's a dumb thing to apologize for and doesn't seem like something that would cause this level of resentment; b) it was true; c) I'm not sorry; and d) I'm not sure that's even what he's upset about. I've tried to query him on several occasions with variations on the theme of, "What's wrong?" including "Are you okay?" "Are you upset about something?" "Do you need to talk?" and one day, quite bluntly, "What crawled up your ass and died lately?" The last one didn't go over so well.

But I'm frustrated. He's not a sulker or a grudge-holder (that's *my* job, as he's so aptly pointed out in the past), so I don't know how to handle this.

I do know I'm not handling it well.

"Can I help you with anything in there?" Jared asks

anxiously while I fumble around in the kitchen, opening and closing cupboards in an attempt to find the dishes and measuring cups and cookware I need to make the very basic chicken recipe printed on the back of the low-sodium (of course) soup can. Embarrassingly enough, I have no idea where anything is in my own kitchen. I mean, I can locate plates, cups, and silverware, but when it comes to digging out cookware, I might as well be a guest. This is Brice's territory, for sure.

Unfortunately, he's overseeing Christmas program rehearsals at the church, which leaves it to me to provide dinner for the three of us tonight. And I just found out a couple of hours ago that there would be three of us at dinner tonight.

In response to Jared's offer—and cringing posture on the other side of the breakfast bar—I say, "No. I've got it. I think. I mean, how hard can it be?"

He smiles encouragingly. "I'm sure you can figure it out. As soon as you find out where everything is."

"I think I have it covered, but thanks, Smart Ass." Mixing together milk and the soup in a large glass bowl, I say, "Actually, while I'm doing this, maybe you can help me with something else."

"Name it."

I tread carefully. "I'm not asking you to tell me anything you're not allowed to tell me, but is something going on at the church that could be causing Brice more distress than usual? Anything you're aware of?"

Frowning, he puts his elbows on the counter and supports his chin with his hand. "Mmmm... just the usual Christmas stuff, I guess. Uhhh..." He taps his cheek with his forefinger. "I've noticed your dad's been around a lot more than usual. That would stress me out, if I were Pastor. Of course, that means I've been making myself scarce, so I have no idea what they're meeting about."

"What have you done now?"

My assumption straightens his back. He drops his hands to the counter. "Now, why do you always think it's my fault? I've been good lately."

I pour the soup mixture over some chicken breasts in a casserole dish. "I'm just kidding. Well, my dad's mere presence is explanation enough for Brice's bad mood lately. Thanks for letting me know."

I double-check the "recipe" to make sure I haven't missed one of the three steps before sliding the dish into the pre-heated oven and setting the timer for thirty-five minutes.

When I turn around to start cleaning up my dirty prep dishes, the look on Jared's face stops me cold. "What?" I ask, hating the sick feeling that's building in the pit of my stomach.

His Adam's apple bobs. "Pastor asked me to dinner tonight, because my vicariate is over at the end of the month."

"Oh, yeah! And then you're done, right? You'll have to let us know when your ordination is. We definitely want to be there," I say lightly, pretending I don't notice that he still looks tremendously sad. Laughing nervously, I toss the soup cans and chicken wrappers in the trash. "I wish I had known this was a celebration meal. I would have brought home something a little nicer."

He shakes his head. "I've been thinking that the ministry isn't really for me—"

"What?"

With a roll of his eyes, he says, "Come on, Peyton. It's pretty obvious to everyone that I'm not cut out for this."

"Why? Because you've made a few innocent mistakes?

You were learning! Don't let assholes like my dad get you down on yourself." I'm furious at the idea that anyone in my family could be responsible for Jared's change of heart. "He's a grudge holder." *Takes one to know one.* "And you got on his bad side big-time with the 'Mafioso middleman' comment. But you were just speaking your mind. That's not a crime! And neither is making some mistakes when you're getting the hang of something new. It's okay not to be perfect, you know."

Scraping his thumbnail against the edge of the counter, he screws his mouth to the side while listening to me but says when I'm finished, "I dunno. It seems like I'm not getting any better at stuff. And I don't know if I really want to do this. I don't know if I *can* do it. I see what Pastor has to put up with day in and day out and it's— It's not what I thought it would be."

"Oh, Jared."

"I'm sorry!" he says miserably. "It seems like all I've done is cause trouble since I got here a year ago. And this is just one more thing. Pastor's not going to be happy to know I've wasted this whole year with him. But I'll be gone soon."

I feel terrible that he thinks we can't wait to be rid of him. Putting the milk in the refrigerator and placing the measuring cup and wire whisk in the sink, I tease, "Well, you've grown on us like a fungus. And you *have* gotten better. You didn't giggle once during your last sermon. And Marilyn says you did a great job at the Advent service last week when I was in the hospital. So, I don't know what you're talking about."

"You're too nice."

"That's definitely *not* one of my problems," I argue.

"I appreciate everything you and Pastor have done for me. And what you've put up with."

"Stop. Just stop." When he gazes forlornly at me, I say, "Let's wait until Brice gets home before you make any hasty decisions. Tell him your worries; give him a chance to advise you about your options. You know, he didn't have a 400-member congregation straight out of seminary. He was a prison chaplain and then an associate pastor first. You can ease into your career."

He nods. "Okay. But this isn't a hasty decision. I've been praying about it for a while."

"Whatever," I dismiss impatiently. "You're freaking out, because your vicariate is ending and your ordination is looming. It's a big step out into the grown-up world, but you're ready."

He just laughs.

"You are!"

Oh, gosh. I wish Brice would get here. I don't know what to say. How do I convince someone young and enthusiastic to go into a line of work that he knows has the potential to suck all that out of him? I feel like I'm trying to sell him something that may not be the best for him. I don't want to be responsible—even partly—for someone being miserable for the rest of his life.

I smile shakily and sit down at the kitchen table, motioning for him to join me. Propping my feet on the chair next to me, I arch my back and rub it. In a disappointingly dead tone of voice, I repeat what Brice has said to me a million times: "It's a calling, not a job."

Slumped next to me, he sighs. "Yeah. And I'm not hearing it. As a matter of fact, I feel like God's shouting at me to run away."

I can't help but laugh at the thought. But then I realize how sad I am at the idea of Jared leaving us. The year has flown by. "So, what's the plan, then, *if* you decide to run away? Will you go back to Alaska?"

He shakes his head. "Nah. I like the Midwest. I've felt at home in St. Louis and Chicago, both. I'll probably stick around here for a while."

My heart lifts slightly at that news. "Really? What will you do?"

"Go back to school?" he answers uncertainly with a shrug. "I like learning. Even if I'm not always very good at it. Anyway, I'll figure something out."

I guess I'd better learn how to cope better with Brice's bad moods, because this news isn't going to improve them one bit.

Later, in bed, I can tell that Brice is awake, but he made it clear with his monosyllabic utterances while we cleaned up the kitchen and got ready for bed after Jared left that he didn't want to talk. About anything. But the silence is stressing me out.

Into the dark bedroom, I ask, "What do you think?"

He pauses so long before saying anything that I think he's going to outright ignore my question. Finally, he says, "About what?"

"Jared!" I say, exasperated with his deliberate obtuseness.

Another long pause and then, "It doesn't matter what I think."

"It matters. He cares. Your arguments for going through with his ordination could have been more persuasive."

"This is between him and God. Period. He has to listen to the quiet voice in his heart."

"That's a cop out. You have a lot of influence over him, probably more than that quiet voice. He looks up to you; he sees how you react to things; he's making this decision based on what he's observed at Messiah." I place my hand over his when he rests it on my belly after receiving a nudge against his side. "Don't you feel responsible at all for this? *I* do! I feel like we— we *broke* him."

After a long-suffering sigh, he replies, "Of course, I do, to a certain extent. But he got a realistic experience during his vicariate. If he feels he can't handle it, then he's right to reconsider the ministry. I think he's still open to going through with his ordination; he just won't be answering calls from congregations anytime soon. And that's okay. That doesn't mean he never will."

I grunt discontentedly, wondering what happened to the guy who told me that he doesn't accept no for an answer. We beat that out of him in a hurry, I guess.

"No use worrying about it," Brice says now.

Sarcastically, I respond, "Oh, okay, then. In that case…"

"I'm tired."

"Whatever."

"You should try to get some sleep."

I flounce against my pillow. "Well, we both know that's probably not going to happen, but you go ahead and sleep for both of us."

"For crying out loud," he mutters. He sits up against the headboard and turns on his bedside lamp. "You want me to stay up all night with you, mulling over all the world's worries? Let's do this. Where shall we start?"

A little (okay, a lot) less gracefully and more slowly, I join him, crossing my arms and resting them between my boobs and my bump. Glaring over at him, I say, "Let's start with you. What the hell's going on with you lately?"

He laughs bitterly. "Hmmm. Let me see: my schedule is crazy, the church budget is messy, and a vicar in whom I've invested a year of energy and effort has decided after interning with me that being a pastor stinks. Now add sleep deprivation, and it's no wonder that I'm a little crabby."

"I'll give you the first two, but you just found out about Jared, and don't even talk to me about sleep deprivation. Anyway, get used to it, because in a few months, you'll look back on this fondly as one of the most rested times of your life."

"At least a baby doesn't keep you awake out of spite."

"I'm not being spiteful!"

"Okay."

"I'm not! I'm just telling you that I won't be getting any sleep."

"And that I'm a horrible husband if I sleep while you're unable to."

"I didn't say that!"

"No, your style is too passive-aggressive for that."

The tears prick my eyes. I turn on my side away from him (even though that's not the "correct" side for me to lie on). "I'm sorry," I choke. "I don't think you're a bad husband for wanting to sleep. Goodnight."

He doesn't move.

As soon as I made the comment about his sleeping enough for both of us, I knew it was a mistake. Before I said it, really. But like a lot of other things I say and do lately, it feels like I'm watching myself from across the room and that I'm not really in control of myself. I'm using all my impulse control lately to govern my diet. There's nothing left over for my other behavior or my mouth. I'm beginning to think they had something right back in the day when they "confined" pregnant women and hid them away from society. In my case, at least, we'd be doing society a major favor.

And he does deserve to sleep. Just because I can't doesn't mean he shouldn't. I'm just frustrated about the situation with Jared and frustrated with Brice's defeatist attitude. And horny (if I'm completely honest).

His light goes off, and he settles under the covers, curling himself around my back. He kisses my shoulder. "I'm sorry."

"Don't be. You're right that it's dumb to worry."

"I hate being short with you and being grumpy all the time, and I'm sorry for acting like I don't care about Jared or that you're not sleeping." He snakes his arm over my side and pulls me closer. "It's my favorite time of year, but I'm being a scrooge, and I hate it."

With supreme effort, I flip over to face him. "I know how you can make it up to me."

He looks confused. "How?"

I rub my foot up and down his leg.

"Oh!" he says. "That!"

"Yes, that."

He winces regretfully. "Maybe tomorrow night? It's been a really long day."

I gulp and smile. "Oh. Yeah. I understand. I just thought… Anyway. Goodnight." I kiss his nose and close my eyes, relieved when he rolls over so I can press my hot face against his back.

I wish I could go to sleep and put an end to this detestable day.

29

FAREWELL

"*W*ell, it's the moment many of you have been waiting for." Jared beams down from the pulpit at the start of his last sermon. "My last Sunday as your humble vicar. My farewell sermon. Pastor Northam was nice—and brave—enough to give me this opportunity to say thanks." He half-turns and looks behind him at Brice, who holds up a hand in a humble wave and chuckles at Jared's self-deprecating humor. Addressing the congregation again, Jared says, "I guess he hasn't learned anything this past year."

I laugh through my tears with the rest of Messiah's members.

When the polite laughter subsides, he continues, "But I have. I've learned a lot. Even though it may not seem like I have. For example, when Mrs. Hanson opened her home to me twelve months ago, I learned that she does *not* like to be called Elizabeth. Where are you, Betty? Ah!" He spots her in the same pew she's inhabited every Sunday for the past seventy-plus years. "There you are! That's right. I was firmly informed of that the first—and only—time I made that mistake. I learned that lesson quickly. 'My name's Betty, young man! If you're going to be impertinent enough to call me by my first name, get it right!'" Speaking of impertinent, he blows her a kiss. She pretends to snatch it from the air and pat it against her cheek.

Well! Who knew that Jared had been shacking up with his ninety-something year old girlfriend for the past year?

"I got it right every time after that. Other lessons weren't as easy to learn." He sobers, looking down at his notes. "No, I did a lot of stumbling and made a lot of messes. I offended people with the things I said and didn't say and did and didn't do." He looks up. "For those of you who fall into any of those categories, I'm truly sorry. Just know that I didn't do anything with malice or out of spite. I'm really that clueless. Pastor can attest to it."

Again, Brice holds up his hand and nods. Maybe they should consider taking this act on the road.

I dab at my eyes while Jared recounts some of his more amusing and harmless blunders. I can't believe he's really going to be gone after today. I think I'm getting a preview of what it must be like to see one of your kids leave the nest. I mean, I know it's not quite the same (or the same at all), but I do feel very protective of him nonetheless. I care what happens to him; I want him to make the right decisions, no matter what he ends up doing after this; I want him to be happy. But most of all, I want him to fondly remember this year. Based on what he's saying up there right now, I think he will, despite all the challenges.

I'm startled from my wandering thoughts at the sound of my name. "Peyton, thanks for sharing your husband with me— Oh, wait. That doesn't sound right." He giggles nervously for the first time in the entire message. Brice drops his head and covers his eyes. "I mean, thanks for being generous with his time, even though you were newlyweds and probably could have done without having me around so much. You made me feel welcome in your home, no matter what was going on. You even cooked for me once or twice, which I understand is a rarity. I'm honored." He puts his hand to his chest, while Nicole nods furiously next to me. I nudge her so she'll stop being such a goober. "And judging by all of the advice you gave me and all the judgment-free listening you did, I can say this: you're going to be a great mom, even if you can't bake a cupcake to save your life. Seriously, people. You should have seen the ones she tried to bake for my birthday. They were so sad!"

"And Pastor. Well, I'd need a lot longer than twelve minutes to say all the thanks I owe you. Don't worry, folks. I won't go over my time limit. That was the first rule Pastor Northam stressed to me: 'Jared, whatever you do, keep the sermons to twelve minutes or less. If it's Christmas or Easter, you may be able to get away with fifteen. But don't push it.'"

Brice shakes his head and rolls his eyes.

"Just kidding, everyone," Jared says, like he needs to make sure no one really thinks Brice said that. "Anyway, at the risk of pulling a Pastor Northam and getting all emotional up here…" He pretends to blot at the corner of his eye with his knuckle. His good-natured teasing about Brice's frequent choke-ups gets the biggest laugh of all. "I do want to give you my sincere thanks for including me in your church family for this past year. It has truly felt like a family, complete with squabbles and forgiveness, trials and tribulations, followed by laughter and fun. The Lord has blessed me with this experience. And I hope my presence here—however chaotic it sometimes could be—was a blessing to you.

"I'll be ordained in early February. You're all invited, of

course. And then I'm going back to school to pursue a doctorate in theology, because I'm really more of a thinker than a shepherd. Not everyone can be both, like Pastor Northam there. I'm not sure everyone here appreciates what a special person it takes to be both. I know I didn't appreciate it until I realized I wasn't one of those people. I just hope it's not taken too much for granted. Every time you feel yourself getting complacent about it, I want you to keep this in mind: you could have a pastor like me." He shudders theatrically. "I know that thought will give some of you nightmares if you dwell on it too much.

"The thing is, the Lord wants us to be generous with one another. He wants us to look upon each other with favor and love and help each other be our best, even when we're not easy to help. Maybe especially if that's the case. When someone is despondent or says they can't do something, He wants us to give them three reasons they can. He wants us to be cheerleaders for each other. He doesn't want us to find fault or nitpick or always put the worst construction on each other's words and actions. He wants us to always give one another the benefit of the doubt. Generosity. When we're generous with our time, our hospitality, our wisdom, and our sympathy and love, we're *living* the Word, and we're Christians in practice, not just in name. Amen."

"Your blood pressure's edging up there again," Dr. Walsh warns at my January appointment as she strips off her latex gloves after my exam. She turns to Brice, as if I'm his child, not his wife. "Are we watching sodium intake?"

He shrugs. "At home, yes. I don't know about other times."

"Gee, thanks, hon, for your faith and support," I say sweetly. To Dr. Walsh, I vow, "*We* are the queen of bland foods, okay? If it tastes good, I throw it away and choose something taste*less*. Happy?"

She chuckles. "Okay. How about stress? Anything about the baby or pregnancy worrying you? If so, let's get it out there and set your mind at ease. Gestational hypertension is serious and can lead to preeclampsia, which is a *very* serious condition. You don't have high protein levels in your urine, so I don't think that's what this is. I think it's good-old fashioned stress."

I shake my head. "I'm not worried. This guy's really active, and I'm not experiencing any symptoms besides backache and insomnia, so there's nothing really new for me to be concerned about."

She taps her chin. "Insomnia, huh?"

"Yep. It's in my chart."

Grabbing control of the mouse next to the wall-mounted computer, she scrolls around and says, "And there it is. Sorry. I missed that. Well, there are some things you can do before bed—natural things—to help. Have you tried drinking warm milk?"

With a wrinkle of my nose, I say, "Yes. Not my favorite remedy. I've also tried warm baths and showers."

Dr. Walsh looks at Brice. "You could do bedtime massages. Of course, sex works for most people, too."

Hmmm... sex. What's that?

Instead of admitting that things are a little dead in that department, though, I simply say, "Okay."

I'm getting fairly used to operating on little-to-no sleep, so I don't think it's worth spending a bunch of time talking about it. Frankly, it's irritating me. I know what (or who) is causing my stress, but I'd have to be a real bitch to tattle on him to the doctor.

Despite his frank apology to me the week before Christmas, his mood has worsened in the ensuing weeks. Exponentially.

Jared's departure bummed him out a lot more than I thought it would. If anything, I thought it would be a relief. But he moped around for days, saying things like, "If Jared were here, we could go do that," or "That would have been a perfect job for Jared." And I swear he got misty-eyed during a jewelry store commercial when the tag line was, "He went to Jared." But maybe I'm projecting my feelings on that last one, because it kind of choked *me* up. The vicar may have been slightly overzealous, but things are a little less cheerful and bright without him. It was impossible to be in a bad mood around him; now, bad moods are a little too possible.

It's not just Jared's absence, though, that's bothering Brice. He feels like a failure where the former vicar is concerned, like he soured the guy on becoming a pastor. And it doesn't matter how many times Jared tried to tell him otherwise; he's convinced he was a poor role model and that Messiah—as a congregation—was a poor witness and didn't offer him a secure and tranquil learning environment.

Our streak of peaceful Sunday dinners ended when Dad recently made the mistake of jokingly inquiring, "Are things almost back to normal now that the dodo bird's flown back to St. Louis?"

Brice stopped chewing, looked up swiftly, stared at Dad for an uncomfortable number of seconds (probably five, but it seemed a whole lot longer), resumed chewing, swallowed, wiped his mouth, and then *finally* said, "I guess I don't know to whom you're referring, Kent."

I thought at first that we were going to be okay, since he was still using contractions, but no sooner had my shoulders relaxed than Brice continued, without waiting for Dad to be more specific, "Because I'm sure you wouldn't speak so uncharitably about someone who devoted a year of his life in service to our church family."

I was torn between warning my husband that calling my dad out in front of everyone in his own home was a bad idea with inevitably ugly results and letting him give Dad the piece of his mind that he deserved. So I just sat there, waiting to see what would happen next. Nobody else seemed to breathe.

Dad blinked hard a couple of times before asserting, "He was an idiot."

Calmly, Brice set his napkin next to his still-full plate, plunked his elbows onto the table, folded his hands, and tilted his head while keeping a disconcertingly intense lock on my dad's eyes. "It's funny you should use that word, Kent, because I've defended you on several occasions when it's been used in reference to you."

Tossing his fork down with a clunk against his plate, Dad replied hotly, "I don't give a damn what anyone thinks about me, and I sure as hell don't need you to defend me to them."

"Duly noted."

"Anyway, who said I was an idiot?" Dad inquired skeptically.

Brice just chuckled, shook his head, and went back to eating, and no matter how much Dad threatened and cajoled, he never said another word on the topic. We left almost immediately after the meal.

Yeah. Not stressful at all.

But with Dr. Walsh, I stick to the tried and true scapegoat, "Work's busy. Maybe I'll just try to go a little slower there. Take more frequent breaks."

She nods. "That's a good idea. I really don't want to put you on bed rest. *You* really don't want me to put you on bed rest. It's not a good time."

From the corner of my eye, I see Brice look at his watch and rub the tops of his legs. He purses his lips, looks up at the ceiling, and crosses his arms over his chest. Reverend Fidgety's squirming gets Dr. Walsh's attention, too. "Uh, all right, then. If that's it, I'll see you in a month. But I want you to take your blood pressure at least once a week—most pharmacies have a free meter you can use—and call me if yours goes higher than 140/90. Got it?"

"Sure thing."

She pats my knee. "Oh, and keep up the good work with

the exercise. Walks on your lunch break; walks in the morning; walks after dinner. And even if you're not sleeping, stay in bed and get as much rest as possible."

"You've got it," I promise.

When she finally leaves, I hop down from the exam table and go about the now-familiar routine of getting dressed, except this time, Brice seems to be trying to hurry things along. He holds out each piece of my clothing for me and shakes it insistently when I don't take it from him as quickly as he wants me to. At the third shake of my shirt while I'm still trying to do up the side buttons on my pants, I snatch it from him and drape it over my shoulder.

Twisted to the side and trying to see around the swell of my breasts to figure out why I can't fasten the buttons (whoever designed these pants obviously had no idea what it's like to be pregnant—probably a man), I ask, "Are you in a hurry? Because if so, please feel free to go. You're making me nervous."

"I have a meeting to get to, but I still have time."

"A meeting? On a Tuesday afternoon?" Tuesday is usually hospital rounds day, which is why we often do our prenatal visits on this day, so he'll be right down the street from the hospital and can go straight there after our appointments.

"It's at the bank," he answers shortly, as if that explains everything.

But now I'm just more confused. I can't think of a single thing going on at church that would require him to meet with the bank. At least not anything I know about.

What if he told me, though, and I was spaced out? I don't want to admit that I have no idea, if that's the case. No, surely I would remember that conversation. Because it would have been a conversation. We haven't really had one of those in a while.

Finally, I get the pants buttoned and pull my shirt over my head. When my head pops through, I say, "Don't get mad, but am I supposed to know about this whole thing at the bank?"

He tilts his head and smiles slightly. Wow. I'd almost forgotten what his smile looked like. I really like it. It's contagious. Even though I'm not sure what's funny, I return the smile while he answers with a question, "Why would I be mad?"

Danger, danger, danger! Do not say the first thing that pops to mind ("Because you seem mad all the time lately"). Keep it on you; don't even mention his mood lately.

Off-handedly, I reply, "I dunno. I've been sort of distracted; I thought maybe I spaced out on a conversation, or something."

Handing me my purse, he says, "Yeah, I've noticed that lately. But, no, I haven't mentioned anything about the bank to you."

What? He's "noticed that lately"? How can he notice something that I just made up for his benefit? *I* haven't been spaced out and distracted; *he* has. And moody and short-tempered and—and distant!

I bite back my outrage and offer, "I guess we both kind of have been. It's been quiet around the house," as we exit the doctor's office.

In the frigid, windy parking lot, he hunches his shoulders around his ears and squints into the wind as he stands with me next to the driver's door of my car. "Anyway, I, uh, probably should tell you about it, but it can wait until tonight."

Considering we're standing in the middle of what feels like a wind tunnel in Antarctica, and he's coatless, I don't have much choice but to agree with him about waiting until later, although I'm dying to know now.

He opens the door to my car, effectively closing the door on the discussion. "I'm going home right after the bank, so I'll have dinner waiting for you when you get home," he says as I sit down behind the wheel.

Putting on a brave face, I reply, "Well, I'll be sure to be home right on time, then; sounds great."

The door and roof serve as handles as he does a modified standing push-up to lean down and give me a chaste kiss on the temple. "I'll see you then." He shuts my door, jams his hands in his trousers pockets, and jogs around the front of my car to get to the driver's side of his. Then, when he notices I'm still watching him after he's gotten behind the wheel and started the engine, he gives me a faint smile before backing out of his parking space and driving away.

I thought of about a hundred possible reasons for Brice to have a meeting at a bank this afternoon, but what he just told me wasn't one of them.

I blink at him and set my fork down precisely on the edge of my plate.

"Now, I can't tell you're rockin' a ten on the freak-out scale, but it's not that big of a deal," he tries to reassure me. I've noticed, however, that he hasn't touched his food. As a matter of fact, his hands are still folded from when we prayed ten minutes ago, before he gave me what I'm assuming is a very dumbed-down account of what happened at the bank and what led to that meeting.

"Getting kicked out of our house is a big deal," I argue.

"We're not getting kicked out of our house," he says in

that tone he uses with members of the youth group when he thinks they're overreacting in typical teenage fashion to something he's said or done in jest. It's his "Stop being so dramatic" tone. I hate it, especially when it's directed at me.

"What do you call it, then?" I challenge.

He thinks about it for a second. "Asset management. This house is church property. The church needs some money, and it owns this house outright, unlike some other parts of the campus, so it makes sense to sell it to free up some cash. That's all. It's nothing personal."

My eyes fill with tears. "Nothing personal? This house is our *home*. I mean, how much do they really expect to get from it? Enough to make a difference? Really? And where are *we* going to live? In the choir loft?"

He laughs. "No."

When I throw my napkin on my plate and say on the verge of panic, "Is the church dying? Is it going under? Is this the beginning of the end? I've gone to Messiah my whole life!" he gets up, switches to the chair next to mine, scoots close to me, and puts his arm around my sagging shoulders.

"Honey, calm down. This is why I haven't mentioned any of this to you; I knew you'd freak out."

I stiffen. "How long has this been going on? How long have you known we were going to be kicked out of our house?"

"We're not—" He stops abruptly, sighs, and answers my original question, "Just a few weeks."

Jerking away from him, I stop crying and stare at him with wide eyes. "A few weeks? Since before Christmas?"

He nods. "Yeah. The trustees, treasurers, elders, and I met and discussed the possibility a couple of weeks before

Christmas. I didn't want to say anything until it was a sure thing, though."

"Wait a second. My dad's known all this time, too?"

"Of course."

"Unbelievable," I mutter. "I can see him being okay with kicking *you* out on your ass, but he's okay with his daughter and grandson being turned out onto the street?"

"Buh-rother."

"I'm serious! Where are we going to live? Huh? If the church is getting rid of this house to liquidate some of its assets—yeah, I know more about money than you may think I do—then how are they going to pay for us to live somewhere else?"

He rubs the back of his neck, looking decidedly less confident. "Well, that's one of the changes." Before I can explode, he rushes on, "We're going to rent one of the other houses the church owns but still pays a mortgage on. Our rent will go toward the mortgage payment."

I swallow loudly. "What? We're going to pay rent to the church?"

"We've discussed something like this before, Peyton. I don't know why you're acting like this is a huge surprise. The thing is—"

"No! I'll tell you what the thing is. The thing is, we discussed moving out of the parsonage and buying our own home someday. On *our* terms. We did *not* talk about being forced from this house into some shit-hole foreclosure property that the church bought to renovate and flip and rent out to a low-income family in a spotty neighborhood, where I'm afraid to come home after dark. I'm not doing it. And let me get this straight."

He props his head on his hand and listens with exaggerated patience.

I jump up from the table and pace the length of the kitchen. "They're going to sell this house out from under us and not only stop providing you a home rent-free but *charge* you rent on one of their fucking *charity* homes? Supplying this house to us is not a *favor* they're doing you; it's part of your salary! Without it, you're essentially taking a pay cut that adds up to thousands of dollars a year, at least! Uh-uh. That makes no sense for us. None whatsoever."

"Are you finished?" he asks calmly.

I seriously consider his question before answering, "No. I'm not finished. I'm pissed off at them—my own father included—for even proposing something like this, but what about you? How could *you* agree to this? And without telling me, without giving me any kind of warning?"

"It's no secret that money is tight. It's been that way for years."

My pacing is making me dizzy, so I stop, but I remain standing and say, "I thought it was getting better, though. We just bought a car! I guess that explains why you tell everyone who comments on my car that we 'got a good deal,' and your Jeep's paid off, like it's any of their business how we pay for things. Do I need to start providing an item-ized list to the treasurer every month about how much I spend on incidentals?"

"Come on."

"This is unfair and cruel and—and selfish of them!"

With his foot, he nudges his original chair further away from the table, closer to my legs, and points to it. "Sit. Down."

"No."

"Yes. Now. You're getting too worked up."

"When were you going to tell me, Brice?" I whine as I reluctantly plop into the seat and brush tears from my face.

"Huh? Were you just going to sedate me on moving day? And then I'd wake up in our new 'home.'" I use air quotes. "And the deed would be done, and there'd be nothing I could do about it?'"

He rolls his eyes. "Yep. That was my plan. Darn. You figured it out." When I just glare at him, he asks, "Are you ready to discuss this like adults now? Because, honestly, I'm about out of patience with your histrionics."

I cross my arms over my chest. "I have every right to be upset about this. And it's disturbing that you're not more upset. You're willing to just take it, no matter what it means for your family, because the Church comes first."

His palm slaps so loudly and so suddenly on the table that I cringe and flinch away.

"Enough!" he growls.

When my heart stops pounding, the tears flow unchecked down my cheeks, partly because he's startled me, and partly because my feelings are hurt at the tone he used and the disgusted look on his face. But I'm quiet and still and force myself to listen to him.

More gently, but still firmly, he says, "God comes first; then you; then our family. And you know this. So stop making it sound like I'm putting everything and everyone else ahead of you, because I'm not. I've spent *days* and *weeks* praying about this; there is no 'taking it' about it. And the elders and trustees and treasurers who are part of your church family have prayerfully considered what's best for all involved, so stop playing the victim. They're taking care of us; and we, in turn, are taking care of the church. Because that's what you do in a family."

"You don't throw your pregnant *sister* out of her warm, safe house," I object quietly. "That's not how you treat family."

"They're not throwing us out. How many times do I have to say it, Peyton? They're *not* throwing us out. Look at me." He grabs the front of the chair in which I'm sitting and pulls it toward him. I screech across the floor before coming to a stop with my knees up against his. He chucks me under the chin to force my head up. Miserably, he says, "It was my idea, okay? I'm the one who proposed all of this; I'm the one who volunteered to give up this house. So, if you're going to be mad at someone, then be mad at me. It's not your dad's fault or any of the other elders or members of the church governing body. *I* told them we have plenty— because we do—and that we don't need to be supported as much as we are by the church—because we don't. But they made me promise that this would only be temporary and that I'd accept my full compensation again as soon as we got out of this rough patch. So, see? They love us and want to do right by us. That's why it was such an easy decision."

"A unilateral decision."

He swallows and nods but maintains, "The right decision."

"But you didn't trust me to come to the same selfless conclusion."

"What? That's not—"

"Yes. Otherwise, you would have shared the decision with me. You would have laid out the facts for me and told me how strongly you felt about doing this, and you would have believed that I could come to the right conclusion, too."

He stares down at his knees, seemingly weighing every word before speaking it. "I was trying to shield you from the stress of making such a difficult decision. It's been stressful to wade through all the pros and cons. And you're not supposed to be worrying right now."

I draw away from him. "Don't you *even*!"

He looks up, confusion in his eyes. "What?"

"How convenient for you to blame the baby for your cutting me out of this decision, because it's too worrisome, but it's okay for me to worry about what an—an ass-face you've been to live with lately! Don't *even* blame the baby!"

Rubbing his face, he claims, "I'm not blaming anyone. I'm explaining why I handled it alone. Your reaction tonight proves my point."

After a dismissive wave at him and the unfairness of this whole situation, I rise from the chair and leave the room. I'm too emotional to effectively defend myself. He's right; I've done nothing but support his argument that I'm irrational and impractical and selfish and incapable of making a mature decision that meets the needs of the greater good.

On my way down the hall toward the bathroom, where I plan to sit in a warm bath for as long as is medically advisable (and maybe a few minutes more, since I'm feeling defiant that way), I hear him call after me, "Peyton! The house we're moving to is actually really nice! And it's right down the street from here! In this same neighborhood! Peyton!"

I'm finished with this conversation, though. To think, I've missed conversing with him. After a talk like that one, I realize it's overrated. Any more like it, and I'll wind up in the hospital for this last trimester.

UNCOMFORTABLE MIRROR

$\mathcal{O}$ur "nice" house is a construction zone.

The first and only time I've visited it (with Jared, not Brice, who was emceeing seniors' Bible trivia night), I stood next to a pile of drywall dust in the middle of the "living room," looking through the bare studs to the "kitchen," with my hand over my mouth as I blinked back tears.

Jared, visiting from St. Louis following his ordination, turned in a circle next to me and said, "Well, silver linings: this house has one more bedroom and one more bathroom than you're used to; you'll get to decorate it however you want; and it'll *probably* be done before the baby's born. Most likely. Maybe."

I wasn't able to respond. I knew if I acknowledged his optimism, I'd break down sobbing. I couldn't imagine the house—which didn't even have toilets yet—would be habitable and ready to receive our son in a couple of months.

When he rushed across the room and said, "Oh, looky! A fireplace!" at what looked like nothing more than a jagged, gaping hole in the far wall, I had to turn around and pick my way carefully back to my car. A few minutes later, he joined me and patted my shoulder. "It's going to be okay, really. Brice won't accept anything less, even if he has to be the one to finish it."

I know deep down he's right. I may have doubts about a lot of things (most things, lately), but I don't doubt Brice's devotion and dedication. If nothing else, it goes against his loyal personality to stop caring. I'm the raisin to his bran. Things are just a little soggy right now.

And whose fault is that? Mine. The old me wouldn't care about the tight budget and the mess and the stress of moving, possibly into an unfinished house, when she's about to pop out a baby. The old me would see this as an adventure. She'd dream big but still be happy when things turned out a little smaller than those dreams. She'd be excited to put her stamp on this place and talk about it incessantly to her amused husband.

But I don't feel at all like the old me. I just feel old. And it has nothing to do with my age.

"You *could* be anemic," Dr. Walsh's nurse reluctantly agrees in a monotone. "*Or* you could be thirty-five weeks pregnant. That kind of takes it out of people."

"Ha!" I chuckle nervously and good-naturedly. "Yeah. How do I figure out which one is the real problem? I'm dying here."

Big sigh. "You're not dying, Mrs. Northam."

"You know what I mean."

"We'll have to do a blood test to check for anemia."

"I'm there. Tell me when."

"I was thinking at your next checkup."

My heart sinks. "Oh. But that's not until next week."

"Mrs. Northam?"

"Yes?"

"You want my blunt advice?"

Not really, but I answer, "Okay," anyway.

"Eat a steak. Or two. Take a brisk walk. Get frisky with your husband. Energy produces energy, you know." When I make noncommittal noises, she adds, "And when we see you next week, we'll do that blood test. I'll make sure Dr. Walsh is aware of your complaint."

Yeah, like my insomnia? I want to ask but don't. Instead, I say sweetly, "I appreciate it. Thanks for your time."

"Uh-huh," she says before hanging up.

Okay, I'd hate me, too.

I have a plan. And I have that bitchy nurse to thank for it, too.

On my way home from work, I stop by the grocery store and pick up two fat steaks (although I'm not planning to eat both of them—one is for my husband, thank you). I'm going to cook these up, and then after dinner, I'm going to drag Brice on a walk with me, and then after that, we're going to come home, and I'm going to make him screw my brains out. That's right, screw me; not make love to me (or "express his love"). I need something a little more invigorating than our usual kiss and cuddle. What is it the English call it? Slap and tickle? Yeah! More like that.

The first niggling of doubt creeps in when I get home and see his Jeep's not in the driveway yet, but I don't despair. If he's going to be markedly late, he always calls or texts me. I'll just get the steaks going and flash fry some spinach while I'm at it. By the time dinner's ready, I'm sure he'll be home. And he'll be so proud that I remembered how to cook this stuff the way he likes it.

As I'm flipping the steaks over, my phone buzzes on the counter. His text says, *You coming to voters' meeting? Starts in 5 min.*

Oh, eff me. I totally forgot about the voters' meeting tonight. Obviously. Well, there's no way I'm going to make it, and this means that he's not going to be home for at least another hour. Shit.

I reply, simply, *No.*

But even this development doesn't discourage me. All is not lost. The food will keep (his will, anyway. I'm eating mine as soon as it's ready, because I'm starving). And I can still take my post-dinner walk. By the time I'm finished cleaning up the kitchen and waddle up to the church, the meeting should be over, and the building will have cleared out, and I'll surprise Brice in his office, and maybe we can do something a little daring and naughty in there. Well, that's a little ambitious, I guess. There's no way he'll agree to that, but he can leave his Jeep at the church, so we can walk home together and convene in our oh-so-usual meeting place. After he eats the delicious meal I've—

Burnt for him. Oh, shit. I transfer the pan from the hot burner to the cold one next to it and wave a towel under the smoke detector, which is shrieking indignantly at me. When the smoke clears, I inspect the damage.

Fortunately, the steaks are only burnt on one side. Seared, I'll call them. And as for the spinach, well, he'll never even miss what he didn't know I attempted and had to throw away. I'll just (a quick look in the cupboards reveals a disappointing selection of canned vegetables) toss these low-sodium green beans in a pot on the stove and call it good. All right, so it's not a gourmet meal. Fortunately, I'm married to a guy who isn't picky. About a lot of things.

Forty-five minutes later, and it's time for me to go rescue

my husband from the inevitable lingerers who corner him and want to invite him over for dinner some night or get his advice about a dispute they're having with their neighbors or discuss a "hypothetical" problem that a "friend" of theirs has. I thought about taking his dinner plate to him, but that would only encourage him to stay longer, so instead I'm using his dinner—among other things—as a motivation for coming home.

Wow. It's such a beautiful night, I observe as I head toward the brightly lit church one block away. Still feels like winter, definitely, but it has that hint of spring promise in the breeze coming off the lake. Before we know it, it'll be spring, officially. The kids in the church will be playing on Little League and school baseball teams and asking us to come to their games. At the first sign of warm weather, we'll be flooded with invitations to backyard barbecues. We might even take the baby to his first Cubs game. He'll look so precious in a tiny pin-striped onesie and an itty-bitty ball cap.

Suddenly it hits me that we probably won't be living in the parsonage anymore by that time, either. Brice told me the other day that they've made some major headway on the construction at the rental house. I haven't had the heart to even drive past there since my first (and only) visit to the place with Jared a couple weeks ago. But according to Brice, it has walls now. And plumbing and wiring (although the utilities haven't been turned on yet).

I'm still sort of in denial about the sale of the parsonage, despite the sign in the yard. It's not like I have a huge affection for the place, either. But like everything else associated with the church, it's been a constant in my life. I remember when Pastor Niedermeyer would have his yearly Super Bowl party there. In that tiny house! We'd all be packed in, watching the game on this tiny TV (at least by today's standards) while his wife would hold court in the kitchen with the people not really interested in the game, stirring the little smokies and cheese dips in the various crock pots plugged into power strips on the counters. (Can you say, "Fire hazard"?)

By the time I was old enough to attend these functions, their only son, Clay, was already grown and out of the house (living in Michigan, I think), but I'd look at the pictures of him and wonder what it must be like to be a pastor's kid, to *live* with a pastor all the time. If someone had told me then that not only would I know what that's like someday, but that I would live in the exact same house, I would have told them they were "retarded" or something equally offensive and disbelieving. Heck, if someone had told me all that just five years ago, I would have reacted the same way.

But this *is* my life now. And that's my house. I wake up in it every single morning. I come home to it every single evening after work. I've made my own life memories within those walls and under that roof. I spent my first night as a married woman in that house. Our first child together was conceived in that house (I'm pretty sure). It may be bland and boring and small, but it's ours. Or was. Or is temporarily. Or something. It's just *sad*.

Pushing through the doors to the church and lumbering my way into Brice's office, I'm halfway into a deep funk with all these maudlin thoughts. I'm relieved that he's not in his office, so I have time to recover a little bit and think happier thoughts and make sure this visit is a *nice* surprise, instead of the usual *"Downer Moment of the Day, brought to you, Pastor Northam, exclusively, every day for the rest of your life by Peyton Northam (nee Stratford). Way to pick a winner!"*

The thought of a voiceover artist saying all that actually

does make me smile a little. I still have a sense of humor, especially when it comes to myself and my quirks and foibles. I just hope Brice still does.

Quite a few cars were out in the lot when I got here, so I'm assuming the meeting is still going on. That means I should probably go to the sanctuary and sit in on the last few minutes. Instead, I sit down on the couch to wait for him.

Something's different in here, but I can't figure it out. The furniture's all arranged the same; the bookshelves hold the same books and pictures and gifts (McDonald's toys and crayon drawings) from the church's youngest members. But it seems cleaner, less cluttered, somehow.

My attention falls on his desk, usually overflowing with papers, sticky notes, coffee mugs, pens, pencils, and books, but which now holds only his computer, monitor, keyboard, mouse, and his desk calendar. It's immaculate! I don't think I've ever seen the actual wooden surface of it before. Looks like someone's nesting.

The only thing seemingly out of place on it is his journal. It's lying face up and wide open, its well-broken spine allowing the pages to flop flat against the gleaming desktop.

Not for the first time, I wonder if he writes *everything* in it, including things like Katy Perry song lyrics. You know, sitting at a stop light on the way to wherever, hear a new K.P. song, gotta record those lyrics so he can sing them in the shower the next morning. Or use them to teach me some sort of philosophical lesson.

Wouldn't that be hilarious if he really did write down stuff like that? I wouldn't put it past him, either. A little peek wouldn't hurt.

I stand up and lean closer to the desk, craning my neck and trying to get a good angle so I can see what's on the exposed pages. No dice. His writing is too tiny. I shuffle even closer when my frontal weight threatens to topple me over if I try to stay in this one spot and lean any further. Then I look over my shoulder at the open door. All clear, but I don't want to take any chances of getting caught reading something that may contain private or confidential information about church members.

Casually, I perch on the corner of the desk, facing away from the journal, as if I just happen to be sitting here, gazing at our wedding photo on his bookshelf, waiting patiently for him. Oh-so-slowly, I half-turn and glance down at the book over my shoulder. And physically flinch when I see, upside down, the word "PREGNANCY" underlined in all-caps, followed by a sentence that ends in four exclamation points.

Unable to fight my curiosity another minute—and throwing caution to the wind—I snatch up the book and read: *"This PREGNANCY is the longest forty weeks of my life!!!"*

I almost laugh out loud. If he only knew how long it feels for *me*. I chuckle at what I assume is his impatience to hold our little guy and be a father in more than name only. Until I read on.

> *Lord, I know all things are possible through You, but I don't know how much more of this I can take. The crying and the mood swings and the hypochondria and on and on and on. It's enough to drive a relatively reasonable man to the brink of insanity. I know she can't help it. Most of the time. She's probably just as frustrated as I am, so I try, try, try to give her the benefit of the doubt and be sympathetic and put myself in her place and all those things that I always preach to everyone else when they're dealing with conflict in their lives, but I'm tired, Lord. I'm tired. I want to spend the next four or five (or Heaven forbid, six... please don't do that to me,*

Lord) weeks hiding under my desk in my office. I dread going home every night. Dread it. I find any possible reason to delay that moment when I walk through the door only to be confronted by her negativity and anger.

Oh. Not nesting. Procrastinating.

I'm always wondering, what's it going to be tonight? Something at work? Something that happened on the drive home? Something I did or said that was done or said so unthinkingly that I don't even remember doing or saying it? Or something I did with the best of intentions that blows up in my face because she's so determined to take everything the wrong way? I just don't know what to do anymore. I've prayed about it a million times, and I'm trying to hear Your answer, but I don't hear it. Maybe no answer is the answer. Maybe You're trying to tell me to shut up and stop complaining to You about something that is the greatest blessing You can bestow on a man. And I know it is, Lord. I know it. I just didn't realize there would be so much payment up-front. I want my wife and best friend back, Lord. Please tell me You'll at least answer that prayer. Let me guess. I have to wait four to six weeks. Okay! If You promise me she'll be back then, I'll try to be patient. I'll be a good, loving, patient, understanding husband. Just, please, keep reminding me that this is temporary. Please—

Quickly, as I hear hurried footsteps and whistling in the hall, I put the notebook back exactly the way I found it and cross the room so that I'm standing as far away from the desk as possible when he enters his office.

I now know I'm not imagining the wariness in his eyes or the forced edge to his smile when he says, "Oh, hey! What brings you here?" He steps forward, grasps my upper arms, kisses my forehead, and then pats my tummy and says, "Hi, bud." Crossing to the desk, he smoothly closes the journal and sits down in his chair.

I don't want to be that person he described. I *never* wanted to be that person. It just… happened. But I let it. And I've made him unhappy. I've assumed his bad moods were the result of things going on here at Messiah, but all this time, it was really *me*.

I'm working so hard to pretend I haven't read what I just read that now I can't remember why I *am* here.

He bobs his head expectantly at me, but when I still say nothing, it seems to make him nervous, so he rushes, "The meeting just ended, but between you and me, you didn't miss much. Although Marilyn made her famous ooey-gooey butter bars, and they were excellent." He pops up. "I'll run down there and get one for you before they're all gone. Hang on."

I hold out a hand and snag his arm on his way past. "No. Thanks. I just ate. I'm not really hungry."

As a matter of fact, I feel pretty sick.

"But there's a separate stomach for dessert," he supplies what I normally say on the topic. His smile fades when he looks more closely at my face. "What's wrong?" The exasperated "now" at the end of the question is probably not as silent as he intended it to be.

Gritting my teeth, I answer, "Nothing. Why does something have to be wrong?"

"You look upset."

I will *not* dwell on something I should have never read, something that was a private "conversation" between him and God, something that was the equivalent of my venting to Mitzi and Jen about my mom or sister or Marshall at the end of a bad day. As a matter of fact, maybe this is God's way of answering Brice's prayer. Now that I've read the

330 | THE SECRET KEEPER CONFINED

journal entry, I can help God answer that prayer. Yeah. I'll use my misdeeds for good.

"Well, I'm not upset," I lie a little more convincingly. "I came here to rescue you from Bart Breaston's detailed description of his latest wood shop accident."

Glancing nervously at the door, he laughs and says, "Shhh! Someone might hear you."

I roll my eyes and concentrate on nothing more than the gratification I get from making him laugh.

"Anyway, you're too late," he says quietly. "I had to hear all about it. And *see* the stump where his finger used to be. Didn't stop me from finishing that ooey-gooey butter bar, though. I am strong."

"Yes, you are," I confirm. "Very." Crossing to the door, I shut it and put my back against it. "Come here."

Without thinking, he does as he's told, but I can tell he's not expecting it when I put my arms around his neck and pull him in (well, as far "in" as I can with this basketball between us) for a very enthusiastic kiss. He tastes like sweetened condensed milk and salty butter. The salt nearly makes my knees give out. Oh, how I've missed it!

"Mmph!" he hums against my mouth. When he tries to pull away, I gently but firmly hang on. "Peyton, there are people still here," he protests rather weakly.

"I know. That's why I closed the door," I reply softly.

He rests more of his weight against me as he relaxes. The baby kicks me, effectively giving him a contact kick. He smiles and puts his forehead against mine. "I love when that happens."

"Stick with me, and it'll happen to you about three hundred times a day."

"I think people would start to stare if we walked around like this all the time."

I laugh and say, "So?" before kissing him again.

This time, he's a lot less resistant. My wool coat rasps against the wooden door as he presses harder against me. After several minutes, he reluctantly pulls back and laughs self-consciously.

"You taste good," I tell him, reaching for him again.

"I told you I'd go get you one of those bars, if you want."

"I'd rather have you, Reverend Hot Stuff."

"Ah." He steps further away from me. "Well. Not here, though."

"Why not?" I whine before reminding myself, *no whining allowed*. "I mean, come on. No one's going to know."

"*I* know. And *you* know how I feel about this."

I sigh, not really surprised by this outcome. Actually, I would have been a lot more shocked if he'd taken me up on the offer. "Fine. Let's go home then."

He backs up to his desk and retrieves his journal, sliding it into his back pocket. "Okay. Just give me a second." When he merely stands there, leaning up against the front of his desk, I'm confused, until I look down.

I shouldn't have looked down. The sight of that only encourages the heretofore-dormant vixen in me. I grin evilly at him and stalk over to him. Okay, you can't stalk when you're thirty-five weeks pregnant. Now I know.) I *amble* over to him.

"Peyton," he pleads, a mock-anguished laugh bubbling out.

I walk between his wide-spread legs and smile against his laughing mouth. "You know you want it."

"That's beside the point."

"No, it *is* the point."

He puts his hands on either side of my face and says, "Nobody can know about this."

My heart races. "I'm not gonna tell!"

"This is very wrong."

"I *know*. I mean, not really." To me, "wrong" is a turn-on. To him, I know it's just the opposite, and if he talks or thinks about it too much, he'll talk himself out of it. And damn it, I want to have sex somewhere besides my bed!

Before the angels on both his shoulders get into a turf war and accidentally make his head explode, I tiptoe and nip at his lips. He smiles in that shy, uncertain way that's like crack for me. I think that's the first thing I fell in love with, followed closely by that ultra-serious look he gets in his eyes right before he says, "I love you," like right now.

I really need to hear it, too.

"I know you do," I tell him and myself. "I love you, too."

He pushes my coat off my shoulders. I let it slide off my arms and onto the floor at my feet. As soon as my hands are clear, I work at the buttons on his black shirt while he lifts his chin and removes his collar, which he sets on the desk behind him. I smooth my palms across the white expanse of t-shirt against his chest and kiss his chin. I can't believe this is happening. I've had about a billion fantasies about this. And if that makes me sick, then call an ambulance. But not right this second. Because right now, I'm busy.

Busy undoing his belt and unbuttoning and unzipping his pants. Then busy unwrapping myself from my side-tie wrap shirt and pulling down my pants with the ridiculous belly panel that never stays up anyway.

"Look at you," he whispers.

"Don't," I half-joke. It's been a long time since I've let him see me close to naked with the lights on. That ended after I nearly fainted when I saw my backside in the mirror one day while getting out of the shower.

Growing up, I was always described as the chubby Stratford girl, even after I really wasn't anymore, but everyone looks chubby next to Nicole, so the label sort of stuck. Well, I'd kill to be "chubby" right now. "Chubby" left the premises about fifty pounds ago.

"Don't be that way," he chides gently, laying both splayed hands on my belly. He kneels down in front of me and kisses it. Then he reclines on the floor and eases me down there with him.

Kissing, kissing, kissing, rubbing, rubbing, rubbing, moaning, moaning, moaning, and then, just as I'm trying to coax him out of more of his clothes, I hear a tapping on the door behind me. At first, I think it's Brice's foot against the door, but then I realize he's no longer wearing his shoes, and his sock-clad foot wouldn't make that noise. Just as I'm coming to the sick realization of what's about to happen, he shoots up into a sitting position and does the most impressive sit-and-reach I've seen since the Presidential physical fitness test in middle school, where Gina Whatsername (she was a gymnast) was able to touch the very far end of the measuring box without a hint of strain. But she didn't have a naked pregnant woman straddling her. I think I would have remembered that.

His palm hits the door where it meets the jamb just as it starts to open. This abrupt motion pushes me off him, and I land with a grunt on one butt cheek on the floor next to his outstretched legs.

"Pastor?" a deep voice I recognize as belonging to Gus, one of the trustees, calls from the other side. "You still in there?"

"Yeah!" he answers, his voice cracking. "But I'm not

decent."

I widen my eyes at him and mouth, *What? Don't tell him that!*

There's a pause while Gus seems to process this answer. "Oh. Everything okay?"

Blushing and sweating, Brice musters a laugh. "Yeah. Just— Trying on some new robes!"

His cringe-worthy lying makes me close my eyes and wince.

Gus buys it, though. "All right. Well, you're the last one here. Just set the alarm and lock the front door when you leave."

"Got it. Thanks, Gus."

"G'night, Pastor."

Neither of us moves until we hear the echo of the front door clicking shut in the otherwise empty building. Then Brice is on his feet, offering me his hand. "Are you okay? I'm so sorry I knocked you over."

Grudgingly letting him pull me up, I say, "I'd rather be knocked over than have Gus Zimmerman see my naked fat ass." As soon as I'm standing, though, I press against him. "Now we're really all alone, though."

"No. That was a sign."

"Yeah, a sign that we have the building to ourselves and don't have to worry anymore," I try to persuade him.

He's already hurriedly tucking and buttoning and zipping and re-collaring, muttering something about "the Lord's house" and "wrong, wrong, wrong," but he doesn't direct any more comments to my argument. Discussion over.

I gather my scattered clothes and get dressed with as much haste and dignity as I can muster, which isn't a lot in either case.

UNINVITED GUEST

The good reverend has his wife back. I'd even say he has his best friend back. Sort of. As far as he knows, he does, anyway. And I guess that's all that matters. He's definitely a lot happier, which makes me happier, which makes life in general happier.

I just wish I had never looked at that stupid journal. I was well on my way to making changes in my behavior without knowing how my husband felt in his own words, words that have been really hurtful and have made me suspicious and have caused me not to be able to take anything he says at face value, always wondering what he's *really* thinking. It's been interesting to see how someone who is such a proven bad liar has learned how to filter his responses so that he's technically never lying but also frequently concealing the whole truth. I won't say "always," because I'm sure that's not the case. Unfortunately, he's so good at it that it's almost impossible to tell the difference.

So when I popped into the drug store down the street from the gallery on my lunch break, and the blood pressure machine gave me the dreaded 141/84 reading, I wasn't all that surprised. It's been edging up a little bit each day. I can actually feel it. I sat there staring at the red digital numbers but made a very uncharacteristic decision not to call the doctor. Just yet. I told myself, *Breathe, think happy thoughts, take it easy this afternoon at work,* don't *think about this reading, and come back after work for one more reading.*

I did just that. And got an even higher result.

At the risk of being dismissed as hypochondriacal, I waited during dinner until after Brice had told me all about his day at work (including an impromptu visit from Jared, who's touring some of the city's universities as he tries to decide which one will get his money when he pursues his Ph.D.) before very casually mentioning, "My blood pressure's higher than Dr. Walsh wants it to be, so I'm going to give her a call in the morning."

The nonchalant tone did the trick. He didn't even look up from his plate when he said, "Okay," with his mouth full.

Whew. It was my duty to tell him, but I'd have hated to disrupt his mastication and digestion with my petty complaints.

When he eventually did look up, I flashed him a reassuring smile.

He wiped his mouth, smiled back, finished his water, and carried his dishes to the sink, where I told him to leave them, because I knew he was in a rush to get back to the church for his catechism class, which meets on Tuesday nights this time of year to avoid conflicting with midweek Lenten services. Gladly taking me up on my offer, he grabbed his jacket from the back of his chair, where he had deposited it only a few minutes earlier, shrugged it on, and kissed my upturned cheek on his way out the door to the garage.

When I heard the garage door thump to a close, I rose and took my time cleaning up the kitchen. As if I had a choice. Everything takes forever lately, because I move so slowly. While cleaning, I tried to think about nothing more taxing than which shows to watch on TV tonight.

Now, the counters and table wiped down, and the leftovers stashed in the fridge, I stare out the window at the budding trees in the dark backyard while letting the steam from the dishwasher give me a free facial. The humid warmth is soothing to the point of hypnosis. I hold onto the edge of the counter to ensure I don't wind up on the tiles.

The doorbell startles me.

Sighing, I make bets with myself about who it could be as I trudge to the door. I've considered door-to-door salesman, Jehovah's witness, any number of people from church "just stopping by," Jared, my sister or my mother (who seem incredibly vigilant and clingy the closer I get to my due date), and a random person asking for directions by the time the bell rings again when I'm halfway to the door.

"Coming!" I sing as pleasantly as possible to the impatient person on the porch. I look through the long window next to the door to get an idea of who's waiting for me (and to paste the appropriate expression on my face) and practically groan out loud when I see it's Justine Heidecker and someone else I can't see but to whom she's talking animatedly.

As soon as I open the door, she stops in the middle of a sentence and says, "There she is!" like I'm a pesky stray sock that she's been trying to track down in a week's worth of laundry.

I smile stiffly, focusing on her face, when I reply, "Here I am." That's when I glance and then do a double-take at the person standing with her: Stefan.

My heart pounds erratically while she prattles on obliviously. "This nice gentleman was asking for you up at the church. Well, actually, he was looking for Pastor Northam, but since he's in class right now, I told him I'd be glad to help him out. And then he said he really wanted to talk to you, anyway, but the church was the only address he had for you and Pastor, so I said, 'Come with me, then!' and now here we are! So…"

I just stare at her while she tells me all this useless information. Part of me is trying to figure out how to explain Stefan to her (or if I even need to), while another part of me is trying to decide if I'm going to slam the door in their faces, while still yet another part of me is paralyzed and can only think, *Fuuuuuuuuuuuuuuuuuuuuuuuuuuuuuuuuuuuuuuuuuck*.

Stefan is the next person to speak. So civilly that I can hardly believe it's his voice (I'm looking around for the ventriloquist with his hand up his ass), he says, "Hi, Peyton. I was in town on business and thought I'd stop in on you and Brice, see how you two are doing."

Turning to his guide, he bows slightly. "Thank you so much, Justine, for your help tonight. And I really hope your little one feels better soon."

She giggles and beams at him. "Oh, he'll be fine. I'm sure he's sleeping soundly for the babysitter right now, but these little colds do have a way of getting nasty, so it's always better to be safe than sorry."

"Absolutely. I'd be the same way, if I were blessed with children of my own." He tilts his head pointedly at me.

"Oh, well, you're still a young guy. Maybe someday you will, Stefan. Anyway! I'd better get back to the church before Pastor's class lets out. I'm supposed to make some announcements to the kids and hand out some flyers about upcoming events." She pats my belly without my permission. "And speaking of upcoming events, I'll see *you* at your baby shower this weekend. I can't wait 'til you see what I got for you! It is precious! Bye now!"

Before I can think of anything to say that would make her stay—I think it's just so foreign for me to want Justine anywhere near me that my brain has short-circuited at the concept—she's in her tank and backing out of the driveway, barreling toward the church.

"Aren't you going to invite me in, Peyton?" Stefan asks in his normal snooty tone.

"Why are you here?" I want to know first.

"I'd like you to answer some questions I have about my baby," he says calmly and simply. "I believe I deserve to know some things, and I believe you owe it to me to tell me those things."

Something about the way he's talking puts me more on guard than usual around him. I make no move to allow him access to the inside of the house. "Why didn't you just call me?" I ask, wishing my heart would return to its normal rate so that I could breathe and speak normally.

He smirks. "That's a little hard to do when someone blocks your number," he says in the same sing-song way one would use to point out some mildly naughty behavior to a child.

Oh. Yeah. I did do that, didn't I? But I had Marshall's blessing! Instead of defending myself to him, I simply say, "Well, you could have emailed me, then."

"Really, Peyton? Don't I deserve a little more than an email on the subject? You've robbed me of one of life's greatest joys: fatherhood."

He looks down at my bump, which I cover protectively with my arms. Wrinkling his nose, he says, "I see you're taking a lot more care with *this* one. Wouldn't want to really piss off God and lose one of his favorite people's babies, huh?"

Now I have no problem stepping back and retreating into the house so I can slam the door in his face. In theory. But in practice, things don't work as smoothly as I'd hoped. My foot catches on the weather stripping that lines the threshold, and I almost go down onto my butt in the entryway. The only thing that saves me is my grip on the doorknob. Unfortunately, that means I pull the door open wide enough to allow him to walk right in.

"Nice place," he says sarcastically, looking around and pretending there's nothing unusual about what's happening. On his way past me, I notice his eyes are bloodshot, and he seems to be walking with exaggerated casualness. That's when I realize he's been drinking. I can't smell it on him, but since he's partial to vodka, it would make sense that I can't.

"Get out," I snarl.

He shakes his head. "Nah. I don't think so. We'll be so much more comfortable talking things over in here." To illustrate his point, he takes a seat on the edge of the couch, his knees pressed together, his hands on his knees. "Now. I think you should get off your feet before you hurt yourself. You seem a bit unsteady. Is that what all that fainting was about last September? Was that little tadpole the reason for that? Because you know, *I* got the blame. Marshall was all up in my business about it."

My phone is in my purse on the counter in the kitchen, but that doesn't stop me from threatening, "I will call the cops on you if you don't leave right now."

"Oh, puh-lease. I just want to talk to you, clear the air, set the record straight, and all that jazz."

Still standing with the door wide open, my hand on the

doorknob, I tell him, "I'm not comfortable being here with you alone."

"Then call your hubby and have him come home to rescue you from the big, bad queen," he snaps. "Because I'm not leaving until you tell me what I came here to find out."

"I don't need rescuing," I say firmly. "What do you want to know?"

"Sit," he commands.

I do, as far away from him as I can possibly be while giving myself a clear path to the still-open door.

When he's satisfied that I'm going to comply with his demands, he smiles. "Now, there's a good girl. You're really making this more painful than it needs to be. I have a feeling that's your modus operandi."

I merely glare at him, so he begins, "Trust me, I tried to get this information from Drex, but he obviously regrets telling me what little he did, because when I followed up with him after my September show, he said the details needed to come from you." He tilts his head and blinks rapidly, smiling sappily. "Isn't that touching? After all the lies you told him and after you smashed his heart into smithereens, he still feels like he owes you that much."

"I'm sure I didn't break his heart," I say with a roll of my eyes.

"You did! I was there! He sat in front of that atrocious painting of you and drank and cried for days. I couldn't get him to do anything. And then just when he started functioning again, he quit. So thanks a lot for that."

My already stressed-out heart aches at the thought of Drex suffering like that because of me, even if I am fairly confident that he was more upset at the knowledge that I slept with and had a baby by Stefan than about our breakup. He hated Stefan with a passion that Christians don't have the luxury of feeling, although I'm getting pretty close to it right now.

Trying to move things along, I prod, "Well, since Drex wasn't willing to talk about me, I think it's only fair that I don't talk about him. What do you want to know about Secret?"

He looks confused for a second, until the confusion turns to amusement, which quickly morphs into disgust. "You named our child 'Secret?' Like the women's antiperspirant? Oh, fuck me. Say that isn't so!"

I blush. "That was her name, yes."

"How… fitting. You know, babies aren't like dogs. It's cruel to name them based on the circumstances surrounding their entry into your life. Secret! My God!"

Out of patience, I say, "Well, then. If that's the only question you have…"

"Nice try." He flicks a blond hank of hair away from his eyes. "How far along were you when *Secret* was born? Was she even a real baby at that point?"

I'm aware that some of what he's saying is purely in an effort to upset me, but that doesn't mean I'm able to moderate my responses. "Moderate" isn't something I've had a grasp of for nearly a year.

"Yes, she was a baby! What the fuck kind of question is that?" I explode.

"A legitimate one! I'm not a religious whack-job like you and your most recent baby-daddy, so I need to know if she was scientifically viable."

I may kill him. I may just go over there and smother him in my considerable cleavage and then leave him for dead on that couch. Giving birth to this baby in prison will be a small price to pay. Actually, the world may thank me. I'll be celebrated as a hero in the media: the murderous mama who relieved society of the real-world, male equivalent of the Wicked Witch of the East. That would be me. I could totally do it, too.

"'Scientifically viable?' If you mean would it have been legal for me to have had an abortion at the time of her birth, then no. So, I guess the answer is, yes, she was scientifically viable." My hands are shaking so badly that I have to hold onto the arms of my chair. "She had arms and legs and organs and eyelids and— and I *delivered* her, Stefan. So, yes, she was a real, 'scientifically viable' *baby*. And I loved her. Even if she did spring from *your* disgusting loins."

He laughs at me. "Oh, ouch. That really hurts, coming from you."

"I'm not saying it to hurt you; I'm saying it so you'll understand the depth of love I felt for her. I loved her so deeply that it didn't matter to me how she was conceived. And I loved her more than myself. A lot more, because I didn't love myself very much at all." When he appears completely unmoved, I shake my head. "Not that I think you could understand, because I don't think you'd ever be capable of loving someone more than yourself."

"Well, you never gave me a chance, now, did you, Little Miss High and Mighty?"

"I was afraid to give you the chance," I concede. "Because I knew you'd not only fail, but you'd make our lives miserable in the process."

He snorts. "Lah-dee-fucking-dah." Smugly, he asks, "Is this what you told Preacher Man? How horrible I was and am? How afraid you were of me? How much of a victim you were? Because I've been trying to figure out how a dirty girl like you could ever convince a man of the cloth to take you on. It must have been the innocent, helpless victim act. I wouldn't put it past you to tell him I raped you. I bet he'd drop your ass like a quarter in the collection plate if he knew the truth, if he knew how you seduced me, how you took me back to your place, how you begged me for more, how you said some of the dirtiest, raunchiest things I've ever heard a woman say. Does he know all that? I bet not. I bet he'd turn as white as that little square on his collar to know what the mother of his child is truly capable of, what she *really* likes."

I shake my head, furious at myself for letting him upset me. Despite the impending tears, I manage to say, "He knows I wasn't a victim. I didn't try to hide who I was from him. But he loves me anyway. He loved *her.*"

"Oh, how sweet.

A sob wrenches its way from deep down against my diaphragm as I remember what it felt like to be me back then. What it was like to have someone like Brice tell me I was worthy of God's love, and then his love.

"Maybe it was wrong to keep her existence from you, but I was so confused and scared at the time. I was just making decisions reflexively and trying to do what I thought was right, what I thought would be easiest in the long run."

"Easiest for you?"

"Yeah! So what? It's not like any of it was going to really be easy. I planned to raise your daughter *alone.* Does that sound easy to you?"

"Sounds like a choice. It's nice that you had options. Meanwhile, I was given nothing but a sad story—more than a year after the fact—about a dead baby who shared half of my DNA."

I wipe tears from under my eyes. "I'm sorry. I can't change what I did. If you want, I can tell you where she's buried. You can pay your respects there. That's what it all comes down to, Stefan. She didn't make it, no matter who knew about her or didn't know about her."

His lips pulled back from his teeth and his nose wrinkled, he simpers, "And if she had lived, she would have had a nice saintly step-daddy to step in—Saint Brice! Willing to take on another man's bastard child, even! Too bad you killed her before he had a chance to really see that good deed to the end."

"Why? Why are you saying these—"

Before I can finish, a winded, sweaty Brice runs through the open front door.

"Oh, and there he is right now, as if we've conjured him just by speaking his name," Stefan sneers. "How god-like."

"I think you need to leave," Brice says steadily.

"Pastor Northam to the rescue!" Stefan, not moving, replies with a laugh. "Your wife is no damsel in distress, Padre, trust me."

"So she's told me. But that does not change the fact that you are here uninvited, and you have overstayed your welcome."

Stefan imitates his stilted, controlled speech. "I am seeking information that is due to me. Overdue, as a matter of fact. And, frankly, I'm sick of you always stepping in and interrupting my attempts to have conversations with your wifey."

Ignoring him and turning his attention to me, my husband asks, "Are you okay? When Justine told me about our 'visitor,' I ran straight here."

"Justine! Now there's a fine, Christian woman," Stefan interjects before I can answer. "I bet she doesn't like it all freaky-deaky, like Peyton here. We did some things that I'm sure would shock the control-top pantyhose off Miss Justine, didn't we, Pey—"

Without warning, Brice grabs hold of Stefan's jacket at the shoulders and drags him over the back of the couch.

Lips pressed tightly together, nostrils flared, and face flushed, he pulls the kicking, laughing unwelcome visitor through the front door and heaves him into the front yard. Before I can even look through the window to see what he's going to do next, he's back in the house, slamming the front door.

I sniffle and quietly say, "He was just leaving."

Bracing his hands on the back of the couch, he looks down his arms while he catches his breath.

Stefan taunts from the front yard, "WWJD, Pastor? I think He'd do your wife!"

"Is this guy for real?" he muses aloud, glaring murderously at the front door. I've never seen him this enraged before.

"He's not worth it," I claim.

"Yeah, Preacher Man! Your wife would teach Jesus a thing or two! But maybe you already know that! Come, Lord Jesus, indeed!"

Keeping my eyes pinned on my lap and trying not to imagine what the neighbors are thinking, I say, "He'll go away if we just ignore him."

"I think that strategy has run its course. I'm pretty sure Jesus would have knocked his block off by now." He tosses me his phone. "Call the police. Now."

"But—"

He yanks open the front door and strides into the middle of the lawn, where Stefan is kneeling. I hurry to the porch to watch, even though I'm not sure I want to see what's about to happen.

"Get up!" he bellows at him. When Stefan doesn't do as he's told, Brice jerks him to his feet by his elbow.

Stefan laughs in his face. "Whatcha gonna do, Preacher Man?"

"I think I'm going to punch you in the face," he answers calmly and honestly.

I gasp, holding my finger above the last "1" in "911" as I watch and wait. I'm not going to summon the police, who will only arrest my husband if he punches that scumbag.

"You would have done it by now," Stefan jeers. "You don't have the balls to punch me. What would all your followers think?"

"I don't have any followers; therefore, if that's the only thing holding me back, you're in trouble, Buddy."

"Whoa-ho! So, just out of curiosity, what do you take more offense to? My comments about your savior or my comments about your wife? Because I'm pretty proud of both."

Hands on hips, Brice chuckles and looks down at his feet. "People have said a lot worse about Jesus Christ."

"Ah. So, it's the comments about Peyton that bother you most. I see. Well…"

"Maybe you should just slither back to New York, while you still have some teeth left in your head."

"You sure like to talk, but you're not much for action."

"I don't *want* to punch you."

"Are you *sure* about that?"

"If I remember from the last time I punched someone, it's not that enjoyable."

Movement across the street grabs my attention. Oh, fuckshitballs. Jared crosses the street and joins Brice in the yard.

"What's up?" he asks, as if the two other guys might be out there stargazing together. "I just got back from dinner with Marilyn. Love her!"

Stefan says, "Who's this, now? Simon Peter?"

That makes both Brice and Jared laugh. This reaction doesn't please Stefan.

"What's so funny?" he asks, showing signs of perturbation for the first time since being literally thrown from our house.

"For someone so godless, you sure do know a lot about Biblical figures," Brice explains his amusement.

Jared answers, "And I was just laughing at how perfectly that kind of sums up our relationship. How'd you know?"

"I don't know anything about you two. But my dad was an Episcopalian minister," Stefan says hotly. "What's it to you?"

"Now *that* is an unexpected layer to your story," Brice says, seeming genuinely interested. "So you've, what…? Devoted your life to going against everything you were raised to believe? How cliché."

"Fuck you. You don't know anything about me."

"I know quite a bit, unfortunately."

"You don't know that my childhood was a living hell. That my parents cared more about the church than they did me. That they disowned me when I told them I'm gay. You don't know any of that."

"I do now. Hmmm…" Brice curls his fingers against his chin. "That's truly awful. I'm sorry you went through that. Still. At some point you have to take responsibility for the person you choose to be."

"Don't fucking preach a sermon to me out on your fucking front lawn with your fucking flunky standing by and your fucking fat-ass wife looking on!"

POW!

Stefan falls to the grass, out cold.

"Shit!" I cry from the front porch, peeking through my fingers.

Brice looks over at Jared, who's shaking his hand and hissing through his teeth.

"Seriously, Jared?"

"Did you hear what he called me? And Peyton? Oh, fudge! That really hurts!" he groans.

"Yeah. You probably broke your ding-danged hand with that little move. Criminy." Brice steps over and looks down at Stefan. "Wow. Is that the first time you've ever punched anyone? Because you got him good. He'll be feeling that for a few days."

"I will, too," Jared says, flexing his fingers. "It doesn't look that painful in the movies."

Squinting toward me and the porch light, Brice says, "Hon, you haven't called the police yet have you?"

Hands still on my face, I shake my head.

"Good. Maybe you should just call Marshall instead. Isn't this *his* artist on our front lawn?"

BIG DAY

Okay. This is the third time she's taken my blood pressure. And the nurse took it twice before this. Between the multiple readings, her utter silence, and the deep crease between her eyes, I'm starting to get a little worried.

"Well?" I finally prompt, when I can't take the suspense anymore.

"What did you say the numbers were last night?" she asks instead of giving me an answer.

I tell her.

She shakes her head once and bites her lip. "It's a lot higher right now. A lot."

"Oh." My heart sinks as I immediately think about calling Marshall at work and breaking the news to him that I'll have to go on bed rest, effective immediately. "I understand," I tell her. "I only have two or three more weeks, right? I've often threatened to stay in bed for that long."

"No, you *don't* understand," she says, putting her hand on my arm. "You need to call your husband and have him meet us at the hospital."

"What? I have to stay in a *hospital bed* for two weeks?"

Writing in my chart and then looking something up on the computer, she answers distractedly, "No. As soon as I can get an open operating theater, you have to have a C-section to have this little guy."

"This news is not helping my blood pressure, Doc," I try to joke.

She smiles sympathetically. "I know. But it'll be fine. You're at thirty-eight weeks, which means the only thing he's doing in there is getting bigger. And putting you both at risk. He'll be much better off out here at this point. Where is Brice, anyway? I think this is the first time you've been here alone. Figures."

And cue the tears. "Oh, shit."

I thought it was odd this morning when he got up way before usual and took his shower without waking me up for our walk, but I didn't question it, because after last night's drama, I was really more interested in sleeping than exercising. And then he said, "Wish me luck," as he leaned down, smelling of minty toothpaste and spicy aftershave, to kiss me goodbye, but I was too sleepy to comprehend what he was talking about. It's not until Dr. Walsh asks me where he is that I remember.

"He's speaking at a conference today in Champaign-Urbana."

She closes her eyes and takes a deep breath. "That's two and a half hours away."

"Easily," I confirm. "But I'll call him right away. We can wait for him, right?"

Putting one hand on each of my shoulders, she looks down into my eyes. "Peyton, I can tell you're about to freak out. If you want to be able to wait for him—and I can't even promise that—then you have to stay calm. No panic attacks. Got it?"

I nod and try to tame my timpani heart, which is beating in double time. "Okay."

"Now. The first opening they have at the hospital is mid-afternoon. That should give him plenty of time to get back. But you need to call him now. Because if something opens up sooner, I'm taking it. This is serious."

I slide down from the exam table, where I've been sitting fully clothed (for once). "Okay. I, uh, I guess I need to go home and get my stuff."

She clucks at me. "Someone else needs to do that for you. You're going to wait for your surgery time in a hospital bed, hooked up to every monitor known to obstetrics. The shuttle will come pick you up. An OB nurse will be waiting for you in the hospital lobby."

"Oh."

"Yeah, 'Oh.' I'm not trying to scare you, because that'll only exacerbate the problem, but yeah. We're not fooling around here."

"Any answer yet?" I ask (more like, beg) Mom.

She shakes her head regretfully at me. "Just stay calm, though. He still has time."

It's been an hour since I've arrived at the hospital, ninety minutes since Dr. Walsh announced today would be our baby's birthday. And we still haven't been able to get in touch with Brice. Mom's taken over the duties of trying to call him, because every time I get his voicemail, alarms go off around me, and the nurse has to come in and reset everything, and she makes notes, and I just know that Dr. Walsh is going to see how often my blood pressure and heart rate spike and make me go into surgery sooner, without Brice. And I just can't let that happen.

But what if it does happen? It *could* happen. Babies are born all the time without their fathers present. I've already done it once. But I didn't think that would happen this time. I thought everything about this time would be different. It needs to be different.

Mom sees panic flit across my face. "Peyton. He'll be here. Are you praying about it?"

A brittle laugh is the only answer I can give her.

"He'd want you to pray about it instead of worrying about it. What is it he said in that sermon a few weeks ago? Why worry when you can pray?"

I don't dare admit to her that I often tune out during his sermons. It's not that they're not interesting, but something always seems to distract me. If it's not a crying kid, it's a piece of his hair that's out of place, or a single word or phrase he says that I know has ticked off one of the usual people who gets ticked off about petty things. And before I know it, he's saying "Amen," and I couldn't repeat the main theme of the sermon if someone were to ask me. Thank goodness, no one's ever asked me.

Now, I just nod at Mom. Brice has said that directly to me several times before, so I don't doubt he's also said it from the pulpit.

"You're still worrying," she accuses, hitting the redial button and holding my phone lightly to her ear so she can listen to the rings. "Pray. Just pray."

I close my eyes and do just that. I pray harder than I have for anything. Anything. Even harder than I did last night when Stefan woke up on our couch and Marshall convinced him not to press charges against Jared, who sat on the loveseat with a bag of ice on his hand.

"Brice! Oh, thank goodness! Where are you…? On the road? Good! Where…? Paxton. Where's that…? Oh." She covers the mouthpiece and relays to me, "About two hours away." To him, she asks, "Haven't you heard your phone ringing…? Oh…. Oh…. Huh-huh…. Well, that's not a very good thing to do when you have a very pregnant wife…. Yeah, we're at the hospital right now…. No, she's not in labor, but you're going to have a baby today…. Very soon. Dr. Walsh told us 2:30…. I know; that's why we've been desperately trying to get ahold of you for the past hour or two!...Well, don't get into an accident. Everything's under control for now. And now that you know, I'm sure Peyton will be a lot more relaxed…. Ha ha ha! Oh, Brice, you're so funny!... No, I won't tell her you said that…. Okay, then. Take care, and we'll see you in a little while. Bye-bye."

As soon as she hangs up, I ask, "What did he say?"

"He said he'll be here as soon as he can," she answers vaguely. "Oh, and that he loves you."

"No," I follow up impatiently. "The thing you told him you wouldn't tell me."

She straightens my blanket and looks at the fetal heart monitor. "Oh, so now you're going to worry about that? Just relax! Try to get some sleep. This is your last chance, you know. Lots of sleepless nights ahead. So exciting!"

She has a point. I'm sure he just said something *hilarious* about my worrywart tendencies. I close my eyes and try to follow her advice. After a few seconds, though, I open them again and ask, "Did he have his phone turned off? Is that why we couldn't get ahold of him?"

She sighs. "No. He left it in his car while he went in to speak. And then he just got on the road without checking to see if he'd missed any calls."

"I'm going to kill him."

"No, you're not. Let's see what's on TV." She grabs the huge remote tethered to the hospital bed and turns on one of those daytime talk shows that features a panel of washed-up celebrity women who talk over each other for an hour in an effort to prove who's the smartest, funniest, deepest, and most maternal. I watch mindlessly for the better part of an hour. Then *The Price is Right* comes on. I listlessly guess the prices, but I'm always off by a long shot. Mom's pretty good, though.

When it's over, she turns off the television and says, "Now, sleep. Brice should be here any minute."

"Mom, I haven't slept in nine months without the help of major intravenous sedatives. There's no way I'm going to be able to fall asleep with all this going on." Nevertheless, I shift into a more comfortable position on my left side, careful of the IV sticking into the top of my hand, readjust my head on the stiff pillow, and close my eyes.

"While you're *resting*, then, I'm going to run down to the cafeteria to get something to drink. I'll be back in twenty minutes."

"Fine."

I'm already ready for her to just go home. It's nothing personal—okay, it's a little personal. Our personalities just don't jibe, and her presence is intensifying the sickening feeling of déjà vu I'm experiencing right now. I can't seem to shake the awful foreboding I have at being in a hospital room with her with my baby's delivery imminent. It's too much like last time.

On that traumatic ultrasound day, when the technician discovered that Secret didn't have a heartbeat, I was brought here. They asked me, "Is there someone you'd like us to call who can be with you during the delivery?" My mom wasn't the first person who came to mind. But the person who did wasn't really an appropriate choice at the time, so I had them call her. My first choice today is the same person I most wanted with me two and a half years ago; only, he's still not here.

Of all the lousy timing! And, again, poor choices on my part. Why didn't I just call Dr. Walsh as soon as I got that first high blood pressure result on my lunch break? If I had, we may have been admitted to the hospital yesterday afternoon; we wouldn't have been home when Stefan dropped by; Jared's hand would still be okay; and Brice would never have gone to stupid Champaign-Urbana to speak at that stupid clergyman's conference—or whatever. To be honest, I wasn't really listening when he told me about it weeks ago. But, no! I had to play it cool and pretend I wasn't worried.

It's all that damn journal's fault, too. The things I read in it weeks ago have been shaping my decisions ever since. I've let it dictate what I say and don't say, what I do and don't do, and even how I feel. I've been walking on eggshells, worried that everything I say and do is getting on Brice's nerves. Well, it's done a number on *my* nerves. And now I'm lying in a hospital bed, alone and scared, worrying that my husband's going to miss the birth of his first—and possibly only—child.

Because let's face it: we don't want to go through this again. It's been thirty-one weeks of Hell. I've turned what should have been a beautiful thing into a nightmare. I took advantage of my husband's sweet, attentive nature and became a tyrant. I'm a horrible person!

That thought, combined with the fear and uncertainty I'm feeling, combined with all the terrifying memories that keep trying to crowd into my mind, produces the first sting of tears in my throat and nose. I keep my eyes closed but don't work too hard to fight the urge to cry. It actually feels kind of good to let it out. After all, only a freak would be okay with the thought that she's evil. It's normal to want to cry at that realization.

Plus, another one of my babies could be in danger because of me. Why can't I get this right? What's wrong with me? Am I so selfish and inherently flawed that I can't even do something as natural as nurture a baby in my own body? Have I somehow subconsciously begrudged my baby the right to treat my body as his own? Have I been funneling toxins in the form of resentment and bitterness to him for nine months? If something happens to him, I'll never forgive myself, no matter how much they try to tell me it's not my fault. I'm not buying it this time. You only get one "bad luck" pass before it's clear that you're the problem.

I think back on all the things I didn't do that I should have. I didn't pray enough, think enough positive thoughts, do enough Kegel exercises, go to the prenatal classes Dr. Walsh recommended, remember to take my prenatal vitamin every day, talk to my belly, or eat right. I definitely didn't eat right. I made a big show of shunning junk food in front of other people, but privately—

"Hey. It's okay. Shhh…" A large hand cups my forehead. "I'm so sorry I didn't have my phone with me. I'm so sorry you had to worry for a second about something as basic as my being here. I should never have gone this morning. I—"

"I ate a bag of Cheetos at lunch Monday!" I wail. "It was a snack-sized bag, but still. I ate them all, and then I drank the crumbs, and I licked the inside of the bag once or twice."

"So?"

"And sometimes when you're not looking, I salt my food. Low-sodium green beans are just so gross!"

He sits down in the chair next to the bed and clutches my hand. "Oh, hon. Who cares?"

"That's why my blood pressure's so high! I've been a salt-cheater ever since I kissed you after you ate that ooey-gooey butter bar." I sniff and sob. "If anything's wrong, it's because I'm selfish. I suck at this mom stuff already, and he's not even born!"

"That's not true at all. You've sacrificed a lot, mostly without complaint."

"Liar."

"No, really!" He leans closer in, putting his forehead against mine and resting his arm on the pillow over my head. "You haven't had a drop of alcohol in more than a year, not even a tiny toast at Christmas. Yeah, I noticed. And I know you were craving beer, because you'd always stop whatever you were doing or saying and stare at the TV when a commercial came on. But you never once complained that you couldn't have any."

"A beer sounds amazing right now."

"I know. I could really use one, too."

"But nobody drinks when they're pregnant. That's not a major accomplishment; that's just a hard and fast rule that everyone follows."

"Not everyone," he argues. "Trust me. And there have been other things. You love hot baths, but you've had to give those up. You said goodbye to your first car. And you haven't worn any of your favorite shoes."

"My fat feet don't fit in them."

"Even if they did, you wouldn't wear them, because you know they're not safe."

I take a deep, shuddering breath. "I've been awful."

I'm actually glad when he doesn't protest that statement right away. I don't want to hear empty platitudes right now. He pauses and then says carefully, "You've had a tough time. And I'm sorry about that. Really. I wish I knew how to make it easier."

"Do you perform lobotomies?" When he laughs at my joke, I give him a watery smile. "I'm so glad you're here."

"I'm glad I'm here, too. Hey." He moves back a few inches and swipes his thumbs under my eyes to brush away my tears. "Today's our son's birthday! What time did Dr. Walsh say we were going to get to meet him? 2:30?"

I nod. "Yeah. Although now that you're here, she may try to do it earlier. She seemed really anxious this morning."

For the first time since arriving, he looks around at all the beeping machines and meters. The blood pressure cuff around my arm buzzes to life, squeezing to the point of pain and then clicking and sighing until it deflates fully. We both stare at the numbers, which are still too high but are lower than they were when I first arrived.

"Everything's going to be fine," he promises. "What's the point in worrying…?"

"When you can pray about it?" I finish for him. "Exactly."

We grasp hands while he does just that, and after he says, "Amen," he points out, "We still have a while to wait, if Dr. Walsh sticks with the original plan. Close your eyes for a few minutes."

"You're not going anywhere, are you?"

He shakes his head and smiles. "Nope. I'll be right here, probably dozing a little myself, to be honest, now that the adrenaline's wearing off."

"I'm sorry I scared you. Not just today, either."

After a quick wink, he says, "Shhh. Rest."

*N*ow *this* is how to have a baby. I could have done without the five minutes of panic and chaos in the OR before they put me completely under, but it's pretty nice to wake up to such a calm, beautiful sight: Brice sitting next to my bed, looking down at a tiny blue-capped bundle in his arms. The large room is dim and quiet and unfamiliar. A closer look reveals that we're not alone; there are several other occupied beds around us, some concealed behind curtains, others (like mine) out in the open, holding recovering new mothers in various states of consciousness.

Brice is completely engrossed in his new son, so I hold as still as possible to watch the two of them for a while through half-open lids. It's not hard to hold still, anyway. Everything from just below my breasts all the way to my toes is numb. It's a warm, pleasant feeling. For now.

Whispering something I can't hear, he traces a knuckle across the baby's forehead. From this angle, I can't see if the baby's eyes are open or closed. Either way, it's the sweetest thing I've ever seen. But I want to hold my baby, so as wonderful as it makes me feel to observe them, I can't stay quiet any longer.

All it takes is a slight clearing of my throat for Brice's eyes to swing up to me. He beams a hundred-watter at me. "Look who I have," he says just above a murmur.

"I see that."

He stands and steps up to the bed rail, placing the sleeping infant in the space between my side and arm. "I just fed him a bottle, so he's pretty content. Not that he's made much of a peep at all."

"What time is it?" I ask, staring into a tiny, serious face so like my husband's that it almost takes my breath away.

He has to repeat himself when I don't listen to his answer the first time. "Just after six."

A nurse bustles over. "I see Mom's awake." While she goes about raising the head of my bed, checking me over, asking me questions about how and what I'm feeling, and intruding in general on my introduction to my son, Brice holds him within arm's reach so that I can stay in contact with him. Finally, she wraps up her exam and promises I'll be moved to a private room within the hour.

As soon as she's gone, I hold my arms out again so the swaddled newborn can be nestled in the crook of them. Before going back to studying his features, though, I tilt my face up and pooch my lips out. Brice smiles, bends at the waist, and presses against my mouth a kiss that surprises me with its intensity.

Breaking away, he says, "You scared me again."

"Bad habit," I reply. "This time, it was him, though, not me." I nod down at the baby, who winces as if in response to a dream. Do babies dream? What about?

Brice shakes his head. "As soon as they got him out, he

was fine; his heart rate returned to normal; his color was good. But you… There was a lot of blood. They had to give you a transfusion. And then they made me leave. You were so pale."

Considering I don't feel any worse than I'd imagine anyone would feel after having her abdomen cut open and a baby pulled from her, this news comes as a surprise. "Wow. I'm glad I slept through all that."

He laughs. "Yeah." Now he glances down at his son. "So, what do you think?"

"He's a keeper," I say.

"No, I mean, what about a name? They keep calling him Baby Boy Northam, and it's kind of sad that he's the only one in the nursery without a name."

I have to try really hard not to laugh at his feeling like his son may be an outcast at such a young age. I turn the newborn around and hold him out in front of me, his head cradled in both of my hands, so we can get a good look at him. We stare down at him for a while.

Finally, I say, "I don't know. I like all the names we've discussed, but he doesn't really look like any of them."

"I was just thinking the same thing," he enthuses, as if our having the same thought is the second miracle of the day.

"Well, that kind of sucks," I state. "I mean, now what?"

"First of all, we need to get the total picture here." He pulls off the knit hat to reveal a perfectly round, black peach-fuzz-covered head. "This is a big decision. He's going to have this name for the rest of his life."

"No pressure."

"Exactly. So, we have to choose wisely."

I kiss the tiny forehead and nuzzle his head with my

nose. Ohhh, that's probably the best feeling I've ever had. And that has to be the best smell in the world.

"Isn't he great?" he breathes. "I can't get over it. Or you. My heart is filled to the max. I feel so blessed."

What he says really strikes a chord. Making sure it fits what I imagine I can already detect to be our son's personality, I look at his mini-Brice, solemn face and suggest, "Max. That's a nice, strong, manly name that the other babies in the nursery can respect. I mean, it's not a Biblical name, but…"

"It's perfect," he immediate finishes. "He's a Max if I ever saw one."

"Just Max, though. Not short for anything."

"Totally. Just Max."

"Max Augustus Northam," I add, checking Brice's reaction.

He nods and bites his lip. "Yeah. Finally something that goes with my dad's name. Doesn't get much more perfect than that."

"Meant to be."

Gently replacing the hat, he says, "I can't wait to tell everyone. Your mom has been particularly persistent with her inquiries."

"It's not going to hurt my feelings if you come right out and say she's annoying the piss out of you about it." I cuddle Max closer and kiss his nose, hoping I never annoy the piss out of him but knowing I will someday.

"I'd never say that."

Of course, he wouldn't. I know he thinks it, though. And probably writes it in his little book.

∽

The hospital room is returning to a homeostasis of sorts after the departure of Jared, Mitzi, and Jen. The only people remaining are Jason and Dustin. Mom, Dad, Nicole, and her brood went to dinner when Mitzi and Jen showed up, since the room was getting a little crowded. Jared was close behind them. And Jason and Dustin just showed up five minutes ago.

When my brother walked in and immediately commandeered Max from Mitzi, it was obvious that no one else was going to hold the baby as long as he was in the room, so my friends promised to visit me when we got settled at home and said their goodbyes. Jared, quite obviously uncomfortable in this setting, congratulated us once more and took his cues from my friends.

Now, Jason's pulling on Max's chin with his index finger, making it appear that the baby is dictating his terms. "'I want a dry diaper every hour, on the hour; I'll eat every two hours, no matter what the time of day or night; and someone will be holding me at all times. Otherwise, you will become quite familiar with the sound of my voice.'"

"He's not your kid," Dustin says, "so I'm pretty sure they're not going to have to be worried about demanding behavior like that."

"I'm not demanding!" Jason protests, laughing.

Dustin shoots his boyfriend a disbelieving look. "Uh, 'I will watch twelve straight hours of football every Saturday and Sunday from September through January, and I will drink only certain types of beer (no lite beer ever) and eat certain types of snacks, or you'll have to put up with my sulking and my constantly checking my iPhone for score updates, even if I'm supposed to be out on a date with my very understanding boyfriend. Oh, and I also want to watch football on Monday and sometimes Thursday evenings. And when it's not football season, I will obsessively follow the NFL draft and plan my fantasy football team for the next year.'"

"Hey, fantasy football is a lot of work," I say in defense of my little brother. "It takes a lot of planning. That's why I don't do it anymore. Took the fun out of watching football."

"As if it's any fun, anyway," Dustin mutters.

Max lets out a warning squeal and winds up for a good cry.

"Now, look. You made the baby cry," Jason scolds.

"He's getting hungry," I explain, after a glance at the clock.

Jason quickly hands him over. "Well, that's where my service ends. I don't have the proper equipment."

I don't, either, apparently. Max has no interest whatsoever in breastfeeding. The nursing coach keeps telling me he'll get the hang of it, eventually, but in the meantime we've had to supplement with bottles (his first two feedings were bottles, since I was still asleep), and now I think he's just thoroughly confused.

In my arms, he quiets.

While shrugging on his jacket, Jason asks, "So what happened to Jared's hand?"

Brice and I exchange nervous glances. Before my husband can tell one of his transparent, awkward lies, I cover quickly. "He's such a klutz. Smashed it in the Jeep's door the other night when Brice took him back to his hotel."

"What a goob!" Jason says, laughing.

I feel sort of guilty for giving Jared such an un-cool cover story, but we all agreed it would be best if nobody knew that the vicar punched someone out in our front yard. It's not very Christian-like. Not that lying is, but…

Dustin pulls on Jason's elbow. "Come on. Don't be mean. Not everyone is as cool as you are. And, anyway, Mitzi doesn't seem to mind. She was all over him."

"She was?" I say so loudly that it startles Max into crying again.

Before Dustin can answer, Jason verifies, "Yeah, as they were all leaving, he totally fed her a line. It was weak and kind of embarrassing."

"What did he say?"

"'You should see the other guy.'" Jason rolls his eyes. "Surely you can teach him something better than that, Brice."

"Yeah," Dustin confirms. "I didn't hear the line, but she was playing with her hair and touching her necklace and giving all the textbook signals of attraction as the three of them were leaving. Watch that space."

Jason sticks a finger in his ear and winces. "Well, Max is obviously ready to chow down, so we'll leave you to it." He leans down and kisses my forehead before tapping his nephew on the nose one more time and leaving with Dustin.

As soon as the nursing coach has gone after we've decided that, once again, Max isn't going to latch on, and we've settled him down with a bottle of expressed breast milk, Brice pulls his journal from his back pocket and settles down on the couch across the room. Lying on his back with his head resting on the arm, he opens to a blank page and begins writing, using his legs bent at the knees as an improvised desk.

"What are you writing?" I can't help but ask, even though I know from past experience that I'm probably better off not knowing.

"Sermon idea."

"About what?"

"About trying to be more understanding towards challenging people. Like Stefan."

I remove the bottle from Max's mouth and prop him up for a burp. He blinks indignantly at me but doesn't cry. Instead, he quickly offers a dry belch that results in painful-sounding hiccups that I hope the next half of the bottle will silence.

Brice smiles faintly at the digestive symphony.

At the risk of ruining such a relaxing family moment, I remind him, "You know I hate when you do that."

"Do what?" he asks distractedly, not pausing in his writing or bothering to look up at me.

"Take something that happens to us and turn it into a sermon! It's one thing to write stuff down in your little diary; although when you leave it wide open on your desk, it becomes a lot less private—" I abruptly shut up when I realize what I've just said.

Now he looks up at me. "What?"

"What?" I try to play innocent and then swiftly change the subject. "Hey, when is your mom getting here? Is she going to wait until we're home from the hospital?"

He's not distracted. "Are you referencing a specific time you've seen my journal open on my desk?" he asks, while tapping his pen against the pages in front of him.

I gaze down into Max's face and reply honestly, "Yes. It was enlightening." I brave a glance at him. When he just stares at me, his expression inscrutable, I rush on, "I mean, I didn't see anything about any church members or anything. I was actually looking to see if you had written down any new Katy Perry lyrics."

Still he says nothing, his jaw set.

"Anyway, no Katy songs. Which was kind of a relief, to

be honest, although it would have been funny. Funnier than what I saw."

His face slackens, despite the fact that I'm keeping my tone light.

Now that it's out, I experience an immense sense of relief akin to farting after holding it in for several hours (gross, but accurate). I'm sick of feeling guilty about reading his journal and keeping it from him. I'm sick of feeling awful about what he wrote. I'm sick of those words haunting me.

Quietly, I tell him, "You know, you should probably keep that thing in a desk drawer. And definitely not open to a page you don't want anyone seeing. I'm assuming that's pretty personal stuff you write in there. Stuff that's between you and God. Venting. Blowing off steam. Privately."

Bringing his chin to rest on his chest, he mumbles, "Yeah."

"Someone not as understanding and wonderful as I am may not put such a diplomatic slant on it. If they were to read it." When he says nothing, I continue, "*And* someone else might not stop at reading just one page. They might go back and read the whole thing, looking for something really juicy."

"Did you see anything 'really juicy' on the page you read?" he asks.

I think for a second and then say, "Nothing I haven't thought about myself, but it was difficult to know you were thinking those same things. It sucks to know your husband doesn't want to come home at night to be with you, because you're so annoying."

"Oh, man! You read *that* entry?" When I nod, he says in a tortured voice, "I'm so sorry. I'm just—oh, man! I'm mortified right now. You must have thought I was such a jerk. An ungrateful, insensitive butthead."

The bottle empty, I set it aside and rest Max on my chest, rubbing and patting his back gently. "Whatever," I say nonchalantly. "It was wrong for me to read it."

"It was wrong for me not to tell you how I was feeling."

"Hmm. I can see where having that conversation waiting for you would really make you dread coming home at night." I look over at him. "I wasn't behaving like an adult. And I was fully aware of that before I read your journal."

He swings his legs around and puts his feet on the floor. Tossing his little book aside, he comes over to me, smoothly removes Max from my chest, and tenderly places the baby in the bassinet on the other side of the bed. Then he sits on the side of the hospital bed and grabs my hand.

"That was weeks ago, you know. In a moment of frustration."

I nod. "I know."

"I haven't felt that way in a while. You've been different lately."

I wish I could tell him that it's because I've grown up or seen the error of my ways; I wish I could say it was easy to change once I knew how much it was bothering him; I wish I could say I *have* changed, but I have to tell him, "Not really. I just haven't been honest with you about how I'm feeling, because I know you don't want to hear it."

At his chagrined expression, I comfort him with the following: "But all that's over now. I mean, even though it feels like there's a tiny football team trampling on my innards with metal cleats, and I'm sure there'll be some hormonal adjustments in the next few weeks, the rest of this ordeal is past. We made it." I smile encouragingly. "Right?"

He shakes his head. "That's not a solution, though. I feel like an utter failure, like I didn't support you the way you needed to be supported, like I contributed to your health complications, like I—"

I drop my head back against the pillow and close my eyes. "Shhh... It doesn't matter. Everything worked out okay."

"No!" He keeps his voice down, but his fierce tone gets my attention. I raise my head and look into his eyes, which are troubled. "I hurt you."

I can't argue with that, so I don't.

He continues, "And that's against the rules. Big time."

His simplified assessment makes me laugh. "I break the rules all the time. Not that that makes it okay."

"I'm sorry," he repeats earnestly, refusing to let me joke it away.

"You can't help how you feel."

"And neither can you." Lowering his eyes, he hypothesizes, "I'm no better than Stefan, taking for granted what you've done for me, for our son—"

"Okay, that's enough." I glance at Max and see he's still sleeping soundly. I wish he'd wake up and cause a diversion. This is just awkward.

"I'm serious!"

I ruffle his hair. "That's what makes it so funny. You couldn't be anything like him if you tried."

When he rests his forehead lightly against my chest, I rub at his hairline on the back of his neck. He shivers slightly.

"I'll make you a deal," I say after a few seconds of searching my own feelings and making sure I'm not committing to something I don't want to do. "Next time we do this, I'll try to be more relaxed and less ugly, and you'll try to be more understanding and gently honest with me if I have trouble meeting that goal."

He looks up at me, his mussed hair making him look slightly deranged. The enormous grin on his face two seconds later doesn't make him look any saner. "Next time?"

I do want to do this again with him. Maybe not the exact same way (definitely not the exact same way), but the past two days have nearly erased all the unpleasantness of the previous several months. I look at Max and think, if I'd only been able to fathom how wonderful it is to hold him and watch him sleep and watch Brice hold him and talk to him and everything else it may have been easier to keep things in perspective. I just had no idea. I thought I did, but my concept of how it would feel was a fraction of what it really is. Now that I do know, I think it'll be a completely different experience next time around.

I nod firmly and repeat, "Next time. If *you* want to do this again."

Craning his neck, he reaches up to kiss me. "I definitely do. Being an only child is kind of the pits."

I laugh at his assessment. "Then we must avoid that for Max at all costs. How many siblings are we talking here?"

With a teasing grin and a shrug, he answers, "We'll leave that up to him. I'm sure six or seven will be plenty of playmates."

My groan makes him snicker. More seriously, he says, "I don't think we should worry about it. I think we'll be blessed with as many or as few children as we're supposed to have."

"I don't want the pastor answer. What's Brice's answer?"

After thinking about it for a second, he says, "As many as we can fully enjoy. If that's two, great. If it's seven..." He takes a deep, steadying breath. "Well, I don't think it'll be seven. But I don't want to be confined to a pre-conceived number. I'd rather just live life and see what happens. Don't you think that's more fun?"

A smile spreads across my face and travels way down into my belly. "Yes. Good answer, Rev."